THE
BERLIN
PACKAGE

D0711185

THE
BERLIN
PACKAGE

A THRILLER

PETER RIVA

YUCCA

Yucca Publishing books may be purchased in bulk at special discounts for sales promotion, corporate gifts, fund-raising, or educational purposes. Special editions can also be created to specifications. For details, contact the Special Sales Department, Yucca Publishing, 307 West 36th Street, 11th Floor, New York, NY 10018 or yucca@skyhorsepublishing.com.

Yucca Publishing® is an imprint of Skyhorse Publishing, Inc.®, a Delaware corporation.

Visit our website at www.yuccapub.com.

10 9 8 7 6 5 4 3 2 1

Library of Congress Cataloging-in-Publication Data is available on file.

Cover design by Karis Drake of subsiststudios
Cover Photo courtesy of Rawpixel

Print ISBN: 978-1-63158-082-6
Ebook ISBN: 978-1-63158-089-5

Printed in the United States of America

Table of Contents

Chapter 1

Nonstop to Tegel

Halfway across the frozen Atlantic on a pitch-black night in March is not the time to have an engine backfire and flameout. Being in a two-engine plane didn't make matters more optimistic for film and television producer Pero Baltazar. He knew the Boeing 767 to be a stable, reliable aircraft, and Pero had flown in them to all corners of the globe. But when the left jet engine coughed out, in a sudden plume of forward blue flame at thirty-nine thousand feet in the dead of a winter's night, Pero started wondering if it had been, actually, wise to shave a few hours off the journey to Berlin by taking the only nonstop any airline offered. Delta had revived the nonstop service because someone in the State Department had leaned on them. Who? The seasoned filmmaker's guess was that it was the returning US ambassador sitting in the row ahead of Pero's seat in first class.

Only slightly worried, Pero's gallows' humor kicked in as he thought to himself, *When this plane hits the water, first class will take on a completely different meaning—first to arrive, first to perish.*

Pero imagined what the two crew members in the cockpit were doing. First, they would have declared an emergency, "Mayday, Mayday," then gotten on with standard emergency procedures, instilled and practiced for hours. The pilot would call out, "Engine restart checklist . . . pressure boost, check . . ." and so on. Pero knew they were busy doing what they were trained to do. The pilot would have immediately trimmed the ship for maximum glide and efficiency, as he sought a planned alternate landing strip, probably Iceland. So, there was nothing that Pero or any other passenger could do except sit, think, pray, and wonder.

While the left engine out the window on his side of the plane sat dumb and useless, the right engine roared, thankfully, full throttle. The plane had only a slight down angle. This is what safety flight paths were designed for—one engine emergency alternate landing fields they were called. And the pilot would search the appropriate one out, somewhat urgently.

Pero was over six feet, and even in first class, his knees were cramped. Like all long distance flyers, he had this yearning to either stand or stretch out. As he stretched, the woman next to him glanced over to see if he had any other intentions. At fifty-five, he thought he had reached the harmless stage in life, replete with graying temples and abundant laugh lines from days in the sun. Yet, he seemed to get more women making passes at him than he did ten years before. He didn't know if it was what one woman called his intense but friendly eyes that contributed to an image of desire for women, but he still thought that his sufficient age would render him harmless. Yet, the mid-thirties woman sitting next to him took less than an hour after take-off to make her intentions plain. While the in-flight meal was being collected, she deliberately dusted crumbs from her ample bosom. The gentle bobbing from her brushing was accompanied by a sly grin. Pero had smiled politely, trying not to encourage. When the engine sputtered, she leaned across, looking out, and grabbed his hand in mock fear. When he patted it like a father would, saying gently, "There, there dear, don't worry," her hand was withdrawn as if stung. Age, Pero's, had brought her to her senses, as was his intention.

When the port engine did not restart, her mock fear became real. She was now holding her own hands in her lap, twisting a ring on her right hand, anxious, looking around the small two rows of first class. Behind him, Pero could also hear that the other passengers behind them in tourist class were fretting.

As he pulled the emergency card from the seat back in front of him, he wondered why he had not left a day ahead of schedule. Berlin always held an attraction. He could have been there by now. It was partially why he had accepted this menial job. He was to produce a second unit movie crew, filming pick-up scenes around Berlin to match the filming taking place on sound stages under the direction of the first unit crew and real director in Hollywood. Besides, Pero had jumped at the chance to spend time with his longtime professional partner, Heep. His friend, Bill "Heep" Heeper, the elegant Dutchman and master cinematographer, would, he hoped, be in Berlin already, waiting for Pero's arrival. And there was another reason, Pero knew he needed to get back in the saddle, get back to work after traumatic events months before.

Suddenly a sound, a feeling, and his thoughts came back to focus on reality. The passengers on the right side were now gesturing and babbling. The right engine had now also coughed once, twice, and then sputtered out. The plane's ambient mechanical sound died. The plane was now a silent eighty-ton glider. Pero thought again about the crew. The cockpit would have an increased sense of urgency: "Mayday, mayday, Delta one-zero-three, heavy, bound for Berlin, both engines out, attempting Reykjavik airfield in a fifteen degree glide . . ." It would be a rough thirty minutes for those pilots.

Thirty minutes, probably not more, he thought, estimating the time for the glide to zero feet and splashdown in the frozen North Atlantic if they could not make Reykjavik.

Pero was frowning and staring absent-mindedly at the emergency card showing lifejacket and raft instructions. His mind was churning—there was something, almost right there, on the edge of his memory.

In seconds, his brain coughed up long-lost trivia, and he took only seconds more to analyze the facts he had remembered. *Maybe they could use a hand . . .*

He had never suffered from copilot's disease—that's the black humor name for a high regard for authority that can get you killed. It started with a British European Airways Trident flight out of London Heathrow in the '70s. There were three full captains in the cockpit, including one traveling in the jump seat just behind the throttles. On takeoff, with engines throttled back for noise abatement, the captain in charge began to have a heart attack. He was frozen with the pain and shock. As the plane leapt further into the air and passed the outer marker of the airport, he should have throttled up. He didn't. The copilot sat there, thinking, "He must know what he's doing." The deadheading captain sitting in the jump seat behind the throttles sat there thinking, "He must know what he's doing." All anyone had to do was push the throttles forward. They had twenty-three seconds to do it. No one did anything. Everyone died. Pero knew that copilot's disease is deadly.

This plane, a longer distance Boeing 767-200ER, had been brought out of retirement—it was in the Herald Tribune article that announced the recommencement of daily nonstop flights. He could see the engine cowling from his window. There was an older, prominent GE logo. That meant she had the GE older engines that operated with a maximum ceiling height of thirty-six thousand feet. Maybe the engines were not broken but had simply exhausted their oxygen intake and had stalled. Like a piston engine, jet engines burn a mixture of fuel—kerosene, jet fuel—and air. As the air gets too thin, the compressor blades inside the engine cannot compress sufficient air to mix with the fuel, and the mixture becomes too rich. Like a choke on a car, the engine will choke out, stall, and backfire. Pero had seen the forward blue flame. It all made sense.

Their flight path was newer than the plane's design, newly planned to allow greater traffic density over the North Atlantic twin-engine safety flight corridor with only so many miles between remote airstrips in case of engine failure. The old flight path had an altitude of thirty-five thousand feet. This newer one mandated thirty-nine thousand feet. The air up here was thinner, much thinner.

Pero rose, inched past his row companion, saying, "Sorry," and walked forward to the galley.

The flight attendant jumped up, "Please sit down sir, right now!"

"Okay, but you must pass this to the flight deck . . ."

"They are busy, please take your seat."

He kept his voice low and calm. "Listen, these are old GE turbofans, model CF6-50 or maybe model CF6-80a, they have an operational ceiling of thirty-six thousand feet. Tell them to restart at that altitude. Don't dump fuel. Purge first, cold start procedure . . ."

"I'll be sure to tell them . . ."

"Listen," he read her nametag, "Paula, your life and mine are at risk here. Tell them exactly what I told you, or we may not have a tomorrow."

"Is there a problem?" A burly man from the tourist section had pushed forward. "Who are you?"

"Pero Baltazar." He looked him square in the face. Pero guessed he was the sky marshal because Paula backed off and let the man take command. Pero also knew he would know his name. It was FAA procedure to tell any onboard security which passenger might have additional authority. With the ambassador on board, they would have checked and rechecked every name, and Pero's would be coded as secret by the State Department and, therefore, trustworthy. There had been an assassination attempt on the ambassador the year before, they would have checked. Or at least Pero hoped they had.

"Okay, bud, you're clear. What gives?"

"I need to help the crew. I may have the answer to our dilemma." He motioned out the window.

The marshal turned to the attendant, "Paula is it? Get them to open the cockpit door. He's got clearance." She looked shocked and picked up the phone.

"Captain, there's a passenger here, okayed by the sky marshal, who has something to tell you."

"Now." Pero said

"Now he says . . . yes, captain." She stood back. The door opened an inch. Pero pulled it all the way open and stepped inside. The copilot turned his head and said, "Spill it."

"Sorry to bother you fellows, but I know this plane of old. It's a recently refurbished two hundred series still with the old GE engines, CF6-50 or CF6-80a right?"

The copilot had been working feverishly on documentation. He flipped through the 3-ring binder that held the SOP (standard operating procedures) and specifications of the plane. He nodded "They're CF6-80a's."

"They have an operational max ceiling of around thirty-six thousand feet."

"What, you're kidding . . . Captain?"

"Check the damn book, Charlie. If he's right, we may yet save this flight."

He leafed through the binder, near the end, "Right here, damn Captain, he's right, it says here op ceiling max three six zero."

The pilot knew what to do. First the radio, "Reykjavík, Delta one-zero-three here. We're descending through flight level three-seven-zero to three-two-zero—clear all traffic." He didn't have to ask them. Once an emergency is declared, if you say "Mayday" even once, the pilot has absolute authority up there.

"Roger Delta one-zero-three, clearing all traffic below."

"Reykjavik, at flight level three-two-zero we will attempt a restart, both engines. Now suspect flight plan conflict operational ceiling capabilities this seven-six-seven dash two hundred ER aircraft and GE CF6-80a power plants."

"Roger Delta one-zero-three. Did we hear right that this is a paper error?"

"Reykjavík, we'll know in a few minutes."

"Roger Delta one-zero-three, traffic below is clear, proceed to flight level three-two-zero."

The pilot put the nose down, began a steeper descent, and said, "If this doesn't work, we'll use the additional speed to regain about half of what we're losing, but it makes a glide to safety unlikely. Hope you're right about this."

The copilot spoke up, "Oh, he's right captain, but can the engines be restarted with the power we have, in this cold?" Pero knew the only power they had now was the auxiliary power unit in the tail still running the plane's systems and ventilation.

"We'll see . . . start pre-heating the compressor now. Number two engine only." Number two was the right engine, the one that was last running and, therefore, warmest.

"Compressor heaters on. Approaching three-two-zero . . ."

"Reykjavík, coming level at three-two-zero. Starting restart starboard engine procedure now."

"Roger Delta one-zero-three, good luck."

With the microphone off, the pilot answered for them all, "Luck has everything to do with it."

Pero watched the two professionals go through the checklist, read gauges, flick switches, and prepare for a cold engine start. The engine caught first time. The pilot increased the power to cruise, not full. They all heard the clapping and cheering in the cabin behind. "Okay, Charlie, now let's see if the other one isn't too damn cold." And they went through the procedure again for the number one engine. It took a little longer, there was an anxious flameout and a second restart, but soon it was running smoothly. Power was back. Passengers were clapping, yelling, cheerful. The copilot patted the throttles, "Atta girl."

The captain wiped his brow and keyed the microphone "Reykjavík, Delta one-zero-three here. Emergency over. Both engines running perfectly. Emergency terminated. Thank you for your assistance."

"Roger Delta one-zero-three, we're all really pleased down here."

"Roger, Reykjavík, us too. Please advise other seven-six-sevens up here our problem."

"Roger Delta one-zero-three, it's being done."

"Delta one-zero-three requesting flight plan alteration to continue at three-two-zero to destination Berlin Tegel. Confirm."

"Roger Delta one-zero-three, we confirm, you are clear to proceed existing flight route at flight level three-two-zero to Berlin Tegel airport. Hand over as route plan to next ATC. Safe journey. Out."

"Thank you Reykjavík, Delta one-zero-three out."

The Captain turned in his seat, facing the copilot "You have her, Charlie." Then he turned further and eyeballed Pero, "And you, mister, just who the hell are you?"

With a chuckle Pero responded, "Just a guy with a memory for details—and who would also rather land safely."

Chapter 2

How'd I Get Here?

As Pero emerged from the flight deck, shutting the door behind him, the sky marshal patted him on the back, and the flight attendant beamed. Pero noticed the closed curtain to tourist class, so presumably no one back there knew he was involved at all. The ambassador had his eyeshades on, and Pero wondered if he had woken during all the clapping. *Maybe he thought the passengers were applauding the movie.*

First class on the JFK to Tegel run was two rows of four seats. The ambassador was sitting front right, with an empty seat next to him, piled with papers and his briefcase. Behind him was a suited man, short haircut, presumably on the ambassador's staff. Pero smiled at his female row mate who had benefited from the commotion and had moved across the aisle and was holding onto the suited man's forearm with pleading sincerity. Pero felt sure he could see the man tense muscles. The woman smiled. Pero was just happy to have his seat and her old one to himself.

As he sat and buckled in, the flight attendant appeared and offered drinks, anything he would like, "I even have some special Cognac if you would?" Her question faded off.

"Yes, thank you, Paula. By the way . . ."

"Yes?"

"You were good there, very cool. Nicely done." Paula was visibly thrilled. Here was the man who had saved them all giving her credit. As Pero removed his shoes and slid one knee over the center armrest, Paula hustled off and fetched his Cognac. Pero thanked her and said he would sleep for a while.

"I don't know how you can, I'm just so excited." Pero nodded and holding the snifter, took a sip of amber liquid, closed his eyes, and sighed. Paula knew the good-bye signs and left him alone.

Alone, why am I so damn alone? He thought. He knew the answer. Finishing the Cognac, he put it on the seat next to him on the emergency card he thankfully would not need. Shutting his eyes, his mind drifted toward sleep, passing remembrances along the way.

Months before, he and his documentary crew had thwarted a terrorist attack in Kenya. There were deaths, killings, and incredible bravery. But what stuck with him the most was that the terrorists had threatened to roast a hundred thousand people alive. *A hundred thousand people or more in a terrible slum outside of Nairobi . . . slums—the concentration camps of the modern age.* The horror of that haunted him, reinforcing his fears for all humanity and, at the same time, labeling his weakness—a feeling of never being able to cope alone. He had involved all his friends, okay, yes they had volunteered, but he knew that he was too insignificant to have succeeded alone. *Alone, why does that word frighten me?*

He opened his eyes and stared at his right arm, already positioned across his chest, under-forearm resting on his heart. *Addiena . . .* On that right under-forearm was tattooed the name of his wife who had died in the Lockerbie disaster. Pero knew his habit of putting her name over his heart was thought of as sweet by his family, but to him it was fierce loyalty to and love for her—so he would not forget. The possibility of forgetting her riddled him with guilt.

Come on Pero, referring to himself in the third perso*n, think about where you are going and the work you need to accomplish. You have to stop wallowing in all this emotion every time something happens!*

Eyes firmly shut, trying to recapture mental level, he went over the events of the week before. He saw himself in his Manhattan Lower East Side apartment, third floor, in the den, clean and dressed after weeks of moping in his pajamas after returning from Kenya. In an effort to snap out of his funk, he dialed his contact number in Washington DC, "Baltazar, P. here, requesting Director Lewis."

"One moment sir."

"Directors office . . ."

"Baltazar here, calling for Mr. Lewis."

"Mr. Lewis is unavailable Mr. Baltazar. You could try calling back this afternoon or maybe trying him on his cell phone, do you have that number?"

"I do. When would that be convenient do you think?"

"He is in congressional hearings today, but I am sure at lunch, say noon, he could take your call." He thanked her and hung up.

Off his computer screen, he read the number of his television agent Dick Tanks, a home number supposedly on Malibu beach. Pero knew it was just a postal drop, that the agent lived in the hills out of sight of the ocean—Hollywood glitter—all that shines is not gold.

Dick answered on the third ring, his voice tired. "Huh, yeah?"

"Morning Dick, Pero here. I am ready to get back to work, find me some."

"Pero? Pero? What're you doing to me, calling at this hour? Christ, what time is it?"

"Time an ambitious agent was up running the beach at Malibu, right Dick?"

"Yeah, yeah, very funny, more like having coffee in Cher's local café. What was it you wanted?"

"Work." Everyone worth anything in television and film has an agent. Those agents do almost nothing, they like to take credit and cash dollar checks. If you don't provide the financial stream, a steady stream for them, they stop you working. Dick worked for DBB, a very powerful Hollywood agency, and they represented Pero, poorly, but then he wasn't exactly ambitious, and they knew that.

"I told you, you've got the new series starting in September . . ."

"Dick, I want something now. I was thinking of calling around."

"Fine, do that, but if you renege on the documentary series with Mary Lever, you'll never . . ." Mary Lever, the *Dinosaur Lady* as the media called her, was a hot property. Pero and Heep had signed her to a thirteen one-hour series for a network. Pero was to be the exec-producer and his friend Heep, the producer/director.

"Save your breath, Dick. I know the score. Remember, Mary is a personal friend." He gave his voice a rough edge, "And if I ask her, she'll drop the series . . ."

"Christ, don't do that!" Dick was wide-awake now. "No, no Pero, it's just that it's a golden opportunity for you, for your career . . ."

"Let's not BS each other here. Look, Dick, I was just after something to get me moving again. I'm a little stagnant, getting rusty, gotta get out, okay?"

"Sure, sure, no offense meant, you know I'm your greatest supporter. I'll find something." He had regained his composure. "I'll call soon, okay? Bye." Unusually, he sounded as if he meant it. Mary Lever must be a huge deal for him. As an agent, maybe he maneuvered himself into a coproducing slot for the bigger bucks and power. Power was the real name of the Hollywood game, not money.

As Pero had warned his agent, he was going to call around, and as Dick hadn't forbidden it, Pero made a few calls to people outside mainstream US television. A Canadian company had something on offer for next month, a ski movie being shot in Banff. A French crew was off to Bali for a butterfly special and, interestingly, Dr. Sylvia Earle was hosting a special on the benefits of drilling platforms and car dumping as new reefs for fish. He asked them all to consider his temporary services.

He called Heep's number in LA and got the machine. Calling Heep's agent, he found out that Heep had just left to shoot in Austria—a commercial, arranged by a European agency. Heep was due back in two to three weeks.

All morning Pero kept calling contacts and emailing his updated bio.

At noon, he called Director Lewis' cell phone. Lewis was terse and business-like. Pero could hear other people and the clink of dishes in the background. "Having lunch with congressional folks?"

"Something like that."

"Just wanted you to know I am back in the saddle. Could you tell me who I report to?" Then remembering, "Hey, nothing like before, just something like a courier job."

"Your usual contact," he meant Tom Baylor, his contact for thirty years, "is still away on medical leave. We'll call you when we're ready but glad you called." He added a few pleasantries for cover about a fictitious wife and kids to mislead whoever he was lunching with and hung up.

A day went by. Pero hit the gym, played squash with the club pro and lost, but not as badly as he might have. He called on his father and mother for dinner, took a friend to lunch, watched the news on BBC America, and, as was his habit, listened to the rest of the real news on Deutsche Welle and Radio Suisse Romande on the Internet. By the time Dick, his agent, called back, he felt connected to the sordid little world again.

"Well, a studio called and asked who we had, and I thought of you . . ." They discussed the details. An independent film company wanted a producer for a second unit shoot, complete with team. The subject was background footage for a feature, meant to be "taking place in Berlin, a throwback to the tensions between East and West."

Especially because they were now the same—Berlin's East and West being terms linked to time already years past. It irked Pero to have this recently graduated business school brat agent—his sockless loafers twitching on his office coffee table no doubt—emphasize the old Cold War status. As if he was even alive when that mattered.

Once, it really did.

As the agent explained, the film was the usual spy flick—a street scene, a chase on foot, and loads of atmosphere shots of a male star riding the old elevated S-Bahn in the cold, "dead-of-winter with frosted glass looking onto some technical museum, very ex-Nazi era" shots.

"Dick, don't they know the S-Bahn has heating?"

"But it was East Germany, they were commies—tough, hard people—they wouldn't have heating, surely?" He said into his head microphone. Pero could hear his breathing beating on the foam microphone cover even three thousand miles away. *Ah, well, if Hollywood wants frosted glass, we'll give them real frosted glass.*

Pero was sure the star actor of this adventure thriller would be pleased to have the "authentic experience," so the celebrity would have a real story to brag about at cocktail parties. He'd be able to tell a long tale of all of fifteen minutes spent suffering for his art, standing on a heating-uncoupled S-Bahn train overlooking the real modern, Technisches Museum entrance. Dick told Pero they had recreated the museum on the sound stage and were building a perfect replica of the S-Bahn station on the back lot at Warner's.

"So do you want it? It pays well enough." They discussed fees and deadlines. A three-week shoot, maximum.

Piece of cake, Pero thought, *don't let him know that.* "Well, sounds harder than you think, the permits alone can be a bitch. And we'll need a really trustworthy DP to pull it off. Someone who's fluent in German." DP meant director of photography or camera operator.

"Christ, we can't make conditions—and why German?" The fact that Dick even asked, affirmed Pero's suspicion the boy was dumb, naïve at best.

"Look, Dick, we're not going to argue this. I know the shooting conditions in Berlin, I know the cops there. One false move, one misunderstanding, and your big Hollywood star will languish for weeks. You want that? You *personally* want that?" He asked it with emphasis. "Who is this guy anyway?"

"They're not telling me, yet, until we reach a deal. Okay, I understand the German angle. Who do you suggest I recommend to them?"

"Bill Heeper." After Pero explained that Heep was over there anyway, Dick agreed and hung up abruptly, as usual, to show he was in control. Or wanted to think he was. Dick knew a movie offer with an anonymous big name film star attached was elevating his agency status with every call. In insisting on a German-speaking DP, he would spin it to seem as if it was his idea, protecting the shoot. If they got Heep, Heep's agent would know better but still go for the pot of gold.

Twenty minutes later, Pero was halfway through a hurried sandwich lunch when Dick called back, "It seems the cameraman they hired has come down with the flu anyway. It's his loss. I suggested Bill Heeper as a replacement as he is already in Vienna shooting a TV commercial. They called his agents and made the arrangements. They were even happy at saving his trans-Atlantic airfare. So, instead, as a personal thank you for you Pero, I got you an upgrade to first class. I set good deal terms with them as well."

Pero was too tired of the pecking-order game not to simply congratulate him. "Well done Dick. Okay, so who's the star?"

"Danny Redmond, it's a career move for him. He's also a backer and producer too. I negotiated directly with him in London." Pero knew right then that Dick's rating at DBB had suddenly shot up. The minor TV agent was dealing with a real movie star, one-on-one.

"Okay, Dick, I'll start the permit process tomorrow bright and early. When do I leave?"

"You can leave—well, it's up to you. We'll send over the script and material by email tonight. The below-the-line expenses are finite. They warned me to keep you in check, you can call the studio contact tomorrow. It'll be in the email. Your billing and expenses must run through this office." That meant DBB was adding a cut. Dick hung up before Pero's laugh of derision could travel down the line to LA.

Business as normal. Time to get rolling. It would take about a day or two to get permits in place, arrange crew, local and Heep's . . . his mind began to compile lists, set priorities. It is what producers do. They juggle facts, permits, people, places, equipment, and money. And they never, hopefully, drop the ball.

The plane hit an air pocket and jostled him out of his reverie. Pero opened his eyes, saw all was calm, and closed them again, determined to get some sleep. *Never drop the ball*, he thought as he dozed off, lounging across the two first-class chairs, the Cognac was unwinding his nerves, *must not drop the ball, this has got to go well, gotta get out of this funk.*

Across the aisle, one seat ahead of him, the ambassador lifted his eyeshade and stared back at Pero, memorizing his face.

Chapter 3

Gedächtniskirche

It was drizzling on final approach. Pero thought, *so what else is new in March in Berlin?* The plane pierced the steel gray skies, settled onto the runway, and taxied to gate fourteen. Tegel is a small airport, not meant for larger mini-jumbos like the 767. Slowly they maneuvered the Boeing snugly into the gateway.

After the usual overly long wait for the luggage to make the fifty-yard trip from the belly, up the conveyor, and onto the carousel, Pero loaded his two bags onto a cart and pushed his baggage cart past the green customs section sign. And he was stopped.

"Kommen sie mit, bitte." The girl with the light green shirt and dark green epaulets smiled thinly and beckoned him toward a mirrored examination room door. Pero pushed his cart obediently. The door clicked shut behind. *"Bitte warten sie hier jetzt,"* telling him to wait. Even using the *bitte* for *please*—the *jetzt* for *now* had the tone of a command. She exited through the only other door, marked Notausgang (exit). Pero noticed it too clicked shut ominously. The one-way mirror there showed his reflection perfectly. No doubt, he was being watched.

About two minutes later, Arnold Phillips entered with a briefcase. "Hello Pero."

Surprised, Pero responded politely, "Arnold, nice to see you too." He decided to skip the obvious questions. Arnold would get down to business soon enough, Pero was sure.

Arnold had known Pero from New York days when he was at the US Embassy at the UN Headquarters. The next time he saw him was an unpleasant experience—for them both—in Nairobi months ago. Arnold had been used by the authorities, trading on their acquaintance, to give Pero false security. However, the fact that Arnold even knew Pero at all had tipped off the terrorists that Pero was a legitimate target. Arnold had been unhappy to be endangering Pero. Pero knew that. Back then, Arnold hadn't known what was going on. Now, however, he looked his old self—healthy, fit, and eager. Maybe a bit too eager. Career government employees are not known for their get up and go. Pero thought he looked edgy.

"Have a seat, Pero." Pero sat. Arnold leaned on Pero's baggage cart, playing with Pero's coat, luggage tags, not making eye contact, generally fiddling, clearly nervous. "I see you have managed to get Local One down in one piece, nice going there, Pero. He's demanding to know who you are, to thank you properly." Local One was coded embassy speak for the ambassador. When the ambassador left Germany, he would be called Berlin One everywhere else, but when he was here, he was Local One, even in dispatches. It told you he was on duty in Berlin.

Local One's real name was Pontnoire, James Pontnoire. He was a career diplomat who had done such an honest and reliable job in Saudi Arabia that Congress could find no fault—though they politically wanted to. And, as these things happen in politics, the State Department was forced to abandon him to what was considered an important country but a backwater diplomatically.

But no posting was backwater to Pontnoire. The man's intellect rose to the occasion, and he became known for funding investigations, initiating probes, and generally raising the media awareness of fascist movements in the EU, mostly stemming out of radical factions unleashed from old Iron Curtain countries. His passion was anti-fascist and no one, nothing, seemed to get in his way. There had been an attempt on his life, raising his media profile considerably and adding to the power of his voice.

He wasn't just a voice. His behind-the-scenes pressuring of the EU and the German Bundt renewed probes into neo-Nazi and fascist organizations, exposing links to terrorism, finding secret funding, and not least, naming names. He didn't limit his criticism to Germany. American politics of the Cold War were, often, fertile resources for his investigations, and he named ex-senators and civil servants who collaborated with known hate groups in the fight against Communism. More than anything else, he was a staunch opponent of any form of racism and so-called neo-nationalists within any country.

All this had a downside. Pontnoire was known to be on his last tour of duty before mandatory retirement in four months. The White House and State Department were tired of hearing complaints from Senate Committees and EU member states. It didn't matter if Pontnoire was right and had, time and again, exposed violent, illegal, groups to justice. In the world of diplomacy, he was a boat rocker on the sea of desired tranquility, even if the tranquility was often pretense.

"Local One has an idea that you could be invited to a cocktail in your honor—to acknowledge your bravery—and wants to call the media. I take it you would rather avoid such attention?"

He knew damn well Pero would. Arnold knew Pero had a sideline with the State Department and the CIA; Arnold had learned that in Nairobi.

"Stop going through my bag Arnold. What gives? And, I hadn't planned only to save your man, Arnold. I was too busy saving my own skin. He was just along for the ride. Pun intended."

"Gotcha. Well, we'll say you've moved on, business to conduct, no media please, so forth. Suit you?"

"That'll be fine, thanks. Oh, and you may want to make sure Delta Air plays this down. Only first-class passengers knew I went into the cockpit, and there were only four of us. They may have seen me come out, there was a lot of clapping and whooping when the engines came back. People make a lot of noise when they think they are *not* going to die. Me? I'd scream just before I died, not much chance after."

"That close was it?"

"Perhaps, I never asked how far the engineless glide could be. The pilots were cool and professional. If Local One wants to make a fuss, make it over them. That'll boost Delta's standings anyway, make sure your flight home is nonstop. You might suggest I was simply a Delta pilot deadheading, out of uniform. Don't make the statement official, how about just a verbal hint?"

"Yeah, that'll work. Okay. Now, on to why I am here. Here's a package." He lifted the briefcase.

Pero hated it already. He was here to film, see Heep, and regain some sort of professional competence, not get back into the game with State so soon. He waved him off. "Oh, no. Who's it for Arnold?"

"You. CIA local station said so on orders from State."

"No, Arnold, *who* did they tell you it was for? Exactly? And any message?"

"No message, just give this to Pero Baltazar, status active, arriving Delta one-zero-three. Told me they picked me so that I could have a chance to square things away with you." Pero thought he was lying. Arnold saw his expression, "No, I understood back there in Nairobi. You knew I had been lied to, just as you were. I appreciated your support Pero afterward when you held me blameless, I really did. I always seem to be saying 'thank you.' Anyway, I am on staff here, two levels below," he meant two levels below Local One, "and I do know you, trust you. This time I was asked, as a personal call because CIA local station knew you would be arriving, and I know you by sight." Arnold paused, seeing Pero's eyes squinting in building disbelief, "No, really, the package arrived from Ulm yesterday morning at my apartment. I stashed it in this briefcase and brought it along. It's just a small package. You want it now? Are we okay?" said earnestly, Arnold desperately wanted Pero to take it, so he proffered it, arms extended.

Oh hell, Pero reluctantly decided to help him out. "Yes, okay, Arnold. Let's have it."

Arnold handed over the briefcase. He didn't take the package out, whatever the package was, he just handed Pero the whole case.

Pero raised his eyebrows. Arnold grinned a little sheepishly. When Pero opened the clasp and peered inside, Arnold took a step back. The package was a plastic bag, empty except for a clearish liquid, no air, and what looked like flakes of paper in suspension. Pero took it out and held it up to the light. "Any idea what I am looking at?"

"Not a clue. It didn't come with any instructions except one: *Radioactive, do not attempt to pass security of any kind.* So I didn't take it into work past security. It's all yours now."

The radioactivity explained Arnold's reluctance to touch the damn thing. It was hot. How hot Pero had no idea. "Gee thanks. No instructions, nothing? No message?" Arnold shook his head. Pero scowled, "Ah, all cloak and dagger, they're at it again. Who am I supposed to give this to? Any idea?"

Again, Arnold shook his head. "Well, I suppose the instructions got lost somehow. Either CIA station or the folks in DC will call you at the hotel, no doubt." He started to get ready to leave.

Pero shook his head. Sarcastically he said, "Gee, thanks Arnold, good to see you again."

"Yeah, I know," Arnold faced him, looking wounded, then changed his expressed to boyish earnest, "and Pero? That was some show your people put on in Nairobi. I never saw any report that credited you, but I just knew it was your show. I heard a rumor you shot someone . . ." Pero shook his head, refusing to comment. "Anyway, in case I don't have a chance to tell you, well done." Arnold rested his hand on the exit door's frosted window, sighed, and said, "Pero you should leave via the customs hall as normal, but put that bag away first. I really don't know how dangerous it is."

Pero thought he meant the radioactive signal, so he stuffed it into his overcoat pocket, put the briefcase on the floor, not wanting any part of it, and draped his coat over the handlebar of the cart away from his body. *Plain site hiding usually works*, he thought and started toward the door. Arnold continued standing next to the other door, not moving to pick up the case. "Me first Pero. Take care, and if you have some free time in the future, we can catch a beer together. I'd like that." He tapped the glass.

"Thanks Arnold, I'll call if I do." Arnold turned around, the door opened, and Pero caught a glimpse of solid green uniform—the uniform of a police officer, not a customs' agent. The door clicked shut behind Arnold. Seconds later, the young customs' woman came in the other door, wiped a chalk line on his two bags, and led him back out to the hall. As he passed her he said, "Auf Wiedersehen."

"Good-bye Mr. Baltazar," she said in a southern drawl.

So, Arnold wasn't here because he alone knew about the delivery. He was here to reassure me, to tell me it was safe. Suddenly Pero didn't feel safe at all. Too many people knew too much, again. Pero liked working alone, safely—carrying something physical, radioactively physical, that loads of people knew was passed to him was not his idea of safe, *not safe at all.*

He pushed the luggage cart that had the usual squeaky wheel through the automatic door past customs, passing around a line of people with boxes tied with string waiting to check in at a Warsaw and Gdansk flight, and walked out to the curb. He spotted the taxi stand on the other side of the arrival and departure circle; cars were parking, driving, and unloading everywhere. He walked the ring outside, all the way around the circle to the taxi rank and handed his luggage to the driver already eagerly opening the trunk. He kept hold of his laptop case and overcoat as he opened the front door and got in.

Most tourists get into the back of the taxi. Years ago, the German taxi drivers would object and try to educate their customers that the front was both more comfortable and afforded a better view. Most tourists were happier in the back avoiding the better view. Driving anywhere in Europe, especially in cities, is, especially for Americans, frightening. Clearances are down to fractions of an inch, and speeds are easily twice the US standard. Many a tourist has arrived at their first foreign hotel white-knuckled, pale, and sweating.

On the other hand, by getting into the front passenger seat, his driver realized that Pero was no tourist and that the tip, built into the taxi fare on the meter, would be small or perhaps—horrors—nothing. If you knew enough to sit in front, you probably knew enough not to tip or at least not to tip heavily.

Pero asked him in his broken German to take him to the Steigenberger, in Los Angeles Platz. That cheered the driver up. At least his passenger wasn't a pauper. The Steigenberger is a good hotel. Not the best, but it had been, for Pero, a haven in Berlin since before the wall came down. They knew him and anyway, four stars was enough for anyone. They assured that the phones and services work well and that the room service is adequate. They were nice there, always welcoming to Pero. There was also no security screen on entry, as there was at the Intercontinental and Bristol hotels. The liquid bag in his pocket was already making problems. *I wonder just how radioactive it is?* The thought popped into his head and made him lift the coat off his lap—well, his groin if he was honest—and place it on the seat behind. He kept his computer bag between his knees, out of harm's way. All he needed was for the damn radiation to erase his hard drive.

The drive to Berlin hadn't changed much. Construction and roadworks were everywhere, but the traffic still moved. Gray skies, gray pavements that a talented writer referred to as the "steel skies of Berlin." Mist sprayed off the grimy tires in front and smeared on the windshield. Out the side window, Pero tried to spot changes in the hodgepodge of architecture, from Weimar to Bauhaus to Communist prefab, mixed with gaily painted overhead water piping installed at a time when underground excavation wasn't permitted by the surrounding East German regime. Hurtling over, around, and through bypasses and intersections, he could see the familiar splashes of green—the little cherished parks West Berlin had mandated to keep the air quality acceptable while they were once just an island lost in the air-polluting sea of an Eastern-Bloc enemy.

Now rebuilt from the ashes of WWII, freed from the yoke of separation and confinement, Berlin had been reborn into a vibrant place of tolerance. If he had to work anywhere in Europe, Pero always knew he could enjoy his time in Berlin.

Pulling up at the hotel entrance, Kamal, the Egyptian head doorman, was waiting by the curb for his taxi. Kamal popped open Pero's door and said, beaming, "Welcome back Mr. Baltazar. It's nice to have you here again."

Pero looked up at the drizzle, held out his hand and said, "Can't you ever stop the rain, Kamal?" He laughed. It was their joke. It always seemed to rain when he arrived in Berlin.

"I'll try, Mr. Baltazar, I'll try. I'll get my wife to cast a spell. We'll see tomorrow." They both laughed at the standard answer. Kamal's wife supposedly did "magic" for a fee, reading fortunes and predicting futures.

Pero asked the driver for a *quittung*, a receipt, for five Euros more than the meter, and the driver smiled and started writing. Pero gave him the cash while Kamal took the bags from the trunk of the taxi and had an assistant porter carry them in.

The year before they had refurbished the lobby. It looked newer, more lacquer and strangely Japanese but no less efficient, nor more efficient for that matter . . . so Pero wondered why they bothered. Hotels get bored with the same old décor. Guests like continuity. *Someday*, he thought, *they'll ask our preference. Renew the mattresses first, then the phones and computer services, then the exercise rooms, then the menu . . . and save the lobby beautification for last.*

Pero checked in, gave his credit card, got it back along with the electronic door key. He was said hello to by the reception desk staff and responded amiably. These were people who knew him over the years. He waved at the staff and turned right toward the elevators. A man sitting and reading a paper folded it and took pace behind him. Kamal speeded the baggage cart with his bags to catch up. He wanted to personally escort Pero to his room, as he always did. The doors opened and they all got in. Pero entered his key into the elevator security slot. He was on the upper floor, the so-called executive floor. To gain access, you need a coded key. Using your sixth-floor door key, the central computer registers your whereabouts—useful for phone call forwarding and other guest services—and security. The other man got in and pressed five, the floor below Pero's. He was well groomed, about five foot ten, black hair, knee length black leather jacket with large pockets, clean shaven, and wore too much aftershave. Pretty pungent it was too.

At his floor, the man got out, turned and looked Pero in the eye, and walked off. Pero noted his expression, not sure why the man had made the effort so blatantly. There was no threat there, just a recording, like a human digital camera with a delay in the shutter.

Once upstairs Kamal got his bags onto the bed, knowing Pero wanted nothing else—Pero could handle it from there on. Kamal took the fifty Euro tip and left smiling and saying thank you. Pero had learned from his grandfather how to tip. "Tip on the way in, not on the way out. That way they know what you are giving them and you'll get better, more faithful service during your stay. And when you get there next time they know the tip is imminent."

Pero did what he always did in any new hotel room. He checked the phone was working, opened the computer, and hooked it up to Wi-Fi. There was no longer any hard LAN in the rooms, but Wi-Fi for e-mail worked well enough for simple emails. The TV screen was showing a personal message, with his name and a greeting. Displayed was, "You have four messages."

Pero pushed the remote buttons for English, then messages and read the four headings as they appeared in descending time order:

1. Bill Heeper called from room 635 9:25 a.m.
2. D. Lewis called at 9:20 a.m.
3. Bill Heeper called at 7:20 a.m.
4. Amogh Ranjeet called at 10:30 p.m. yesterday

One by one, he clicked on each, the first three had no message or call back number. D. Lewis was CIA Langley, the director, but why would he be using a landline? Heep's earliest message first told him he was on his way, and the second message was that he had arrived and to call when he could. Pero planned to call him later. There was a worrying message from Amogh "Please call as soon as possible." Something was wrong. Amogh must have called Pero's office in New York to get this contact. If he was calling from Nairobi, something was wrong. Amogh was reliable, totally so, together they had thwarted part of the terrorist attack in Kenya. Pero's junior by almost thirty years, Amogh had proved himself equal in times of need or danger.

Pero called him first. "Hi Amogh, Pero here, got your message, I am in Berlin. What's wrong?"

"Pero, good of you to call. Been a bit of a disaster here. Mbuno's wife, Niamba, got hit by a matatu." Mbuno was Pero's oldest friend in Kenya, a safari guide who had saved Pero's life, all too often. A chief, a *mzee*, of his clan the Waliangulu, Mbuno's reputation as the premier wildlife and safari scout was legendary. Pero wasn't about to let him down. Amogh was explaining that a dilapidated empty matatu truck-bus had sideswiped her badly as she was walking back from a *dukka* (a shop). "She's in the Kenyatta Hospital, pathetic care I am afraid. Doctors are not sure. My father and mother—we're all hoping you could intervene . . ."

"Amogh, I can and would be pleased to help. What's the issue?" Pero knew Amogh's parents, Prabir Ranjeet and his wife, Acira, would be able to fund anything necessary.

"It is Mbuno—he is reluctant to impose . . ."

"Tell him he is hurting his friend by not asking for help. Did we all not ask for his help when needed? Tell him it is a matter of honor and that he cannot let me down."

"I will . . ."

"And Amogh, money no object. Can you arrange transport to another hospital? The Aga Khan or the Nairobi? I prefer the Aga Khan, it's more modern."

"That can be arranged. Mbuno's with Niamba, and he seems very low."

"What are Niamba's injuries like?"

"Crushed pelvis, mainly. They say she's stable but not getting better. They are blaming it on her age . . . but I fear it could be more serious."

"Okay, if the doctor team at the Aga Khan needs it, get an air ambulance flight out, Brit Air would be best, and have her taken to London. Use the SOS people out of London. They can arrange everything. I have those details on my computer here, and I'll send them on to you—same email address?" Amogh said yes. "Okay then, fine, take this down . . ." He gave him his private Amex card followed by his private Visa card numbers, including all the expiration dates and those annoying little security numbers. "Spend anything you need to. If I need to come down there, call back and I'll fly in."

"Okay, Pero, will do, but what hospital in London?"

"Ask the Italian doctor, the one in the Aga Khan. Anything he says goes, okay?"

"Very good, Mr. Pero, I know the man. Glad I reached you. But Mbuno may not want to leave her . . ." Amogh sounded doubtful he could convince Mbuno of anything.

"Look, Amogh, promise Mbuno as much honey as I can buy. It'll make him know I'm serious." Pero remembered that Mbuno loved honey on toast every morning. "And buy him a ticket as well, but for God's sake, get your father to fit him out with some warm clothes. Please tell him I ask him, humbly, to accept this help, it's my honor at stake, it's my turn to save his life for a change. He'll understand. Could you get someone to go along to help them both?"

"Well, I could go. I have friends from LSE I could stay with." LSE is the London School of Economics in London where Amogh had attended school on a secret scholarship arranged by Pero. Perhaps not so secret as Amogh had figured it out many months before.

"That's great, Amogh, thanks."

"Not a bit, Mr. Pero, thank you. But I'll pay my own way, least I can do."

"Thanks, but don't let money stand in the way of helping them, okay? First class for Mbuno on the same plane as Niamba, okay? Here's my mobile number, twenty-four hours a day," and he gave him his European cell phone.

"Lot of numbers to remember—what?"

Pero laughed, he knew the financial whiz kid Amogh could handle anything with numbers.

Amogh chuckled in response, "Don't worry, wrote them all down. Bye for now," he laughed and hung up. Amogh may have been young, but he was efficient and competent and knew he could rely on Pero just as Pero could rely on him. Their joint near-death experience in Nairobi in air-to-air combat with the terrorists had bonded them for life. Besides, Amogh could organize anything. Pero knew he could handle this. He just hoped Mbuno would agree.

His next call was to Lewis, but not on the house phone. He grabbed the coat, pocket gurgling with the liquid and made his way down and out of the hotel. In his other pocket, he had a special issue satellite phone as well as his local cell phone.

He turned right out the door, waved to Kamal, and made a right at the corner. He walked the two blocks to the Wilhelm-Gedächtniskirche, the "wedding cake" church, knowing it would be busy with tourists and students. It always was.

The church had been bombed out during the Second World War, but its hollow remains stood proud as the old pre-WWII center of cultural Germany and, for many years, the hub of West Berlin. Pero walked past the ugly concrete box outside, remembering that inside it was lovely, serene. He marveled that in the fifties people were in a hurry to erect replacement monuments. And in a hurry, they often botched it.

Behind the old church were street food stands with vendors of *shashlik*, sausages, and *kartoffeln* (potatoes). These spicy kebabs of pork, greasy paprika or curry sausages, and applesauce-covered potatoes are popular. Everyone was milling about so no one would pay attention to one more tourist blabbing away on a cell phone, even if the phone had an odd-looking antenna. Pero bought a greasy looking sausage, *currywurst*. It was surprisingly good.

The satellite phone he used was not a standard model. It was illegal. It has a second amplitude modulator. Press 9-1-1 and you get CIA Headquarters. Langley, scrambled, direct. It was a perfect signal, always. They listened, you spoke, they double clicked off when you told them to. It was how you knew they had heard you. It used the President's backup frequency, channel four. You didn't use it for long. You had better not.

He heard it connect while he still had hot sausage in his mouth. Swallowing quickly, "Baltazar, P. On site in Berlin. Returning Mr. Lewis' call."

"Stand by." He waited.

They repeated, "Stand by."

Oh damn, he forgot they wanted his agreement. It was unusual to have a conversation about this thing. Give me instructions or listen to his field report and hang up, that's the norm. It seemed they wanted to chat. He wished they didn't. It meant something was wrong. He had hoped all he was being asked to do was to act as a postman with the liquid bag. "Yes, of course, I will stand by." The seconds clicked on his watch, approaching noon. He ate another piece of sausage.

"Lewis here, please state your location."

"Good afternoon Director. I'm standing by the Gedächtniskirche in Berlin, in a crowd of people, tourists and students eating cheap, greasy food. I am. they are."

"Any tail?" He was all business.

This was the second time he had talked to him in months, and again Lewis was terse. This must mean that either Lewis was troubled and was being overly efficient or Pero was in the doghouse for some unknown reason. *Perfect*, Pero thought, *then I can resign*. "Yes, recently seen but not presently aware of his presence." He gave a description.

"Not one of ours. Be careful. Where's the packet?" It wasn't a packet. A packet was pure information. This was a package. He should know that. *What the hell's going on?*

"I have no packet."

"Repeat that."

"I have no packet."

"Were you contacted by Phillips at," he spoke off to one side "what was the name?" he heard a voice, and he repeated it "Tegel?"

"I met with him and he made no mention of a packet. He specifically had no message for me. He specifically said there was no message. He gave me a package."

"Repeat that." Pero did. Lewis' voice grew more urgent. "Your articles are still active," he meant Pero was still authorized, and he had agreed to the terms of employment as an active field agent, "and we want you . . ."

In desperation, on the last mission, the CIA upped his grade to field agent, or what Heep teased Pero later was really 007 status. To be sure, some of the events that unfolded were almost spy agent like, with guns and danger to all. But, to his innermost core, Pero was uncomfortable with the added authority and the danger it brought.

"Hold it, Lewis. Article thirty-four states the agent has the right to declare himself unfit. I now do so."

"What are you playing at Baltazar? You have the package . . ."

Pero wanted to make himself perfectly understood, "Yeah, now let me make this clear. Clearly a package you knew nothing about. Clearly, I'm involved in something already, with no briefing, no assignment beforehand. Clearly, I was even being followed by a 'not ours' and presumably you expect one of ours to be following me as well since you asked for a description. Clearly, you sent Arnold Phillips on the face of it because I know him, but he's not carrying a packet but a package. He's your man, and he's either not following orders or your chain has broken down. I'm in the line of fire—and I hope that's not literal. I was not ready for this. I'm not a field agent really. If anything at all," he stressed the at all, "I was merely a gofer, a messenger boy before. That field agent stint was a one-off. Are we clear on that?"

"You did well on that assignment . . ."

"What so-called assignment? I was dumped in the deep end and to save my skin I agreed to proceed."

"You mean to save everyone's skin, don't you? I seem to remember your words," Lewis stressed the next word, "Clearly."

"Okay, big deal, I was appalled at the possibility of failure when you had no one else on hand, so we all agreed to step into the fray. Let's not forget that, everything was done with my friends' help and agreement. I couldn't have done and didn't do it without them." A group of unlikely looking tourists—too old, all men—was elbowing their way through the students. Pero decided to move across the street, toward the zoo and aquarium a few blocks away. "I'm walking, I'm getting a bit exposed just standing here arguing with you. If you have something to tell me, do it openly and let me assess if I can help," he paused again for emphasis, "at all." As he walked, he dropped the rest of the sausage in the garbage bin.

Pero could tell by Lewis' returning pause that he was wondering if he could order Pero back into his command. Sense prevailed. "Oh, well, here goes. If you hadn't done so well before . . . Phillips was supposed to be given, sent from a field agent who's down . . ." he meant hurt, injured, or sick, "a paper message with a photograph to pass on to you. You were to read the message, study the photograph, and give them back to him. Your instructions were to verify that information and run the message home to me." He paused and Pero said nothing. *Make the bastard finish*, Pero thought. "Okay, Phillips never got back to the embassy after Tegel. Missing. He handed you a package. Can you describe the package?"

"You first."

Lewis hadn't expected that. *How many variables were there here?* Pero thought. "The only one in play is a vacuum packed solution of liquid with paper particles inside. Radioactive. It's missing." There were no variables, he got it right first time.

"From where?"

"Mannheim Air Force Base, Military Intel, Unit twenty."

"I have it, I think. Arnold said it was sent from Ulm."

"That fits. The field agent carrying it went out of play on the train between Nuremberg and Frankfurt. That train passes through Ulm."

"Where is he? The agent?"

"We don't know." Lewis' answer also confirmed to Pero that the field agent was a 'he' and not the southern drawl woman in customs.

"What exactly is this blob? Oh, and how dangerous is it?"

"Radioactivity is minimal we've been assured, the liquid is heavy water, absorbs emissions, stabilizes nuclear reactors. The particles are decomposed labels, half-life fifty-four years. Is it safe?"

Pero wondered about that too. Heavy water stabilized unstable radioactive emissions, but it was hardly liquid lead. There would be contamination here, but how much? He had no idea. Still, heavy water was better protection than nothing. It should make it safe to handle. He hoped. Lewis was waiting for an answer . . . "It's in my pocket, physically safe. Where was it supposed to go? And why did Arnold have it at all?"

"I cannot answer the Arnold part yet. The sample, that's what it is, floating in the heavy water, needed to get to the Max Planck Institute for typing, to see what isotope it matches. So far, the isotope looks like nothing produced in any reactor we know of."

"What's the isotope?"

"Uranium 234."

A loyal reader of Scientific American, Pero knew what that was. "A bit ancient isn't it? Natural or man-made?"

"Enhanced, man-made. The label was not found on the sample."

Oh, this is getting interesting. Pero asked, "What label?"

"The label in the heavy water."

"You mean the bits of paper, fragments floating in the water?"

"It must have begun to deteriorate. Yes, that paper is, or was, a label."

Pero told him to wait. He had reached the aquarium and put the phone, still on, in his pocket.

"*Ein mal, bitte*," and the woman sold him an entry ticket. He walked into the exhibit building, dark and mysterious, underwater gloom punctuated by glowing glass panes, each with a different aquatic scene. He had been here many times before. Just past the Cichlid's tank, ten-inch marbled Oscars, fins waving gently in an Amazon floodwater simulation. He turned around to see who came in next. Just some kids and parents. No one suspicious. He took the first exit to the left and walked out of the aquarium into the zoo next door. He pulled out the phone. "Sorry about that, took a detour inside and checked for a tail. I am clear, I think."

"I am still here Baltazar, next time ring off and call back." Lewis was reminding Pero of the status of this phone line, none too pleased by the delay. Lewis took a breath, "Okay, here's what else we know, it was going to be in your written instructions. The label was found on the bottom of some gold bars the US Treasury was swapping via a Swiss bank and a dealer. The radioactivity set off alarms in Zurich airport when the shipment arrived. The Swiss searched the gold bars—nothing unusual about them but then they found those labels, some of them fragments on the bottom of a few bars. When they scraped them off and ran them through the X-ray machine, the screen went black, indicating radioactivity; the gold was mostly clean of any more particles or labels. They took the bits of paper to a decontamination center and bagged it in heavy water. A week later, the sample went missing from their evidence room. We suspect the Pentagon had it removed.

A week ago, we got a call from Mil Intel asking us to collect the bag and have it tested for origin of source. They had tried and failed. They needed our help."

"What was the rest of the packet? What was I supposed to be reading and passing on?"

"The rest was a request to the Max Planck scientist, Doctor Juren Schmidt, he's a sleeper, one of ours. His image was in the photo." Lewis meant he was a detainee of the CIA.

"So why did he get the package, or was he supposed to get the package, and what's Arnold's role? Did you brief him and if not, who did?"

"I called him at home, but he was briefed by Station." He meant Berlin Station, the CIA agent in the embassy. "Station is also missing. We suspect foul play."

"So, let's recap," Pero was getting angry, "Arnold slipped me a package that he shouldn't have had in the first place, sent to me by Station, who's missing as is Arnold now, in the airport with at least two other witnesses . . ."

"Describe witnesses."

Pero gave him the description of the police officer spotted through Arnold's exit door as best he could. "And there's a southern American accent woman, dressed as customs . . ." And he gave him her description.

"Sounds like Station and her escort. It's a mandate in Berlin. Police accompany embassy officials when they are going about the city. There have been terrorist threats against personnel." So, it meant a federal official was impersonating a police officer in uniform or had borrowed someone, probably from German Internal Security.

Into Pero's head popped a children's book, *this just keeps on getting curiouser and curiouser*. "Okay, now what? I have a hot package, and surely you don't expect me to go to the Max Planck anymore, do you?"

"Stand by for a moment, there's a wire coming in from Station." He heard him talking, his hand over the mouthpiece.

It's a mistake, really. The microphones that are designed to work so far away from your mouth are tuned, finely tuned, for voice frequencies. It's like talking on a cell phone while on the toilet, never a good idea, every sound carries, perfectly. Pero could hear Lewis talking, muffled, but clearly "He placed the phone where? Why did he do that? What do you mean she's on the autobahn heading for Mannheim? With both the cop and Phillips? Who told her to do that? Can we speak to her? No? Well, try, damn it!" He lifted his hand. "Station is out of the area, I am not sure why. You cannot rely on her."

"I heard all that, careful with your open microphone. Mannheim . . . it's the autobahn to the Institute, isn't it?"

"Yes."

"Well, perhaps she's leading them astray . . . whoever they are, perhaps they think she's still got the package."

"Damn, okay, good thinking. Okay, that leaves you in the clear."

"No, it doesn't, it means my tail is just a little looser. Now let's get rid of this thing, and I can go back to normal work. Oh, and remember, I am not a field agent."

"Well, you think like one. Okay, here goes. As radioactive as it is, it cannot be sent, no mail, FedEx, DHL, no air courier. Borders, post offices, planes, truck transport—all are insecure with loads of radioactivity screening. Max Planck is out. The lab we wanted to use as a backup is CERN in Geneva. Any ideas?"

It took Pero ten seconds of hard thinking. "Maybe—two. One, I would have to carry the package there. And I will need to talk to a friend to confirm an idea. If he agrees, we'll need a little leverage in Hollywood. So, two, can you buy me time in Hollywood on the job I'm on?"

"That's an easy one. Yes. What do you need?"

"Hollywood leverage, I need time from them on this assignment—I assume you know all about it by now."

"As I said, that's an easy one. We do have your filming details. We'll handle this through the banks, put pressure in the right place. The film people will do exactly what you ask." He was right, banks controlled Hollywood production. If he could leverage the banks— Pero was sure he could because the CIA exerted pressure globally through the banks and World Trade Organization—then no producer would argue with a money source.

"Okay, let me see what I need on that, exactly." Pero thought for a moment, he could hear the little satellite connection clicks in the background. "Lewis, can you make sure the film company that I am here for understands that I am golden, can do what I please as far as time is concerned? Specifically, I want to have them understand that the clock, financial clock, is not ticking if I spend more time or money."

"Can do. Will do. We'll make the financing via Germany solid, without limit. It will act as cover for extra time. Citibank had once wanted to underwrite your film it says here, so we can make them step up to the plate, put the pressure on, via them."

"Wow, that's fast. Okay, the second part is trickier. I want to stash this somewhere for a week to ten days. Let the trail go cold."

"I was not sure I can agree with that. Where did you have in mind?" Pero didn't want to tell him. There were leaks possible. Already there had been swaps in director's orders, people moving all over the map and, really, he was sitting with the hot potato. When the music stopped—and it would when they caught up with Station and Arnold—he didn't want to be left holding the bag.

"Is there some kind of rush, I mean besides the action everyone has sprung to? Whatever the paper is inside here, it was there for a long time, on that gold bar, no?"

"About fifty plus years or more as best we can tell."

"Okay then, let's slow this down and cause the opposition to rush about, exposing themselves. Gives us time to think."

"Spoken like a field agent."

"I am not. I only want to get on with my normal work. The crew is here, permits in place, and the talent arrives tonight, I think. If I take off running now, it'll tip everybody off. By the way, who is the opposition?"

"We're not sure. It's either an inside or a slightly outside operation." He meant no foreign government. Inside meant a rival firm or spy group. Outside meant rogue ops, possibly terrorists or criminals. "So will you tell me where you will stash it? Is it safe?"

"No and yes in that order. But I need one final piece of information. What residue is now on my clothing?"

"Our people here say negligible, but it's possible. The high Zurich readings might have been an anomaly."

"Great. I'll lose this coat in case it sets off a detector somewhere. And maybe my clothes. You'll get the bill. Look, this is getting suspicious, there's a zookeeper eyeing me. These apes can hold my attention only so long."

"Okay, but be careful and report in hourly." Two clicks and he was gone. *Hourly? No way.* Pero needed to get back to normal life and fast.

Folding away the phone, he went over to the keeper and asked him "*Kann ich gehen nacht eine mal im aquarium? Hier ist meine billet.*" he showed his ticket and asked him if he could get back inside through the exit door. He shook his head and told me it wasn't normal. Pero explained he had taken the door outside so his phone would work and so he would *nicht disturbieren* (not disturb) *die anderen leute* (the other people). The keeper nodded, mumbled something about damn *handies* (cell phones), and pulled out the passkey. Opening the door, he motioned Pero in, who then thanked him profusely. He wasn't being facetious, he thought he had spotted a tail coming through the brick and carved stone main entrance archway of the zoo about 100 yards away. The jacket looked familiar from the Steigenberger. He was sure the tail hadn't seen him yet.

Once inside the aquarium he quickly turned left and opened the door marked Verboten.

Years ago, he had watched feeding time at the arowana and arapaima tank. The aquarium keeper had arranged a school group standing in front of the giant glass that held these five-foot freshwater prehistoric fish before the keeper went through the verboten door. Inside the tank, the fish snaked around the surface, effortless and graceful, silver scales shining. They had no need for camouflage. They had speed and could eat most anything in their huge, gaping, articulated mouths: frogs, birds, fish, insects—anything coming near the surface was potential prey to be swallowed whole. The demonstration the keeper arranged was to show their agility and appetite. The aquarium was only half-full of water, the upper half being a natural jungle scene with moss and plants. The keeper, behind the scenes, opened an upper door and released three little chicks. The chicks hopped about on the leaves. As soon as they showed themselves to the water below, the fifty-pound silver sides snake-like arapaima struck and swallowed the chick whole. It was all over quickly, no feathers, a little splash that made the kids draw back. The arapaima moved its neck muscles as its teeth, in its throat, disposed of dinner. The other two chicks went just as quickly.

In this land of horrible children's tales, the demonstration had the desired effect. Horror, fear, and nightmares. Raw nature.

Pero knew where to stash this heavy water bag. He opened the trapdoor above the arapaima tank and lifted the healthiest potted plant, chosen on the assumption that it wouldn't need replacing any time soon. He dropped the bag in and repotted the plant, then closed the trapdoor, exited the keeper's door and resumed his tour of the aquarium. No one saw him, there wasn't even a child visiting the darkened labyrinth.

Next, he needed to get rid of the coat and satellite phone. He needed to be clean, squeaky clean, in case he was apprehended. Exiting the aquarium, he headed back to the Gedächtniskirche. He had seen a beggar there and planned to give him a newer coat, even if it might have a little residual radioactivity. Pero knew cloth does not hold contamination very well.

Chapter 4

Tempelhof

Pero walked back from the church, now chilled by the March damp and breeze. He had liked that coat and needed to replace it quickly. He turned up his jacket collar. On the way past the bookstore on the Kurfurstendamm, he dropped the satellite phone into the blue dumpster of the street sweeper, first pushing 999 to disable and erase the memory chips. He heard the crackle of electronic destruction. Even if someone found it, it was useless and untraceable.

Thankfully, the doorman Kamal was off helping a busload of tourists, so he turned unseen into the building and went straight to the elevators. The newspaper reader who had been sitting in the lobby on his arrival wasn't sitting there anymore. Pero saw the woman behind the desk recognize him and pick up the phone, but Pero didn't stop.

At his door, he could hear the phone already ringing. It was Heep, "Pero, where have you been? They said you checked in over an hour ago." Pero told him he had to run an errand and to join him for a drink or coffee in the executive lounge. The sixth floor had a small private sitting room for their elite guests. Well, maybe not elite, just those with the right color credit card who wanted peace and quiet.

Five minutes later the two old friends were hugging and patting each other on the back. Heep's finger now sported a gold band. He held his hand up, wiggling the fingers. "You're kidding, without me? And Mary—our crocodile and dinosaur lady—and you? When?" Heep had gotten married, again. Heep was a recidivist husband—trying it over and over again.

"A month ago. We tried to invite you, but you were not taking calls after the first week, remember? And, anyway, I didn't want to tell you on the phone last week."

The two old friends sat, ordered tea, and talked about life and the aftermath of Kenya. When the pleasantries were over, Pero gave him the news of Niamba, Mbuno's wife. Heep was shocked, not about a matatu bus hitting someone along the road, but that it was her. She was a kind, gentle, aging woman, as spiritual as her husband was vital. Heep thought what Pero had arranged was the best one could do. "Amogh will handle it, he's great like that. When will you know where he's taken her?"

"I expect he'll call," he patted a cell phone in his jacket pocket, "anytime he's ready." For a while, they discussed the upcoming shoot. All the shots were supposed to be without dialog but to include ambient sound. "Who'd you get to record sound?"

Heep told Pero he couldn't bring his regular commercial crew. "They're still shooting the Tyrolean second unit shots for that damn car commercial. Stupidest job I ever took. The client has no idea that a Cadillac Escalade looks stupid on a winding alpine road, the damn thing's so wide it doesn't even fit into one lane! Honestly, Pero, you'd think they would figure this stuff out before spending a million bucks shipping three cars and our team over here to shoot this in," he paused for effect, "wait for it," pausing again, smiling, "you'll love this—IMAX."

Pero nearly fell off his armchair. That was perhaps the stupidest thing he'd ever heard. A couple of million bucks for an IMAX shot that cannot be edited to suit TV? How many people did they think would get to see it? What a bad return on their money.

Anticipating, Heep answered his unspoken question: "It's for the Detroit Car Show only. Five days, sexy men models and all, promoting the mommy car line. It's the car launch, new model, in luscious pearl pink color. Yech." They were both laughing by then at the absurdity of it all. Sometimes Hollywood is only surpassed in arrogant stupidity by the twentysomethings, the hotshot creative team, at ad agencies.

Pero needed to know Heep's availability, "How much more do you have to shoot? Do you have to go back?"

Heep explained he'd completed his bit, the rest were helicopter shots and a few static set-ups for the product photographers to fill the brochures. He thought the whole thing should be wrapped up by the same time this job was, say a few weeks, tops.

Pero seemed satisfied. "Ever work with Danny Redmond?" The movie star was an unknown quantity to Pero, and he was sure Heep, who shot movies from time to time, would have a better idea about Redmond. A man with boyish good looks, now all of thirty-two, he was once a party animal, according to *People* magazine. In the past three years, he had steadied down, took up serious reading—or so the magazines would have everyone think. And there had even been an appearance on Oprah where they discussed his ten favorite books, most of which were classics in translation. He had done a few great action films and then some colossal failures, yet he always looked good. But in truth, Redmond had few acting skills.

Heep explained, "So he has dropped out of films for about a year and went to hone his craft on the London stage. You know, the usual thing, proving and growing on stage where audiences are demanding but not rude for established stars who need to become real actors."

"I met him at the Emmy's. He was with that beautiful wife of his. He seemed genuine. He loves our wildlife programs." It was Heep and Pero's specialty, producing animal series, like *Edge of the Wild.* They had been due to tape those episodes again in the next months, but the show had been canceled, to be replaced by a thirteen-part series of prime-time one-hour specials starring Mary Lever, the Crocodile Lady. Pero was the executive producer for the series, and Heep had taken over as the producer, Pero's old job, in addition to his usual role as director. Pero hadn't felt up to it when it was all being negotiated over the past few months by their respective agents. Refusing calls, he had told his lawyer to quietly tell Heep to make any deal he could. Heep did. It was a doozy, making them both more money than usual. Mary was hot, and they had signed her up. The industry knew they were damn good at wildlife shooting—the best, well, not exactly—David Attenborough and the BBC could still run rings around them, but that brass ring was always an encouragement, not a competition.

Pero said, "I hope Danny will like the crap they've written for him. Did you read that stuff?" Pero knew Heep had been emailed a copy of the script. "The last thing we need is a script re-write, new demands every day, delaying permits and schedules. The Mayor's office likes a tight and accurate shoot schedule, you know that." Heep nodded. Pero asked him, "You got the equipment squared away?"

"Well, we had an idea that I floated past the studio and Pederson a week ago." Heep meant the film's director. "Then he called Redmond in London." That got Pero's attention. Heep continued, "Look, I explained I want to shoot this hand-held, not Steadicam, real *Funeral in Berlin* type of tension, off balance. Redmond loved the idea—that he's like Richard Burton's character, seedy, a washed up spy, haunted, but sharp. He's supposed to be drugged, not knowing where he is, riding the S-Bahn until he sees something familiar . . ." He meant the trimotor plane hanging above the Technisches Museum, "that's why he gets off there. We'll have to catch the reflection in the glass as he sees it. Then as he gets into the entrance, the perspective changes as the girl sees him." They were building the set for that shot with her, in Hollywood right now. "The train yard may now also be needed for a running scene, I got a fax . . ."

"Oh, they're pushing us already, more shots?" Pero asked.

"Well, yes, we may shoot the train shunting yard out the back of the museum for the chase sequence. But here's some good news, they cut one scene for us—they don't need the transfer from the U-Bahn subway, to the elevated S-Bahn train. They think the audience will just think the inside train goes outside." Pero's mouth was open. "Yes, Pero, I know, the S-Bahn is yellow and the U-Bahn is . . ."

"Orange. No wait, don't tell me, they've repainted the U-Bahn to yellow." Heep nodded. Pero shook his head in amusement. "Okay, that'll work, I suppose, but Heep you better make sure they know the carriage is a different shape and size."

"We'll shoot it tight so we'll never see it whole. And I'll get extra shots, in case, with the size clearly shown using the tripod, full Panavision, in case they need to make a continuity cutaway." They went on like this for a half hour or more. For them, business came first. They were professionals and liked their work. At the end, there was a pause as they finished a second small pot of tea.

Pero was waiting for it as Heep asked, "So, any other side to this trip I should know about?"

Pero had promised him never to lie again. In Kenya Heep and the crew had learned the truth of his secret sideline. Back then, if it had upset Heep to think Pero had a secret from him, neither Heep nor the crew showed it. Their loyalty and friendship had come on strong. "Not until we're done here, I hope. I had a delivery this morning at the airport coming off my flight, but I arranged for a ten-day delay. Should be okay."

"If not, count me in. It is good work. Worth doing. If I can help, you have only to allow me, no asking required."

Pero was touched, "I'll keep that in mind. It's already messy—they wanted me to transport something. It's not what I was trained to do and besides, I am not the agent type, don't you think?"

"You did all right Pero. I am no judge of other missions— isn't that what they're called? But we did all right. You produced us well, as you always do."

"Yes, we did all right, but it was an emergency. And in those situations, people sometimes go beyond their talents and, well, we got lucky."

"Luck or not, Pero, you produced us, and we stopped the bastards. Are you up against anything like that now, already?"

"Oh no, it's just a small screw up. I called a time-out for me to do this shoot and to allow matters to resolve a bit without me. Lewis, remember him?" Heep nodded, "Well, Lewis was not pleased, but he knew I was right. Sometimes slowing down produces more sure results."

"You still, what was it, a field agent? Or have you reverted to the other?"

"Gofer? I tried doing that, going back, I told Lewis. At the moment, I am halfway between a mail carrier waiting to deliver if and when I am damn good and ready. Neither snow nor sleet nor dead of night has any interest to me, I am more your kind of lazy mail carrier. If they don't like that, tough. When the time is right, I'll deliver the package."

"Where to?"

But Pero told him not to ask too many questions. If he needed him involved, he would tell him. Otherwise, it was safer for them all to put it aside and get on with filming. Heep agreed, with a sigh of relief.

As Danny Redmond—and his circus entourage no doubt—would arrive that afternoon, late, they decided on a dinnertime and place. Heep told Pero he'd meet their sound technician and assistant later over dinner. Heep was handling the camera himself.

Pero debated going to the airport to pick the actor up, so he called the production coordinator's office in London to ask. They informed Pero that Danny Redmond was being met, for security reasons, by "someone from the Mayor's office." Pero had once had that experience and knew what was in store.

Germans take celebrity—political and artistic—seriously. If asked for discretion, they will just watch covertly. But if asked for protection or if they think it's needed, they will put on a display of an ostentatious bodyguard elite that is unrivaled anywhere in the world. To be really showy and effective, they provided a large escort, loads of flashing lights, screaming vehicles, a variety of transport from motorcycles—big fat BMW superbikes—to gleaming black paint and black-windowed limousines and green and white BMW or Porsche souped-up police cars. Each has a siren and uses it. Each has lights, top, front, and back, and they use them.

Then, just to outdo every other police force in the world providing first class security, this procession of vehicles does not proceed at twenty, thirty, or forty miles per hour like the US President's cavalcade. Oh, no, they literally put the pedal to the metal and roar through the streets. The drivers are race-trained on the famed Nurburgring racing course as well an anti-terrorist secret facility outside Koln. The key to success is the motorcycles.

For Danny Redmond it went smoothly. They collected him at the arrivals and loaded him and his team into the black limousine. Once the car doors were shut, the engines were revved and the ten or so cops with the machine guns stood around keeping everyone away. At the same time, the motorcycles, roared off in pairs, at least four sets of them. The clock started ticking, engines idling. At twenty seconds, the limo started off—one police car in front, one at the rear—full speed ahead. Down the ramp from Tegel airport, the lead white and green police BMW hit seventy-five or eighty, still accelerating, followed by the limo three meters behind, on the bumper. By the time they got on the short stretch of the autobahn, the convoy was doing a steady 110 mph. The motorcycles were nowhere to be seen. As the autobahn ended and the first intersection approached, the convoy slowed—if it can be called that—to around eighty-five and kept that speed until the destination was reached. Every intersection was clear because two motorcycles blocked the side roads, helmeted super-cops staring down any potential transgressor. As the convoy passed, the motorcycle cops fired up and screamed up alongside the cavalcade doing well over 120, leap-frogging their colleagues to cut off traffic four more intersections ahead.

And so it continued, with the motorcycles blocking traffic, zooming ahead, and the convoy maintaining an incredible speed—bursting through traffic that had been moved aside, screaming past pedestrians pulled back from the curb, and zipping, inches on either side, at break-neck speed through city thoroughfares. Danny Redmond only knew they had arrived when he saw the lead motorcycles perfectly positioned, in pairs, calmly parked. His limo brakes would then have been applied strongly bringing the car to a smooth but sharp stop. Then the doors were snapped open, and another guard of machine gun toting police, already there, were standing at attention, controlling passers-by keen on seeing who the big shot was.

Danny Redmond's cavalcade had arrived.

He exited the car and stepped onto the sidewalk looking for someone to talk to, perhaps to shake hands with. There was no one to thank. The whole manner of the police declared, "No fuss please, we're professionals."

There was no doubt that Danny Redmond was charismatic. After he had stepped away from his convoy, followed by three of his entourage, he saw motorcycle police and his driver give each other the thumbs up, pleased with their performance.

As Danny went into the hotel, below Pero's sixth-floor window, the police car twirling lights still flashed on and off like press flashbulbs. Inside, the hotel staff pranced about trying to get closer and cater to his every whim. The elevator had been stalled by the manager, with a key, who then personally escorted Redmond upstairs, riddling him with the usual pleasantries. "How good to have you stay with us. Did you have a pleasant flight?" that sort of thing. It was not as if Danny Redmond wouldn't have heard it all before.

The three people walking with him, presumably his "people," tried to keep their position of authority by elbowing anyone who impeded their progress down the middle of the hall. "Please, please, Mr. Redmond has had a long journey; he needs to be left alone." A tourist and his wife started to come out of their room, and they were pressed back inside as the Redmond tide swept past. Pero was watching all this from his door, next to Redmond's suite. Pero had booked rooms for Redmond's entourage on a floor below with no passkey for this floor. Pero too needed peace and quiet time with the star, to make sure they could achieve what the film needed, not what a celebrity's entourage could take hours to bitch about. Redmond was a producer on the film and word had reached Pero that he was hands-on. Heep's room was ten doors down from the suite and Pero saw him standing in the doorway grinning, shaking his head, as they passed him.

As Redmond got to his door, the manager already had the key out and was ready to do his "voila" gesture. *Yeah, it's a room, what a surprise*, Pero saw in Redmond's eyes—it was what Pero was thinking too. Pero smiled.

Redmond smiled back and turned to the manager. "Mr. Gestler, isn't it? You are very kind to take all this trouble. What a lovely . . ." The rest was lost as they pressed on into the room. Pero stood there watching ten people follow them in. It was going to be crowded in there. He glanced at Heep, who was still shaking his head. The noises from inside were gaining strength, the door re-opened, "And if you wouldn't mind personally showing my assistants their rooms?" The manager nodded and started to say something. Danny cut him off, "Yes, yes, that's wonderful, Herr Gestler, I would consider it a personal favor if you would ensure they have every service they require. I will be busy this evening and will not want to be disturbed," and here he paused for effect, looking as well at his assistants before adding, "by anyone." It was a command performance. Everyone had left his room and he stood in the doorway, arms up over his head, hands on the doorframe, physically occupying the space. Even with the good looks, charm, and radiant smile, it was prime ape behavior. It said, "This is mine, now go away." They all left, like good little chimps.

He looked over at Heep and back at Redmond. They all smiled, nodded. Redmond was a take-charge guy. "Ten minutes? I need the bathroom, then we'll talk. That's the lounge over there, right, next to the elevators?" Pero nodded. "Fine, see you then."

Before he could shut his door, Pero's cell phone buzzed. He looked at the screen and frowned. Heep saw and came over, fast. It was Amogh. Pero clicked on the speakerphone. "Go ahead, Amogh," who started speaking as the two went into Pero's room and let the door shut behind.

"Things are going better. We moved her to the Aga Kahn . . ."

"That was fast!"

"Yeah, well, it was either that or watch Mbuno eviscerate the incompetent doctors. One of them had the stupidity to say that it may be Niamba's time to die . . . Mbuno went over to the bed, clicked off the side rail and started to lift her up to take her away, tubes and all, somewhere, who knows. They thought they would restrain him. The first doctor, an Asian, quite large and heavy, smacked his head on the door as Mbuno open-palm blocked him across the room. The old boy is strong. Before a real fracas started, he had a nasty looking knife out, and the doctors were calling for security . . . I arrived just then. It took some of your dollars to make them all calm down . . . I paid the bill there even though it was free for an honorary colonel's wife. Hope you don't mind."

"No, not at all, please go on."

"We lifted her up on a stretcher, Mbuno and me. She's in great pain, with a pelvic superstructure—little steel rods like a cage holding her crushed pelvis open. Something about it preventing her bleeding to death if it falls inward. I had called the Aga for their ambulance, and it showed up with your Italian doctor, Rinaldi by name, good young blood, well trained, something about being trained in a place called Waid, in Switzerland. He's a trauma specialist. His records say so.

Anyway, Rinaldi took charge and she's over there, at the Aga Khan, now being prodded and tested. Something about blood in her urine they don't like."

"How's Mbuno in all this?"

"Ah, yes, Mbuno. Well, here's his message to you . . ." he imitated the Kenyan bush accent flawlessly, "'Bwana Pero, it is more than my life you are saving. Again." And then he smiled at me, wide, teeth and all. Most odd. You understand that?"

"Yeah, it's our private thing." Heep was smiling too.

"Heep here, Amogh, good to hear from you. Thanks for looking after the *mzee* and his wife; you're doing a great job."

"Hello there Heep old fellow. By the way, Rinaldi says he appreciates your offer of transport if it's something he doesn't want to handle here. But, you know, it would have to be pretty serious. He has that new operating theater and some young lions for doctors. Quite the talk of the Nairobi ladies they are too."

"Well, as long as Niamba is getting the best attention, that's all that matters. Will you call back when you have news of Rinaldi's diagnosis? And give Niamba our best?"

"Will do. Don't worry too much; things are pretty well under control for the moment. My parents have turned up and are arguing over who's going to pay the bill. They say they want to. I told them I was taking orders from you, but you know father, he feels it is his duty to help. Anyway, we'll manage. Got to go, they're signaling. More later. Bye." And he hung up. Heep tilted his head as if to say, it's the best we can expect. Pero nodded. Without a word, Heep went back to his room. Both of them were worried about their friend's wife. And for their friend Mbuno as well, for he and his wife were inseparable, they talked every day whenever they had been on safari with Mbuno. It was a ritual. Rituals are danger-ous when broken.

In the lounge ten minutes later, Danny Redmond walked in and the waitress sprinted to help him choose a table. He walked over to where Heep and Pero were already seated. She shot the two a glance of newfound respect. Redmond had changed into jeans and a cashmere V-neck sweater, no shirt, and a gold wristwatch. He had socks on. Definitely not creepy Hollywood.

"Heep, how are you?" Danny extended his hand.

"Fine Danny, may I introduce Pero Baltazar?" It was Heep's formal Dutch upbringing. Pero stood and extended his hand. It was a firm handshake yet without muscle—no test, no statement.

"I've heard all about you, even saw a bootleg copy of your latest croc footage, incredible. Other people, like *National Geographic*, are pretty miffed to lose Mary Lever as on-camera talent, although your new network seems pleased. I met with them last week. I'm doing a Christmas special appeal—Diabetes—for them and they promised Mary in a supporting role."

"Heep, here, may or may not like that. He's the producer of her new series. Husband too."

"That so? Well, damn, everyone's loss, your gain. She's a firecracker. Camera loves her." Pero got the impression he was evaluating her professionally, not as a man. Pero wanted to find out, to make sure Heep didn't get jealous. He had a tendency to be the type.

"She is a great gal," Pero said casually.

"I wouldn't know, haven't met her. Maybe one day you'll introduce me, Heep?" His interest was professional. It was a good sign. A man with his charisma should—and he did—know the power of the weapon he wielded. Turn off the personal charm; keep it clean, professional, and friendly.

"Danny, anytime, Mary would be pleased to meet you too." The drinks arrived; Heep had his habitual evening beer. In Germany, it was always Weissbier, almost clear in taste and color.

Danny got down to business, "The script they sent you fellows? It's crap. The movie is about a quarter shot, and I've asked the studio to fire Pederson." The director was going? Not a good sign. Pero needed this work—and the week away from that bag of heavy water. "The revised script arrives tonight on my plane into Tempelhof from England . . ." He looked at his watch, "In about an hour. Secretly, for a week I've had Stan Letterman working at his country home in Cornwall. He's bringing it."

Stan Letterman was a two-time Oscar winner, very high-powered and well respected. Pero had heard he didn't hire on to fix a script for under a cool million. Power is measured by money in Hollywood—what you could make or stop other people making. Letterman was at the top of that game for a scriptwriter. "The studio was on board with the concept, but I was having problems. You see, with my plan I'm using my own money—and not only to pay Stan—but the truth is I don't have the twenty-five million dollar deficit financing, at the minimum, we would need. Plus I needed to dump Pedersen— he's a great action director, but not serious enough for this. He's still box-office gold but what he had in mind for this movie might not be." He turned to Heep. "It was your entire fault really; you gave me the idea, that *Funeral in Berlin* pitch. The studio and distributors said they wished that was what they had originally green-lighted . . . And the studio said I was nuts to want to take what we have—the sets are still up—and remake it. The studio and distribution money boys finally said no, even though studio creative said okay."

With a premonition, Pero guessed what might be coming . . . Redmond turned toward him, turned on the whole charm, smiled, and said, "Then, three hours ago I get a call telling me that they give be a complete green-light. Pedersen's gone and everything I wanted, especially an extra fifty million dollars and deficit-financing if needed—all no problem. Seems someone wants the second unit team to have a free hand here in Berlin. They wanted that so bad they rubber-stamped anything I wanted as long as it kept Berlin on schedule and a priority. New banks put up the cash immediately, no meetings, nothing. A phone call and it was done. So, I took a little advantage and sold the studio the whole plan, you two attached. Hope you don't mind?"

Pero didn't want to answer that. He wasn't sure how much trouble he was in with Lewis in Langley. Fifty million dollars? Would the CIA have to put up money like that, just to buy a week? Or was it just leverage, not cash? So he dodged Redmond's question with another "Who'd you get to take over as director?"

"He's sitting right here, next to the two producers." He saw Heep's shoulders square up. "Yeah, you Heep. It was your idea, your vision. Ever since you talked to me, I've been screening everything you've shot on a laptop link with the studio. Time you made that feature film you're always skirting."

Unsure, Heep asked very quietly, "And the studio is okay with this?"

"Look, I am the producer, and I okayed it, and all our agents at DBB agreed as long as the money was there. They see this as my climb back into their pocket after my stage time-out in London. They're sick of me earning fifty pounds a night in . . . What did they call it? Oh yeah, 'a dusty, run-down rat trap in the land of Shakespeare whose actors can't earn their way out of a paper bag.' Subtle, aren't they? Anyway, since twenty-five million of the budget is mine, and fifty million dollars is now guaranteed studio financing, and the rest, including the deficit financing and distribution fees, are all assured by the banks, I can pretty much do what I want without the studio's bullshit. Once the banks rubber-stamped anything we wanted here in Berlin, it sealed the deal. Once we shoot here—what *we* want to shoot—there's only one way to finish the picture: with you still at the helm and Letterman's script, which just was approved."

Heep raised his eyebrows. His worry was equally Pero's: could this all be happening so quickly?

Redmond knew they were skeptical, "Yeah, guys, really, they read the script treatment overnight, amazing. "Wow" and "gee" were the descriptive words they used—deep thinkers all. Let's hope when you get the full script tonight, you'll agree." The two men were silent.

Redmond's aura deflated a little. He slowed down and talked—a man telling his secrets—it was no act. "Look, Heep, I know I've taken everything for granted, and Pero, whatever friends you have in high places—and I figured it had to be you, not Heep—am I right? No, don't tell me. Look, I am not stupid enough to think you can't also pull the plug on this one just as quick. Whatever role you want here, it's yours, as long as you're aboard. But Heep was right about the story—the look, the feel we should be filming. Damn, look guys, I saw a chance and took it." He wasn't apologizing; it was a statement of cold fact.

Pero felt it was time to let him off the hook. He knew Heep too well not to make this easy on them all. Money wasn't an issue here, for any of them. Danny had made that clear. This was a creative thing, a chance. "Danny—and I speak for my friend here as well since he's just too dumbstruck to say it—I think we'll work as a team, just fine. I'll produce locally for you and Heep, it's my pleasure." And he stuck out his hand. Danny took it, saw the acceptance in Heep's eyes, and pumped it up and down, a child-like enthusiasm very evident. Suddenly, he was in control of his destiny, the last card played in a game of chance, and he had that glow of a gambler who had won, and won big. It was written all over his face. Of course, that's because he's an actor. They have those open, demonstrative faces, sometimes without knowing. It's what makes the twenty-foot blow-up on screen work so effectively.

"Pero, won't you take on the job all the way through?"

"You don't need me for that and, anyway, I have an aversion to Hollywood." And he added, "Boss."

Redmond laughed hard, openly, and deeply, "You're not getting off that easy. I was making you a producer, full salary and control with me, just us two. Heep trusts you, I now see and know that much." He suddenly got serious, "Look, word is something happened on your last shoot, no one will say what, but it's clear you're a team. If I lose you, we may lose this incredible chance. No way. It's both of you or nothing." Pero started to interrupt. Redmond waved him off. "No, listen. You're the producer. Heep's the director, a team. I am sure of that. If you want no part of Hollywood, that's okay. I can handle that end. If you agree to sole-produce the European part of this shoot, I can handle the rest. But you're Heep's insurance, his protection, a full producer with a fifty percent say. That okay?"

Pero thought about it for about five seconds, just long enough to give the impression it was an important decision, not long enough to create doubt. "Agreed." As he said it, he realized that he had already mentally agreed to any request Redmond would make.

Redmond started laughing. The man's charm was overwhelming.

Heep just sat there looking at his wedding band, shaking his head. "I think I'll call Mary and tell her the good news." He got up, patted Danny on the shoulder, slowly, by way of thanks and confirmation, and left the lounge. Heep was a modest man. Pero knew he had always wanted to direct a feature. Heep had the best eye of anyone he had ever worked with. A Renoir or Cartier-Bresson kind of eye, seeing immediately what others would only see a day later in the memory of their mind's eye. The quick, the hard-to-visualize, never eluded him. It made his "vision," on film or TV, stand out, head and shoulders, above the rest. Pero was a fan and Heep knew it.

Pero suggested the new two coproducers drink up and get over to Tempelhof to pick up the script by Letterman before dinner—together. No one mentioned money. Without a word, they knew that the money side would be when put on paper, fair and honest. This was unlike most Hollywood business where "Have your agent call my agent" would proceed weeks of posturing for status advantage over small details. The three men skipped the power dance because, sitting there in the lounge on the sixth floor, all three knew it was not necessary. Expert evaluation was their stock in trade, what kept them at the top of their professions.

But then they were, in spirit and flesh, in Berlin—the land of the culturally possible.

* * *

Tempelhof Airport is in the south central part of Berlin, smack dab in the center of the newly growing, renovating, city. It was built in the Bauhaus school of architecture shortly before Hitler's rise to power. Bauhaus is the school where form follows function. Design for function almost always requires clean sight lines, efficient layout, and a mono-focus quest for perfection without embellishment. Most people associate the style with Hitler's era because, well, it was still new then. But, Hitler hated the modern architecture of the Bauhaus school; it was too angular, too modern. He preferred the neo-classical, and lots of old-world elegance; it tended to suit his dreams of Cesarean grandeur better.

Tempelhof is the blueprint for all the world's airports. Modeled on the classic train station—buy a ticket, go to the platform gate, check your ticket, board your train—Tempelhof was designed for efficiency with a massive central hall and doors that lead to the gates. The front of the building has all clean lines. The back of the building is angular but spread out as a horseshoe, creating a covered harbor for the planes that you would walk to. In the age of the separate covered Jetway and noise abatement, Tempelhof became inefficient, and in the 1990s it was shut down for commercial traffic. As valuable land, it is a ping-pong ball in a game of political aspirations—developers set against preservationists. Pero had seen Tempelhof from the air before his landing at Tegel. He could see there were still open fields around the runway, virtually untouched. But he knew only a few flights drifted in and out every day—mostly turboprops, many of them ministerial flights, and the airport now only had a skeleton staff to service the mostly private planes.

Danny's private plane was due in from London at 8:00 p.m. and as far as they knew, should be on time. Pero showed Danny around the airport, discussing the history, showing him the famous sculpture in front by the parking lot. It is a half arc, the other half perfectly aligned in Frankfurt, the other port of the Airlift. Two halves of the Air Bridge so vital to Berlin at one time.

Pero had disguised Danny Redmond pretty well—public appearances for one so famous could cause havoc. Redmond was used to pretending to be someone else. Disguise doesn't so much matter visually as it does for posture. Pero put a matchbook in Danny's right shoe and lent him a sweater and a pair of sunglasses—full tint. With the matchbox in his shoe, his gait was changed. Danny added a slump to his normally square shoulders, and he passed inspection. With a coat and hat, even Kamal didn't spot him, making a fuss over Pero instead since he wasn't wearing a coat, as they came out for a taxi. "Mr. Baltazar, Sir, you want me to lend you a coat?" Pero thanked him and declined.

Tomorrow, Pero thought, *I really needed to buy a new one.*

Danny's voice was world famous, so Pero had told him not to speak in public, even in the taxi. Danny seemed to be enjoying the role-playing.

After the tourist tour of the almost empty airport, Pero took him up to the second floor, looking out the windows at the plane arrival area, the horseshoe harbor. It was dark and the thirties' yellow hue floodlights created weak pools of light, like polka dots, on the concrete basin in front of them. They were alone so Danny could speak. "It's no accident you took me up here, is it?"

"It does add character to anything in a script."

"Yeah, let's see what Letterman has to say. Is all your and Heep's knowledge like this?" He waved his hands at the atmosphere in front and then, turning, behind us at the main hall.

"If we can help, sure. It's your call, how much or how little you want."

Danny simply nodded and went on looking out the window. The first script Pero had seen, now completely re-written he expected, had a chase scene down Unter den Linden Street. The film was supposed to be taking place thirty years ago. Unter den Linden was in East Berlin then, the action wasn't supposed to be. Danny might have been thinking similar thoughts.

"If the chase were here, we could have interfering crowds, not simply people trying to go about their own business." He meant that people in an airport mostly stand around, bored. If a cop yells to stop, they might lend a hand, adding to the hero's jeopardy. It was a good thought. On a public street, people tend to shy away. Human nature.

"Yes, and the transfer to the U-Bahn here is more believable. You passed it on the way up, about a quarter of a mile back. Running distance." Again, he nodded.

Pensive, they watched in silence. A plane landing left to right into the wind touched down safely and disappeared from view. Moments later, pools of lights appeared stage left. The whole scene looked like a stage. The pools evolved into shafts that made their way stage right followed by the plane. The modern plane's lights obliterated the solid oily black of the concrete harbor before them. "Need to make sure we get dimmer lights on a plane if we film this. It was better before." Pero's turn to nod.

They walked down the concrete steps and Pero could sense apprehension, Danny's hand on the railing . . . He stopped, took it off, stared at it, and put it back on. "Goebbels, Himmler, and Hitler probably used this same banister, touched where I have touched."

"Yes, but do remember we're in Germany. It has been disinfected, oh I don't know, a million times since then." Pero laughed. They continued on down.

Suddenly three men, burly men, leather jacket sleeves bulging, climbed the bottom three steps and blocked the bottom of the stairway. "*Was wollen sie?*" (what do you want), Pero challenged them, offense is often the best, well, offense. He had a major world star here, unprotected, he was not about to allow a kidnapping or robbery.

"*Sie müssen gehen raus.*" It was a command, flatly given, hand in pocket. They were being told to leave. The man was staring at Pero.

"Pero?" Danny asked.

"They want me or us, to leave." *Sie* could mean *you* plural. Pero looked at the man who had spoken. "Wieso?" Why so?

"*Sie müssen, jetzt.*"

Pero translated for Danny, "Seems we must, now, no explanation." He faced them: "Gut, ja doc, war müssen unto war gehen. Nicht mit fliegen?" *Good, yes so, we must get going. Not by flying?*

"Nein. Sie Kane gehen" then a deliberate pause, "mit taxi." Telling them to leave via taxi was said with a snarl. Pero sensed a trap.

"Gentlemen, I have no idea who you are, but if you stand aside, we'll be on our way." They understood English perfectly well. The man and his friends parted, one on one side of the stairway, two on the other—the doors to a trap. Pero turned to Danny, "These gentlemen mean business. I suggest we take their advice and go *down* quickly." Danny nodded, taking cues from Pero, who had seen Danny's eye flick on Pero's clenched fist, the one hidden by his side away from the assailants.

As they started down the steps getting closer, a tall man in an orange ski jacket suddenly rounded the left corner under the stairway yelling "Danny! Danny, where the hell are you?" The two men on Pero's side were distracted, turning to see who was speaking behind them. The leader on the right, the one who had spoken, was about to shout them a warning when Danny's fist connected between cheekbone and lower jaw. Danny jumped, fist first, full weight—the man took all one hundred and eighty pounds accelerating, as Galileo had proved, with the full effect of gravity. Pero heard bones snap and the man's head swiveled, hard.

The two on Pero's side didn't have time to react. Pero jumped, letting gravity take his weight and height down the steps. He hit one on the side of the neck, although he was aiming at the man's temple. Pero's aim was off because he was concentrating on kneeing the other one anywhere, as long as he made contact. The three men made a tumbled mess at the bottom of the stairs, but the two adversaries were more hurt than Pero was. One was semi-conscious, and the other was curled over in a ball. Pero's knee had made contact, by chance, with the man's groin as he turned to face his attacker. Pero disentangled himself and yelled "Police!" as loudly as he could and turned to see that Danny was standing, calmly, over his unconscious prey.

Danny noted Pero's look of astonishment. "What, you think months of martial arts training for all those films didn't give me any ability? First time I've made contact in anger, though. My knuckles hurt. I mean really hurt. Damn."

"Not as much as his jaw I suspect. Looks shattered." There was a pool of blood and teeth. Steady unconscious breathing was making little crimson ripples.

Two police officers came at a run, hands on guns. Danny, hat off, shoulders squared, standing tall, had resumed his famous persona. Pero was worried about shock. But so far, Danny looked capable.

They recognized him and took charge. In his broken German, Pero started to explain before they arrested the wrong people. "Diese drei leute . . ." *These three men . . .* he calmly explained that "they were going to rob us or maybe try to hurt us. They were, what's the word? *Drohen* is threat. Drohen?"

"Sie drohen sie?" *They threatened you?* He nodded, looked at Danny, and he nodded, thankfully. The two near Pero's side were getting up, one shaking his head, the other red in the face. They started to protest, and they were told to be quiet. One officer got on the phone and called for medical assistance. When he was done, he reached down and went through Danny's victim's pockets. He pulled out a wallet and passed it to his colleague. The leather jacket was padded down. He stopped, reached inside, and pulled out a revolver. Both officers drew their guns and barked orders to the other two attackers. They got on their knees and assumed the position, hands on head. Handcuffs were quickly applied. Their pockets were searched and wallets taken. Again, each man had been carrying a small pistol. They all looked like .22 caliber to Pero, Berettas he thought. The cops called the weapons into police central. Major help was on the way.

Letterman was standing there in his orange ski jacket, pencil in hand, scribbling away on a notepad. Danny and Pero were explaining, Pero translating, as best he could, that they had no idea who they were or what they wanted. They had simply told us to leave the airport and threatened us. One of the handcuffed thugs asked why we had attacked them, and he was told to shut up. The police compared their wallets. Each had the necessary national identity cards. Each had corporate identity card: TruVereinsbank. They were bank employees. And they had permits to carry the guns.

Chapter 5

TruVereinsbank

The two producers spent the next hour in an airport office as senior police officers arrived and questioned them, together and separately. Danny's hand was attended to by a police medic, bandaged and pronounced unbroken, although it was already swelling and sore. He was told to apply ice and was given little sympathy, but he was not dealt with unkindly. Danny was on the verge of shock, Pero had seen the other hand tremble. It took all of his acting skill to remain calm.

The head of the police team told them little. Clearly worried about the tourist trade implications of a famous star being accosted in a famous landmark, the police chief asked and Danny agreed that he wanted no publicity. Pero told them that went for him as well. Danny confirmed Letterman would keep quiet. There weren't many people at the airport, he was sure the police could keep a lid on things. This wasn't America, no one wanted fifteen minutes of fame that accompanied a lifetime of police anger.

Pero listened as best he could to the officers talking among themselves. There were ten of them by this time, on cell phones and comparing notes. The name TruVereinsbank was often repeated, as was Geschäftsführer (CEO) Tische, when a cell phone was passed over to the head of the group. After speaking with him, the cop stared at the cell phone and angrily pushed the off button muttering "verdammt Stasi!" *Damn Stasi.* That was enough for Pero. His blood was now running colder.

Eventually, they were free to go. They knew where the two men lived and what they were doing. The police chief told them that if the three thugs wanted to press charges, they would be forced to make contact again. The way he explained it, Pero knew he already knew they would never do any such thing. No doubt the Geschäftsführer, Mr. Tische, had told him that.

Danny couldn't leave it alone. "Aren't you charging them?"

"With what would you like me to charge them, Herr Redmond?" Give Danny his due, he regrouped fast. He didn't answer. He got the point. They had permits for those guns, they were bank employees, one of the largest banks at that, formed out of the absorption of the eastern half of Germany and all that implied.

The police were through with the two men, for a while anyway, "You are ordered not to leave the country without permission. You must not change address without telling us. If you fail to obey these instructions, you will be arrested. Now go back to your hotel." Walking back toward the plane to see Letterman off, Danny told him, again, to keep quiet. Nodding vigorously, Letterman professed he only made notes to enhance the script "You guys have no idea what this means to me, actual violence, real blood, real cops . . . I'll refine the script now, it'll be real." He said it with emphasis.

Pero called the hotel for a car after first getting approval from an officer. Within ten minutes, a junior officer told them the hotel car was waiting outside. They didn't stay to see the small jet off. Danny's hand was trembling as he got into the car.

Pero knew that Danny could use events as publicity. Pero hoped he would have the sense to wait until they were finished filming in Berlin. Pero didn't want to cross the police. He didn't want more enemies.

On the way back to the hotel, Danny held his injured hand in his lap and asked Pero to give him the background. The lack of an arrest for those who attacked him was troubling to him. It took Pero the entire ride to explain, so first he started with a little background.

"Okay, Danny, let's start with Frankfurt. Frankfurt is the banking and financial capital of Germany—Wall Street and Manhattan rolled into one. What is less well known was that in the nineties, the large Frankfurt banks assumed the assets of the former East German State Bank as well as the largest GDR—that's the German Democratic Republic—anyway, their nationalized industry company, was called the Treuhand for short. In the absorption, the GDR banks installed their representatives on the boards of the Frankfurt banks and the companies with whom they did business. In short, the Frankfurt banks controlled all the money and industry (Treuhand) in East Germany. However, many of the lower-level employees from East Germany came with those deals. Since the East German State Bank and the Treuhand were part of the East German government, the absorption of employees by established Frankfurt banks became a pipeline to full Western business access for many of the power elite of East Germany—converted communists all. Everyone of them gets a new Mercedes and a new power base."

What worried Pero more was the police officer's use of the word "Stasi." He wanted to make sure Danny understood the real danger there. "You know he used the word Stasi?" Danny nodded. "Well, the Stasi are another matter entirely. At the end of the Second World War, the chaos in Germany had to be controlled. Nowadays, we think that Nazi Germany was conquered and, overnight, gave up violence. Tell that to the soldiers who were castrated six months after the end of the war, in the dead of night, by masked gangs or to the US regional commander in Berlin whose house and family were blown to smithereens in 1947—A note sent to authorities with a swastika proclaiming credit. There was a serious insurgency, as it is now called by the media. The Allies quickly realized they needed inside help to control the seething, starving, and vengeful population. They thought about it—while the folks back home wanted the troops back on the farm. Without the political will from Washington to fund a total takeover of all levels of the German government, the Marshall Plan was hatched to much fanfare. That plan was simplistic: America funded the rebuilding of West Germany, which grew into a democratic, open, and free state that agreed, in principle, with her conquerors. That was the public side.

"What was hidden was the simultaneous enlisting—and forgiving—of the SS and Gestapo officers still alive. No Nuremberg trials for them, no sirree. On the American side, the ex-Nazi enforcers were absorbed by the CIA, the OSS as it was then, and Military Intelligence. The British were more reluctant, but still, dozens made their way into the spy operations necessary to penetrate the developing Iron Curtain. The French murdered all they could, but some French SS Nazis were allowed to return home to France, under assumed names or with erased files. Some SS were allowed to rise to great political heights, like Kurt Waldheim of the UN. Later, even after he was exposed and suspected of war crimes . . . remember he was elected the president of Austria? And that was with his photo in an SS uniform on the front page of every newspaper. So much for that country's change of values."

The hotel car rounded the corner approaching Los Angeles Platz and their hotel, so Pero hurried on, "The Russians, on the other hand, filled with hatred for the carnage they had been subjected to, wanted nothing to do with the German people except to keep them as good worker slaves. Subjugation of that nation was the goal, old Gestapo and SS were the tools, Stasi was the new name. They were the East German Ministry for State Secrets, die Ministerium für Staatssicherheit—Stasi for short. And they were formed up with a recently ex-SS major as the head, no pretense there and grew like a virus to infect every aspect of people's daily lives. Everyone informed on everyone else. People were carted away in the dead of night. Families were terrorized. Order was maintained, *perfekt*. Here we are years after the fall of the Wall and the Stasi records are still being cataloged and read, open to citizens to see who informed on whom and why some went to jail for no reason other than malicious gossip."

Danny was appalled, "Christ, didn't we . . . didn't they learn anything?"

"It didn't matter if anyone knew better. The machine was put in place with an iron fist. And like all good German quasi-military outfits, the Stasi kept a paper trail of everything. Why shouldn't they, since they believed, *they knew*, they were dealing from right? Might makes right in the mind of the absolute power user. It was the Nazi work ethic applied to a false communist structure. In East Germany, some things got worse, not better after 1945."

"And after the Wall came down?"

"Yeah, well, after the fall of the wall, the Stasi had to find a new home. Some moved naturally into new forms of mafia criminal organizations. Others stayed with their bosses and now worked as security for large corporations. And banks."

The car stopped, and the driver jumped out to open the door. Kamal was there and immediately saw that Pero motioned to Danny coming out after him. Kamal helped Danny emerge, saying, "Herr Redmond, welcome back." Danny nodded. The driver looked Pero in the eye and said, "Thank you," with more sincerity that Pero thought normal.

The driver smiled and said, "I escaped next to Checkpoint Charlie fifteen years ago. It is good to know someone still cares." With that, he walked around the car, saluted, got in and drove off before Danny and Pero could reach the revolving door.

Danny seemed deflated as they crossed to the elevators. Pero used the house phone quickly to ask Heep to be waiting.

Adrenalin is a curious hormone. It gives you primordial strength or fortitude to submit to what would be if you thought about it, terrible, overwhelming ordeals. Then, after, as it ebbs out of your system, you feel low, crushed, tired beyond whatever has happened. Shock can set in. If you are suffering from depression or taking other medication, the effects could be worse. Fatal even. Pero hoped Danny wasn't on anything. The elevator seemed to take forever.

As the ding sounded and the doors opened, Danny walked as if in a sleep into the elevator. Heep was there, riding down to the lobby, to escort them up. As the doors to the sixth floor opened and the corridor was clear, they walked to Danny's room, opened his door with the passkey Heep had gotten, got him in, and sat him down. As the door shut, Danny leaned forward, put his head in his hands, and sobbed.

He looked at Heep. He looked at Pero. His eyes asked, *would you?* Pero nodded and looked at Heep and explained, "Yes, three men. Danny took one out with some sort of Kung Fu flying fist move. Shattered the man's jaw. The problem is they were armed, with permits, work for TruVereinsbank. We have no idea what they wanted, except to have us leave the airport."

"It's my fault." Through his sobs now, Danny was confessing. Emotional outpourings are usual with the aftereffects of battle.

"No, Danny, they . . ."

"No, Pero," he lifted his head, "it's really my fault. You heard his name?"

"Whose?"

Danny stumbled over the title, "That *guess-shaft-furor* Tische, you heard his name?" Pero nodded. "I didn't recognize the name of the bank, *true*-whatever it is, but his name I remember. Before I left London, that man was threatening our financing move back to the Dresdner Bank as our new backers—your bank—Citicorp wanted. Tische wanted the previous deficit financing the studio had arranged with him when he replaced Dresdner two weeks ago. But when Citibank reinforced Dresdner today, a take it or not deal with the open guarantee, I called him and told him he was out again. He yelled at me, threatened me with ruin. Said I'd be sorry. I told him not to try those Nazi tactics with me. And hung up. This was my payback."

Pero needed to get Danny back on track here, without revealing anything. He'd do that later with Heep. But he also needed something answered as well.

"Danny, you are wrong. It's a coincidence. They only wanted us to leave. Had I known they were legitimate employees, I would never have attacked them. I thought they were after you, a kidnapping or something. As the police chief said, I was stupid to take you out unescorted. That won't happen again." Time for the question. "Danny, when did you decide to work with TruVereinsbank?"

"The studio hired Dresdner for deficit financing after they, sorry you, applied for permits to film in Berlin weeks ago. Then within twenty-four hours, TruVereinsbank called and said they were replacing Dresdner—that it was a condition to get our permits. They said Berlin's mayor's office said so. We checked. Dresdner wasn't happy but confirmed they were replaced. But then today, before I left London, Dresdner Bank called and said they could now get permission, all our coverage. Just as well because the Chancellor's office had ordered Berlin to comply . . . so I thought about changing back to them with a better interest rate. And then when Citicorp called and named Dresdner as their usual partners, it just sealed it for me . . . a lower interest rate, accommodating Citicorp and all. Anyway, Dresdner assured me they had control of the permits and the new deal in place. So I called Tische and fired him."

Pero quickly added it all up. *So, TruVereinsbank had muscled their way in, using the Berlin permits and someone in the Mayor's office. That was what . . . just under two weeks ago, after he filed the permits with the Berlin mayor's office? About the same time, my name first became involved.*

Pero was now sure. He alone was a target, likely the only target.

Danny wasn't responding to anything meant to lift his spirits. He was sinking deeper and deeper. Pero and Heep needed him back on track and fast. Pero felt it was time to use his father's method, so he raised his voice and tried to sound authoritarian. "Look Danny, snap out of it! One. You acquitted yourself well. The man was a specialist bodyguard, and you took him down and out, one blow. Two. They never explained themselves and never meant to. Three. They wanted to frighten us . . . why we don't know and don't care. Four. They didn't succeed unless you sit there bawling anymore."

Heep shot Pero a look of horror. You don't talk to Hollywood superstars like this. Not if you wanted to work ever again.

Redmond looked up. Anger filled his eyes. He stood, fists clenched . . . then just as suddenly, he smiled, that smile of charm that won over audiences the world over. He grabbed Pero and hugged him. Pero hugged him back. "Well, you are one strange person Pero. But I can't think of anyone I'd like on my side more." He paused and took a deep breath. "Ah, fuck it. We're alive and we have a film to make. How about you, Heep?"

"Well, except for added police security and delays this may cause, and that ugly hand . . ." Danny's hand was seriously red now. "We're in the clear. I say *thank God* you two are okay. Now, tell me all about it, and if we can use any of it . . ." They resumed normal business, planning for the next day. Instead of meeting the crew and going out to dinner, they offered the crew a rain check and ordered room service, plus plenty of ice for Danny's hand. Danny wouldn't be filmed until tomorrow afternoon, so they had the morning to ready the crew at the museum location during setup. Right, then they needed to get the production and their heads in order.

That evening, the longer Danny worked on the film—reading out portions of Letterman's script: the Berlin sections, the new Paris sections where the hero would have a taxi cab chase down the Champs Elysees—the more he resumed being Danny Redmond, superstar. And he inadvertently gave Pero what he needed if he was going to escape to finish the delivery business of the damned package.

When people push, either you can let them roll over you or you can push back, so they say. Pero? He would rather let them push dead air. He wanted to be out of the way whenever possible. He was a coward at heart, and so he was going to dump the package and let people chase somewhere else. In his mind, it sounded like a plan. Besides, he now really wanted to make this film.

Later, alone in his room, he called the embassy number he had memorized before he threw away his satellite phone. "Baltazar, P. here. Could I speak with Station?"

"One moment." He waited until he heard the clicks of connection and then an American ringtone.

"Lewis here, not a secure line."

"Uh, developments. Request means." *Means* was a code word for means of communication.

"Shaving kit." And the line clicked off.

Pero went into the bathroom and checked his shaving kit. Nothing there. He had to think this through. *What did he mean?* He sat on the bed, looking at his unpacked bags. *Was it only this morning he arrived?* On top of the luggage was his canvas carryall with his straw basket he was making. Basket weaving was his hobby, so he needed a large holdall on long flights to hold all the straw. *Let's see what's in here . . . basket stuff, reading material from the plane and—hold it—a shaving kit from first class.* He reached in and took out the triangular blue case with Delta's logo embossed on the plastic cover. He had never taken one from this flight, and this was an old one from when they used to give them away regularly. Inside was a small radio, a duplicate satellite radio. He wondered when they stuck that in his bag. Then he remembered Arnold's fidgeting with his hand luggage at the airport in the custom's room. Arnold had planted it. And he remembered overhearing Lewis' background questioning "He placed the phone where? Why did he do that?" Now he knew what that all meant.

Pero went over and opened the window. Or thought he did. The handle moved from down to sideways and the window pitched down toward him. Realizing, rather forgetfully, that it was one of those European dual-hinged windows, he pushed it shut, moved the handle back down and then fully up, activating the left side hinges. It swung open. He extended the radio's antenna and stuck it out the window. He pushed the buttons and Lewis answered.

"Report. You were supposed to call hourly."

"Sorry, I ditched the other phone. I didn't want to be caught with either the radioactive coat or phone. I had a tail and needed to be squeaky clean."

"Understood. You are using Station's phone. Report status and package whereabouts."

"Hidden in arapaima tank, bottom of a potted plant, aquarium, Berlin . . ."

"Aram . . . what?"

"It's a fish display, arapaima and arowana aquarium display. You go behind the scenes, open the trapdoor, and it's the plant on the left. I lifted it up and stuck the bag in there. It should be safe for at least a week."

"Okay, got that." He sounded bemused. "Proceed."

"I was accosted by three suspected ex-Stasi, TruVereinsbank employees, all armed, at Tempelhof. I was there with Danny Redmond to pick up a script from an incoming private flight. The man carrying it is called Letterman . . . scriptwriter. Never saw the pilots, Redmond's plane. A scuffle ensued. Redmond broke one man's jaw. I slowed the other two down, enough that the police could take over. No charges filed, police are hushing it up . . . our advantage that there would be adverse negative publicity for the City of Berlin *if* Redmond is involved in a mugging, especially ex-Stasi mugging . . . if the papers got hold of that. Filming will continue tomorrow at Technisches Museum. Suspect full police bodyguard. End report."

"Been busy, haven't you." It wasn't a question. "Our Berlin Station *and* the policeman *and* Phillips have all now disappeared. Reports are coming in of a car pileup on an autobahn. We're monitoring. Set your satellite phone to vibrate. It is a new five-band model, automatic. I can ring you on the cell band, scrambled. To scramble your end, you need to press five-five-five after answering same as always."

"Question: How did anyone know I was on the Delta flight and why would they care?" It had been bothering Pero all day. The tail was at the airport or at least waiting for him at the hotel. They knew he was involved before he did for Christ's sake. Redmond's confirmation about the financing in Germany with TruVereinsbank confirmed that.

"Bothers me too. While you were on the flight, we activated you, not before, but it was discussed ten days before . . . after you called in. I'll investigate that."

Pero thought, *Oh great, there was a leak in the CIA?*

"Phillips was on hold to pass a packet to you, not the package. Station must have changed the plan, last minute. We need to ask her why and what. As to why they were after you, it's simple. They wanted to make sure you didn't have the package and if you did, presumably, to get it back. Who they are is a puzzle, your clue TruVereinsbank, may give us a lead. There are some ex-German Democratic Republic senior spies—*Stasi* all—in that organization enjoying a capitalist lifestyle. Doesn't mean they are not still engaged." He meant engaged in spying.

"You got Citibank to endorse this picture?" Lewis said he did. "Well, TruVereinsbank was not the previous studio financing partner. However, TruVereinsbank used their extortion leverage with Berlin politicians. TruVereinsbank came on— muscled themselves in—at exactly the same time I was asked to produce second unit filming here. The key was timing of my involvement. Then Redmond and Citibank—endorsed by you—replaced them with Dresdner Bank."

"Why threaten you or be threatened by your involvement at that time? We weren't controlling you then. They should threaten Citibank if it's about money, not Redmond."

"Except that Redmond now controls this, he's the producer, loads of his money. They must know that. And yet I had the impression the thugs were talking to me, telling me—just me—to get out. The *get out* had a wider meaning than just leave the airport."

"What you say could still make Redmond a target, we'll check, but somehow I doubt it. Being after you matches the airport and aquarium tail profile. What we need to unravel and what has puzzled us is why a few flakes of paper, radioactive paper, on some old gold should trigger such violent reactions—not just against you but Station as well."

"Well, the same could be said for the CIA. Why did you decide to ask Mil Intel to steal the sample from the Zurich police?"

"That wasn't this office." The line went quiet. It had deep meaning to Pero.

"Oh, great, I am in the middle of an inter-CIA battle?" As he now suspected.

"As best I can tell. Yes." He said *I* not *we*, directors never get personal. This one was. It was troubling. And useful.

"Who ordered the lifting of the sample?"

"The orders came from the NSA" the National Security Administration, controlled by the White House, "and were handled by the director general's office. The Military Intelligence folks were brought in because it was a clandestine op with a short fuse. They have active ops in Germany, and we do not any longer." He was unusually forthcoming. "You realize you are being provided all this as a field agent in briefing?"

"Yes, I assumed as much, not happy, but I get that. After this evening, I figured as much. I'll need to brief Heep, he's here with me."

"Oh, no! Not that again!" A pause. "Damn, I can't dissuade you. Okay, he did well last time and sometimes you show a tendency not to think for yourself." Pero took that comment on the chin. "But you must not involve Redmond. Our records show he is unstable, not reliable." Not reliable to the CIA meant not discrete, their worst fear. "We need you to get the sample to CERN sap." He pronounced ASAP the military way, *sap*, not the letters. "The answer to why and what we're up against must lie in that sample. You need to get moving. We may not have a week."

"There may be a way, leaving tomorrow night. I'll advise when I am sure." Pero guessed why the hurry now, Lewis was reminding him there was tons of interest in this package, sudden, quick, interest, with ex-Stasi in play. There might be wholesale slaughter if people got desperate. Things were happening, had been for weeks—only Pero had not known it. His idea of slowing things down had only made the other side, or sides, speed up. That meant something was planned, and there was a timetable Lewis and Pero had no idea of. "If you get an idea of timetable on this, whatever it is, will you promise to tell me?"

A pause. An agent doesn't ask for promises from a director. He knew Lewis knew that. Pero knew he was asking beyond duty, he was calling in a favor, a personal favor. "Yes." Two clicks and Lewis was gone.

It was time to brief Heep. Fully.

Chapter 6

Technisches Museum

Six-thirty in the morning, two cups of strong Assam tea to wake Pero up, everyone, collected, and they were off. The police had called ten minutes after his hotel wake-up call, which meant they had agents in place to monitor the official schedule and fit in with it. Kind of them, as it saved Pero calling them and asking for exactly the sort of protection he now craved for the crew. Heep looked happier that morning seeing all the green uniform jackets around.

That was an improvement over the night before when Heep had not been happy when Pero had briefed him and used that dreaded word. Heep understood it wasn't Pero's doing, but now they were dealing with Stasi—it was the only word Heep focused on. For a Hollander, whose family suffered mightily at the hands of the Gestapo and SS, his hatred and fear of those Stasi, who had inherited the means and power, not to mention moral ethic . . . well, when Heep was frightened, he was very apt to be violent, and damn the consequences.

Pero suddenly realized that if Heep had been at the airport, on learning the attackers were Stasi, he would have taken their guns and shot them dead. It is hard for anyone to understand who did not have firsthand memories of relatives tortured, imprisoned, and gassed. Pero had seen the lifelong hatred before. Not everyone can be a Simon Wiesenthal or a Beate Klarsfeld—patient, dedicated, and just. The rest of humanity is more human, always wanting an eye for an eye.

Now in the cold light of a Berlin morning, Heep was calmer and only wanted to know how to help. Pero told him he needed cover to leave that evening. "Don't ask where, just cover for me."

"How long?"

Pero explained he expected two days; he didn't explain that CERN might not work out that fast. After tossing possibilities back and forward between them, Heep finally suggested that he string a yarn. He would tell Redmond that he could handle the next two days of the shoot in Berlin alone, helped by their new assistant, while Pero leap-frogged to Paris to pick up permits that would be needed there. Heep would emphasize that shutting down the Champs Elysees at 5:00 a.m. was a major political undertaking and could take a few weeks of paperwork, best started face-to-face. Then when Redmond took ownership of that idea, he would suggest Pero go off to undertake that essential film permit work in Paris and Pero could agree, reluctantly.

Secretly, Heep and Pero knew that Paris was only a one-hour phone call to arrange the Champs Elysees' shoot. They had longstanding contacts there. After thirty years at their craft and trade, they better had. Redmond might know they had contacts, but he wouldn't, couldn't, imagine they could do it so easily. Only in France could you pull strings like that, though. As Heep said, "Film art—cinéma—rules in Paris baby, ah oui!"

At the Technisches Museum, which had been closed to the public for the day, equipment boxes arrived in vans. Pero had ordered the tools of the trade and the support crew on the phone from New York—old, experienced hands all. He recognized two grips from a documentary they had shot three years before. The prop man was new to Pero, but the grips knew him well and vouched for him. Pero and Heep didn't need a lighting technician until they would get to the interiors to match the sets in LA. If Heep needed exterior ambient light reflectors, the crew could handle them. Pero had ordered an even dozen reflectors, to be on the safe side. This was big budget moviemaking on the fly—and still on the cheap. Compared to an L.A. production, they were operating on a shoestring, with only thirty men and women, some days less.

However, big moviemaking on the cheap or not, Pero spent production money and sent a grip to KaDeWe, a big department store on the Kurfurstendamm, to buy him a new coat, something for winter. The man came back an hour later with a Johnny Hilfiger ski parka, day-glow green. Before Pero could send him back with it, the man reversed it and the inside was dark blue, very subdued. The grip was smiling, *hah*, *hah* his expression said. Pero went along with the joke and smiled.

The assistant producer/assistant DP was Thomas (pronounced toe-maas) Wiedemann, always reliable and thinking ahead. Usually a TV production employee, Pero had always wanted to elevate him to a bigger job. This was Thomas' golden opportunity, and he beamed and pumped Pero's hand in thanks. Heep knew him and liked him too. Pero knew Thomas would cover for him while he was off to Paris, *kein probleme*.

Danny Redmond's three assistants were in charge of wardrobe and acting and served as his lackeys—something they were, all three, good at. And Danny seemed to sideline them whenever he could, which was fine with Pero and Heep. Heep had packed Danny's hand in ice the night before, over dinner in his room, and that morning the knuckles still looked raw and red, perfect for the part. "We'll have to match that in LA, let's take a few shots" His assistant took a dozen or so digital images.

The police were also there in force, maybe twenty of them. They knew their job and moved out of camera range if anyone brought a camera up or looked through a viewfinder at a scene to be shot. Three of them had machine guns.

Pero had never met the camera crew Heep had arranged. They consisted of two trusted hands Heep had worked with often. Ludwig Reber, second assistant DP, was the "most reliable damn film and lens changer at the ARRI Factory." ARRI manufactures the best movie camera equipment since 1917. Heep had once been an apprentice there and relied on them for equipment and support staff when the shoot had to be perfect, first time, every time.

Heep's vision for the film, now that he was the director, was to shoot this as he would a wildlife documentary—visceral, full of tension, creating the feeling that the cameraman would not know what was happening or about to happen and had simply gone with the flow, captured the action as if by accident. It was no accident, of course, but carefully thought out by Heep. No sticks (tripods), no dollies, no tracks, no Steadicam. Everything handheld. Heep's hands were the best damn Steadicam ever built, but human, not machine, creating a visual edge. The hero—Redmond—was human, he underwent human emotions in his spy mission, and the plot developed according to those emotions. Letterman's wonderful work on the script made this clear; no longer did emotions alter to fit the plot as in most action films. To make this succeed, the team had to increase the usable film to shooting ratio to documentary levels, say one usable foot for every twenty feet shot—something that is expensive with 35 mm film. By reducing the production personnel, they hoped they could keep on budget. It all rested on Heep's ability and Redmond's newfound talent honed on the London stage.

For sound, Heep had hired a woman he had worked with before, a German technical sound expert, Susanna Reidermaier. As Pero and Heep walked over to meet her, Heep explained: "Pero, she's about as good a boom operator as we've ever worked with. Her technical skill is first class. She's a little temperamental, try not to boss her around."

"She works for you. I'll stay away then . . ."

"No, it's not that, she just has had some tough breaks. She's perfect for this job, she won't let us down."

"Has she ever before?" As a producer, the last thing he wanted was a weak link on a location shot.

"No, but she's tough on the outside and jelly inside. Family tragedy. I'll vouch for her. And besides, she's brought her invention, a very special new microphone."

As soon as Pero saw her, he felt she seemed familiar somehow. She was about thirty-five, pretty with an hourglass figure and stood just above five and a half feet. She had an open face and quizzical blue eyes. She was assessing Pero, Redmond, the police officers, everyone, every chance she got. It did not make Pero uneasy; she seemed a kind person, just unsure, perhaps just wanting to make sure of her surroundings, to know who to trust. He instinctively liked her, as it seemed to him that she wore her emotions out in the open.

He had seen the same querying look once, that quizzical behavior, in a Bonobo ape.

Close relatives of chimpanzees, the Bonobo are a matriarchal society, very rare, in Tanzania, last seen by Pero on a guided video tour with Mbuno. The males hunt for the females' food and are rewarded with sexual favors. The Bonobo are seen as the closest relatives to human anthropology, much more so than chimps or gorillas. By allowing the males to hunt for food, the females can stay at home and safely raise the young. Sex is the tool, offspring and family generational safety the reward. Affection and loyalty, often tribal monogamy, become commonplace.

Two years ago, they were filming them when one Bonobo female came to Mbuno's attention. She had lost her suitor to a leopard or some predator. She was alone, unprotected, and mistreated—no male to protect her or hunt for her food. One day a group of young males approached her, and she fought them off. She accepted no fruit or leaves, in case it meant having to perform sexually. She was skeptical, only trusting her fellow females. She accepted their grooming and when finally starving, shared their food leftovers. After a while, a few weeks, one female introduced a new male to her, gently. She looked at him with those same quizzical eyes Pero saw Suzanna now displayed. After a period of sitting, sharing his food, a week or so, they consummated their relationship, gently. After that, she was his, heart and soul. Moreover, their sexual relations were anything but gentle after that. Mbuno found it equally amusing as well as right and proper. He explained why to Pero, "A bond, open trust takes time Mr. Pero, it takes time." In a short while, the Bonobo female got very fat and content on her suitor's eager, repeated, foraging. Subsequently, the male Bonobo wore a familiar expression of pride and ego.

Pero shook his head, clearing the memory. Heep was elbowing him in the side. "Hey, Pero, have a look at what Susanna has brought, you gotta see this." Heep was so excited he skipped the introduction. Pero and Susanna shook hands while Heep and Danny were fussing with the hero's costume's collar, on a much worn looking leather jacket, US Air Force around 1965. Heep said, "Okay, Danny put it on." He slipped the jacket on.

Susanna walked away and put on headphones. Danny said, "testing, one two three." Susanna walked back, pulled the lapel back and, with her fingernail, seemed to turn some hidden screw.

"Try it again." She walked away.

"Testing one two three." Danny looked at her.

"Is that all you know how to say?" She asked.

Danny instantly became Richard Burton in manner and voice: "One Christmas was so much like another, in those years around the sea town corner now and out of all sound except the distant speaking of the voices I sometimes hear a moment before sleep, that I can never remember whether it snowed for six days and six nights when I was twelve or whether it snowed for twelve days and twelve nights when I was six. All the Christmases roll down toward the two-tongued sea, like a cold and headlong moon bundling down the sky that was our street; and we stopped at the rim of the ice-edged fish-freezing waves, and I plunge my hands in the snow and bring out whatever I can find . . ." He paused, "That do you?"

Susanna was astonished. They all were. They had just been given a private audience to the presence of Dylan Thomas. Danny had become Dylan Thomas—he spoke like him in that singsong Welsh accent, and he stood like him, cocky, assured, on the edge of wanting to run away. It was the way Richard Burton had played him, but Burton had done *Under Milk Wood*, not a *Child's Christmas in Wales*. Pero asked, "Danny, you've been practicing, taking the concept for this film a little further, haven't you?"

He grinned, "Seen *Funeral in Berlin* over and over, listened to *Under Milk Wood* like it's in my head. I figured that if he could pull off something he hadn't done before, playing a spy, but similar to something else he had done, well, maybe we'll pull this off. I got the BBC to record it for me and help. In return, they get my recording for next Christmas, free. They were happy and so am I. The radio sound record-ist there," Pero noted he used the BBC correct title, "had worked with both Richard Burton and Dylan Thomas. He really helped."

Heep asked worriedly, "You planning to play this in charac-ter, a Welsh role?"

"No. To understand the man, Burton, his movement, I had to trace his mental footsteps. First part's over. Now this movie, built on his performance in *Funeral*, will be the second part, time to show what I can do for the part. It's a fine bal-ance to make the character my own, build my own character." He turned to Heep, "If you see me screw up, see too much Burton or not enough depth, tell me, okay, Mr. Director?" They all laughed. It was encouraging. Danny wasn't anything like the Hollywood action man they had been expecting. He had worked at this, wanted this to be right. He would succeed. Now there was no doubt in Pero's mind or Heep's.

But then Pero had a strange thought. "Wait, you don't mean to tell me that lapel microphone will be used for these scenes. Surely it's only a backup; it'll have too much ambient noise, LA will go nuts."

Susanna walked over, calmly, and put the headphones over his ears, pulled out a cigarette pocket-sized digital recorder and pressed a few buttons, suddenly, there came the purest recording of Danny's voice, "One Christmas was so much like another, in those years around the sea town corner now and out of all sound . . ." *Impossible*, Pero thought. Better than any boom microphone, clearer than on a sound stage, it was truly amazing. Yes, he could hear other ambient sounds, but natural, far off, unrecognizable. Taking off the headphones he asked, "How's this possible?"

In clipped English, speaking in a professional monotone, Susanna explained, "Neue technology Herr Baltazar, Non-Dynamic-Insulating-Oscillating technology, NDIO as an acronym," she paused and scowled, "since you Americans like them so much."

All Pero could think of was the Swahili for *yes*, *ndiyo*. He thought he saw that in Heep's eyes since he too nodded.

Suzanna, however, did not approve of doubting Americans. She continued, "A monofilament of organic fiber, grown to match the tuning of the human ear, is placed across a magnetic oscillator, placed within a half meter of the object it is supposed to record—not the voice box, just the object. Technology does the rest. The filters, I built myself, they are complicated but stable. The programming I borrowed from friends in Stuttgart at the university. They are complicated differentiation equations to allow for separation of ambient noise. But, you will note that there are no anti-waves here, Mr. Baltazar." She said anti-waves like an insult. No doubt, she hated sound wave technology built on those principles. "I have perfected the first studio quality hidden microphone recording system."

Pero had to ask because what he had seen and heard was so incredible, "How hidden?" They walked over to Danny. She showed Pero the thread, sewn in a straight line into his collar, just beneath the fabric, almost invisible. The control box was not a box at all. Inside the jacket was a flat card, about half the size of a credit card and thinner. A little six-centimeter wire dangled down his jacket. "Well, that's amazing!"

She smiled.

"I can see a flaw, however."

Heep shot Pero a glance of warning. Danny looked puzzled and Susanna looked like her internal boiler was being turned up as her face flushed. Heep wondered how close she was to blowing.

Pero deliberately used a serious tone, "Have you considered properly," he paused, she glared, "if you are properly prepared," he paused for another moment, she shifted her shoulders, "for the nightmare of total, unbridled success? Have you given any thought to what it truly means to be a worldwide success, a multimillionaire?" Having gotten the joke, Heep and Danny laughed; Heep patted her on the shoulders.

Susanna lowered her head and said nothing. She looked a little lost.

Suddenly ashamed for teasing her, Pero said, "Look, I am sorry Susanna. I just meant to compliment you really. And, please, my name is not Mr. Baltazar, it's Pero. I would be honored if you would call me Pero." She looked at him hard, gauging his words. "And I am honored to be in the presence of such genius. Your family will be proud." It was a bit patronizing, he knew, but she seemed to need assurance, even so obvious a compliment—creative geniuses usually need reassurance.

Staring into his face, she suddenly sniffed a little and ran off, crying. Heep said, "She'll be fine Pero. I did warn you to go easy. She's been working on this for ten years, got kicked out of school, missed her doctorate, they had so little confidence in her. Her marriage failed—he was an idiot from Miami—and a bunch of us have been secretly funding her. That's why she became a sound tech on films and TV, to earn money. This microphone? She built it in memory of her mother. She calls it the SilkeWire."

Suddenly it dawned on Pero where he had seen the face before.

"Oh damn, Heep!" Pero looked at Danny, "Do you understand?" Danny shook his head. "Remember about twelve years ago there was a terrorist attack on a bus in Lebanon on the way to Syria? It was a splinter group, a sect of the Hezbollah who conducted the attack; there was a renowned Hezbollah higher-up on board. In the attack, they captured a German journalist, unrecognized as such initially, Silke Reidermaier. For four weeks everyone assumed she was dead, but secretly she was recording every day—a diary . . ."

"Oh God yes, I remember, she recounted the beatings, the rapes, and torture . . . that tape played everywhere."

"Right. When they found her secret recorder, they beheaded her and sent the tapes with her head to prove their ruthlessness. It backfired. Hezbollah cleaned house, killed them all. They even returned the woman's equipment and clothing, as if that would help. How old was Susanna back then, twenty-two?"

Heep said, "Maybe twenty-three. I'll see if she's okay in a moment . . ."

But just then, Susanna came striding back. "I was not having you men standing there discussing me . . . oh, I know you are, don't deny it." She stared at Pero "Either you are the biggest fool there ever was or you're perhaps the kindest man I've met."

"Both," he said. Heep chimed in his agreement. They all laughed, even Susanna.

Danny coughed to clear the air and said, "Now that it's all settled, and I am miked for God's sake, can we practice this scene?" And so they got down to business—rehearsing, blocking the scenes, talking professional, and all the while, the police kept observing, never intruding. The public was nowhere to be seen.

But just after lunch, just as they were getting ready to film, a man arrived with his own police escort.

One of Danny's assistants came over to tell Pero that he had company. "There's a Mr. Tische to see you, seems important." He gestured to the large man wearing a black cashmere coat standing with the police. The police officer who came with him, a new face, had more bars and a gold cluster on his coat. Brass. Pero told the assistant to tell them he'd be right with them.

Pero went, slowly, into the museum foyer where Heep was setting Danny up for the scene, walking it through. He interrupted him. "It's an emergency Danny, sorry." Danny nodded okay and went off studying the script. Pero pulled Heep aside.

Pero explained what he wanted, and then Heep called Susanna over and gave her instructions in his fluent German. It's an interesting language. What Heep said were simple instructions, but they had the whip of authority and urgency. Susanna did as he asked, no questions. There was a moment when she looked up into Pero's face with a furrowed brow, but he patted her arm to tell her not to worry. She shied back. Five minutes later, Pero was back outside, to greet Geschäftsführer Tische of the TruVereinsbank.

The man's face was full with a wide jaw. His ears were big, his slicked hair combed over a balding head. His eyes were coal and close set. Even at over seventy, his shoulders were wide, his hands thrust with purpose in his camelhair coat pockets, and later Pero could only describe his stance as powerful. This was a man used to giving orders.

He got right to business. "Herr Baltazar, is there nicht somewhere privat we can talk?"

"How about in the museum? It's closed to the public."

"Proceed." His police officer looked to accompany them, but Tische motioned him to stand there and wait. There was no doubt who had the authority. The police that came with him were solely under his control.

They walked past Heep, with headphones on, and Danny Redmond. Geschäftsführer Tische had no interest in either; Pero doubted he recognized Danny or wanted to. He had that sort of disdain for being anywhere as commonplace or public as this, a place where people were working. Pero guided him to the right as they entered the museum foyer, over the cut wooden block flooring that made no echo of their footsteps into the first of the two great train halls.

The Technisches Museum houses all sorts of technical marvels, from computers to telephones, from bikes to cars, from gliders to planes, from models of boats to ships. For Pero, the most interesting were the trains. The museum was cobbled up from the ashes of WWII, in a declining industrial Berlin. An old railway locomotive yard, with two locomotive sheds, each in an arc, one next to the other, converted to hold some of the industrial world's most marvelous steam engines.

Steam engines are living things. It's not that diesel and electric engines aren't massive, fast, and powerful. They are. But steam is a force, an energy that turns a lump of iron into a living, breathing, snorting, thing of iron, brass, and steel beauty. You can smell a steam engine, smell its vapors—the overheated oil in its bearing and the ashes in its boiler. All these mingle to one distinctive odor.

To see a steam engine powering along the track is to understand the age of the train, to feel the romance of the rails. To ride on the fireman's platform is to ride the back of a steel whale.

In this one museum are some of the finest designs of locomotives ever assembled. As good, in its way, as the Louvre or the MET are to art, so too, the Technisches Museum can show you the best of the best of German train engineering from the mid-1800s through to the present.

And then, *then*, in the middle you come to the prized pieces, the '30s Weimar Republic locomotives with their speed, clean lines and elegance, all art deco and ready to be admired. Next to them are the trains of the Third Reich, swastikas and all, ready to be feared. Power, speed, and capability oozing from every rivet, every polished knob, with massive wheels, they seem all efficiency coupled with might. In the middle of those dark, threatening machines was a cold, dark lesson.

Before Berlin public money can be spent on a museum, it has to demonstrate that it serves the greater good. It was voted on, democratically, that the greater good of the German people must be continuing reminders of their past, WWII to be exact, the concentration camps to be precise. For its respectful reminder, the directors of the Technisches Museum chose to place, in the middle of all that Nazi glory and steel and power and might, one lonely boxcar, one human cattle car. Children visiting the museum jump up and down, from one locomotive to another and, suddenly, find themselves in this strange wooden box, complete with photographs on the inside of humans being herded to camps. It put the use of technical ability in perspective and was, for Pero, one of the most poignant atrocity memorials he had seen.

He walked Herr Tische quietly past the trains, turned left down between the Swastika adorned locomotive on the left and turned right, up the stairs and into the cattle car. The entrance was low as was the roof. They both barely could stand upright. "Now, Herr Tische, how can I help you? It is private here, not a sound except for ghosts."

Tische's voice had a two-tone resonance, at once clipped, clear, and powerful and yet floating on a guttural carrier sound coming from deep in his throat. "A melodramatic touch Mr. Baltazar, so American of you. My parents traveled in one of these, so if anything, you help my position without knowing it."

"As guests or hosts?"

Tische's face reddened. "Don't play games you are ill-equipped to win, Mr. Baltazar."

"I was not the one who sent three thugs to roust us at an airport Mr. Tische. I was not the one playing games." He decided to take a chance, a wild guess, "And I was not the one who, how shall I put this, interdicted US and German government employees on an autobahn yesterday."

Tische's eyes came up too quickly He knew. Pero now knew he knew. "Both were most unfortunate. It was not supposed to happen on the autobahn. They were supposed to slow and give up the . . . what do you people call these things . . . ah yes, the package."

"What package?"

"I said, don't play games with me, Mr. Baltazar. Your coat, given to that bum, gives you away. It had a detectable signature. I hope you don't want children, I am sure the bum didn't."

Pero caught the tense. Had they killed the homeless man? He decided to string Tische along, "Ah, that package, the one I refused to keep. The one I forced that idiot Arnold to take back after he had stuffed it in my coat pocket. It's not my job, being a courier. I don't do that."

"So you gave it back?" Pero guessed Tische wanted to know if it was in that car accident.

"Yes, that is not my job. Besides, I am here to film, I had no idea they were even going to contact me."

"Mr. Phillips seemed happy on leaving the airport, he did not look like a man who was, shall we say, turned down."

"Oh, he agreed to help after the filming was over . . ."

"You are lying. Mr. Baltazar, where is the package. It was not in the car." Tische was getting angry, he leaned forward, backing Pero into the wall, making his threat clear, and he was bulky, heavier than Pero was. His teeth showed in a snarl, "We are not like those Arabish idiotin in Kenya. We will not be stopped so easily." Instantly, Pero realized that Tische had connected all the dots about him, about Pero thwarting the Arab's terrorist plans in Kenya. Hell, he had better intel sources than Pero did. This was serious. Tische was almost salivating, "Do you think we care if we exterminate you and Mr. Heeper, as well as that buffoon actor? My employee has a fractured jaw. If I allow him, later, he will kill that man as easily as I could kill you now." Suddenly there was a six-inch steel blade aimed at the fatal region of Pero's liver. It was poking his new ski anorak, the outer skin of which made a little plop sound as the tip pierced the Gore-Tex.

Oh my God, I am going to die right here, all for a lousy package! His thoughts caused his voice to waver, showing his fear, "What exactly do you want then?"

"The package."

"You know I don't have it. I gave it back to Arnold for God's sake. If I had it, any detector could spot it in an instant if what you say is true. I assume that's why you think it wasn't in the car wreck?" Pero needed to put doubt into his head. Tische nodded, so Pero continued, "Well, maybe they missed detecting it or maybe it wasn't even them in the car . . ."

"It was clean, the car. And it was the three embassy people, one diplomat, one CIA operative, very pretty I was told, and one Internal German Sicherheitsbeauftragter." (*security officer*) "Our men shot them and their car crashed and burst into flame. I was not planning to lose them so quickly." Pero had the idea that a lengthy torture was probably a forte of his.

"Look, if I don't have it, and you don't have it, is there anyone else who could have taken it?" Pero saw it, he saw it in Tische's eyes. There was a third side to this battle, a second opponent Tische was waging war against, it was the doubt Pero needed him to think about. But Tische was smarter than that.

"Then we do not need you. Good-bye Mr. Baltaz . . ." he backed Pero up against the wall, the cattle timbers pressing his back as Tische slowly pressed the blade into Pero. Even with Pero's two hands also gripping the man's hand holding the knife handle, Pero couldn't stop him. Tische was too fanatical, his bulk and the strength of his pure hatred and pleasure combined were overwhelming. He was drooling, *For God's sake! He wants to kill me, he is enjoying this!* Pero thought. He felt the blade slowly inch through the coat and begin to slice into his skin.

"*Halt! Lassen dieses mann, jetzt!*" Stop, let go this man, now! It was Heep, to the rescue. With him was Susanna, clicking away on a digital camera, flash punctuating the darkness of the cattle car.

Tische pulled the blade back, out of Pero's skin and jacket and it disappeared into the folds of the overcoat like it had never been. Pero guessed the camera wouldn't have caught the sheen of the blade.

Tische put his face next to Pero's, very sensual, very intimate, licked his lips and whispered "Gut, it is not over, but for now, gut genug" *(good enough)*. "You will remember. I give you two days to comply or we will have them all killed. And all your little friends from Kenya—especially the one you call your friend . . ." Pero knew he meant Mbuno, "and his wife who is not quite dead, yet, and," he paused, smiling, "Yes, and your parents for good measure, we can kill them all." With that, he spun around and walked off.

Heep wanted to stop him, but Pero told him to let him go. As frightened as he was, he knew this enemy. Pero was in no doubt that his use of the word "we," when he could have said, "I," meant there were others. Pero needed to watch this man, his enemy's main protagonist, or else a stranger could come out of nowhere, silently replace Tische, and kill them all, as promised.

Behind Heep and Susanna waited the police officer that Tische had arrived with. Turning, Tische instructed him, "*Wir verlassen,* Hans" (We're leaving, Hans).

"*Jawohl, mein chef*" (Certainly, boss). And they strode away as if nothing had happened. They were untouchable, their whole manner said so. The other police guarding the film location saluted as they passed.

"Heep, Susanna, say nothing to anybody."

Chapter 7

Moscow Express

The flash pictures showed nothing. They were back in the hotel, the day's filming having finished on a high, everything "in the can" was perfect, and Danny looked really wonderful as the star he was. He retired for the night as Heep and Pero stayed up late, planning the next day's filming scheduled for eight the next morning, minus Pero. He planned to catch the 1:30 a.m. train to Paris that night.

Heep wasn't happy. "Pero, you need to have a doctor stitch that up." They were finally alone in Pero's room. Pero peeled off the gaffers' tape he had used as an emergency Bandaid. The wound began to weep again. He covered the slit with a clean hotel facecloth to soak up the blood.

"If you'll give me a hand, we can shut the cut here with superglue. I need to get a move on tonight."

"Oh, okay," Heep said reluctantly. They went into the bathroom. Pero lifted off the blood-soaked towel. He thought, *the wound should be pretty much clean by now, blood is a good cleanser.* He asked Heep to squirt superglue right along the slice. It burned like hell. It was about a half-inch deep, nothing vital was hit as they could see only surface flesh, no internal dark purple tissue. However, Pero had squirmed when Tische stuck him and that made the cut wider. While they worked, they reviewed. "Tische had never moved, steady as a rock, I must have sliced myself, he only meant to pierce me, not slice me."

"Oh, good, that mitigates the bastard, does it?"

"No, but . . ."

"No 'buts' Pero, he meant to kill you right then and there. God, did you see his face? He was drooling!" Heep's face expressed disgust.

"I know, his breath smelled of rotten teeth or meat, it reminded me of a brute animal, something wild we've filmed, a big cat maybe or a hyena."

"You're right Pero. Hyena, definitely, hyena. He had that killing lust they get when they know they can't be stopped. Big jaws, powerful shoulders, hyenas are more dangerous than any lion."

"Well, hyena or not, Tische is a serious threat to us all. Danny's on his radar too after Tempelhof . . ." He glanced a warning at Heep.

"Yeah, and that means all of us, I get it." The superglue started to set under the incandescent lights of the bathroom. It wasn't pretty, but it was together, as good as a butterfly bandage. "That'll do," Heep said. "But you need to take some antibiotics, I'll go get some."

He was back in a half minute. Much to Pero's surprise, Susanna was with him. Pero was busy trying to wipe down the sink in the bathroom where he had dripped on the floor. She pushed Pero out of the way and took over. She finished with the sink and sank to her knees, wiping the floor. She asked, "And *vat* do you want me to do with the recording?"

"Heep?"

"Look, Pero, I could listen, but I have no idea how to record with the damn thing."

Pero asked Susanna "Did you listen?"

"Ja. Had to. As Heep said, you are an idiot. But brave. Why did you not call out for help?"

"I guessed Heep would be on the way."

"Well, I would have been sooner Pero if I had known there was a blade involved, you never gave me a clue." Pero had forgotten that sound doesn't always conjure up images. "It was only when he said *good-bye* that way that we guessed what he was up to, not how. What a vicious bastard." Heep handed Pero the prescription pill bottle, "Here, take two now and one every six hours. If the damn thing gets puffy, see a doctor fast. The blood supply there goes right to the heart, don't mess around."

Susanna got up off her knees. The place was pretty clean. "So, *vat* am I to be doing with the recording?"

"Oh, hell, Lewis is not going to like this." Heep squinted his eyes and tilted his head questioningly. Pero nodded, "Yeah, him again."

Pero pulled out a cell phone, walked to the window, and Susana peered over his shoulder at his hands as he activated the cell phone programming. Pero thought she was just nosey when it came to her technology field. He listened. It rang. When he heard static, he pressed 5-5-5. Lewis's voice came in clear: "Where the hell have you been? We've been trying to reach you." Damn, he forgot to set the ringer. Its fail-safe setting was to keep the ringer off while they were filming. Lewis had told Pero, but he had forgotten.

"Sorry, sorry. Look, there's been action here, I need to report. Okay, if I put this on speaker?" And, not waiting for Lewis' okay, he proceeded to do so.

"No, no it is . . ." Lewis paused, "Ah . . . It's already on speaker isn't it?"

"Yes. Heep's here and we have a new member, Susanna Reidermaier daughter of Silke Reidermaier." He saw Susanna flinch at her mother's name. "I trust her with my life, she's reliable." He used the CIA term to reassure Lewis. It didn't much. And Susanna looked at him with that quizzical look again.

"Damn Baltazar, what's the point of having secrets if you are always going to involve anybody you are standing next to?"

"Heep here. Pero's been stabbed, he's bleed . . ."

Pero interrupted, "I am okay. Lewis, look, I didn't ask for this. I specifically asked not to have this happen again. Two weeks, within minutes of me getting this job offer out of the blue . . ." He stopped. He had gotten this offer unexpectedly, he didn't normally do film work and yet only his agent knew he was not working. "Wait Lewis, wait, this is crucial. Here, talk to Heep, he'll fill you in and Susanna can play you a recording. Heep give me your room key." He did and Pero ran out the door.

In Heep's room, he called his agent in LA on the room phone. Dick's phone rang twice, his assistant answered. Pero was told she would give him a message that he was otherwise engaged. "Then tell him this, unless he's talking to me within five seconds, I am going to tell Danny Redmond and the studio that he tried to screw this deal and I'll make sure Dick never works in LA again. Oh, and tell him his client—now *the full producer of Danny's new film—is* on the line."

He counted mentally. *And a one and a two . . .*

"Pero, how great of you to call. What's this about producing? With Danny?" He said it as if he was on first name terms with Redmond. Dick was TV, second-tier reality TV, he would kiss the ground Redmond walked on to advance his career.

"Cut the crap Dick. Now get this, I *am* the producer, sole sharing with Redmond. Full studio and bank backing made the deal last night . . . no, don't interrupt or you're fired. I need a complete and honest answer from you, your job depends on it. Ready?"

Dick said, meekly, he was.

"Fine, where exactly did the second unit work offer come from? Exactly?"

"Well, as I told you, the studio called and asked who we had, and I thought of you . . ."

"Okay, you're fired, you're lying."

"No, no please Pero, I'm sorry. You want the real truth?" *Was there any other kind, slime ball?* Pero thought. "We suggested Tommy Lewis, you know him, he's good, he is . . . well, anyway I suggested him. They, the studio had to get approval. About an hour later they called back to say they had a pre-approved name, yours."

"Dick, who was approving the name?"

"Why their new financial partner in Germany, of course, they need financing approval sometimes. I have the deal memo here someplace . . . yes, here it is a *troove-er-ee-ins* bank." TruVereinsbank. It all fit.

"Dick, you're not fired. But any deal Redmond puts before you, you agree to sight unseen, got that?" Pero wanted to make damn sure Dick did not change anything Danny wanted. "If I hear you changed one comma of any contract you're no longer my agent, got that?" He could hear Dick mumbling. Time to drop the financial hammer to make sure Dick did as he was told, "Oh, and Dick, check my employment and financial rating with Citibank, you might be shocked. I could buy your agency for cash. Bye." Pero knew if he asked the bankers, Director Lewis' standing orders with Citibank would make Dick's hair stand on end. Pero would appear golden, platinum, for once in his career, absolutely bankable. *Might as well play the Hollywood power card*, Pero thought.

He ran back to his room. They were just finishing playing the recording to the open phone on the desk. It made his flesh crawl. "*Y*ou will remember. I give you two days to comply or we will have them all killed. And all your little friends from Kenya—especially the one you call your friend and his wife who is not quite dead, yet, and . . . Yes, and your parents for good measure, we can kill them all." The recording playback stopped.

The phone speaker responded first, "We need that recording digitally transmitted, can do?"

"Pero here Lewis, yes," he could see Susanna nodding "we'll do that. First, you need to know that Tische's company was the one who asked my agent for me by name two weeks ago. I thought his name came into it after I filed for Berlin permits. But my agent, Dick Tank, just confirmed my name was floated to him, not by him, and I was chosen *before* we filed those permits. So they knew I was on that plane, and get this, it's important, they planned for me to be here, they set me up before I knew you would need me. So, why the hell did you choose me?"

"Oh, damn, it's too obvious. Shit. Why? Because you reported that you were traveling, as all operatives must. We simply matched your itinerary with the need for a packet transmission."

Pero told Suzanna and Heep that a packet is papers only.

Lewis continued, "Right, we here never planned a package delivery, that was Station's doing, we think."

Pero was beginning to connect the dots, "Yeah, but think about it. They knew your procedures. They got me to go on this shoot. I then inform you that I am going to Berlin. Presto, and then you have a sudden need for my services. Tag, I was it. And this means they know that I once—just once—was an operative. Look, that was only one time, ever. And we were all exposed, it was way too public." Lewis and Heep knew Pero meant Kenya, Suzanna looked perplexed. "And Tische specifically named Heep and my friends in Kenya. It fits; he may be doing business with al-Qaeda."

"Why?" Lewis asked.

"I don't know yet, but the only other source would be you, Lewis. You didn't tell him, did you?"

"No. I did not." It was a flat no, backed up by the single person pronoun, emphasized singular.

"So, let's look at something else. Somehow, they knew the CIA was moving something, right? So when did someone order Mil Intel to lift the sample?"

"Sixteen days ago. But it was fourteen days ago that Mil Intel called us in." Lewis paused. "Oh, Christ. Once we knew we would regain possession of the package, we knew we needed to handle it. Congressional cutbacks, you see, so we need to use agents in place, no plane fares if we can help it. That meant Berlin Station, but Station has a German cop attached twenty-four seven. If we have a cheaper alternative, we have to use that, someone there already on their own buck . . . Oh God, sorry, Pero, Tische only knew our internal intel, our procedures, maybe a leak from Berlin Station. It's not an al-Qaeda link. We set you up and didn't know it."

"No you didn't Lewis, someone else there at CIA did, told Tische what the schedule was, no way he could have found out your decision to lift the sample without an inside informant. It was his mentioning my parents that just tipped me off really, it just took a while to sink in. No way has al-Qaeda known about my parents, they wouldn't care. Only your files have my parent's information. And I suspect that the inside informant is part of the same team that's also in the field, looking for this stuff. Why they are looking, I don't know. But if this leak was passing information to the likes of Tische, he would, could, have people in the field watching us all. Who are you reporting to?"

"Don't go there, I cannot answer that question."

"Well, if you cannot answer, you can at least think. Work it out. Someone in State or CIA Headquarters is passing information to Tische." Pero paused. "What the hell's in that bag of heavy water that's so damned important?"

"You had better find out. It all hinges on that answer."

"Okay, I was leaving tonight and, before you ask, I am not telling you. Sorry. Here's what I need you to do, field agent instructions . . ." Heep shook his head and Susanna looked even more puzzled. Pero waved his hand at them to dismiss worries and to help his concentration.

"Welcome back," Lewis said.

"Yeah, well I quit for good after this, quit the whole thing. Got that? First, I need you to find out who handled the gold shipment and where it is now. I suspect the Swiss will have refused it and it'll be on its way home, or, wait, somewhere else, a new buyer . . . watch for a TruVereinsbank connection here, Lewis. It may be simple, but errors sometimes are. Okay, second, I need to make sure my parents, Mary Lever, the playwright Letterman in London, and the entire crew here, and especially don't forget Susanna, and my friends in Kenya are protected. I can't go and do this thing unless you take care of them."

"Agreed. We have command and control synchronicity with the security forces in Germany. I am pulling the gloves off this one, budget be damned."

"Don't you like being used?"

There was a pause. "I see what you mean, don't rub it in. We screwed this up. So I'll cover your back." There it was again, the singular, not plural, pronoun. "I will have the police replaced—especially as Heeper told me who Tische came to the Museum with—an ex-Stasi of the worst kind, we've got records on him. We'll put a crack team in place. Same for Letterman in London. For Kenya, all we need to do is tip off the President. He has got national heroes there and there are some crack troops we've trained, anti-terrorist experts trained in Socorro, New Mexico. They'll do. Your parents, they're on US soil, and I'll have to ask the FBI. It may take time. May I suggest a private team? You pay, we'll refund?"

"Agreed. But you have to put them in place, here's my dad's private number."

"We have it, in case something should happen to you, we keep those up to date. Now, Mary Lever . . . may I suggest that she goes to her uncle? That Nigerian muscleman friend of yours is still with him, he'll protect her." Heep nodded. Pero and Heep both trusted the ex-soldier, Kweno Usman, he had saved Mary once before. So, Pero confirmed that would be fine. "Anything else Baltazar?"

"Yeah, tell me how to pick a lock in the dark." Lewis knew it was a joke question. Two clicks, he was gone.

Susanna looked at Pero and Heep and said, "You are both crazy. Al-Qaeda before and now you are going up against *die Stasi*?"

"Look, Susanna, I didn't want this deal, but we're in it. I did, yes I did put my friends in danger back in Kenya. I still cannot forgive myself for that, even though they agreed to it," he looked at Heep, who was nodding, "and yes, thank God they supported me. We won, in the end, but people were hurt. I am still sad about what could have happened. But the truth is, if I can do good in the world, it is what my father once called my duty to do so." Pero sat on the edge of the desk, a little exhausted. The memory of the risks taken in Kenya still weighed heavily on him. "But we have a chance here. We have a sample of some paper bits in heavy water—the stuff in the water is radioactive, and it was stuck to some gold being sent from the US Treasury to Switzerland. Apparently, they swap gold all the time, different types, different needs. Anyway, there's this portion of a paper label—that's what Arnold said— Arnold from the US embassy who stuck the damn thing in my coat pocket without me knowing. Okay, the gold label and radioactivity . . . As soon as the Swiss spot and tag it, all hell breaks loose. Days after, but maybe the same day, a man deliberately puts in motion a sequence that will result in my being in Berlin, vulnerable and exposed and not knowing a damn thing. Think about it, it's brilliant. The CIA think they have a clandestine operative, me, and send me to do a simple job. But I was not clandestine, the bad guys are working with knowledge from someone else at the CIA or State. Their intel from someone in DC marked me, only me, to them, and so anything I do is, in effect, transparent to them. Then Station in Berlin, that's the CIA desk person here, changes the plan and has Arnold give me the package. Okay, they think, now get the package. But I don't have the package and meanwhile Station and her police escort—and a friend of mine—were chased down the autobahn and possibly killed. Stasi behave in Stasi ways, too heavy-handed for the new Germany. You heard him . . ." he pointed to the tape recorder, "Tische as much as said so.

"Now, he has no lead to the package, but he has me in his sights. He can squeeze that trigger anytime he wants, but he doesn't . . . yet, and he won't . . . I don't think. He wants me to take him to the package."

Susanna was aghast, "He nearly kill you, yes? He stabbed you."

"Yeah, that was blood lust, Heep, and you saved the day. But now he's keeping me on the loose so I can show them around a bit more. That's why I need to run and run fast. But one more thing . . . I know some things Tische doesn't. I know where the bag is and where it needs to go. And I know how to hide it." He turned to Heep, "You got one of those lead-lined bags for film shipments?" Heep's face lit up. "Yes, it's simple, isn't it? No one uses them anymore. They're not sold because there are such problems with security at airports. But I am going by train, no screening. Anyone with a radiation wand could pass it up and down me, and they shouldn't get a beep. I hope."

The next half hour was spent getting Pero ready. It was critical that he leave so they could simply get back to filming routine. The less suspicion, the better. *The less stress on them, the better too*, Pero thought.

They could talk on the phone the next day. Pero had a plan for that call to be untraceable to him. He'd ask Lewis to bounce any call via Bombay—just to rub it in if anyone was monitoring his calls—and he was sure they would be. Pero had realized that Tische was just too resourceful. And he had no illusions about the so-called unbreakable State or CIA phone coding anymore. If there was an inside man at the CIA, Tische didn't need the code, he could probably get the transcript in plain English by email.

Pondering all these pitfalls, Pero suddenly had a frightening thought, *Damn, maybe he's getting the one we just had—right now, on feedback from inside the CIA. They know I am leaving, but . . .* He paused, shook his head, *think Pero, did I? Nope, I didn't tell them how, thank God. But I'll have to watch for tails.*

Pero took Heep's lead bag, a small one, and folded it into the pocket of the ski parka, which he wore blue side out. He had passport, phone, cards, and all the cash the three had, about two thousand dollars. It should prove to be more than he would need. He took a small Longchamp bag, the ones you get at airports that fold up into nothing, and stuffed in extra sweaters, a few towels, two free hotel shower caps, the toothbrush kit the hotel always supplied, and some underwear and socks. A traveler must have luggage not to be suspicious. It was time to go.

Heep clapped Pero on the back as he handed him the normal cell phone. They both looked at it, knowing that news of Mbuno's wife was overdue. Heep tried to allay Pero's fears, "I'll call them first thing, redial should work to Amogh, it's worth a try. He'd have called if there were anything you needed to do. Take it easy. And take care, Pero."

Susanna took his special phone and started pressing buttons, holding hers end to end with his. Pero had no idea what she was doing except that the infrared connection was on. While she was busy, she asked, "Mary Lever, she is your wife?"

"No, my wife's dead." Even to Pero, that sounded callous. His face, however, showed sadness that Suzanna could not misinterpret. Pero continued, "Sorry, Mary is Heep's wife. Why?"

"You were protecting her." She was staring into his eyes. She wanted to ask a different question, her eyes said so.

"Yes. She's a friend, a good one. And now Heep's wife. I owe her that."

"So, your wife is Addiena? I see the name on your arm when you are taking off your shirt in the bathroom." She was blushing.

"Yes, that was her."

"She is a lucky woman."

"Was, Addiena died."

"*Ja, so?* She was and is a lucky woman." Then, all businesslike again, she handed Pero the phone and said, "Please to come back safe. It is secure, *perfekt* secure, to his handy," she nodded to her cell phone, "I programmed it in." She turned and left the room in a hurry. Pero stared at Heep.

"It's up to you Pero, and this one is special. I think she likes you."

Damn, Pero thought, *all I need are complications*, as if he didn't have enough already.

* * *

It's a strange thing. Hotels protect their guests from intruders but extruders—if that is a term that can be used—have free rein. Pero knew the police were in the lobby so he took the elevator to the second floor, the elevator registering his sixth-floor special key card, went to the pool area which was still open, and swiped in there as well. The cops would have seen his room card swipe twice on the security screen. He must be in the pool area, second floor. All's well.

He pretended to go to the changing rooms and simply walked through the one-way *Nur Notausgang* door (no exit). This lead to the back stairway, which was connected to the old casino next door, and another one-way door to the garbage alley behind. There he climbed over the iron gate and dropped onto the pavement. He walked away normally, just another person making their way somewhere with a bag. The matchbook in his shoe annoyed him, causing a desired limp. Danny's little trick might just make him unrecognizable. Most surveillance depends on seeing a familiar pace, recognizable pace and tempo. Pero was aware he was taking shorter steps as well.

They don't secure aquariums like art museums. They should sometimes. The valuable last breeding chances are in there. This time he wasn't complaining. Pero scaled the wall to the zoo using the zoo animal sculptures laid into the brick wall. One tow on the baby Rhino's nose, the next foot onto its mother's back and, presto, he was over. Then he simply broke the lock to the aquarium exit door, the one he had used before, with Heep's toolkit hammer and screwdriver, the way New York car thieves do. Nothing pretty. Get in, do your thing, get out. He had seen there were no wires yesterday on the hinge section or the doorjamb. Training sometimes kicks in, sometimes it doesn't. That time it had, so he thanked God or rather his instructors. *God or instructors, they're the same*, popped into his head.

The bag was where he had left it. But the plant had wilted. That puzzled him. Suddenly glad of Heep's lead bag, he said sorry to the swishing arowana who looked hungrily at his fingers and stuffed the radioactive bag into the lead pouch, folding over the metal top.

Then it was back to the wall and . . . damn, no rhino sculptures this side. He dragged over a bench and stood it on end. It made noise, but no one seemed to care, no guards to be seen. Strangely the animals were quiet, even the chimps didn't call out, but they watched carefully, their eyes boring into the back of his head. Maybe they identified with one of their own making a break from prison and didn't want to squeal. He was over with no one in sight and walked the two blocks to the old Zoologischer Garten train station.

Once upon a time, this was the prime station for West Berlin. Now it was relegated to drug dealers, urine smells, and students looking to score hashish. He climbed the steps two at a time to the platform, thirty feet above the street, and waited. The night Moscow-Paris Express, stopping at Kiev, Warsaw, Berlin, and Paris was due within an hour. Pero chose a dark corner and waited. No one else came up the steps, and the platform was empty.

The train was, as expected, late. It had stopped at the newer, renovated Lehrter Bahnhof, an eight-story monster station of glass and steel in that new breed of architecture that astounds and gives one the feeling that, surely, Berlin has limitless resources. Lehrter is in the center of Berlin and the Zoologischer Garten station is now only a curved, slow, pass-through for international trains, no stopping.

But he knew that the old station was on that very sharp curve, necessary from the days when trains had to turn around within the city limits to go back the way they had come, back to the West. Through trains now had to slow drastically. He also knew that the Russian carriages still had hinged doors with actual handles. European trains, in the liability-free world Pero lived in, had abolished handles, the doors shutting when the guard pressed a button. The Russian sleeper carriages should, if he guessed right, have a step he could jump onto and a handle he could open. Once inside he'd pay the fare. He slipped his trouser belt through the handles of the Longchamp bag and refastened it, creating what amounted to a large bum bag. And waited.

Plans don't always go the way people want them to. The train wasn't slowing as much as he thought it would, maybe still doing twenty-five mph. Pero could not run that fast, so he worried and calculated that he really had to time it right.

From his vantage point on the inside of the curve, he could see the line of railcars squealing their way around the station curve, illuminated by the garish neon beer and kebabs signs one level below the platform. The Russian sleeper cars, old-fashioned, boxy, and a dark brown color, not the red or dark blue with a white stripe of the German carriages, were at the rear. The second to last looked like a very old sleeper, with two iron steps below the door. He started his run as it reached the middle of the length of the platform and missed the first door. He kept running as hard as he could. He felt the superglued wound split a little, that warm sensation of blood leaking but kept going. As he reached the end of the platform, with an imminent thirty-foot plunge off the end, he leapt for the last door.

His foot slipped. He thought, *Oh, you're kidding* . . . knowing it was a cliché, but his foot did slip. His right hand held onto the door handle, which was slowly pivoting down. If it turned all the way down, it was a toss-up what would happen first: either the door would open—throwing him off completely—or his hand would slip off the vertical open position, and he'd plunge to the street below. Either way, his plan to get aboard wasn't going well.

His other hand, flailing about, made contact with the top metal step, he slipped his fingers into the grille and pulled up, hard. Like a mountain climber, he got one knee on the bottom step and using the one good handhold, changed his right grip from the door handle to grab the vertical handrail next to the doorway instead. Then he pulled himself upright. There he was, standing on the bottom step, panting hard, holding both handrails now either side, catching his breath. The Longchamp bag was still held secure by his belt and bouncing in the wind behind his rear. The train began to accelerate in preparation for the express corridor toward Koln when a woman's face loomed over him in the door's window and the door began to swing open—toward his right arm!

There was nothing else to do. He let go of the right side handrail, swung his body out of the way of the opening door and as soon as it was open, swung his leg and arm inside. He grabbed the doorjamb. In a continuous movement, he then let go of the left handrail and pivoted his left side in through the door. Smiling, the only thought he had was of a circus act. *Ta da!*

Thankfully, though, his acrobatic tricks were done for the night. He was in, safe and sound. The door latched shut behind him. The *little mother* Russian carriage guard was less amused. She reached up and slapped his face, hard.

Chapter 8

Jura

He was pushed down the corridor of the Russian sleeper car by the five-foot barrel of a woman in a floral nylon smock over her blue Russian train service uniform, complete with aluminum buttons. They were fastened up to her neck, fat spilling over the tight collar. Her hair was covered by a scarf, tied under her chin, framing fat cheeks, now glowing red from the exertion of surprise and of pushing Pero before her.

Her responsibility was this first-class carriage and Pero was clearly not first-class material, so out! "выйдите, не позволенный, выйдите." *Get out, forbidden, get out!*

He tried protesting in halting Russian, "ïîæàëóéñòà, небольшое-количество-мать, ждите, нет, ïîæàëóéñòà." *Please, little mother, wait, no, please . . .*

They neared the end of the car, adjoining the next car, which was a Deutsche Bahn (German Rail) company car. There he would be subject to a rule-biding, strict, train guard who would, no doubt, throw him off the train at the next opportunity, or worse, call the police. Pero finally physically resisted the little mother, twisted to face her, stuck his hand in his pocket, and drew out a dollar bill. He didn't know which one he had grabbed. It turned out to be a hundred dollar bill. He waved it in front of her. She stopped.

"для какой?" *For what?* She folded her arms, an imposing authority.

"кровать, кровать к Парижу." *A bed, just a bed to Paris.*

"нет, нет, нет!" *No, no, no!* She wanted no part of him, but he could see her eyes fixated on the money.

"двести долларов?" *Two hundred dollars?*

She hesitated. "Евро." *Euro.* Pero nodded and pulled out the Euros and she snatched them. Then she grabbed his sleeve, checked the corridor anxiously behind him in case another conductor was coming, and now like a sweet, affectionate granny shooing him back to bed after a nightmare, she opened 5a–5b, with her passkey. In a conspiratorial whisper and lots of hand gestures, she gave him instructions, "Останьтесь дома там." *Stay in there.* She put her hands in prayer to one ear, pretending to sleep. "Париж," Paris, "Я пробуждаю Вас." *I wake.* She pointed to her watch at the six, "шесть часов?" *Six o'clock?*

He nodded and thanked her, smiling happily. She smiled back, patted his chest, withdrew, and locked the door. He could open it from his side, no problem. But he put the chain on anyway.

The wood paneling modeled after the Grandes Wagon-Lits of the 1950s was well oiled and polished, making the cabin smell of linseed, as *little mother* did. The bottom bed was folded down and made up with crisp Siberian linen, thick and smooth. They often left a bed ready for late-night unexpected guests, although not those who stowed away as he had. He took off the coat, removed the bag from his belt, toed off his shoes, and made himself at home. Somehow, taking off his shoes always changed his mental pace. Now, if he only had slippers, he could pretend he was vacationing or at home. He smiled, realizing humans were such creatures of habit.

The train left the last of the track points of Berlin, so the swaying reduced and it picked up speed. He found the catch for the sink and folded it down, revealing the two taps and the soap dish, a piece of soap wrapped in paper, waiting. The polished copper basin had no plughole, as usual. To empty the sink, you folded it up, and the water went down a drain onto the tracks clickity-clacking below. He washed his face and hands, cleaning up as best he could. Then he gingerly lifted his shirt. There was a nasty red stain just coming through the hand towel he had left there, stolen from the Steigenberger. In his pocket was the superglue. He took it out and unscrewed the top. The tip was solid. It never ceased to amaze him that the manufacturers of superglue cannot make a reusable container. *One use and it glues itself shut!*

He bit through the top with his teeth. It stuck his lip to a tooth. As he pried that off, it hurt. Checking the mirror, he pulled the towel away from the wound and saw that it was leaking, slightly, not too bad, about only half was open again, only about half as deep as the cut. He quickly glued it back shut.

Looking at the tiny tube, he stuck the cap back on hard, hoping he might get one more use. He contemplated biting through the other side next time. He was vaguely aware that superglue was consuming way too much of his thinking. He realized it was shock. This was normal. Mundane things become overly important as shock approaches.

He quickly cleaned up the surrounding area, wiping the blood off his stomach with another facecloth from the Steigenberger. He patted the area dry. It wasn't seeping, a good sign. He took off his trousers and slipped into the sheets, placing the crisp linen floor mat over his stomach, just in case.

He had five hours to Paris, almost, and he wanted to sleep deep, but he couldn't lie on his stomach as usual, his arm with Addiena's tattooed name against his heart. So he folded his arms and drifted off to a somewhat fitful sleep, the adrenaline still keeping him awake. With discipline, he stayed that way, like an Egyptian mummy as the train screamed into the night. There was no passport control for anyone. This was now an inter-European Union train with little, if any, customs. He was sure his *little mother* would keep quiet, so finally he slept shallowly through every stop, every jostle. Adrenaline consumed, he finally zoned out.

But her knock on the door with "Париж!" *Paris!* woke him quickly. He looked out the window. The train was just beginning to wind its way through the various points and sidings outside the station, the Gare de l'Est. He figured they had about ten minutes to go.

The wound had not bled. He brushed his teeth, put any soiled linen in a Steigenberger shower cap in his bag, and stole the clean hand towel from the cabin. Then, in a fit of remorse, he left the one hundred dollar bill to cover. No way he was going to make *little mother* pay for the loss. He washed, took his antibiotic, got dressed, zipped up the coat, and looked at himself in the mirror. He was ready. He opened the door and stepped into the corridor, joining the other passengers getting ready to depart. The *little mother* spotted him and nodded, even gave a little smile. Taking her smile as approval, he was sure he must look cleaner, less suspicious.

They pulled slowly into the station, a head stop, and he deliberately went out the farther door, away from the station. He wanted to pass her and say one more "ïíæàëёóéñòà, небольшое-количество-мать." *Thank you, little mother.* She smiled wider, cackled, and reached up to smack him on the back as he passed. He pretended to stumble because of her heavy hand, and she laughed. As he stepped down from the train, he smiled back through the window and waved good-bye. Her face pressed next to the train window, she waved until he was out of sight.

He took the mid-platform stairway that connected directly with the Metro and passed through the station quickly, going about his business. He bought an allez simple (*one way, second class*) for the Metro from the ticket window and went down the long corridor and stairs to the number four line, making sure he got the direction, Porte d'Orléans. The Paris Metro never tells you what compass direction the trains go, just what the end station is. You have to memorize not only the station you wanted to change at but also the name of the stations for the direction.

He got on the number four Metro just as the buzzer was sounding. This being rush hour at a major station, the pneu-matic-powered barrier was beginning to move as he ran past and boarded the train as the doors opened. No one followed. At Chatelet, he changed, taking the long hike again to connect to the number one Metro going toward Chateau de Vincennes. At the Gare de Lyon, he got off again and climbed the stairs into one of Europe's busiest stations. It was 7:12 a.m. He had to hurry.

While he had been waiting at the Zoologischer Garten sta-tion, he had used the Internet connection on his phone to get the schedule of the TGV, Train à Grand Vitesse (high-speed train), to Lausanne in Switzerland. Lausanne would have no intelligence connection to the package he was carrying, so he felt sure Lausanne couldn't, wouldn't be watched. He didn't make a TGV reservation on his phone on the Internet in Berlin in case that gave them—whoever "them" were—time to react and catch up to him.

However, the TGV does require both a reservation and a ticket. No *little mother* nonsense with the fastest train service in Europe. The TGV is a welded-track super train reaching up to two hundred miles per hour. They are smooth, prompt, and efficient. They also allow customs and immigration officials to come on board to interview and check passengers if a border is to be crossed. Customs and Immigration were due to come on board in Frasne before Vallorbe on the French border with Switzerland.

He went to the TGV *guichet*, the special ticket office for the TGV, and asked for a reservation and ticket for the 7:24 TGV to Lausanne. *"C'est complet monsieur."* It was full.

"Premiere classe?" He asked if first class was free.

"Ah, il en reste, c'est 234 Euro, s'il vous plait." First was available, he paid her the money. Pero went to Track 16. The guard at the door of his carriage checked his seat reservation and ticket, and he boarded the train and walked to the dining car. He was hungry and, besides, he could look around, watching to see if anyone else would board in the three minutes left. No one he recognized did. There were no late sprinters either. The train left the station on time.

His phone vibrated in his trouser pocket. Taking it out, he looked at the screen. It was a cell call. He put it to his ear and pressed the green button. He heard static. He tried the 5-5-5.

"Hello? Is that you Pero?" The voice was Heep's, tinny but clear enough. It was as if he was listening down a tin can and string walkie-talkie set from his childhood.

"Hi Heep. Everything okay?"

"I have news. Susanna says relax, the phone is secure. I am using hers. She knows these mathematical things, I think you can trust her, it's her code."

"Yes I do, absolutely. Go on."

"Okay. The big news is that Mbuno's wife is okay. Rinaldi found a ruptured bladder. It's repaired, the whole thing stabilized and she'll be fine but sore. They say rehab will start next week, and she'll need a wheelchair for about four weeks, crutches after that. But she'll be okay. Rinaldi took you at your word, well Ranjeet's word, and used your money to fly in a team from London. They did the surgery. Now Mbuno's hanging around, not sure what to do. He's charming with the staff at the Aga Khan, but it won't last. Amogh suggests you find him something to do, like scouting out some leopards or something. I know we have nothing on the cards there," Heep meant in production planning for Mary's new show that was months away, "but I did suggest that maybe you'll want to send him to Langani to see if the dugong are accessible. What do you think?"

The dugong were Africa's version of the manatee, but they were the real origin of the mermaid myth because, unlike the Manatee who has one rounded flat tail similar to the beaver, the one thousand pound dugong has a tail similar to a Dolphin. Pero told Heep it was a good idea but that he was still worried for Mbuno and Niamba's safety using a code phrase of "your friends" meaning Tische's thugs. They had him rattled.

"Heep, I think we need to move them." Heep started to object, Pero cut him off, "Now, Heep, hear me out. Are those doctors still there? Let's blow the money and transport Niamba to Europe, wherever the doctor says, keep them both in the same care. I am sure they can arrange an air ambulance for her, maybe with Ranjeet and Mbuno escorting them. Ranjeet has friends at the LSE," Pero meant the London School of Economics where Ranjeet had studied, "and he can take precautions. I'll try to call him later when I am clear. You understand?"

Heep responded, sounding worried, "It's that serious? You think they would still go after Mbuno and Niamba?"

"I cannot take the chance. We," he stressed the "we." "We cannot take the chance, agreed?" Heep signed and agreed. "So, can you get that moving quickly? Tische will be watching the Nairobi connection and he'll expect me to want to protect my friends there. Let's give him that impression, no the assurance, that he has me frightened and at the same time move them from Kenya to a secure location—and then call Lewis and tell him he's got to protect them there. The US Embassy can even post Marines, just protect them, okay?"

Again, Heep said he'd handle it but added, "If you fly Mbuno out of Nairobi, everyone will know."

"Not if they use an air ambulance, a private flight . . . can you tell Ranjeet that? Tell him money no object."

"You are running up quite a bill with the doctors . . ."

"I don't care. One, we need to be seen as keeping them safe and two, we need to have them safe, and three, we might need to have Ranjeet and Mbuno nearby. I am beginning to think we may need them."

Heep's next sigh could be heard clearly, "Oh, shit, you're that worried? Please tell me you'll get rid of that package and make sure Tische knows you have given it away and we're done."

"Yes, Heep, that's the plan, but this was all set up too carefully. Something, some plan, is being produced here—just like a rival film that now includes all of us whether we like it or not. Yes, I'll run my delivery errand, but somehow if it gets complicated, I'd prefer to have Mbuno and maybe Ranjeet handy if only to help you and me figure things out. Between us we might prevail here."

Heep said a reluctant okay and then got the conversation down to normal work, as much to avoid the tension of Pero's plans as to ward off the uncertainty they were facing. Normalcy is de-stressing, "Now, the shoot today and tomorrow . . ." and for the next twenty minutes, as the TGV train rolled slowly out of Paris, they discussed production business. Thomas, standing in for Pero as the producer, was being efficient and Danny really got along with him, no problems. The police had called ten minutes after hotel wake-up calls that morning, at 6:10 and wanted to know where Mr. Baltazar was. As they had planned, Danny told them he was production planning for Paris, in Paris. No doubt, Mr. Tische would know by now. Pero realized that Heep forgot to wonder how the police knew he was gone. Heep pressed on, "Hey, Pero, you okay? How's the cut?"

"Doing fine, not sore, and thanks for the pills." The phone went dead. As cell phone conversations went, it was stable. When the TGV got up to speed leaving Paris, it had become sketchy and finally cut out. Pero guessed they were doing about a hundred and fifty miles per hour. It was just under three hours to Vallorbe. Thirty-five minutes less for Frasne. If he got off in Frasne, it would be suspicious. If he got off in Vallorbe, he'd be on the border and open to questions he didn't want to answer—especially concerning his package. So he decided to wait and see how many got off in Frasne, if that would be his best bet. If there were a crowd of, say, tourists, he would mix in. If not, he'd stay on board until Vallorbe and take his chances. In any event, he was not going to Lausanne, which was too risky. The Swiss have excellent, hidden detectors. He didn't fully trust his lead bag—or a body search—not to reveal all. The Swiss would arrest him and maybe charge him with theft of police property just to make his life complete.

Pero went back to his seat. It was in the second of the first-class carriages, nearest the dining car. The through traffic was continuous, people walking back and forth, lurching with the train swaying, grabbing onto others' headrests, apologizing for tapping a passenger's shoe. He was in a four-seat section, facing an empty seat with a woman diagonally opposite. She was facing the direction of travel. He settled in to doze and think, shutting his eyes.

Lost in his thoughts an odor snapped him back to reality. Without moving, eyes half closed, he just saw that the shoes were passing off to his right going toward the front of the train. Nothing remarkable about the shoes but the odor was unmistakable. It belonged to the man with the paper in the elevator of the Steigenberger, he was sure. Pero waited until he was twenty or thirty seconds past his seat. Next, a group of women with cameras and fanny packs ambled in the man's same direction followed by the *garde de train* (train guard) asking to see the women's tickets. The *garde de train* examined their papers and explained that there was no second class this side of the dining car or in the direction they were going. Pero knew the women could be lost, but aftershave man wasn't. He was looking for Pero, he was sure. It all fit. The conversation with Langley, somehow Tische had already found out he was going to CERN. *That was how the Berlin police knew to ask my whereabouts this morning.* Tische already had his stooges on the trains to Geneva and Switzerland. They must have spotted Pero at the station ticket office. Damn TGV for needing an advance reservation. And suddenly another piece of the puzzle clicked into place. He thought *they didn't need to watch the airport security, that would mean a quick computer check of the passenger manifest and that would do it. That and a metal detector being set off by either the lead bag or the plastic one. Damn.*

Pero needed to figure out if the man thought Pero knew he was being watched. So Pero stood and walked away from the tourists, the ticket collector, and the aftershave man—toward the dining car.

Dining cars on TGVs have two sections, sitting or a standing bar. He stood. *"Donnez-moi un coca, s'il vous plait."* He bought a Coke. He could use the caffeine and the sugar. In the reflection of the polished chrome surrounding the bar, he watched behind, checking for movement. He didn't expect anything violent, but he wanted to know if the man came back this way. For almost an hour, he didn't. As they were approaching Dijon, he suddenly appeared, Pero saw his reflection in the polished bar handrail. The man didn't see Pero looking at him. But it was obvious that the man needed to keep Pero in view in case Pero alighted from the train, so he had to come looking. Not knowing Pero could see him in the chrome, he brushed on past—giving Pero a whiff of that odor—and went toward the dining table area. He took a seat facing Pero as far away as possible and started to study the menu all too attentively.

Pero had calculated his chances. He realized it was vital to find out if the man knew Pero had spotted him because any feint Pero wanted to do to throw him off his trail depended on knowing if the man thought Pero knew he was there. If the man thought Pero knew he was being tailed, he'd keep his distance and Pero had a chance. So, he wanted the man to suspect that Pero might know, but not be sure. Pero wanted Mr. Aftershave to keep his distance but not think his cover was totally blown, which would cause him to do something rash, like a swift knife attack. The man must suspect Pero was carrying the package. Why else would he be aboard? And Tische only wanted the package, what happened to Pero was irrelevant, at least that's what Pero hoped—and feared. The Museum stabbing had taught him at least that much.

Surely, he thought, *with aftershave that strong. He must know he's blown. On the other hand, anyone who wears that much aftershave will have no sense of smell anyway, they might not think it is so obvious.*

So Pero made a plan. He would strike up a conversation with the next person to stand next to him at the bar, offer to buy them a drink, and get their name. Suddenly, a woman stood next to him and, in very broken Franglais asked for a "Deux bottles of l'eau, please and, eh, and . . . Oh damn."

"Can I help you?"

She looked at Pero. "Yes, please, I left my phrase computer packed in the suitcase, and I don't want to rummage for it on the train. It's so crowded, you know, and the porter charges three Euros for carrying each bag. Can you imagine? Almost five dollars for each bag! I remember when I was a girl—I came over here with my parents when I was six—the porters were happy with twenty-five cents!" And she went on and on. Smiling, he let her and, in a few moments, got her name— Margarete Tribbet from Connecticut. She was on a trip with her friends, two of them. Money wasn't going very far. He seized the opportunity.

"Margarete, I am on a company expense account. I will never see the bill. Why don't we just have lunch together? I mean you and all your friends," he quickly added, she didn't seem to be the type looking for a romantic encounter. "I'll pay the bill, my treat, I'll give the waiter over there the money. You can start without me, I have a quick call to make and no cell phones allowed in the dining car, you know." She nodded. "I'll be back as soon as I can. We have about three hours to go before Lausanne, so it'll be fun, you can tell me where you've been and where you're going. I may have some suggestions." She protested, but it didn't take long to convince her. He suggested she go back to her friends and bring them here, into the dining car, and they would have an early lunch, late breakfast, "It'll be an American brunch, but that's our secret from the French, okay?" She nodded eagerly.

He called the headwaiter over and handed him two hundred Euros. He explained that the woman, Margarete—she said hello, and he did that little French head bow—and his friends would be having lunch on him. "Vous pouvez les servir avec ça et garder le reste pour vous. D'accord?" *Take their order with this money and keep the balance for you.* The waiter was very happy, his smile said so. The menu for three might run to just over a hundred Euros. It was still breakfast or snack time. White tablecloths would not be used on this train that would arrive before lunch in Lausanne. Pero hoped Margarete enjoyed her brunch. She looked happy enough. "See you shortly Margarete, go get your friends, grab a table. It's all arranged and paid for!"

Margarete was beaming, almost giggly, "Thank you, it's so kind. Can I bring the maps, so you can show me things to see? That all right?"

"It's fine, off you go before the place fills up and you can't get a table."

As she ambled down the car toward second class, he timed, in his head as he looked innocently at the half-finished drink in front of him, when she would be about next to the after-shave man. He looked up, stared after her, and called out, loud enough, "Margarete, don't be long, the place will fill up soon." She gave Pero a quizzical look, waved, and walked off more quickly. Pero saw what he needed to.

When the man looked up at her, she was standing just past his table. As Pero called out, he ducked and turned to avoid Pero seeing him.

A man who thinks you know who he is will hide. The man who is sure will stare you down. Pero thought, *the man who thinks you have no idea won't move and will avoid your eyes, since sudden ducking and hiding it gives him away.* Now he knew what he knew and vice versa. The man wasn't sure Pero knew it was him, but he suspected Pero might. The doubt in Mr. Aftershave's head was perfect for Pero's plan.

Calmly, Pero went back to his seat and dozed off. He set his mental alarm for ten minutes before Frasne, twenty minutes past Dole. His thoughts as he fell asleep? *Who was this stinker?* The gray cells in the brain sent their wake-up call. Out of his reverie, he looked at his watch. In ten minutes, they would pull into Frasne. He had a game of chicken to try.

TGVs don't stop very well and they have poor acceleration compared to normal trains. They are designed for few stops and high speed, not local traffic. The TGV line to Lausanne is one of the slowest because of the number of stops, as well as the twisty pass over the Jura and down to Lake Leman, also known as Lake Geneva. So, to minimize delays, the short stops in smaller towns, to take on Customs and Immigration officials, were limited to under thirty seconds.

In Frasne, as the wheels stopped, Pero suddenly got up, went to the door, and as soon as it opened, got off. He looked left up the train. Nothing. He heard the door closing warning whistle and the beep behind him. Nothing. Pero stayed still at the open door, level with the platform. Just as the doors began to close, the man stepped out, level with Pero but one car away. The doors closed. But not Pero's door. It jammed, oscillating open, shutting, open, confused by his small bag blocking the doorjamb. Too late, Mr. Aftershave's door was sealed, fully shut, so he ran at Pero. As Pero's door recycled open, he stepped back inside, lifting his bag out of the way, and it shut solid. The man's hands banged on the glass as the train began to move. Pero watched through the departing window as the man pulled out a phone.

Pero went and joined Margarete and her friends in the dining car. He ordered and paid for champagne. They had a party. When the French Immigration people came around, all their American passports were seen together, no problem, no suspicion. About twenty minutes later, as they train approached Vallorbe, he excused himself, went back to first class, grabbed his bag and, when it stopped, stepped off the TGV.

Vallorbe, in France, is a mostly a way station for important trains, the boarding point for officials going in either direction. Pero watched the Swiss immigration and custom's officers get on board, ready to check papers as the train would pass that invisible Swiss border, just ten minutes down the line, winding through the snow-covered valleys.

But here, still in France, as Pero's breath steamed the air as he walked down the stairs and under the tracks, through the underpass, and up again. There were no customs. How could there be, he had come from Paris and was still in France. No control, no suspicion, no need to worry. Pero walked over to the restrooms. Inside, in the warm, he waited. Two minutes later, he emerged and Vallorbe station had resumed its sleepy way station appearance. No one was moving. It was 11:10 a.m., a time when Vallorbe was hardly a hive of activity.

In that tiny community, situated on the northern side of the Jura range, a row of mountains eroded by glaciation to resemble massive rolling hills, Pero faced his next task alone. He needed to steal a car.

Chapter 9

CERN

There is something about a Deux Chevaux 2CV, made by Citroen, the idiosyncratic French car company. The translation is *two horses*, meaning it has a two horsepower motor. It has hugely reliable components, a capable motor, and a wonderful, springy suspension. Like a Model T, it can be driven anywhere and often is. It is, like other Gallic icons, unrivaled for function and affection.

The stationmaster's and the delivery van of the *laiterie* (milk and cheese shop) were both 2CVs. They were parked side-by-side, both were warm to the touch. The gas tanks of 2CVs are under the rear. The gasoline sloshes back and forth. You can hear it. If it is a loud slosh, it's nearly empty. The station master's, with its SNCF labeling (Société Nationale des Chemins de Fer Français) rocked easily on the soft springs, with just a little slosh, telling Pero it was full. The laiterie van was not. Pero would have preferred it the other way around, but the stationmaster's was the one to borrow. It is not hard to steal a 2CV. There is no steering lock, no gearbox lock. You take the two wires under the metal dash by the driver's knees, the green and the black, and you connect them. Then you open up the engine compartment and hold your Swiss Army knife, two blades open, one each side, across the solenoid terminals and touch the engine block for ground. The engine turns and starts. You get in, you drive off. Nothing hurried.

There was no face pressed up against a frosted window of the train station or shops next door. No one was looking, just the station cat basking in the morning sun on the granite steps, nonplussed.

Pero took the road north, back toward Métabief. He had taken a *Ski France* brochure off the rack in the ticket area in the Gare de Lyon. It showed him the roads he needed to start with but not the little lanes and slip roads he remembered from his childhood.

He had walked these mountains when he was in school on the shores of Lac Leman. The Jura had been so glacially eroded there was even a glacier depression on the top, forming a series of lakes—the largest of which was Lac de Joux, where several Swiss watch manufacturers' component plants were located: Omega, Tissot, Swatch, Jaeger leCoultre and Patek Philippe to name a few. Pi (π) and Rolex are nearby as well. The air is clean, the altitude favorable, and when the factories were built, there were virtually no taxes.

This area is in Zone Franche. Zone Franche is not strictly Switzerland. It's in a no man's land between France and Switzerland. The currency, communications, immigration, and laws are French, the tax laws and sovereignty are Swiss. It's a compromise instead of a confrontation. It's been that way since the 1700s. The Canton de Vaud, a Swiss Canton, has a divided people, proud to be Vaudois—a people of the Jura region. On the French side, their cousins are the people of the Haute Jura—the high Jura. CERN lies at the bottom of the

Zone Franche, near Geneva. Pero planned to drive near there, walk the last mile or two, and bluff his way in.

At Métabief, he took the small road to Mouthe and onto Saint-Laurent-en-Grandvaux. There he turned by the church heading south through Morez toward Les Rousses. In Les Rousses, he remembered there was a sort of border crossing, French customs only because it connected to Divonne-les-Bains, a spa town, whose waters contain very rare salts that are said to be good for the liver or kidneys. *Or was it the pancreas?* It also had a gambling casino famous for fleecing the really addicted gambling rich, some as much as a million dollars a night.

Instead of passing through that frontier gate, Pero took the country lane. It was quite muddy, with snow still piled up in the shade but no match for a 2CV. He drove onto Lamoura and then left onto the road for Mijoux, climbing the backside of the Jura, passing the π factory just before you reach Col de La Faucille. In March there was no more skiing, the snow on the pistes had melted at this lower altitude, so there were no tourists and no need for a French frontier guard. He drove down the Lac Leman side of the Jura, through Gex and took the back road to Ornex, about three miles from the backside of CERN and four miles from Switzerland proper. He parked the car under some trees by the town cemetery, put two hundred Euros on the driver's seat with a "merci" written on a bit of paper, and proceeded on foot.

About two miles down the road, he walked straight at the guard tower he could see through the forest trees. It was about a mile away. The earth between the trees and the gate was covered with gray-brown grass, kept short. He knew that the old cyclotron atom smasher was under his feet. The targets were in the buildings behind the guard tower. It was gray and two stories high with ground-level windows and cameras sticking out all around the top of its square stucco sides. He remembered it was the seldom-used north gate of CERN, used only for deliveries and emergencies. His professor at school had once asked for directions on a school outing. Since he considered his current need an emergency, he proceeded boldly up to the tower and rang the bell. When in this part of the world, Pero knew it was critical to appear calm and very civilized.

"Oui?" Came the tinny voice.

In answer, he explained in fluent French, with a slight Vaudois accent, that he had a breakdown and that he had a friend that worked inside. "Could he come to give me a hand?"

"Qui es?" *Who is it?* So Pero explained that Professor Samuel Turner would, he was sure, be prepared to help. He was told to wait. Before long, the voice changed, this time more authoritarian, "Qui etes vous?" *Who are you?* That was not a good sign. Pero knew that Professor Turner would, right now, be seeing the video image on a window on his office computer . . . unless he was not there. With nothing to lose, Pero decided to continue the pretense that he was sure that his friend was there.

Looking into the camera lens he said in English: "Sam, it's me, Pero Baltazar, can't you get off your bony ass and come and help me you, *giraffe* you?" At school they had been part of a clique, a gang of five all told. Pero was nicknamed otter and Sam was giraffe. The rest of the childhood friends made up a sort of zoo.

"Attendez-la." *Wait there.*

A Swiss police officer appeared at the other side of the gate. He seemed to be waiting for something. In a minute or two, a small golf cart approached from a concrete bunker about 200 yards away. Pero saw his friend, all six feet eight inches of him, folded to fit under the plastic roof, giant hands gripping the wheel.

As Sam approached the gate, he handed the police officer his ID card. It was swiped in a portable carrier attached to the police officer's belt. "Hello Pero, fancy meeting you here. Boney ass, huh? Broken down?"

"Yeah, if I could just get a lift into Geneva, I can have someone go and collect the rental. I left it back there about a mile this side of Ornex," he lied for the cop. "Anyway, I remembered you worked here and thought le giraffe, he'll help me out."

"Eh, you expect me to help out the slippery la loutre?" (*otter*) "Well . . ." he milked the pause, "oh, why not? C'est bon chef, vous pouvez le faire entrer, c'est bien mon ami d'école." He vouched for Pero as his friend from school. The police officer looked annoyed. No doubt, looking at Samuel, he thought, *what a geek*. Pero didn't see a geek, he saw what the British called a boffin. A man so deeply committed and talented in his branch of science—nuclear physics—that reality had slipped sideways. His tie was askew, his shirt had one sleeve up, one down, and he noticed Sam had his V-neck sweater inside out. No doubt, his socks wouldn't match either. Pero didn't care, it was his mind and friendship he came for.

The gate opened, Sam and Pero climbed into the golf cart, and they slowly ambled away. "Thanks Sam."

"Yeah, when you used our secret code words," he meant *skinny ass*, "I took a moment to realize what was going on. It's been twenty years, hasn't it?"

"A bit more. You're looking well."

"You too. Sorry about your wife, *Addiena*. I meant to write, but then months went by before I found the reminder on my desk. Sorry."

"It's okay, I know you. You liked her, I figured you'd miss her too. Sharing the loss with friends at the time always helped, but it doesn't matter. I knew how you'd feel. Anyway, sharing at the time didn't reduce the longing later. I still miss her."

"Yeah, sorry. She was great. If it weren't you, I would have asked her. And before you say it, there are a couple of other friends, especially Lion who would have fought you for her. Yeah, but she only had eyes for you. Oh, damn, Pero, sorry again. I've been saving that up." They pulled into a little golf cart bay under the concrete overhang of the research facility. Sam got out and plugged the cart in, recharging the batteries. "So, what's going on and how can I help?"

"Sam, I know I used our code, but I'll consider you've fulfilled any commitment or promise we once had just by listening to me. It's a long story, and I don't know if you can—or should help. It could be dangerous. Can we speak alone?"

By then they were walking down a neon-lit, concrete corridor with pipes that ran along the walls. Some technicians pushed or squeezed past. Everyone seemed to have a task at hand, a schedule to keep. It was never a nosy place, CERN. Too many dedicated, mono-focused scientists for internal politics.

"It's two-fifteen Pero, it's lunch time, no one will be back until four. Anyway, this is my lab here—the whole shebang, so I can send them all away if they butt in. Often do. Prefer working on my own."

"You always did Sam. But then you did finish your work in five minutes when we took the whole evening."

"Not the damn French idioms. Still haven't gotten the hang of them. Luckily everyone here speaks English, the language of my trade, well, apart from math that is."

Anytime he'd ever been in CERN—the first time was twenty-two years ago to be exact—there had been pipes in every corridor with wires inside, all rainbow colors, and aluminum and plastic pipes that were written upon and, sometimes, tagged. The whole building was one electronic erector set. At the end of the corridor was a twelve-foot sphere filled with a light blue clear liquid. Sam explained, "New liquid helium bubble target. Interesting results. The Mesons we accelerate don't seem to hit anything, making energy calculations difficult. I was trying to ionize it, like the sun but not thermal-reactive, to see if that causes a more dense target. If it works, we'll be able to trace light emitting quarks, especially those that jump time and space. Interesting . . ." he was losing Pero. Sam's brain thrived in complex calculations and theory—far away from the mundane moments of life.

Pero needed him to focus, "Sam, are you with me here?"

"Sorry, Pero. Shoot." He was still looking at the bubble chamber.

"My story involves a matter of life and death. So far, it's a dozen or so people at risk. But I suspect it may involve exponentials of that number."

Sam's head snapped around. Pero used a term, "exponential." That would mean something special to the mathematician in Sam. "Explain." Now Sam was in "input" mode, staring at Pero's face intently. Whenever they had a problem at school, Sam would say, "Explain." And the other students would relate all they knew. Sam would do the calculations and give them the answers or at least the odds of success. He was a certifiable genius without ego, a rare combination.

Pero pulled out the lead bag and rolled back the flap. A small light on the ceiling immediately started flashing. Sam put his giant hand over Pero's, stopping him, calmly but firmly. "Not here, unstable environment."

Pero folded the lead top back over and they walked a few more hundred meters, through underground corridors, until they got to a large steel door. Sam pushed the key code buttons and pulled the door open revealing a one-desk office and lab cluttered with an eccentricity Pero hadn't seen since dorm days. Sam's domain. The door swung shut automatically behind them. Sam walked over to a clear-sided box and simply said, "It's got a lead crystal liner." He took the film bag from Pero and put it inside as if it was a newborn baby, shut the lid, and put his hands into rubber gloves attached to the box. Talking to Pero as he opened the lead film bag, he extracted the vacuum bag containing the liquid. "Pero what the hell have you got here? It's so damn hot the hydrogen radiation sensor went off as you opened the outer bag. It's outgassing, for Christ's sake. And it's got to have a radiation signature, giving off rems like crazy, to set that detector off."

"It's a bag someone asked me to carry to the Max Planck labs in Germany for analysis. Something went wrong, there have been killings. We need to know a few things in order to find out what's so damn interesting about this material. We need to know what the hell it is, and then I'll be able to figure out what to do. Sam, I am pretty sure I need to take the damn thing back with me and give it to someone. It must look untouched."

"No way. It's not leaving here. It'll kill you in time. This outer bag, what is it? Lead?" Pero nodded. "Yeah, well, look . . ." Sam peeled its plastic outer layer revealing white powder, dust, "See? It's already breaking down, it's not pure lead anyway. It's an alloy, fine for film safe x-ray machines but not this. Two days, max, the whole bag will turn to dust."

"Can't you examine its signature or whatever, without opening the plastic bag and spilling the heavy water?"

"You mean it's not the liquid that's giving off these rems? It's the crap floating around in there? Christ, it must be really hot." He peered closer. "There are less than one point five grams in there, I'll bet." He picked up a portable meter inside the plastic box, held it against the vacuum bag, and then tilted it to let Pero see. The needle held steady at three hundred rem or 3MSV.

Pero had no clue what the reading meant. "Bad is it?"

"About a full year's worth of normal radiation exposure every one second. Nasty stuff. Now, tell me exactly, what am I looking at?"

"Apparently a label that came off some gold being shipped from a US Treasury gold deposit to Zurich. It set off the Swiss sensors at Zurich airport. They bagged it in heavy water . . ."

"Christ, that's what this is? Paper? And I was getting a reading, any damn reading? Holy cow . . . " Pulling his hands out of the gloves, he swiveled the chair, entered an equation on the computer, pressed enter a few times, clicked this icon and that one—then swiveled back to face Pero: "You have thermonuclear fissionable material in there. It can't be just the paper. It has to be what the paper holds." He was getting excited but disappointed. "Look, Pero, I may have to give this stuff back to you. If I keep it here, there are procedures. No telling what it will do to destabilize years of research. No way the Planck people could have handled this, they'd even have had trouble handling it as far as he has. This here is a new type ten-b shielded box, real secret lead and depleted deuterium Plexiglass. We're clear here, safe." He took a deep breath as if about to take a plunge. "Now, how the hell do I help you? And who are you nowadays?"

"Sam, I can't answer that. I am just the same old me, but I've been given this damn thing, and I need to work it out. All I can promise is that it's not illegal. But, if you can help me know what it is, then maybe I'll be able to give you some answers."

Sam went into one of his eyes-closed-thinking modes that Pero remembered so well from school, so Pero waited, absolutely still. If Sam couldn't tell what it was, Pero had no idea what to do next.

Sam shook his head and then smiled. "Ok, Pero, let's make a few assumptions. Anything that's in there is uniform, original.

We're probably not dealing with contaminants, except for the paper or what the paper was saturated with. Paper won't hold radioactivity. The heavy water we can discount. Therefore, we don't need a large sample. And, if I give it back to you, you will need to track where it goes because, Pero, one stick of dynamite attached to this stuff and you could pollute a major city's water supply for God knows how long. We okay so far?" Pero swallowed and quickly nodded in agreement.

"Okay, then here's what I propose. I have a sample needler. I don't know how it will work with this bag, a police sample bag I assume as it looks like one. We had a case in here once, many years ago, some stolen plutonium and flakes in a plastic evidence bag. Anyway, if it reseals, then all will be well, if not, we'll catch it in a basin and decide what to do next. Agreed?" Pero nodded. Sam was in command.

"Sam, don't you want the whole story?"

"Look, otter, I know you. If you're doing this—well, it must be right." Reaching over, he put his hand on Pero's shoulder. "It's dangerous, very, very dangerous, but if it's you, it's right. But I don't think I want to know too much. If it goes wrong, at least I can claim some sort of scientific curiosity but no involvement." He looked sad. No, more than sad.

"This stuff frightens you, doesn't it Sam?"

"It's why I was working here and not in Los Alamos. I want to uncover nature's secrets, not use them to kill. This stuff you have here? It's killing material, I am certain of that. Massive killing material. Evil."

Slipping his hands back into the rubber gloves, he put the vacuum bag back into the deteriorating lead film bag. He muttered something about a little protection being better than none. Then he opened the box and reaching over, took a glass bowl, and placed it inside the box. Then walking to the other side of this small lab, he brought back what looked like a pistol. In the place of a barrel was a long needle. He put that in the box. "And you'll need a better bag. Let me see, where was that Russian bag they sent?" He rummaged through drawers in his desk. "Ah, here it is." And he put that in. "Lead balls, millions of tiny ones, loads of surface to deflect the radiation, better design than we have, frankly," and shut the lid.

He opened the film bag, extracted the vacuum bag again, and taking the pistol-like tool, stuck the ultrathin needle all the way in and squeezed the trigger. He withdrew the needle. Suddenly a drop fell into the waiting bowl, but the bag held, resealed itself. Sam smiled. "Must be a Mylar bag. Police did a good job, looks like—ah, no wait, they would have had Max at the University of Zurich handle it, I'm certain. He's the only one with heavy water around there." He jumped up, lifted the computer screen, and took one of the phone books from underneath. Sam was so tall he had the monitor raised up with phone books. Handing one to Pero he said, "See if you can find his number if we need to ask him anything."

The directory was titled *IAEA Directory, Worldwide* and had the slogan "Atoms for Peace" diagonally across its cover. The IAEA is the International Atomic Energy Agency. It's a branch of the UN headquartered in Vienna, Austria. They track and log every safe atomic use, worldwide. Pero looked up the University of Zurich and quickly found only one professor, first name Max, in their nuclear medicine Center for Radiopharmaceutical Sciences. He told Sam he had the number. Sam responded with, "We'll call him in a moment." Pero wasn't sure he wanted Sam to do that at all.

Sam was busy concentrating. With his hands in the box, he took the resealed police vacuum bag and placed it in the Russian lead bag, cloth covered and sealed it up.

He peered inside through the glass, making sure he had what he wanted. "See, Pero, there's debris in the collection chamber of the syringe? Okay, now to flush." He clicked on an orange icon on the computer and a red liquid sprayed the inside walls of the chamber. "Iodine," he told me. The red spray was followed by clear liquid vapor. The washing stopped and it seemed to have a drying cycle underway. Like a washing machine, it went through its thing. The empty rubber gloves were moving their fingers all by themselves and looked a bit eerie. There was a small digital timer on the screen, showing 5:35 counting down; a little more than five minutes to go. Pero was shifting his weight from side to side in anticipation. "We have to wait Pero, or I can't handle that sample."

"No, that's fine Sam. I was just amazed. Will we be able to tell where it came from? So far, I've been told that it's U234, unstable, and from no known reactor."

"They couldn't match output signature?"

"Nope. But I suspect they were limited in their lab." He watched Sam's face.

He frowned, nodded, and said, "Then it's time to tell me which lab they used, Pero."

Pero trusted *le giraffe*, always did. He used to protect smaller kids and never, never once, turned away a kid in need. He was that type—geeky, strong, stable, and kind. His only flaw was curiosity. Pero had welcomed that right now, and Sam had a better brain than he to figure this thing out. "Labs in Mannheim. Mil Intel stole it from the Zurich police evidence room . . ."

"They did them a favor, they'd all be showing symptoms by now."

"Well, they stole it for someone, ordered from Washington, and tested it in government labs in Mannheim."

"Ah . . . the Air Force labs, pretty sophisticated. They deal with atomic triggers for the nukes they keep there. We're not supposed to know, but scientists are recruited from time to time. Their specialty is pretty obvious. Hmm, if they couldn't identify it . . ." Sam was, if anything, the master of logic, "Then maybe it's from a time before they built the damn things," he meant nukes. "A lot of that pre-reactor material is logged here, all the way back to some of Marie Curie's lab samples. It was how pre-CERN got its first funding, from the watch industry—the radium used with paint to make the numbers glow at night was originally developed from a Marie Curie sample. We'll see if we have a match in a minute."

"Thanks, Sam, but I really don't want . . ." he cut Pero off with a wave of his hand. Pero wanted to keep Sam from getting too deeply involved. To Pero, that seemed increasingly impossible.

"But, Pero, the gold part has me confused. Let's assume they had this label on some gold. Odds are the whole thing was radiated, you're just seeing the label, but the gold will be contaminated as well. It may not give off as many rems, though. The salts—like you'd find in printer's inks—tend to absorb vast amounts of radioactivity, a factor of two hundred or more compared to gold, I think.

"But it's pointless radiating gold like this unless you want to declare it useless for the jewelry industry. But sitting in a bank as an asset, it'll never be used, so no one would care. Why radiate it? And when? You remember Goldfinger? The premise was silly. Anyway, gold would delay the half-life, acting as a shield." Pero remembered giraffe standing up in the movie theater in 1965 telling the audience "Who cares? Radiate the ingots, they're only an asset, no one will be handling them." James Bond couldn't hear him. A theater full of students didn't want to. They all told him to shut up and sit down, peppering him with candies.

"Sam, I don't have answers, I only have threats to me and my friends, real and serious." Pero lifted his shirt and showed him the healing wound.

He peered, close. "Nasty. Hurt much? What did you do, glue it together?"

"Yes, superglue." Sam laughed. Pero gave a lopsided smile, "Yeah, well, Sam, it was all I had."

"You were always practical Pero, you can figure anything out. Infected?" He pressed the skin around the cut.

"Ouch, no, not yet, but I think it is beginning to be. I am taking antibiotics."

"Good idea. How'd you get it?"

"You really want to know? Your innocence story won't wash if I tell you."

"Pero, this stuff is too hot to pretend scientific curiosity anymore. I should have hit that button," he pointed to a blue button by the doorway frame, "a few minutes ago when I took a reading. It's the protocol here. But I know you. So, shoot, we're in this together now."

Oh, no, Pero thought, *here we go again. Friends who ask to be involved. Let's hope I didn't endanger this kind soul, at least unnecessarily.* Pointing at the wound area, "The head of the TruVereinsbank did that yesterday. A man called Tische. He's ex-Stasi, or anyway I think he's somehow connected with them. He wants the sample back or everyone dies."

"Pero, if you give this back to him, more will die. Let's find out what it is first, then we can go from there. Hey, while the box is drying, maybe we can find out if we can see anything." He put his hands back in the gloves and removed the vacuum bag from the Russian lead bag. He placed it up against the left side of the box. He removed his hands.

From across the room, he brought a stereoscope with a downlight. He placed it up against the box and adjusted the diopters, got the focus clear.

"Holy shit." He sat down. His face was white. "Pero, tell me what you see."

Pero peered into the eyepieces. He was looking at a Swastika, surrounded by a circle. There was a portion of one next to that. The piece they were looking at was maybe a sixteenth of an inch wide stuck to the inside of the vacuum bag. It looked, to Pero anyway, like a portion of a finely printed official something . . . a bank note. It had to be. "It's maybe a Reich Mark?"

"Pero, now is the moment you hope Tim Berners-Lee's new program works."

Tim Berners-Lee was the inventor of the World Wide Web—spawning the Internet, mapping pathways and methods of handling packets of information across a net of like-thinking computers. Pero smiled and asked, "What is the *wunderkind's* new invention?"

"Un-traceability of requests. No traces, none. It doesn't use code, it doesn't mask, it simply cleans up after itself, erasing all trails, like a scout covers horse trails with a branch of leaves, only much more perfectly. He's given it a nickname: Tonto. He's a Lone Ranger fan."

Sam typed in a search on the CERN home page and, in seconds, a list of possible answers came up, appearing as icons. He ran his pointer over them, one at a time. As he did so, a window appeared with the contents listed . . . a search engine within a search engine. "Ah, here we are." He double clicked. A page filled the screen, he clicked on an entry, and there on the screen was a picture of a Reich Mark. He zoomed into a corner and, matching what they had both seen, the little swastikas were all neat and tidy in a row, black on a red background.

While Sam put his hands back into the gloves and re-bagged the sample, he said, "Pero, the junk in here is, at least in part, money. Nazi money from pre-1945. It's not a label unless they used money as a label, which I doubt." The clock timer got down to zero. "Okay, now. Let's see if we can analyze the sample." He lifted out the needler and motioned Pero over to the other side of the lab. Inset in the wall was a gold-mirrored window, semi-transparent. He flicked a few switches, and it became smokily transparent. "Not as good as the Type Ten-B box glass, but effective shielding, effective enough I think for this small sample." He inserted the needle into a rubber plug in the wall and pressed the trigger forward, releasing the sample into . . . where?

"Sam, where's it going?"

"This is connected to a spectrometer, a separator and sequencer and, a radiometer. All automatic, our latest toy. We love it. We'll get the reading over there," he nodded his head back at the computer, now balanced more precariously than before on the remaining directories. "If it's known to us, we'll find a match. Now, what it is, exactly that the paper has absorbed, that's a mystery, so far. You know, putting it into the heavy water may have been a very bad idea. Sometimes fissionable material is best left alone, not turned into a solvent. The good doctor at Zurich would have no way of knowing that. He doesn't usually play with nuke material." They went back to the computer, sat on the stools, and waited. After a moment's silence, Sam asked, "You met anyone since?" Both men knew he mean since Pero's wife had passed.

"No, I don't think so. *Addiena* was unique."

"Yeah, well stop trying to replace her." It was a simple, scientific, logical statement.

"How about you Sam?"

"Yeah, one of the technicians here and I were close for a while. She went off with the aluminum supplier, guy who sold us more tubes for the accelerator." He meant the impeccably fabricated conduits with a perfect vacuum inside, surrounded by powerful electromagnets. Inside the tubes, Sam's stream of electrons or protons or whatever whizzed around at near the speed of light before impacting on the target—like the helium bubble they had walked past before. "Zarah wasn't happy with my work hours." He smiled, "Who is? That and I am always broke."

"You are known for it, Sam, always were." He had a habit of buying stuff he needed for his passion, to hell with budgets. Pero was pretty sure the equipment he could see all around in the office room was Sam's. It had that feeling of Sam, a bit untidy but very efficient, strung together loosely but strong, reliable.

"Yeah, well, I don't mind being poor, but a little sex now and then doesn't hurt." Then he remembered something. "Zarah used to complain that I shouted out equations in my sleep. It freaked her out." He laughed. "It got worse, I asked her to write them down, they could be useful. That's when she left. So I got a voice-activated tape recorder instead."

"Stranger bedfellow." They were both laughing. The years peeled away, they were teenagers again, sharing secrets. Pero had an idea he could pay Sam back a little.

"Sam, while we're waiting for your gadgets to do their thing, want to have a look at something?" He took out the special phone. "I don't know how it was done, but the infrared port was used to encrypt this, something fancy—right up your alley, heavy math."

Sam took the phone and put it on the desk. From the center drawer he took out a wire with a USB plug and stuck it in the front of the computer. The other end was a red ball. "Infrared USB port." He explained. He clicked the mouse to activate a recording program, infrared selected as in-port, and then pressed a few buttons on the phone. Nothing happened. "Whoever did this was good. It's not on the sim card, it's internal. Let's try . . ." He pressed a few more buttons. Nothing happened. "Hmm . . . no, wait, it can't be that easy . . ." he pressed a few more buttons and moved the satellite antenna at the same time. Suddenly a stream of data poured onto his screen. "This is clever, really clever. He wrote code to prevent this being used by the satellite phone, only by the cell phone, but it's invisible unless the satellite antenna is up and the satellite functions are *not* working. A fail-safe dead end. Clever man, clever. Now, let's see what we have pulled off . . ." he started scrolling down the code on his screen. Suddenly he stopped and turned to face Pero.

"Pero, where did you get this?" His voice wasn't, angry but it wasn't friendly either.

Pero knew better than to lie to his friend. "Sam, there's a new woman, not a man, who's working on a film project I am producing in Berlin. She's a genius with sound. She programmed his phone so that the cell phone would also be encrypted. The other part is State or CIA, I suspect, their phone."

He breathed out. "You're CIA or State?" Pero nodded. "Me too. Been writing this stuff for them for twenty years. That's my code I am looking at, but it's been altered. It is genius all right and," he was peering at the screen, nose almost touching, "Pero, if I didn't have this, I couldn't break it. Rotating integers, binary logarithms. NSA ain't going to like this one bit." The National Security Agency had massive supercomputers checking every phone call, every email for terrorist or other information. *Electronic intel* they called it. Pero called it a total wiretap—congressional authorization intact.

"Sam, don't stop her. Okay? Say nothing, please. She's okay, one of us." Pero used the term the friends had used way back when to tell their other friends that they had a new friend they could trust. "I'll make sure you meet her when this is over. You can exchange codes."

"She cute?" That was Sam, through and through. Always eager, always, well, a boy.

"Yeah Sam, she's cute, very."

"Oh damn, I see it in your eyes, you're making a play for her. Oh, no Pero, not twice. First you get *Addiena* now you've got . . . hell, what's her name anyway?"

"Susanna Reidermaier."

"Young, tall, boobs?"

Pero answered automatically. "Yes, no, yes. Ah, can we get back to business?" He had seen the screen change over Sam's shoulder.

"Yeah, sorry. But you will tell me later, won't you, and her eyes?"

"Oh, an amazing blue . . . damn. Sam, won't you ever grow up?" He smiled at his friend who was such a teenager at heart.

"Oh, God, I hope not. I'll stop wondering then, hate that." He got busy with the computer.

In a few minutes, he had rearranged long complex chemical equations on the screen overlapping one with another. Although Pero had no idea what they meant, it was plain to see Sam was moving an equation from a library list on the left and dropping it over the blinking equation on the right. Suddenly, he dropped one over, and the blinking stopped and the computer gave a significant sounding beep. "There's one." He carried on. Within ten minutes, he had all three matches. "Okay, now let's see the history of these little beauties. He clicked on each library match on the left, pushed the F-six and the screen went blank for a second. Then up popped an Internet browser and then an Adobe Acrobat reader . . . six windows cascaded across the screen. He read them off from the top, one web page and the longer pdf file read in Acrobat to match.

"Okay, the first one is an analysis of the primary ingredient here, common calcium salt, calcium carbonate, common to the Alps, Northern Alps, the border of Switzerland and Germany. Not the Italian stuff, which has sulfur in it, the Dolomites and all that. The pdf says it is common enough in the Jura too. The whole of Lac Leman and Lake Constance is full of the stuff, soluble in water. This is what's melted in that heavy water in your bag. It's highly radioactive, contaminated. But stable even if it kills you.

"The second one is a signature of Uranium 234 straight out of the textbook, nothing fancy—but there's not much Uranium here, it's hardly distinguishable from the melted salts in the heavy water. That salt can absorb anything really, concentrated, deadly. The isotope signature shows the Uranium was crudely refined—see?" he pointed at the screen, but Pero couldn't see anything understandable. "There are tons of impurities. It's why I can get such a perfect match. This stuff matches the sample Niels Bohr took when he escaped from Denmark to the US. It's Nazi experimental stuff. They stopped that program in 1943 . . . lack of scientists. Some key scientists they mistakenly sent to concentration camps where they died. Others, like Bohr, were helped to escape by the partisans and the Allies. Bohr, in case you've forgotten your physics lessons, Monsieur Baltazar," he imitated their physics teacher, "was the inventor of heavy water, which made all of our research possible. Without him we'd all go the way of Marie Curie, radiated to death."

Pero felt like teasing Sam, "And the third Sam? Monsieur Turner qui, encore, dors en classe!" Pero imitated the same teacher reprimanding Sam, constantly, for sleeping in class. Sam often did, only because he was so far ahead of the curriculum anyway. The teacher knew it, but it was a love-hate thing. That same teacher had, in an unexpected gesture, written to CERN that they should grab Sam at age eighteen before the US military did. He knew a superb mind when he taught one. And Vietnam was hardly the place for a gangly six foot eight genius. Pure science was.

"Ah, Monsieur Baltazar, the third one, there's the problem. It's from here. Or it was. It's watch-making grade radium that we used to supply before World War Two, before we became CERN. As I told you, it's a Marie Curie legacy, radium used in watches. It even has paint residue in it."

"What the hell have we got here? It's a mess, Sam."

"Ah, all is not as foggy as it seems. Discounting the calcium for a moment, even though it's the most deadly thing in the room . . . let's ask our friend here," he patted the screen "to combine the two—leave out the paint sampling—and treat them as one sample for a match." He did so. "And voila! It's the Nazi thermonuclear signature, the one they shut down in 1943. The half-life is short, but not exponential, early stuff, very radioactive. And look, Pero, here's a note with a hypertext . . ."

"No, Sam, don't!" Too late.

He had clicked on the hypertext link. It connected the computer to something and then the screen went blank. An anti-virus program came up and said it was locking the computer from intruders, suggesting a purge, scan for viruses, and re-boot. They looked at each other. Sam shrugged. Suddenly, a ringing started in the desk drawer. Sam looked at Pero and raised his eyebrows. He took out a phone similar to the type Pero had shown him but one that had no satellite connection, cell only. He opened the lid, placed it on the desk, and keyed the speakerphone. He wanted Pero to hear.

"Turner, S. here."

"We had an intruder probe from CERN. Can you advise?

"No. Who's that?"

"Control."

"Control who?" There was no answer.

"Standby." He nodded, same as Pero. Pero knew what was coming. "Standby," they repeated, waiting.

"Oh, yes, sorry, standing by."

Now Pero took up his phone, punched in his number, and placed it on the desk next to Sam's, speaker on. What happened next was a farce. Pero's phone connected and it could be heard ringing somewhere distant. It was answered and only static could be heard. Pero keyed 5-5-5 and said his name, "Baltazar, P. here."

Sam's phone's speaker said, "Who?"

Pero's phone responded, "Lewis here, report."

Sam's phone's voice asked, quite irate, "Lewis, who Lewis? Turner respond."

Sam obliged, "Turner, S. here."

Pero decided to confuse the issue, "Baltazar, P. here."

Lewis' voice sounded worried, "Baltazar who's Turner?"

Sam's contact wasn't too happy either, "Turner who's Lewis, who's Baltazar? Report."

"Gentlemen," Pero began, "you are talking on cell phones on speaker in the lab of one Professor Sam Turner at CERN in Geneva. I am Pero Baltazar. Director Lewis is State and CIA Langley." He looked at his friend, "Sam, any idea where, who, your phone is connected to?"

"Langley as well, but sometimes I get different people. But my director is called, let me see, I had that here somewhere . . ." He flipped noisily through some notes on a clipboard.

Sam's phone piped up, "Oh Christ, I am Director Bergen, for Christ's sake, can't you ever remember my name?" Sam was smiling. He'd done it on purpose. He shook his head, he hunched his shoulders silently laughing.

"Bergen, Bergen?" Lewis was angry, "What the hell are you doing involved in ops, your job is communications, not ops!"

Bergen responded, "I am not involved! My codifier, the best we have, is Turner at CERN, he called me."

Sam got professional, "Not true Bergen, you called me because there was a hypertext link to CIA that called for a computer phishing probe which my computer rejected, no probe effective. Then you called me asking me if I knew anything. Now why would there be a link to you, in communications, regarding a sixty-year-old data file at CERN?"

Bergen responded, "I didn't know why. I was called, by upstairs, to find out. The data transferred to me included the links for me to decode. Your computer-blocking program? It has your IP address. I know it by heart. So I called you. Besides, you are CERN's best, aren't you? And you're one of us."

"Lewis, Baltazar here. Listen, this *quote* upstairs *end quote* . . . it couldn't be the same one who's giving you directives, the one you wouldn't tell me the name of, could it?"

"Wait." He suspected they were talking on an internal phone. Lewis' connection had gone quiet. Bergen's was muffled, he had his thumb over the microphone. Sam keyed a few buttons and put the USB red ball next to the phone's infrared port. He smiled at Pero and mouthed "recording." They waited a minute or so.

"Lewis here, you can shut the other phone, we're getting feedback, Bergen and I are on together, conference call." Sam shut his phone down. "Okay, Baltazar, you've broken all the rules again. You're going to kill me with all this stress. Now, what the hell were you looking at when the computer cut off the fish or whatever it's called?"

Sam and he explained together. He explained his end, and Pero explained his. Lewis summed it up to be sure he understood: "So, you have a sample of a bank note that turns out to be soaked in radioactive something and now has salts, you say? Well, those salts are local calcium carbonate and you have other things in there: U234, and radium as used in watches, provided by the pre-CERN labs to the watch industry. Only not to the watch industry alone was it Turner?"

"Hang on, the computer is coming back up after a dump. I'll use Tonto . . ."

"Who's he? Not someone else Baltazar!"

Pero explained, "No, no one Lewis, relax. It's a new program, untraceable."

Sam continued, "As I was saying, I'll enter in the radium pre-CERN supply data, and in case you don't know, yes my predecessors here at CERN supplied this stuff all around the world. But the handling agents, pre-World War Two, were always the same. CERN's export partner was J. Mengele & Sohne, Bayern, Germany."

Lewis had the rest of the puzzle "The chemist, J. Mengele's son was the famous doctor butchering kids, twins, in concentration camps. His brother Aldon, also a chemist, conducted the nuclear refining for the Third Reich. He died in 1944, radiation poisoning."

"I am surprised he lasted that long." Sam was telling them this stuff was hot.

"His supplies and samples were never recovered."

Pero chimed in, "How much are we talking about?" Pero had an idea why, suddenly, this stuff was important.

"About two to three tons as best we can tell." Lewis was shuffling through papers, they could clearly hear him.

"Mass? Density?"

"I have no idea."

Sam chimed in: "Almost like lead."

"And the boss who is telling you men in Langley to quicken the pace?"

Bergen answered before Lewis could cut him off, "The DG . . . what Charles, what? I don't have secrets from his man, he's too valuable." He meant Sam, who smiled and folded his arms. *Hah!* His manner said. Bergen had revealed it was the director general who had received the direct computer warning from Sam's computer. And that meant the link, as fast as it was, had to be for his eyes only. It was no wonder Lewis had been reluctant to tell Pero who was pulling the strings. If the director general was involved, the White House was involved. Directly involved.

"Look, Lewis," Pero began "You've got to think ahead of the curve here. The label turned out to be a portion of a Reich's Mark. So ask yourself what was hidden as an asset near the end of the war, what would the Nazis have realized was the super weapon by then? And where would they have hidden this asset? And with what other assets?"

Sam understood immediately, "Okay, I get it, they hid the Uranium with the gold in a cave somewhere, maybe that cave had water dripping or even flooding it, hence the calcium carbonate. I read about one gold stash like that once in '52, only accessible in winter when it was frozen. The US Treasury team could hack it out, but at least it was not underwater. The rest of the year the cave was flooded, impenetrable."

Lewis chimed in, "Anyway, I see the point. This is gold that was with that radioactive stuff, maybe also with some loot. But why all the sudden interest?"

"Why, Lewis, why? Because it is obvious. The gold and the Uranium are one and the same. The gold wasn't contaminated with the Uranium and radium. The uranium is inside the gold, the gold is shielding it. It's Sam who gave me the clue here. He told me that gold acts as a delay to radioactive exposure. There are gold-coated windows all around here, like astronaut's visors, that rely on that ability. The Nazis must have known that." Sam was nodding. Pero told them, "Sam's nodding. He agrees, he's the expert. And, his guess? The radium was used to mark the gold. In the dark you could tell what is what, which is just gold and which is gold covered uranium."

Sam corrected him, "No Pero, bad guess . . . the radium was in the gold, that's how they refined it. It's complicated, but the radium acted as a chemical catalyst in the enrichment process back then. It made it very unstable, loads of rems given off. In time the whole shipment would glow in the dark, gold or no gold. I'll bet it's glowing away right now."

"And can this stuff make a bomb? Is it that quality?" Pero asked Sam.

"I don't like this field, so I keep up on it. Once it could have been used that way, the signature says it still is, just, but the yield is inefficient, like the first bomb, Fat Boy, all over again. And you need a delivery system for a big metal bomb weighing three tons to deliver one megaton of explosion. It is not worth it. The only nations with that kind of delivery system already have bombs much more efficient. And you can't use it for something small, like NATO's howitzer shells, it wouldn't trigger properly."

To Pero, then, it seemed useless, a relic of the past. "That means they're covering up other deeds, it's the only reason I can think anyone would bother if the stuff's useless."

Sam shook his head, "It's not useless for a dirty bomb, which would work quite well." A dirty bomb is the nightmare of security forces everywhere. One dirty bomb in New York and downtown Manhattan would be off limits for decades.

"Okay, there's that. But Tische is not a terrorist. He may be supplying them, though." Another thought occurred to Pero. "Who ordered the gold to be shipped? I'll bet it was a mistake. Find out, will you?"

Lewis chimed in, "Okay, I'll do that. And your thinking on the money, the notes?"

"Find out if there were cases with Reich Marks and maybe printing plates, something like that, with any cache uncovered by the Army. Call the Treasury or the Pentagon, or better yet, just call the Pentagon historian. My father was with counterintelligence for a while so he may be able to help here. Somebody should know this cache. Even if the gold went somewhere else, we know these gold-uranium bars had money—by then useless money—shipped with them? That must have been unusual. You find the place this money came from and you'll know who handled it. Maybe then we'll know who has designs on it now and why."

"Okay, Baltazar." It was Bergen.

Lewis was trying to get control, "No, not okay anything, you're not ops, stay out of this."

Pero changed the subject, "And another thing: I was followed on the TGV down here. Paris was my known destination but known only to you Lewis. Tische's people acted very quickly. That means they and their informants in DC are in crisis mode. I still don't know why. So, I think it's safe to assume, now, that Tische or the DG or whoever has an agent or agents watching CERN at this time. If it's CIA, could you find out and try to calm things down? We're on the same side after all. No?"

The silence was deafening.

"Lewis, are you there?"

"Yes."

"Can you answer that?"

"No."

"Can you find out if signals or any instructions have been passed to a field agent or worse," Pero meant an assassin, "in this region this morning?"

The two men in Washington engaged in an argument. Bergen and Lewis answered together, stumbling over each other. Lewis won out "I told you before, you are not in ops. Okay, Baltazar, I'll call back with the answer." Before he could hang up, Sam and Pero heard Bergen's voice saying, "But it is my department . . . and I have passed the DG's orders to Switzerland . . ." The phone went dead. Pero picked his up and dropped it into his parka jacket.

All the while Pero was working it out. Bergen was head of communications. If there was a second agenda here, the communications people should be able to track a call—or be the ones who sent it. The DG shouldn't have any way to order a CIA operative in the field unless it was through communications.

"Okay, that was fun," Sam said, "now let's see what they said to each other . . ." He keyed the computer recorder and played the voice tape. It was muffled. He stopped it, set some sliding icon switcher, an equalizer, and replayed the recording. Lewis's voice came in clearly enough:

"Paul, you can't tell them. For Christ's sake, we've got dead agents in the field, Berlin Station One, I might add, plus one level 3 and a German Internal Security man, plus one field agent missing four days now. We've got agents trying to recover the sample my man has taken to your man at CERN. I didn't know Baltazar knew your man or that your codifier was even there. You never filed that with me . . ."

Bergen's voice was louder: "I didn't have to."

"Okay, but if you blab to anyone, the DG will shut this down, and we'll never get this solved. And I am not sure either of our men are safe either. There have been real threats. And the DG is not telling us anything, yet we report to him!"

"Okay, Charles, but I want in, you understand, all the way in." Pero and Sam heard Lewis agree. "Okay, I'll tell the DG the CERN lead was nothing, a mistake by a Google random hit." Lewis agreed and then it went back to an open line.

Lewis and Bergen were obviously old hands. As Sam and Pero discussed them, as best they could, Sam revealed that he had known Bergen for over ten years. "Bergen trusts no one. If he is suddenly trusting your Lewis, it had to be a good sign."

Pero explained that he knew Lewis from an anti-terrorist plot in Kenya but did not elaborate further. He confirmed to Sam that he trusted Lewis, completely after that—if not the CIA.

Sam asked for the highlights of Kenya, "I really need to see the depth here Pero . . ."

So Pero briefed Sam on Kenya, the highlights only as requested. Even the highlights were impressive. "Wow, when this is over, let's meet and discuss that again over some beers. Sounds exciting!" Pero told him not to hold his breath if the beer was the only enticement. The old friends laughed. "On the other hand," said Pero, "If it were a meal at that little restaurant halfway up to the Col de la Faucille, on a sunny Saturday afternoon, I'd give in." It was an old haunt and the best food on the side of the Jura overlooking the lake, the city of Geneva, and the shimmering massif of Mont Blanc.

What was more urgent was their discussion that there was a conspiratorial aspect to all this that Lewis and Bergen were acting behind the DG's back. Sam said that the DG was a political appointment, CIA and State directors were permanent staff. "And remember that the DG could have agents in the field with terminal orders—orders to kill if necessary—to recover your sample, the package. With Tische and possibly the DG against you, well maybe us, the chances are getting slim we'll get away with this."

"But why do they want the sample? If it were me, I'd forget it and take the gold."

"Pero, there's also one thing we didn't tell them about poor Max Bierbaum in Zurich."

"Yeah, call him while I call my film team. You can warn him. Don't tell him anything, no info, okay? What can you do if he's exposed?" Pero meant exposed to the radiation.

"He is, I am sure. He just won't expect it or else he would never have released that sample. I'll tell him to do the same thing I was going to do with you." He reached into a Red Cross cabinet on the wall and took out a glass bottle. Inside were little red pills behind brown glass. The lettering was Cyrillic. "Leftover souvenir from Chernobyl, iodine tablets, good ones. If they had given the people these on day one, fifty thousand would still be alive today. Take two a day for a month, your nails might get brittle but take the pills. Okay?"

Pero said he would. While Sam started calling Max, Pero keyed the address book on his phone and saw Susanna's number. She had placed it there. He pushed the green call button. When it answered, he heard static and pressed 5-5-5, Susanna answered.

"Pero, *sie*? Is that *sie*?" She sounded desperate, speaking half German, half English.

"Yes, are you all right?"

"*Nein*. No, no. They . . . they have been kidnaped. Ich habe eine, a message for you. Dreißig Stunden, sorry, thirty hours. Das ist alles. Oh, sorry again," he heard a little sob, "it is all it says. It is all they wrote."

Chapter 10

In the Lab

"But are you okay, Susanna?" To Pero, it sounded like her world was imploding.

"Nein, nein, I am not. The police are all over. I left the museum shoot *immediat* after Herr Redmond and Heep were *entführt*, kidnappen. I have been trying to call you for over ten minutes. I could not call you before, the polizei officier was keeping an eye. I do not trust anyone. I cannot. Except my sister Bertha," Susanna pronounced it *Bear-ta*, "Bertha is living here in Berlin, she is agreeing to coming over immediat. While I try to call you again and again, she has arrived. She is here with me now. I do not want to be alone."

"Okay, easy does it. Tell me what happened, slowly. I need to understand everything."

"It is just like my mother again. Demands, unknown peoples, they are going to die and, scheiße, I cannot save them."

Pero almost yelled down the line to try to instill confidence, "Susanna, hey, please, listen to me. Yes, we can, I know we will, we will save them."

Sam concluded his call with Max in Zurich, and Pero waved him over, keying the speaker. Pero was still trying to calm Susanna, "Together Susanna, together, we can save them, you have my word." He heard her breathe loudly, pause, and still he could hear her sobbing lightly. He put the phone on the desk as he introduced her to Sam. "Susanna, listen, here's my close childhood friend, Sam."

Sam looked at Pero, pointed at the phone and mouthed "That the one?" Pero nodded. He mouthed, "Oh," his brow was furrowed.

Pero shook his head, as much to clear it as to get Sam on track, "Sam, get your phone working again, Langley needs to hear this. Susanna, let your sister hear on speaker, okay?"

"*Ja*, here . . . can you hear me?" He told her they could.

Sam's phone connected, Berger answered. Sam told him to conference Lewis urgently. Lewis came on immediately. Pero told them to listen; stay quiet and listen.

"Okay, Susanna, from the top, everyone is listening—and remember, you've got the resource of the US government, but what's more, you have the best mind in Europe sitting next to me—I mean Sam."

"*Nein, nein, ist das meine schwester* . . . my sister Bertha." No, that's my sister.

Sam knew the name. "Not Bertha Reidermaier, the chemist?"

"Yes, it is she. I am with her now. She is also listening."

"Hallo." Bertha's voice came in. She had a thicker accent.

Lewis chimed in "Oh my God not another . . ."

Sam answered for them all, "Can it Director Lewis, please. If Bertha Reidermaier will help, we have a brain trust here you could never, in a million years, call on. Now, Susanna and Bertha, on the line we have two people, one is Director Lewis of the CIA, the other is my contact who is in communications there too,

Director Berger. Both are top level. Now, fellows in Washington, you have here as a Nobel candidate within two years. Makes my bunch at CERN look like students. Sorry, Doctor Reidermaier, and please proceed, Susanna, if I may call you that."

"And, Susanna, remember you have my word." Pero reiterated, "We'll get them back, somehow. So, from the top, please . . ."

"Okay." They could all hear her take a deep breath. "We had finished filming the second S-Bahn scene, Herr Redmond coming down the metal scaffolding stairs to the museum, you know, scenes Three-B and Four-A, mit ambient light. Then Herr Tische shows up mit die polizeibeamter—how you say it? Police officer? Police boss? So, they yell at Heep—want to know where you are—and Herr Redmond goes over to see what is wrong. Herr Redmond tells Herr Tische that his bank is out, to leave us alone and to leave the closed set. Herr Redmond thought it was about the money for the film financing. Die polizeibeamter, he then bedrohen Herr Redmond, no, sorry, threaten him. He told Herr Redmond, he is not to talk in dieser weise to a senior German citizen of good standing. Heep gets Herr Redmond quieter, less angry. Then Herr Tische and die Polizeibeamter leave, we think. The other three police officers on the set seemed happy they leave. One of them tells Heep, who speaks fluent German, Berlin German . . . Did you know . . . that der name von polizeibeamter is Oberlutenant Hans Paltzer, he was an East Berliner definitely, ex-Stasi, an offizier, they do not trust him.

"So, we go back to filming. It is mittagessenbruch, ah . . . yes, lunch break. Herr Redmond and Heep are in their trailer reviewing video. The police are keeping good security, we think."

Every modern film camera comes with a side-by-side video feed, so you can see the day's shoot immediately. It was normal for Heep and Danny to review tape in private.

She continued, still upset, Pero could hear it in her voice, "The crew and I, we set up for the afternoon, still keine, sorry, no Herr Redmond or Heep. I go to find them. They are not there." She took another breath. "There is blood on the floor, a lot of blood, and a note. I took the note before the police could find it. I have it here. Can I fax it?"

Sam gave her the number, reading it off a label on the machine next to his computer. He said, "But not on an open fax Susanna." Sam was smart. He didn't know where they were, but if the fax machine was included in the private hotel room, security was okay, but not if she would send it downstairs to the switchboard.

Susanna's answer was strong, "I may be in shock, but I am not stupid." Sam looked chastened. Pero patted his shoulder. "I have a hand scanner and *die faxe* will come from my computer. I reduced the image. *Das original* is about forty-five by twenty-five centimeters. It should be arriving . . . about . . . now." A fax paper started to come out of Sam's fax in the lab. "Anyway, here is what it says . . . thirty hours. *Das ist alles.*" Nothing else.

Sam brought it over. "She's right, that's all it says. I've pushed resend to you, Berger." On the speaker, Berger responded with thanks.

Pero looked at it. Something was missing: corners—the paper wasn't square, it was a special shape. "Susanna, where was the paper, exactly?"

"On the floor next to the blood." That was no help.

"Susanna, anything on the other side?"

"It is just a papierortmatte, a restaurant paper, how you say it? A place paper? For under your dish. It has a logo on it: Borchardt."

Pero realized immediately, it was a place mat from Borchardt on Französische Strasse in what was once East Berlin. He knew right then, the thirty hours matched the timing, it was a dinner reservation invitation from Tische: Borchardt Restaurant, Berlin, tomorrow night. Bring sample was also in the invitation—unwritten, maybe—but there just the same. He explained to all who were listening. Berlin it was, the sample was Tische's party favor.

How to get Heep and Danny back? Pero had no idea. And why do they want the sample so bad? The thought nagged at him. His brain plagued with questions, he blurted one out, "Why was Nazi gold in the US in the first place, in a US Treasury Deposit in Manhattan?"

Lewis had the answer. "The gold teeth deposit, that's what it is called. I got the info just now from the State Department, who were busy denying any knowledge up until now. Before 1950, the Counterintelligence Center, known as the CIC, picked it up and sent a sample to Fort Knox for assay, and then the whole shipment was sent to the US as part repayment of the German war debt. War spoils in effect. Fort Knox assayed it and came up with impurities. Calcium impurities, human tooth, as well as some alloy residue. They put two and two together—exterminated Jews' teeth fillings—and told the Treasury to sell it, dump it. Apparently, they didn't. A man called Fellars, working with the Marshall Plan and the OSS, didn't want to lose the asset. He was funding both, the Plan and the OSS, which was, by 1948, the CIA—as well as advising MacArthur on his chances to run for President. Anyway, Fellars stashed it in the US Treasury deposit vault in lower Manhattan. He considered it a US asset, Jewish teeth gold or not.

"Then, it seems, two months ago that building was scheduled for renovation. They inventory the contents, preparing to move it to another location and, on examining the gold, see it is reddish. Red gold has a value twenty percent higher on the open jewelry market. A young, inexperienced Treasury officer takes it upon himself to assay the gold and make the US Treasury a profit, swapping red gold at $470 an ounce for regular plain yellow gold he could buy at $418 an ounce. So he posted the sale quantity as a lot on an Internet precious metal commodities auction site. It became a plain metals' auction. He says he didn't realize the significance of the assay description. But Jewish groups did. They had seen such red gold before when Stalin sold some. Some of that Stalin gold actually had mercury fillings still embedded. So they guessed where the US gold also came from.

"The Jewish groups have forced questions now being asked in closed session in the Senate, right now. That's why State was able to admit it to us. But, in all honestly, it's hardly a secret inside the government anymore."

Pero responded with anger, "Well, it's a secret to us, shameful in fact. But what about the radioactivity, didn't they know about that?"

"I was coming to that . . . Anyway, so the gold is already sold and shipped to Switzerland, a precious metals' dealer, very reputable. It's shipped, gone. Jewish groups are angry, blaming the Swiss. The Swiss are sick of people accusing them of being anti-Semitic and insist it leaves. The rest you know. It has been refused. It sits in a customs bond, technically outside of Switzerland."

"So, why don't they ship it back?"

"The metal dealer had paid for it, it's his technically. But now he wants rid of it. He knows it could develop into a lengthy law case and be bad for Switzerland with the Jewish complication. The US Treasury doesn't want to give the money back nor get tainted gold—remember they know it's tainted now because of the concentration camps' connection via Stalin's history. To make matters worse, some Senators may use this to leverage the CIA. They do have access to CIC documents from 1947, and that would still embarrass the CIA of today no end, so Treasury has asked State to push the Swiss to dump it on the dealer. No one that we know of has any idea about the radiation. They're all playing hardball. And without evidence—meaning that sample you have there—the Swiss police cannot hold the gold, nor will a Judge give them a court order to re-examine the shipment. Lawyers in Zurich, we think, taking orders from the Treasury, are blocking that, maybe CIA operatives helping. To sum up: the gold is not in Switzerland, it's in no-man's-land."

Lewis wasn't through, "If the evidence you have pointing to a different history doesn't turn up within forty-eight hours, then the dealer can sell and ship it onwards, so the Zurich judge says. If the dealer doesn't sell it on, our sources say he's bankrupt. He has demanded in an open fax . . . Bergen got a copy . . . that the US to take it back because the police say it's tainted! Bergen and I think it means he knows it is tainted with Uranium, but unless someone knows about the sample you are holding, anyone else would think he's talking about the Jewish concentration teeth knowledge again.

"But, get this—the US Treasury and the State Department claim it was sold, period, good gold, good-bye." Or did he mean *good buy*? "If State is also involved, it means the White House is involved. I suspect it's the Jewish teeth connection. If there's no evidence on US soil for the Jewish groups other than CIC documents, but that can take months. Everyone here will want this to disappear—including anyone holding a noisemaker. Like the package you are holding. Remember, once it moves again, Treasury can always claim that the gold they sold was different, there's been a confusion. Out of sight, out of mind, even if the original Treasury assay was suspicious. No evidence, or a switched trail, equals a clean record. So State, Treasury, the dealer, maybe even the Swiss government, wants this gold to disappear or change ownership." Lewis was still fired up, almost as if he were telling this story for the first time, putting it all together for them all. "And get this, our sources say the police haven't questioned the dealer. He may not have known it was tainted beforehand—but he damn well knew when they wouldn't give it to him. And then about thirty minutes ago, the dealer got an offer—out of the blue—for fifty-five dollars a troy ounce more than the dealer paid for it. Just enough to look legit for a supposed company in Thailand, big jewelry region, trinkets. Seems almost legit for some very red gold."

"What's the real value?" Pero asked.

"Bergen intercepted that email as well, NSA helped. A cool cash offer of twenty and a half million. Plus shipping, air-freight. They say they'll send a plane."

Pero was willing to bet they would. "Lewis, I'll wager you anything you like that TruVereinsbank is putting up the money. Once they get that gold, Heep and Danny may be expendable. As well as us. We're the only ones who know what's inside. The inside is worth a hell of a lot more than twenty million."

Bergen answered, "About ten times that. And geopolitical advantage. The Thailand buyer may be a front for North Korea. But there is no way to move that much radioactive material from Europe."

Pero shook his head, the stakes were huge, "Look, let me think about that. Meanwhile, can you think of a way to stall that sale to Thailand? It may be the only bargaining chip we have."

Lewis was firm. "Oh yes, I can." He didn't say we. Lewis was getting personal again.

Pero clapped his hands, "Okay, I've got this far, it's time I made my way back to Berlin with the sample." Then he winked at Sam.

Giraffe looked at his friend and shook his head. "Pero, you said people were following you. All they need to do is catch you and take the sample. Maybe we could use some help?" He nodded toward the open phone, the one to Washington.

Pero was sure there was too little time for that. "Sam, I need to find out where the operative is—the one I am sure is watching CERN. They knew I was headed here, right? Then, *we* need to find out where they're holding Heep and Danny." He moved closer to the speakerphone to make his voice louder. "And although we need to know the DG's involvement here, Lewis, for God's sake don't tell the DG anything, you or Bergen."

They both agreed, immediately. It was not that Pero thought the DG was in on this uranium scheme, he was probably working on suppressing the Jewish gold angle for the White House. But Pero had a plan slowly percolating through his gray cells. He thought he knew how to get the bag back to Tische in exchange for Danny and Heep, or find out how to rescue them before the CIA or the Swiss police made them expendable by allowing the gold to disappear. For his plan to work, he needed silence, no feeding information back to Tische, via the DG—White House or not.

What had suddenly dawned on Pero was that he had figured out why—*how*—nations would pay through the nose for this cloaked uranium.

But before he stopped the phone calls, to bolster Susanna's confidence and to release some of his adrenalin, Pero ripped into Lewis for not having protected Heep and Danny in time. It was petty, he knew, but in truth, he knew he was more than a little scared. When scared it helps to yell at somebody. Lewis was simply at the receiving end. Pero finished with, "Those were field agent instructions, and you were supposed to comply."

Lewis replied somewhat meekly, sounding sincerely sorry, but explained he had no Station anymore in Berlin, so men were on the way from Frankfurt and Koln. It didn't help. Lewis knew he had had almost an hour, and had blown the chance to protect them.

Pero warned him not to make the same mistake again, reminded him to protect Susanna and Bertha, then pressed "end" and closed the phone down. Lewis and Bergen might be mad, so be it.

Meanwhile, Pero's brain concentrated on his new tack . . . some of the truth he now felt sure he had figured out. And now was the time to try to unravel all the clues. He felt sure they were all there, ready to be put in order. How better to do this puzzle work than with three of the finest minds in Europe?

What he had suddenly realized was that the idea of shipping disguised gold could be an amateur play, one bound to fail now that people knew the gold was to be watched. He needed to be sure. The phone to Berlin was still up but silent.

"Everybody, you still there?" He heard their replies clearly. "Okay, now, all of you, don't say anything, just listen . . . I have an idea of what's happening here. Just listen and then I'll ask for comments, clearer thinking. Ready?" The two Berlin voices on the speakerphone said they were and Sam nodded. "Okay, good . . . here goes . . .

"The IAEA—the International Atomic Energy Agency—is a policing body as well as a negotiating autocracy. Some of the finest legal minds have helped craft the UN treaties over the years, from SALT to other nuclear limitation treaties. I met Gurdon Wattles once, brilliant mind, drew up the SALT Treaty. Anyway, the IAEA also monitors and detects agreements for normal use. For example, if a French reactor was installed in Iran, you want to make sure that the natural output of that electricity generating plant is measured and cataloged.

Reactors produce electricity and they produce depleted uranium and they produce the building blocks for nuclear arms: enhanced, condensed, uranium. If it's a plutonium reactor, the output is even more valuable as an arms' supply source.

"Okay, the IAEA comes along and scientifically knows— measures and monitors—how many tons of radioactive material goes in and then comes out of these plants. It all ships in the form of rods, each rod is a set size, right?"

Berta confirmed, as did Sam.

Pero continued, "Right. It's science, not guesswork. They measure the output, four in, four out, they measure the shipment, they count the rods, and the rods sit underwater in safe storage in giant heavy water baths. Then, they put cameras and inspectors on the whole thing. Nothing gets by them. Libya, Iraq, Iran, China, India, Pakistan, South Africa, Syria, Lebanon, Kazakhstan, Vietnam . . . the list of the countries they monitor is long and their task is never done. I know, we did a documentary on them." He paused, "Anyway . . .

"Now, imagine you have a ton of non-rod-shaped, radioactive material that would have a rem signature almost like the spent rods give off but with reduced radioactivity. Ton for ton, if made into rods, the same stuff would appear to be similar to the fuel rods from those nuclear plants. Maybe seen underwater they would seem exactly the same. Right? The dummy stuff could still have tons of rems streaming off its shiny surface and yet be useless for real bomb making. It won't be plutonium, but without a chemical test, who would know the difference?" He paused, took a breath while Sam looked increasingly concerned. "To transform the Treasury gold-covered uranium into bomb material, you would have to run the gamut of every other monitored piece of equipment to make such bomb material. Like refining plants and loads of centrifuges. Like Iran. Right? You'd stand out as if trying to make bomb material simply because of the handling, refining you would have to do to transform the poor quality Nazi uranium.

"And who could you sell it to as it is? Worthless old Nazi uranium? Rogue nations or terrorists to make a dirty bomb? Hardly worth the effort because it won't make an efficient detonable bomb. Would it make a good dirty bomb? Yes, but not cheaper than stealing, say, the nuclear waste material from one good-sized metropolitan city hospital.

"But, imagine if you turn it into unstable but not very dangerous fuel rods, pretending to be lethal spent fuel rods. The newly made fake reactor rods made with Nazi Uranium would give off tons of rems but pack no punch because they're not plutonium but old unstable Uranium. Hey, but if those rods, those dummy rods made of Nazi uranium, were in a bath of heavy water mixed in with real plutonium rods, don't you agree they then could hide the sheep among the wolves?" Pero was getting worked up by his own imagination. "But what about the wolves you swap your sheep for. Right? You can swap the uranium rods out for new, really lethal, reactor plutonium residue. The old Uranium masquerading as plutonium. The real plutonium rods now encased in, I don't know, a repeat of gold sheathing? Those ingots—or even the plutonium rods in a smuggled shipment, could be sold to Libya, Iraq, Iran, North Korea, or to criminals, or rogue military states . . . the list is, sadly, frightening."

"Mein gott . . ." was heard from the phone speaker while Sam was still shaking his head.

Pero continued, "The IAEA would conduct its inventory in the heavy water bath, measure the radiation in that spent-fuel-rods heavy water tank the size of a gymnasium, and all would appear to be normal or close to it. Right?" Sam was nodding, Pero told the Berlin phone, "Sam agrees. So, meanwhile a ton of real, potent, bomb-grade plutonium would be secretly whisked away to a deep subsoil lab some-where. Perhaps even ex-Soviet scientists could be doing what they have done for forty years, only for more money: making bombs. Sophisticated, lethal, world-politics' altering, power-ful atomic bombs."

Sam, sitting very still, his eyes half-closed, still said nothing. Susanna and Bertha Reidermaier in Berlin were now similarly quiet. Only the faint crackle and hum of the speakerphone punctuated the quiet.

Pero hadn't wanted to tell Langley. If they knew of or believed his version of the real use of the shipment of gold and uranium, every agency resource would kick in, and they would consider the loss of his friends as unfortunate collateral damage on a path to crush Tische and whomever he was working with or for. Pero desperately felt he needed to save his friends. Surely, there would be time for CIA action and recovery of the uranium and plutonium later if Pero calculated correctly. Moving tons of material takes time. Tische had made one mistake, he had set a deadline of thirty hours, thirty hours was way too short to move that uranium. Pero felt he had time to save his friends.

Sam was the first to speak up. "Christ Pero, you're a devi-ous bastard. It would work, damn it, it would work. Oh, good God damn I hate these people."

"Who Sam?" the speakerphone broadcast.

"Scientists making the damn things. Think I hate the politi-cians and those power-mad thugs? No, they're more human than the scientists who spend a lifetime learning secrets of the universe, speaking the language of God, math, and then they allow them-selves to build something that can vaporize fellow living beings. They make me so damn angry." He smashed his fist on the table and dented the metal top. Sam was a very strong man.

Bertha chimed in, "Ja, it ist vat we fight against every day. Not to have science used by these people."

Sam continued, all business now, "Pero, if what you say is true, if it is even possibly true, we need to think this through. First, they would have to smelt the gold and extract the uranium. The density of the uranium would sink in a smelter and you could pour off the gold. But there is no place I know that could do this, every worker would die within hours, as you smelt the ingots. Even here we could not do an ounce in our ovens and shop."

Bertha wanted to know: "Where is here please?"

Sam answered "CERN, Geneva."

"*Ach*, dat Professor Sam Turner." She said it in a way that reminded Pero of someone who was tasting a new dish, savoring every morsel. "Das forschungspapier, research paper you presented in Rio last year, it was good but *ihr* displacement theory is wrong *mit* the chemical equations you used. I have data for you to help better erklären sie" (*explain it*). Sam was looking very intense, he grabbed a pen like he was expecting this pre-Nobel scientist to dictate.

Pero interrupted, "People, can we stay on point here?" Sam nodded, and he heard two "*ja's*" from the speaker. "Okay, Sam, what would you need? Heat, a pot, some shaper for the rods— I assume it would have to be recast into rods, the uranium?"

"Yes, it would have to be, but not molded, they would need to extrude it, five centimeters in diameter to match, to pass visual inspection."

"Okay. What plant would have an automated smelter and an extruder that size?" Pero referred to a pressure squirter that forces, extrudes, molten material—whether plastic or metal— through a hole of a certain size. Windowpane extruders are flat, those for metal rods are perfectly circular.

Samuel was shaking his head, "But they would not be able to separate . . ." He paused and smacked a hand on his thigh, "Ah, but they don't care, do they, Pero? It is the uranium they want, the rest—the gold—can be wasted, right? The gold has a value way less than the illegal value of the uranium—not to mention plutonium. And later, anyway, all they have to do is cast that residue gold into ingots and sell it off. It's not the damn gold they want, it is the fake rods! Christ, they can sell those rods for millions, maybe even billions, to countries wanting to swap the old uranium rods for plutonium that would escape IAEA scrutiny." Sam was shaking his head. "But still I do not know of a smelter that could handle all this, let alone an extruder."

"Think my friend, who smelts stuff in this region? And who did we see on a school field trip years ago making gears that start as an extruded bar of any diameter?"

Sam's eyes widened, "Damn, you're right, the watch companies. They have automatic smelters, untouched by human hands to make sure the watch parts are perfectly true and pure steel. A fine steel extruder handles much higher temperatures than ones for uranium or gold, it could work."

"What about the plants around here?" Sam knew the region better than Pero.

"No way, Pero. We're in charge of water and soil contamination for this whole region because of our work here at CERN. That was the deal. We take samples and fly helicopters for air sampling up and down this region, from Lyon to Lausanne and over the lake. If anything were being done in this region, we'd know it. Couldn't they simply be doing this overseas? Maybe Thailand?"

"You ever hear of a watch factory in Thailand? It would stick out like a sore thumb. No, it has to be here, where a factory would be only one among many. I am sure it's here, and I'll tell you why. Because if any radioactivity escaped the plant, they would have a perfect excuse: the radium in the dials, years of watch making pollution. One declaration of 'Oops,' and

Switzerland would close ranks to avoid unemployment or col-
lapse of the watch business. Wouldn't the Swiss want to mask
a small air or water leak?"

"Yes, and for that reason no one in the watch industry
dares use the stuff, not since 1982 when the entire watch
industry had to stop using it, it was causing cancers. So it's a
dead end."

"Is it? When did Tische start funding this little venture?
Let's say they—the Stasi—started their operation in the '50s
or '60s, wouldn't it have been reasonable, back then, for the
locals to expect a little leakage now and then?"

"Pero, you're getting too far away from reality here. If they
are still doing this or preparing to with this shipment you're
thinking, about . . . no, no . . . current environmental laws
would make them stand out, no matter how careful they were.
And besides, how could they get the gold into such a plant
without anyone knowing? You saw what happened when we
even opened your bag."

"I don't know, but TruVereinsbank does—Tische is desperate, exposed, relying on Stasi contacts and muscle. That level
of desperation can only mean he's got something already in
operation, already underway, already—maybe for years—doing
exactly this. Twenty million or ten times that is not sufficient
reason for his desperation."

The phone emitted the two women's agreement and cha-
grin. Sam sat on the edge of the desk, looking dejected.

Pero laughed, "Come on people, we're figuring this out.
Don't lose hope. Now let's hope Lewis comes back with something we can use, Thailand or not."

Bertha, the expert chemist, suddenly added, "Scheiße . . . und
you have another Problem. Cadmium. Nuclear rods require cadmium for the making of them. Ach, what is the word for ablauf?"

"Flow." Susanna translated.

"Ja, flow. Not a catalyst, but cadmium molecules will be rejected by the molten uranium or plutonium and will migrate to the outside, acting as a lubricant for die extraktion. It is an old process. New rod processors use magnetic extruders. There are only four of those in the world. If you are right and these ingots will be made into nuclear fuel rods in a watch factory, Wird hat müssen, sorry, they must have cadmium for the process."

"Okay, it's worth a shot. We'll look for that when we get a hot trail, or . . . wait! Maybe that is the trail. Good job Bertha! Sam, you and Bertha work on shipments of cadmium into Switzerland first, then spread your search outward. Me, I have to get going. I have a date in Berlin. If I hear anything from Lewis about TruVereinsbank, I will call one of you, right away. Then they will call another, and then that person will call another and so on. We'll make a telephone tree, okay?" Everyone said yes.

Sam asked, "Now, how are you going to get out of here? How can I help?"

Pero had a plan. It was simple. "Ah ha! Watch!"

Pero told Susanna—still on the coded phone, "Susanna, I am going to hang up and call you on the hotel room phone . . ."

"Why, why not call me on your handy? Heep left it on the table."

Ah, Tische left it behind. So that wasn't an accident. Pero also knew Tische had probably copied the SIM card and would be tapping the line. Good. "Susanna that's perfect, we're winning already. I am going to call that cell phone and lie to you, just play along, they'll be listening, I'm sure. Do an act: you are completely distraught, you are crying. Okay? Just agree to anything I say."

"I won't have to pretend very hard. I still feel *Drohend*," (threatened).

"Chin up, Susanna, this will work fine. And when I leave, keep Sam and Bertha talking on the secure phone, his, he's got one like mine."

"Are you all CIA?"

"Yes and no, he'll explain later . . . here's his number, he's infrared ported your code to his phone so it will work safe and secure." And Sam read out his cell phone number, along with the 5-5-5 sequence.

They all hung up. Pero told Sam to run the cleaning cycle that sounded like a washing machine in the sample box as background noise, and Pero called her again, on the open cell phone. "Susanna . . ." She burst into tears telling him about the kidnapping all over again. He got her calmed down, she was doing a perfect job. It was his turn, "Okay, I was just arriving in Lausanne . . ." On his schedule, it was time for the second TGV to arrive from Paris, "I got off the first because I was being followed and then took the next one." He gambled that the aftershave man he suckered off the train had moved heaven and earth to catch up with him while he was, supposedly, waiting at Vallorbe to catch the next train. He went on, "I am taking the next train to Geneva, to go to CERN and give them the bag. They can give it to the police." That should make Tische pay attention. "I'll call you after I get there."

She was into her part now, "What about Heep and Danny?"

"I have something Tische will want more than this dumb bag. I know what he's doing and where. He'll want me more than them." It was a bluff, but he knew Tische would use Heep and Danny as bargaining chips to get Pero to reveal everything. He was counting on it. He'd expect Pero to ask to speak with or see them, and he intended to do just that.

Wait, he thought, *there's something else he'll expect.* "Susanna, has Amogh called?" Her answer was a surprise.

"Yes, apparently someone called Mbuno is trying to thank you, his wife is doing fine, but he needs to talk to you."

"Okay, I'll call him, don't worry I'll call you back within the next two hours. Bye."

Then Pero immediately called her back on the other coded phone, on speaker, and congratulated her. She told him a man in a green coat had arrived, German Internal Security, with a man showing ID from the US embassy, to protect her."

Sam mouthed: Lewis' people?

Susanna answered his silent question, "Bertha is calling the embassy to verify . . . yes confirmed. I am feeling safer, danke Pero, danke fur alles." *Thank you for everything.*

"No, Susanna, it is I who thank you and also apologize. Please don't cry anymore." He could just imagine the tears in those blue eyes. "I will, forever, be sorry I got you into this mess."

"Forever sounds," she inhaled "hopeful. Bye." Then she hung up. Sam gave Pero a teenage look and snicker saying lucky devil.

Pero? He was puzzled. What had he said to encourage her? And yet, he felt that little pang you do when an adventure may be beginning. Hopeful. Hope. It was a good word under the circumstances.

"Come on Sam, I need to get out of here." Sam handed Pero the sample from the box in the film bag inside the Russian bag. Pero grabbed the phone and his train bag.

As they walked back the way they had come in, locking the lab behind him, Sam was worried about something. "Pero your clothing is contaminated. That many rems, it's bound to be. Look, there's a gym here. We scientists need to exercise occasionally. They have a locker full of gear to borrow. No one remembers to bring sweats and such. We can give you a change . . ."

"No, they need to see me in the same clothing."

"Well okay, but how about putting a track suit in that bag and when you're done doing whatever it is you plan to do, you can change?"

"Okay, Sam, I won't argue. Lead the way." They turned sharp right and three doors down was a small gym and sauna closet. On one wall were lockers. Sam went to the first one and after a few seconds, brought out an Adidas gray suit, black stripe down the leg. "That's about right, I think. Remember to ditch the coat and underwear. You're stuck with the shoes and socks." Pero opened the bag and took out the shower cap with the blood-soaked towel. "*Merde* Pero, that's nasty! You lose that much blood?"

"It looks bad, never mind. Throw these out, will you? Don't want to attract too much attention."

Sam took a corner of the shower cap and, at arm's length, went to the last locker and dropped it on the floor. "Doctor Marc's closet, he's in America for two weeks. Plenty of time to get this mess cleaned up later."

"Okay, let's go, I have a train to catch. And when I call, you hop the next flight to Berlin, agreed?"

"Yeah, I get to meet Bertha, oh and your Susanna . . ."

"She's not *my* Susanna. Behave will you?"

"Well, not yet she isn't, but there's hope. No?"

Pero thought Sam was, always, a boy at heart—adult smart, but a child emotionally.

* * *

Nyon is the canton capital, a small town on Lac Leman, in the State of Vaud before one enters the Canton de Genève when the lake changes name to Lake Geneva. Pero stood on the platform, *direction Genève*, and waited for the local train, due in three minutes. He had driven with Sam in that silly cart back to the car, hot-wired it again, Sam shook his finger at Pero. Then, Pero drove cross-country through Grilly and into Divonne and ditched the car again, making sure the note and compensation money was on the driver's seat again.

In Divonne, he hired a taxi and turned south to Nyon. He was then in Switzerland proper. Passport control south of Divonne was simple, the Russian bag giving him confidence. As it turned out, he didn't need. No one even looked.

As the train pulled into Nyon station, he opened the door and got on. No one else got on, and he didn't spot anyone on the train who seemed interested. The trick was to get to Geneva station and spot someone, have them see that he spotted them, and run back the way he came. Then he would have time to lose them. He was gambling that any Stasi from Berlin would not know the region as he did from his school days.

If Tische thought he was running toward CERN—Lausanne-Geneva then onto CERN—Tische would think his course of action was clear: get Pero, get the sample. Meanwhile, Sam would be free to travel, and Tische wouldn't know they knew what the sample was. It was the only advantage they had—their knowledge and Tische's false assumption.

As he alighted from the train in Geneva, he spotted the tail but made sure the man didn't know he knew. Pero kept his face open and innocent. The open call to Susanna had worked. He took the steps down, used the tunnel passageway, and walked back up into the main ticket hall where the information counter was. He needed the tail to follow, so he took his time. As he asked the information attendant questions about CERN, he palmed the timetable for the intercity trains in Switzerland and slipped it into his pocket. He glanced above his head at the track and time of departure/arrival board with the ever-present accurate railroad clock face. Quickly looking away, he calculated he had forty-five seconds until the express train to Basel departed. That would do.

Switzerland runs on time. If the station clock said 17:14:15, that was the exact time. If the Basel train left at 17:15, he had forty-five seconds. Simple as that. Geneva was a head stop, the train would, always, leave on time.

As he turned, he spotted them, two of them and made deliberate eye contact. They wore the same leather coats he was familiar with from Tempelhof. In Switzerland, they looked out of place. Way too fascist. One was covering the street entrance, the other the platform access. Pero put a look of shock on his face.

They didn't know the station. Behind the information and ticket hall was the second hall with the down ramp to the second under-track tunnel, with access to the quays. Pero ran as fast as he could. They followed. As he rounded the corner into the second hall, he ran into a third man, knocking him flat. The two behind him started yelling. Pero vaguely saw the man he had knocked down had wiring in his teeth and stitches on his cheek. *Danny's victim*. He stretched his legs.

Pero had never been a very good runner. He was muscular, at least his legs were, and he could sprint, but one hundred yards and he could be toast. He had fifty more to go, and he was already out of breath. As he reached the banister for track number four and started to climb, two steps at a time, one of them reached him from behind and pulled on his jacket. Pero did what any self-respecting operative would do. He turned and kicked the man in the face. Someone blew a whistle. Pero started yelling "Au voleurs, au voleurs!" *Thief, thief!* His accent was local, so help was immediate. A woman with an umbrella was the final insult to the hardened Stasi. She whacked him as he tried to board the moving train, right on Pero's heels.

Pero saw his assailant tumble over. Pero was clear. The train accelerated with usual Swiss efficiency, plenty of hydro-electric power. *Pour it on, please, Mr. Engineer.*

This train ticket collector was, déjà vu, not amused, they never are with rowdy behavior on their trains. He was taller and thinner than the *little mother* from the night before, but the anger was real. Unlike her, he could not be bribed. Try and you'll be arrested. In Switzerland, you're guilty until proven innocent. With what he was carrying, he'd spend quite a long time in jail.

Pero had to explain himself, so he lied. He said he had pulled a wodge of money out of his pocket, just like this and as he was about to buy a ticket and they had seen his cash. The conductor scolded him, took the requisite second-class fare to Basel, and told Pero to sit down and not cause any more of a disturbance for the ninety-minute ride to Basel.

"Oui, monsieur, merci. Je m'excuse . . ." What Pero didn't explain was that he'd be getting off before Basel at Bulle.

Bulle was the gateway to Saanenland. Pero needed trans-portation to Berlin. He was sure all the airports would be watched now. But Gstaad is in Saanenland. Her residents, the truly rich, had loads of private planes at Saanen, where the single runway airport was laid out, running along the valley floor beneath towering skiing mountains. In Bulle, he could get a taxi to Saanen. And in Saanen, hopefully, a private plane for hire.

Pero had an hour left on the train. Time to change and try to call Nairobi. It was late, but he felt sure Amogh and Mbuno could still be at the Aga Kahn Hospital.

Chapter 11

Mbuno

Swiss trains have an aura of privacy, like Swiss banks. Cell phones are considered rude interruptions to the stately, silent, powerful means of transportation. Like steamships passing over land, the trains in Switzerland may come in different sizes and shapes, exhibit different speeds and levels of comfort, but they all share one thing in common: they are the finest in the world. There are narrow-gage mountain trains, winding their way up picture-perfect passes, in and out of snow, taking you to alpine retreats. There are *rapides* running along valleys between mountain ranges, with supervised kindergarten carriages to allow parents a moment of peace—in a different part of the train. There are dining cars that compete for Michelin Guide ratings. If a Swiss train is ever late, you know it originated in Italy or France. The last time a Swiss origin train was late an avalanche was the cause. An act of God. Anything short of that is controlled—Swiss efficiency.

Pero needed to call Mbuno. Amogh, really, and hope then to get Mbuno, but he didn't know if he would have to shout to be heard. Moving cell phones and very long distance calls are not always compatible. So as not to disturb *les autres passengers*, he walked off to the restroom with his bag, intending to change and call at the same time.

The toilet was small, just a metal toilet and a tiny sink. He stripped off, stuffed the clothing he was wearing into the bag, donned the tracksuit, and reversed the coat—green day-glow side out. Next chance he got, he'd throw the contents of the bag away. The Russian radioactive bag he kept in the coat pocket. The older train carriage had an end-of-carriage jump seat for passenger overspill or for people with muddy shoes. Swiss allow for people's desire for cleanliness.

He sat down and realized he was feeling tired. And he was hungry. The food cart woman, pushing her assortment of "sandwiches, bonbons, cola, chocolat" should be along soon. Sam had given Pero two hundred Swiss francs, so he took out a ten franc bill and kept it handy.

He scrolled the phone address list to Amogh and pushed send. After two tries, the phone rang and Amogh answered, "Hello?"

"Hello Amogh. Pero here. Sorry to have been out of touch."

"Ah, Pero, good of you to call. There's good news and not so good news. First the not so good news: you are about thirty-five thousand dollars down. Is that all right? I really am terribly sorry."

"Hey, that's fine. The results you got at the Aga mean the money was well spent. Anything more you need, don't hesitate."

"Ah, then can I have a new car? The Porsche is getting a bit long in the tooth."

For him to make jokes meant things were going very well. "Sure, Amogh, I'll authorize that, in trade for the portrait over your father's desk." Mr. Ranjeet had a pencil portrait done by

Hemingway of the Maasai—he had found it in a Nairobi auction of a deceased white hunter's effects. It was wonderful and had twelve lines by Hemingway on a Maasai's trustworthiness and friendship.

Amogh was chuckling, "Not for sale, but I could ask him to leave it to you in his will. Now, really, for the good news: Mama Mbuno—that's how the hospital is referring to her by the way, never by her name—is doing fine. She's got no fever, the infection seems on the mend, and what's really wonderful is she's feeling strong enough to suggest that Mbuno go home for the night. No way, he's still here charming the nurses." It was two hours later in Nairobi, past eight, past Mbuno's normal bedtime of darkness, Pero was sure of that.

"You're kidding? She's feeling that well? That's marvelous."

"Yes, but she'll needs tons of rehabilitation. The doctors now call it rehab. Seems she'll need a good deal of special rehab at that. The two doctors you flew in—yeah, sorry that's part of the bill—anyway those two fellows say that the best place is in Italy, south of Rome, on the coast. Problem is, I can't see them being separated. They are talking about five weeks at least. Her hips are mending, but walking will be painful for a while."

"They don't know the Waliangulu. She'll be walking fine in three weeks. Look, make sure Mbuno goes with her . . . book them in together. That part of the world will be warm enough, I expect."

"Yes, well . . . I have to say the two *dottori*, as they're called here, are very fond of Signore et Signora Mbuno. I am sure they'd look after them if you're sure. There is the question of convincing Mbuno."

If something happened to him, Pero wanted to make sure this was arranged. Convalescence, with proper care, was essential for her—and for his friend. Mbuno may make a poor nursemaid, and Pero knew her pride would suffer if she made him one. Recovery was essential for their happiness. Pero knew it was an African thing, if anything can be so generalized to be called after a continent. Pride and responsibility. A closeness to nature that expects, no demands, self-reliance in all people. Waliangulus have this self-respect in abundance. They had earned it over hundreds of thousands of years. "Is Mbuno around?"

"I'll get him, hold on." He heard Amogh calling down an echoing hall to Mbuno. There was the shuffling of sandals on hospital linoleum—Pero remembered that Mbuno always drags his feet indoors, never in the bush. Pero had never figured out why, wondering if it was maybe the unnatural evenness of the floor.

"Mr. Pero, bwana?"

"*Ndiyo* Mbuno. How are you? And your good woman wife?"

"She is most better." He pronounced it betta. "You have saved me bwana, again, but this time it is not a life I can repay. But I am most happy."

"Mbuno, there is a time to stop keeping count. There is nothing, not one thing, I could or would not do for you and your family. It is my own life I am saving."

"These things are not said between morani or mzee like us." morani are warriors, mzee elders.

"Well, although I am not in Kenya right now, friend, part of me always is. So please accept my apologies."

"No, I do not. Do not apologize, tafadhali," *please*. "You are right in what you say, we must stop to keep count. It has been a game. The game must stop. Brothers do not keep count."

"Mbuno, I am honored. Asanti sana." *Thank you very much.* It was not an idle thing for him to include Pero in his family. This wasn't a Western use of the word *brother*, it was deep, primordial, and blood strong.

Mbuno imitated Pero's voice: "You are most welcome." And he laughed. Pero did not think he had ever heard Mbuno laugh that way aloud. He joined in.

"Mbuno, there is another matter. Would you and your wife, whenever the dottori . . . you know who I mean?"

"Ndiyo, I do."

"When they say it is all right for your wife to travel, would you consider going to Italy—to a place to make Niamba much better? I could join you there."

"The dottori say she will be permitted to leave in one week if there is no infection. My brother asks me to go this place?"

Pero had no idea of the protocol here. Family structure is a rigid matter in Waliangulu tribal life. "Your little brother advises you to go and adds that he thinks it is wise. And he hopes you will agree."

"It will help you?" Mbuno visibly wanted an excuse now. An excuse to agree to Pero's request. Mbuno must have known he couldn't handle her recovery for himself.

"Ndiyo."

"It will help Niamba?"

"I am certain it will make her strong again."

"Is it not too many shillings?"

"No, my older brother, that is the easiest part. The difficult part will be the plane ride, which will be painful for Niamba, and the strangeness of the land by the ocean, in Italy."

"Will they have fish? Niamba likes fish."

"Ndiyo, they have wonderful fish, hundreds of types, she can have any she likes."

A man of decision, Mbuno's voice grew decisive, "Good, I think this place near the ocean will be good for her. I agree. I will tell the dottori and Mr. Amogh that we will be going. Will you come here to this place to safari with us?"

The train rattled over the points in Morges and brought Pero back to reality. "Maybe Mbuno, but I have work to finish here . . ."

"Is it as before Pero?" He did not call him Mr. Pero or Bwana Pero. After more than two decades, their relationship had changed, permanently.

The train passed through a short tunnel and Pero lost signal for a second, it came back ". . . said, is it like before with the Arabs?"

Pero couldn't lie to him. "Ndiyo, but not Arabs this time, more like Nazis, you know the Germans during the last Great War?"

"I do. Do you need me there Pero?"

Pero thought for a moment. He felt he could use some of Mbuno's famous logic and bushcraft, but he couldn't endanger Mbuno in this strange element. Mbuno had proved himself in the bush hundreds of times. Civilization, so-called, might overwhelm his survival talents.

But where Pero saw confusion, Mbuno saw clarity. When Pero saw simplicity, Mbuno gave him perspective. Mbuno knew the law of the jungle—all the animals including man— better than any. Pero needed advice.

"Mbuno, the people, or rather the man who threatens us, the one we're up against is a very, very powerful man, more powerful than Moi was." Moi was the ex-president of Kenya, thoroughly corrupt and, often, brutal. "He was head or part of the Stasi, a communist secret police force. He now controls a bank and employees, almost a small private army, like a tribe. These men are all dangerous, killers, violent people."

"Shufti?"

"Yes, but much more focused, much more, what's the word . . . capable. And they have police who are corrupt on their side."

"This is not good Pero. You should run away, right now."

"Yes, except they've kidnapped Heep and another innocent man. I need to find them and rescue them. And I need to stop this man—he has material to make a large bomb."

"This man, is he like an animal? Is he, in your dreams, an animal?" Waliangulu felt that dreams were prescient—they told you what you needed to know. What Pero was up against had given Heep and Pero the impression of a hyena. A ravenous, determined, fierce and, above all, cunning hyena. He told Mbuno. It was his subconscious thought in Berlin perhaps, not a dream, but that's close enough. He hoped.

"Ah, that is most bad. The hyena always has special place he keeps food, a meat locker the British call it. It is like the crocodile who never eat fresh meat. They put it in the special place, always the same special place, and eat it later. Hyenas never change the special place for their food, the kill they have carried away, even if they know you have found them there. They will die protecting it. It is how we track and kill hyena."

"Do they have more than one place?"

"Oh yes, but the hyena is not like the crocodile who fills one place and then fills the next on the river bottom. The hyena will, many times, put one type of kill meat in one cave or hole in the ground, and another animal meat in another place. He is always very careful, he never mixes them up. If you are looking for our friend Heep and this other man, look in the hyena's meat locker where he keeps the same type of meat." Pero was suddenly sure that this hyena's "meat" was everything to do with the gold and uranium.

It was the clarity he needed.

Now, he needed to find out Tische's contacts, his "lairs," that could lead him to where Tische had stashed Heep and Danny. Because he now firmly believed that Tische would have stashed them with the gold/uranium project. He also will have stashed them safely because he might need them to bargain with Pero or whomever. "*Asanti sana* Mbuno, I think you have helped, *asanti, asanti.*"

"Good. Is Miss Mary also in danger?" Mbuno knew Heep and Mary Lever were married.

"No, she is at least safe in Florida with Pastor Threte . . ." he let his voice hang.

"Ah, is there another, perhaps another woman in danger? It is always most difficult when a woman suffers, is it not?"

"It is. This time there is another woman—who reminds me of that Bonobo female. You remember? We filmed her for two weeks, and you had tracked her for a month or so."

"*Ndiyo*, I do, she was special."

"Well, Susanna, that's her name, is not in immediate danger, but she is involved. If I don't get this right . . . I only have thirty hours."

"You will, we will." Mbuno paused. "Brother, you will now take an order from me. Arrange for a flight for me to you. Immediately."

"Mbuno I can't ask . . ."

"You do not ask, I tell. Niamba is safe here with dottori and Amogh. Amogh and dottori will keep guard and transport to safari place by the sea where I will join them. You give order, they will follow. Now you follow my order. I leave tonight, will go to airport immediately."

Pero heard the determination, understood the new relationship was already being tested. Pero's big brother was to be obeyed. He had no option but to agree. He did so, explaining that Amogh would have to get him to the airport and buy the ticket.

"Ndiyo, he has that fast car. He will take me to Langata," to his home in Giraffe Manor, "I will get passport and clothing Amogh's father already sent over last time you were here, and then we go to Nairobi Airport. Where do I fly to?"

"Take the next flight to Zurich, Switzerland. It leaves late, around nine-thirty I think. I can meet you there, in Zurich. It lands around three-thirty a.m. If I do not show up, call Mr. Lewis—remember him?" Mbuno said he did. "Here's the number . . ." and Pero read it to him twice until he was sure Mbuno had it accurately. "You must travel first class. It will help with Swiss immigration. Ask Amogh to give you one thousand dollars, he can get it from his father."

"Ndiyo. All will be done as you say. Now, brother, hear me: you are a brave morani. But remember, that if I had lost Niamba, I would be like you, my little brother, lone." He meant lone, not alone or lonely, but acting as one, not part of a pair. Lone described Pero's status perfectly. "It is not good to be a lone morani. It is time for you to bring a woman fruit." There it was, the second time in the day, advice, logical, clear, and impossible to fathom. *Maybe when this is all over . . .* Until then, Pero decided to try to put it out of his mind.

Chapter 12

Saanen

The train pulled into Bulle Station. Pero alighted on the platform, watched other passengers get off and some get on, ducked away from the overhead lights behind a pillar, and waited until the train pulled out, proceeding on to Basel. When the platform was empty, he made his way to the nearest telephone box and called a local taxi, selected at random from the public phone book. When the taxi pulled up five minutes later, Pero still didn't see anyone around. Bulle isn't exactly a buzzing metropolis at 6:30 p.m. in the dark.

The ride to Saanen was cold and snowy. The driver had studded tires—Pero had asked when he booked him—and the journey, past Gruyère (where they make the cheese) was made in under ninety minutes. Pero had the taxi drop him at the Saanen Bahnhof, the station for the picturesque narrow-gage MOB mountain train.

A block over, he went into the Saanerhof, the largest local hotel, into the *stube* (a café bar restaurant). Pero needed to waste time until Saanen's residents went off to bed around ten p.m. Besides, he was still hungry. So he ordered a full hot meal; soup followed by *geschnetzeltes mit rosti* and then *crème caramel*. The soup was potato leek. The sliced, sautéed veal was smothered in cream, and the fried potatoes called rosti, like hash browns, were crisp and wonderful. The Swiss may not change menus often, but Pero thought *who cares when the quality is this good?* The *crème caramel* was, he admitted to himself, perhaps overdoing it, but he justified the extravagance by saying to himself that he needed the sugar.

The meal finished, he added up the little paper receipts that had been accumulating in a shot glass as the courses arrived. He paid his bill—the tip is always included in Switzerland—by leaving the correct change on the table. It was only then he realized he was seriously tired.

He remembered that he still needed to acquire a ski jacket—at night when everything was already closed. Making his way to the toilets, as any dinner guest would, down to the Saanerhof basement, the ski room next to the public toilets was piled with guests' skis, poles, and boots. Guests came in from skiing, dumped their equipment in the ski room, and walked upstairs in stocking feet to a warm shower or bath. As he expected, there was always some tourist who didn't want to take their ski jacket, which might be damp from skiing, to their room. Indeed, there was a selection, all the latest designs. Saanenland was trendy. He chose a Head ski suit model nearest his size because it also had zip up over-pants, to cover his tracksuit. The Russian bag stayed in his green coat pocket, under the other jacket.

The ski-room had its own outside door. He left quietly. He needed to see what companies' aircraft were at the airport. The walk, a mile or so over the train tracks, past the lumber mill in the cold March evening air kept him alert and awake.

Pero was concerned he wouldn't know who owned which plane by the tail registration number any more than he could tell one car from another by their license plates. In the Saanerhof stube, gossip among locals had been in Schweizer-Deutsch, the local version of German with a heavy accent. Mostly, the locals assumed that no outsider could understand. And they were right. Mountain valley people, isolated from one another, develop strange variations in dialect that make comprehension difficult. However, people's names are always recognizable. So when he heard the name Sergio Negroni, he knew which jet should be, if Sergio were still in the region, at the airport. Sergio was celebrity famous for flying his own Boeing BBJ (Boeing Business Jet), a remodeled Boeing 737. There surely couldn't be too many of those around. So if there was one BBJ there, it was likely to be Sergio's.

Pero was right. He saw it there, parked on the apron in front of the service hangar, next to the glider hangars. It was illuminated—tail showing a logo, a scrolled white SN with Italian green as a background. It looked very elegant. Sergio was simply rich. Olive oil rich, originally daddy's olive oil that Sergio had nurtured into a global empire of gourmet kitchen supplies, mostly packaged in China. His BBJ was ultra-long range. He was known, so it said in People Magazine, to week-end in Gstaad, a few miles from Saanen, and still get to work in Shanghai on Monday. Friday he'd be back partying. Sergio was the real jet set, a modern international business tycoon.

He was also Pero's old roommate. It was Sam who referred to Sergio as the lion that gave Pero the idea to go to Saanen and see if Sergio was around or if not, would Sergio at least know of some rich personal jet he could hire. *Maybe my luck's holding* . . . Way back then, in his school days, Sergio was, sim-ply, *le lion*, at the time always the brave one. Pero could use that sort of help.

As he trudged toward the plane, Pero knew Sam would already be fully engaged in helping. Sam's hatred for the misuse of "the secrets of the universe" as he called nuclear science, made him fully commit before Pero even had to ask.

Sergio, on the other hand, would have no such burning passion. Pero was hoping that the tycoon would still be, after all the years, that brave, reckless adventurer he was when Pero knew him best.

Walking around the perimeter of the airfield and away from the lights, he crossed to the flight center, ambling slowly so as not to arouse suspicion. The tower was halfway up the mountainside dominating the airstrip. The hut where you filed a flight plan, got a machine to dispense hot chocolate or coffee, or simply sat waiting for your private pilot to finish paperwork was mid-way down the airfield and guarded. The police officer on duty asked him for his identity papers. He showed him his passport. When asked what he was doing there as the airport was closed for the night and no flights expected, Pero told the officer he wanted a walk. Then he suggested that while they were both there and it was getting cold, perhaps he could get them both a hot something to drink? Would the officer care to join him?

He would. They went in and Pero put the two franc coin in the machine and asked the police officer his choice. "Choc Ovo." Chocolate Ovomaltine it was. Pero then pushed the correct buttons to order a second one. The altitude, cold, and Ovomaltine were always perfect combinations. For over an hour, the two sat there on the leather couches drinking and discussing skiing and Pero's history in the region. He knew the officer would be curious and Pero had nothing in that time period of his life to hide. As in most villages, they had acquaintances in common. The young man's father was the brother of the ski-lift operator on the Wispile in Gstaad. They happily discussed the years before the lift was installed, when Pero and his fellow students all had to uptrack, putting fur pelts on the bottom of skis and walking up the mountain, a thousand meters up, to have one run down per afternoon. The younger man was just old enough to remember 1963, being born in fifty even.

When Pero's cell phone rang, the officer got up and told Pero to stay and finish his call in the warmth. As the officer was leaving to retake his patrol position outside, Pero thanked him and answered the call. "Hello?" He pretended the signal wasn't strong enough, looked at the phone keypad, and secretly with his thumb, keyed 5-5-5. He listened again.

The officer, standing in the open door, was making sure Pero heard someone. He gave a little wave and went back outside, the door smoothly shutting off the cold of the night air.

"Baltazar, P. here, go ahead."

"Susanna here. My sister has something to tell you." She handed over the phone.

"Bertha here. It is a, how do you say fremder beruf, ach, ja, a strange profession you have Herr Baltazar."

"Call me Pero, please."

Bertha let it all tumble out in a rush, "Ja Wohl. Susanna and I have initiated a search mit die Internet and then we call a colleague in Paris. He is metals Spezialist, and we have confirmed the cadmium and some cesium—cesium is also used to improve the cadmium's properties for the flow ... have been recently purchased in Switzerland. Twelve shipments in the past month. Five were to the electronics company Bosch, but we think they are for coating of rotors in electric motors. Two were for RINCO, expert welders for hydroelectric generatoren. Both these companies have regular shipments every month, every year. Und so, that left five shipments. Only two of those were ordered in the past two weeks, making them more likely, we feel. Now, we have kalkuliert, Susanna and I, mit talking mit Herr Professor Turner, the amount of cadmium one would need with cesium and the amount without cesium as a reactor to convert one ton of uranium. Aber, neither shipment was enough to convert a ton of uranium. We are sorry."

Listening intently, Pero realized he had made a mistake. "Bertha, the shipment was for a ton, total weight, gold and uranium. If the gold were taken away, how much Uranium would be left?"

"It is impossible to say. Let me see . . ." she was talking with Susanna, quickly in German. "Ja, ja, gut . . . Mr. Balta . . . sorry, Pero, yes, if you assume half the weight, either shipment is just enough. If you assume one-third, by weight, then it is more likely. That would be enough protective gold too, and we discuss this ratio with Herr Professor before," she meant Sam, "to cover an exchange of plutonium or uranium. Und so mit a third of a ton you have enough to process into, ah, approximately, twenty or thirty fuel rods, which would release in a . . . a swap you say . . .? A swap to make maybe ten conventional thermonuclear devices, as your government calls them, of five megatons each. I call them what they are." She said it with distaste, like Sam had before, "atombomben."

"That many? God, that's terrible, that damn many bombs, five megatons, each? Christ!" Pero said and meant it. Pausing to collect himself after such a shock, he asked, "Okay, where were those two shipments made?"

"One was made to Geneva," Pero's hopes soared, "but it went to the Albert Schweitzer University in Geneva. For medical uses we think. They have an extruder, for pipes used in making water purification filters, but probably not suitable in *strongness* you say? Not for this type of application.

"One other went to Brinker Metallarbeiten Fabrik B.V., a metal works, in Schaffhausen. They do not do any extruding. They prepare raw metals, metallelementet, for coating. They import precious metals und chrome, make special formulas, specializing in medical instruments . . . the coatings are for. We do not think it is them either. They have no smelter, we checked. They grind and prepare mixtures, little ball bearings or flakes, only mit verhältnissen, sorry, only with proportions for clients to smelt in their own factory. They are an old company, very well regarded in the medical field."

Pero thought, damn. "Do you, or did Sam, think of anything else?"

"No sorry, we did not. Oh, and Herr Professor wanted you to know he is on his way to Berlin, via Paris. He will arrive this night, late. He could not reach your phone, it was always busy. He wanted to remind you to have a shower and change your clothings. Und to please take your pills." There was a background comment. "Ah, und Susanna wants to know what pills."

"Please tell her I am taking the antibiotic, the wound is still doing fine. Sam also gave me some iodine pills . . ."

"Oh, Gott und Himmel." He heard her tell Susanna.

"Listen, listen, he gave them to me as a precaution, there's nothing wrong." Even to Pero, his own voice sounded desperate, trying to will Susanna not to worry.

"Susanna is not happy, she says you are *ein dummer mann*, a stupid man, a . . . What?" he could hear Susanna speaking, "Yes, also a brave man but now more stupid than brave. She says you are playing . . . how do you say it? With fire? Yes, with fire. She says you must stop. *Nein, nein . . . Ach, genug.* Here she is . . ." he heard the phone being passed.

"Pero? You . . . you . . ." she gave up, Pero heard her inhale a deep breath, "Please to be careful."

"I will." And they left it at there. There was little else to say as they both realized that what could be done was being done. The sorrow in her voice was also troubling to Pero, then the phone line went dead.

Time to call Sergio Negroni and borrow his jet. Pero knew the old four-digit local phone number by heart. It had always been the same since they were fourteen when they partied at Sergio's parent's chalet on the side of the hill overlooking Gstaad. Most winter outings the boys had to confine themselves to the Hi-Fi Disco in the Gstaad Palace, and its lesser cousin, in the ping-pong room in the basement that they affectionately called the Lo-Fi.

The new Gstaad numbers were now three digits longer, all unique to Gstaad, so Pero added the three, dialed all seven, and the phone answered on the first ring. "Good evening. Can I help you?" It was the suave voice of Sergio's butler.

"Is Mr. Negroni in? It's Pero Baltazar calling. It's urgent. We're old friends."

"One moment sir."

"Pero? Pero, is that you? Where the hell in God's name are you?"

"In Saanen, at the airport."

"Great, I'll send the car, be there in fifteen minutes . . ."

"No wait, Monsieur le Lion, I need you to get off your bony ass and come here in about an hour. Can do?" There was a pause and the line went dead.

Pero immediately called Lewis. He explained to him that Sam was on his way to Berlin. He still felt he couldn't explain what Bertha and Susanna had discovered because, as he was increasingly sure, the thought of all that weapons-grade substitute uranium being processed and shipped would cause the CIA to act immediately, thereby pushing the safety of Heep and Danny into obscurity. He could see it from Lewis and Bergen's point of view. The CIA would be concentrating on the greater good. But Pero guessed he still had at least twenty hours to play with. Tische wanted to get the sample, the package, the police evidence, from Pero—at the rendezvous time and place he had set. By now Tische would know, or at least think, that Pero hadn't made it to CERN. He would also assume Pero still had the bag. But only Pero, Sam, and his two new friends in Berlin knew what it contained, what it meant. Tische didn't know they knew nor did he know that anyone knew the truth about the gold, especially not DC. As far as Tische was concerned, the package only contained evidence linking him to something dangerous to his liberty and enterprise.

The fact that Tische could not know that Pero and his friends knew what the package really was, that was their only real advantage over Tische. That and a serious brain trust helping the friends think straight and hopefully get ahead of Tische's plans.

Lewis was concerned that Pero wasn't making progress getting to Berlin. The CIA and German Internal Security were conducting probes—as Tische would expect, no doubt. "Had there been none, he would have gotten more nervous and would have run to hide, permanently, and probably made your friends disappear," Lewis explained.

Pero agreed. "We needed him thinking he is winning—just. But not enough to dispose of the kidnapping evidence . . . Danny and Heep." Lewis agreed. "Your people have intel for me on TruVereinsbank yet?"

"It's a list, a long, long list. TruVereinsbank owns or controls or Tische sits on the board of over two hundred companies. Some are in China and Shanghai but nothing in Thailand. Some are, well, everywhere. The shipping agency that sent the gold from New York? They own them. The online metals auction company the Treasury idiot used to sell the gold? They have a majority share. Some of their companies are . . . how can I say this? Familiar." He used a word, like the CIA's use of the word "reliable," meaning discrete. "Familiar" to the CIA meant well known to the CIA, sometimes partners.

"How familiar?"

"Very. Funded." *Oh damn, and double damn*, he thought realizing that TruVereinsbank was a funded partner with CIA holdings. The slush fund. Direct contact with the DG was more than possible.

"Lewis, I don't want to upset the CIA's applecart here, but they've chosen a strange bedfellow. I can't tell you why, yet, but trust me . . . you may want to check every one of those familiar connections."

"Yeah, if they're anything like the gold-uranium deal, we need to. I can't take this upstairs yet, I need proof."

"If I can find Heep and Redmond, you'll get your proof. We are working on it."

"I have additional information on Tische. You are dealing with a nasty fellow, he is ex-Stasi, came with the nationalized business entity, Treuhand, when some of the assets were parcelled out to the Vereinsbank, making it TruVereinsbank. Tische only became Tische in 1987. Before that, his last name was Aue, Stasi Oberführer Heinrich Aue. His father, Sergeant Joseph Aue, was an informant and source to CIC, the pre-CIA, after the end of the war. CIC took charge of him from the Seventh Army prison camp in 1946. Aue disappeared from records shortly thereafter, presumed, according to the open CIA internal records, to be back in East Germany, Russian side. Pero, many of the SS officers assumed the rank of foot soldiers to escape war crimes trials. If they had information to trade . . ."

"Or gold."

"Yes, or gold. CIC was in charge of that. But I think he, this Aue, could have been in the West and changed his name or had *someone* cleanse his records. But why did the son—and there's a daughter by the way—stay in the East? I was going to access Aue's records, but they have a red line in the computer here."

"What does that mean?"

"State secrets. If I probe that, it will mean the DG will find out."

They were both silent, there wasn't much more to say. Pero ran over the details in his mind again, *A father who was probably an SS officer pretending to be a non-com, as many of them did, who traded the whereabouts of Nazi gold to CIC—who then liberated the gold and used it to fund the most clandestine CIA operations—and no doubt still does.* "Lewis, see if you can locate the daughter, maybe there's a lead there." Was there anything else he needed? Yes, there was, he just couldn't really access it on this phone. But he needed to try anyway. So he asked him, "Can you simply read all those company ties of TruVereinsbank and boards Tische sits on, starting with the ones in Switzerland?"

"They're only in alphabetical order, not importance, so I'll go down the list for you picking those out when I see something significant. Okay, let me see, there's . . . *Almvier GmbH* in Konstanz, *Arcadia Promotions SA* in Morges, and, ah, there are no more "A's"—as he started into "B," Pero stopped him. Lewis had made the solid connection.

"Stop. I am going to Schaffhausen, *Brinker Metallarbeiten Fabrik*. That has to be it. Get me anything you can. And Lewis, those are field agent instructions, no delays."

Lewis' voice had a hard edge, "I got the lecture last time. We'll talk about that later unless the director general cancels your appointment. But tell me, how did you associate Brinker. What is it you know that you are not telling us?"

Pero responded harshly, "Not now, Baltazar out." Two clicks and Lewis was cut off. A half hour later Sergio's Porsche Cayenne roared into the parking lot outside and the police guard saluted, smartly.

Chapter 13

Schaffhausen

His elegant northern Italian accent still made Pero chuckle. The finest schools, the best elocution lessons, and he still spoke English with an Italian accent. "Da boney ass? Twenty years . . . no, we saw each other in LA ten years ago, very brief, but all *dese* years and you expect me to jump because of a teenage oath?"

"You're here, aren't you?"

"Okay, so I am here. Now what?"

"Now, my old and trusted friend, le giraffe, and I humbly ask you to take off your mantle of world business leader and help us save people from dying and, perhaps, millions from catastrophe." Shocked, Sergio looked at Pero, saw Pero was serious, and buckled his knees to sit on the couch, shaking his head.

Pero waited until Sergio went through the thought process, the same one he always had done as a kid. *Am I being used? What's in it for me? How can I stay the leader?* And then, *I can relax, this is my trusted friend.*

So, like Sam before, Pero told him the whole story, everything he knew. Sergio's eyes sparkled. Not admiration, more like, *you've been doing things, daring things.* Pero saw the gleam in Sergio's eyes and knew then that Sergio would want in. Besides, Pero had just the plan to let Sergio take all the credit if it all worked out. Old friends are reliable, especially if you knew them as well as that little gang knew each other. Their tight, teen boarding school did all that—all is revealed, trust is born and never dies.

The BBJ took off fifteen minutes later. The flight plan was filed en route, to Zurich, the nearest large public airport, for a quick stop. Sergio Negroni was the sole pilot, there wasn't any better. Pero sat right seat. Once they were aloft, he told Pero it was only a fifteen-minute flight and put it on autopilot. "Hand me that case, will you Pero?" Pero passed over the standard pilot's map case. From inside, Sergio pulled out a Panasonic Toughbook tablet computer. He used his finger as the mouse and soon had selected the Schaffhausen region. He punched up the map. "Jeppesen maps, worldwide, every airfield, all the frequencies. Zurich I know by heart. We need to make a decision pretty soon if we're going to divert to Schaffhausen, not Berlin, after Zurich. Only one airfield in Schaffhausen there that can handle this plane. See?" He pointed at the map.

Pero could tell by Sergio's voice he was bragging, as usual, le lion never changes. But what he was bragging about escaped Pero for the moment. "Yeah, you're brilliant, got that, but can you or can't you set us down in Schaffhausen?"

"No, is impossible, see the time *conditzione?* No runway lights, no services. Cannot do." He kept Pero waiting for effect. "But *we will do*, you wait, you see. Now we land in Zurich. What you collecting there?"

"A friend, a master tracker from safari." And Pero explained Mbuno's, capabilities.

Sergio was skeptical, "But this ain't Africa, and he'll be out of his depth. No way he's gonna be useful here."

"It's his thinking I need. He understands animals—all animals, especially human animals—better than anyone I know. Having him here might make all the difference. Do you mind bringing him aboard?"

"Nah, he's a friend of yours, he's welcome. And I'll be interested to see if your otter skills are still good . . . you used to be good at scheming." And he laughed.

Touchdown at Zurich was uneventful. As they pulled off the active runway, the little van with the flashing yellow light and illuminated Follow Me sign led them toward the private hangers' side of the field. Sergio got on the radio, gave his call sign and said, "Zurich Tower, request parking and refueling near the main terminal. We're here to collect an incoming passenger from Nairobi and will request immediate take off once he comes aboard, bound for Saanen, return."

"Zurich Tower here, hold current position." They did, waiting. The Follow Me van turned toward the main terminal as the radio squawked, "Zurich Tower here, follow the leader to park at Terminal B and shut down."

Sergio confirmed and did mostly as he was told. Shutting down the engines, he told Pero, "We can restart without their generator, but I'll have the tanks filled. That'll be normal." Pero went to the main hatch, rotated the handle, and as the door came open, the steps emerged from the hold below and extended to the tarmac. As he was about to descend, he told Sergio he should be back within the hour or two, hopefully. Sergio called back, "Make sure you do. I'll have to shut down all the systems if any longer and then I might need de-icing, it's getting cold."

Pero sprinted in the frigid night air to the man emerging from the Follow Me van and got directions to collect a passenger from the Nairobi flight. The man told him that it would land in a few hours and then asked if the pilot had authority for fees and charges. Pero assured him Sergio did with a laugh, "The pilot? He owns the BBJ."

Then Pero went into the terminal warmth, found a quiet corner, and got some shuteye.

Mbuno, emerging from the customs hall carrying only a straw basket of effects, was smiling while two very pretty air hostesses, either side, were chatting across him. Pero approached and said, "Welcome, Mbuno, good to see you."

"Ndiyo, Pero." He turned to the two women and, reaching into his straw bag, took out and handed each one a small leafy packet tied with raffia. They looked at each other with puzzled looks. Mbuno explained, slowly, "It is honey. A young Okiek boy collected it for me yesterday. I do not need it as my friend," he gestured at Pero, "is here and he always has honey for me." The two women were busy saying thank you, one gave him a kiss on the cheek, he nodded and further explained, "It is very good honey, Okiek honey, it is very sweet."

Pero wanted to get a move on, "Thank you, ladies, come on you old mzee you, let's get going, your private jet awaits . . ." And he led Mbuno away, waving at the pretty women, toward the BBJ waiting on the terminal apron, the refueling tanker pulling away.

Mbuno stopped at the bottom of Sergio's jet, looking up. "It is safe?" Pero assured him is was, that it was a private jet belonging to the pilot, an old school friend called Sergio, who had the nickname le lion. Mbuno nodded and started to climb the stairs, "Lion always like to make a show, prove how powerful they are. But lion are trustworthy, that is good."

"Yeah, well my nickname in school was otter . . ."

Mbuno stopped climbing the stems, lowered his head, and gave a chuckle. "Ah, yes, otter. Always capable, always making what you call plans. Very hard to catch. Bad eating."

Pero coughed, "Just as well . . ."

Sergio and Mbuno shook hands on the flight deck, and Sergio asked Pero if they could, please, leave immediately, "I'm getting flak from the tower." Pero gave him a thumbs up, pulled open the jump seat, and settled Mbuno in place. Sergio soon got the port engine running smoothly, so then he started the starboard engine. As Pero settled into the right seat, they taxied to the end of the late night runway. Brakes applied, tower called, Sergio then ran up both engines, went through all the pre-flight checks, and got permission to roll.

Seconds later, they were in the air gaining altitude. Pero asked, "What's the plan for Schaffhausen?" Sergio put his finger to his lips. He called Zurich ATC and told them he was experiencing a minor problem with pressurization, and that he was descending to a lower altitude. They asked if he was declaring an emergency. He said no, but he needed to descend to a lower altitude to make sure there was none. The Swiss hate emergencies. He assured them he would sort it out over Lake Constance, away from housing, and then report back to them. "Ten minutes, maybe fifteen, before I call you back." They agreed, and he swung the plane over to the north, left and descended. Even at night Pero could make out the shores of Lake Constance, it was the only place that had no lights, was jet black. As they loitered over the lake at 6,000 feet, Sergio entered in the GPS coordinates of the runway, beginning and end, into the onboard computer. "Flying by instruments, using GPS, have to do this all the time in China, real bad ATC there."

Then turning them eastward again, he passed over the edge of the lake and, immediately, Zurich ATC asked where he was going. He said, very calmly, "Busy, Mayday . . ." and switched off the radio. He made a controlled descent, checked headings, watching the blinking GPS indicator. "Good to within eight feet, very reliable, especially here. In China, it's twenty feet."

At the end of the most nerve-wracking thirty seconds of Pero's life of flying, seemingly flying blind, he saw houses pass beneath the nose. Sergio suddenly flicked on the landing lights, pulled the nose up, and eased the throttles back. He was committed to landing.

Before them was . . . nothing, then grass, then an outer marker of sorts. On either side, there were faint lights from street lamps and houses. The wheels touched just as Pero saw runway under the landing lights. Sergio applied the brakes hard and the full reverse thrusters. They stopped before the end, on the warning stripes, and taxied to the very end of the strip. Sergio swung the plane to the right, got two wheels on the grass, and did a U-turn to point back the way they had come. "Taking off will be easier."

Mbuno, behind Sergio, said as if talking to a child, "Lion, they always show off."

Sergio laughed, turned on the radio, and called Zurich ATC. "Sorry Zurich, we had what I thought was a problem. We're down safe in Schaffhausen, turned around, ready for take-off. The problem appears to be a faulty circuit breaker. We're fixing it. Can you give us a half an hour before we take-off? We need to take a breath."

Zurich Air Traffic Control was less inclined to let matters pass. On the cockpit speaker came an authoritarian voice telling the plane to await the arrival of the police. Sergio blithely said, "fine" and switched off. "We've got about a half hour, let's go." He switched everything off, leaving the plane in darkness, inside and out. They made their way to the door and extended the steps.

"Where are we, Sergio?"

Le lion's timing for a boast was always impeccable: "Welcome to Brinker's private airfield. No reception committee I see. Pity." As he said that, he took out a pistol from the hidden cabinet next to the door and handed it to Pero. "Your show. Useful in some places I travel to. You never know." Pero suddenly realized that Mbuno's assessment of Lion was perhaps too accurate. To make his fears worse, he suddenly remembered that le Lion's favorite films were always James Bond.

Pero handed his gun to Mbuno, who checked for safety and stuck it in his belt. Sergio's raised eyebrows and nod to Pero showed he was reassessing his evaluation of Mbuno.

Brinker Metallarbeiten Fabrik had its own longish runway. It made sense when Pero thought about it, as they shipped precious metals and very valuable cargo to all parts of the world. This way they could avoid the expense of handling agents at commercial airports.

It also meant Tische could ship contraband cargo, slipping in and out of there virtually undetected. About two hundred meters away, behind a double chain link fence was a huge, unlit factory complete with smokestacks. In the distance was a car park and access to the main road. Closer to the runway, on their side, were low-level, modern, buildings with their own, taller security fences through which the runway taxiway ran. They could see loading docks for trucks and well-lit open concrete aprons. The apron sign said Brinker in bold letters. In the middle of those buildings was an aircraft hangar where the taxiway headed. This was the exit ramp from the runway, and it dead-ended at those low-level buildings and the hangar.

They sprinted across the runway in the dark toward the gate by the side of the taxiway that lead back to the hangar and loading docks midway down the runway. The gate opened into the Brinker compound. There was no guard at the gate, but they could see lights coming on, a garage doorway being opened, and inside lights flooding a parking lot. Then, they could hear voices in the cool pre-morning air. Negroni took a cell phone from his pocket and made a call as they watched the Brinker men gather forces: "André? Bonsoir, c'est Sergio Negroni, I have a problem . . ."

Le Lion explained that he had needed to divert to Brinker Metallarbeiten Fabrik in Schaffhausen to use the private runway but landed safely, thank you, "but now armed men are threatening us and . . ." Taking out his gun, he squeezed off a shot, "they're firing at us." After listening and saying grazie a few times, he hung up.

After they had heard the shot, Mbuno and Pero looked across at the Brinker forces who were wondering what to do. Pero quietly asked, "Who's André?"

Sergio kept his eyes focused forward and whispered, "Guest at my chalet. He's sort of head of the Swiss Internal Police, Major André Schmitz." Pero knew that colonel was the highest rank in Switzerland, so the rank of major was pretty high. Sergio interrupted Pero's thoughts, "So, help is on the way, hopefully before Zurich ATC sends local cops. Now, what do you want to do until they get here?"

"Rescue my friends. If Mbuno is right, this is a hyena meat locker."

Sergio looked even more confused but shrugged his shoulders in acceptance. "You have interesting friends, old amigo."

The three made their way, crouching, running across the grass and over some train tracks and approached the car park, out of the line of sight of the open garage. There were four more garage doors in the back of the building facing them, but only the one was open with five men standing, pointing at the plane, talking, and gesturing. Pero shot a glance back. The plane was visible by the black silhouette blocking the slight glow of early morning, which highlighted its shape against the factory on the other side of the runway about a half-mile away. Pero, Sergio, and Mbuno waited until the Brinker security men made their minds up, piled into an open truck, and sped off toward the plane's position on the airfield. They had left the garage door open, and the space appeared empty.

The three men watched the truck go far enough down the taxiway before they ran into the garage and then went into the back of the building. Pero was somewhat thinking aloud, "Mbuno, if you were hiding someone here, someone you had kidnapped, where would you put them?"

Mbuno responded, "Somewhere . . . where most factory workers from the factory complex never go. Somewhere not used very much."

Sergio nodded and chimed in, "I think we should go to the fire station, look at a map or plan of this factory . . . I know there will be a building plan, there is always . . . cost me a fortune every time I build a factory."

Mbuno nodded and followed as Sergio led the way toward the front of the building.

In the front lobby, behind waist-high frosted glass, they saw the security station with a man standing facing the main entrance doors, looking at monitors, his back to them. As the three were behind the reception guard, he never looked back at them but stared instead, intently, at the screens and through the glass entrance doors at the front parking lot. An open door off to the left, on their other side of the security partition separating them from the security guard, had Feuerkontrolle (fire control) in red lettering. Hiding under the frosted glass, the three crouched and crept past the man's back and into the room.

Sergio put his hand on the plan, stroked the aluminum panel, read the Swiss German captions for each station, and finally said, in a whisper, "Here, here I think, Pero. See the sign for toxic chemicals? Let's try here first. Nothing else fits."

As silently as possible, they passed down two corridors—Pero in his ski suit making nylon on nylon noises that seemed to him to be loud enough to wake the dead, Mbuno in his Chinese rubber-soled sneakers slightly squeaking on the polished floor, and Sergio in Gucci loafers with a tinkling buckle. They made an odd trio. Maybe it was that oddness that gave them the edge. Pero certainly saw the surprise on another guard's face before Mbuno dropped him with the handle of the gun. Sergio, who was a black belt and had always been athletic, was surprised that this small old man had moved so quickly and decidedly. Sergio shook his head and patted Mbuno on the back, "Grazie."

Carefully, they tested the door the guard was stationed at. It was locked. His pockets had no key. "It means there's someone inside, another guard maybe." Sergio whispered, "We need to get him to open up. That door looks solid."

"Agreed, but what do you suggest?" Pero whispered back. "It isn't like we've been very stealthy so far. There's the plane, the call to the police—ah, are those their sirens now? Hear them?" Pero frowned and then shook his head to clear his thoughts. "Change gears, Mbuno, give Sergio the gun." He did. "Now, let's make a real racket." The guard on the ground was not coming to. Pero went over and threw the nearest fire alarm. All hell broke loose—lights, sirens, everything one would imagine. Pero counted to ten to himself, mouthing the numbers silently as he folded fingers. Sergio watched the corridor they had come down, pistol ready.

Mbuno dragged the unconscious guard out of sight around a corner as Sergio and Pero flattened against the wall, out of the line of sight. At the count of ten Pero banged on the door and yelled *"Feuer! Feuer! Jeder aus!"* Fire! Fire! Everyone out! The police sirens were loud, obviously outside the main door now. Pero realized that it helped that police and fire sirens were almost the same in Switzerland.

Immediately, they heard the door being unlatched.

With the chain on, the man looked around. Not seeing anyone, the guard shut the door and removed the chain. As the door opened, Sergio stuck the pistol in the man's face, poking one eye, and told him to *setzen sie (sit)*. He did as he was told, he couldn't have been older than twenty. Behind him was a security door with a keypad. No one else was around. "Sprechen Sie Englisch?" asking him if he spoke English. In his Swiss accent, he said he did, so Sergio pressed on, "Who is in there?"

He said the men who were working there had gone to their hotel for the night. There were valuables in there. He was guarding them. After more questions, it was clear he had no code for the door lock. The guards, being cooperative, were desperately affirming that only the two Germans did. Pero thought, *Germans working in Switzerland? A bit unusual* . . . The guard wanted to know if he could leave because of the fire. Pero told him to stay seated, the police were coming. "There are men trapped in there, being held prisoner, we need to get them out." The guard looked shocked.

"What now?" Sergio asked.

"I am thinking." They had only moments, Pero was sure of that. Mbuno's evaluation of the hyena came into his mind. The hyena would put everything together, keep like with like—it could be . . . "Watch the corridor, hold this guy here. If the cops come, give up. No gunplay okay?" Sergio nodded. "Mbuno come with me . . ."

Pero went over to the keypad and tried 2-3-4. Nothing happened.

"Press the pound key between tries, it clears the memory." Sergio called back. He obviously was familiar with such keypads.

Pero tried U (the number 8) 2-3-4, nothing happened. The young Swiss guard spoke up, eagerly, "It's eight numbers, I've seen them put them in." Pero tried 8 (for T) 4 (for i) 7 (for s) 2 (for c) 4 (for h) and 2-3-4. Tische 2-3-4. The door lock clicked open.

Mbuno and Pero saw two men, obviously Danny and Heep, bound, sitting in chairs, each with a full rubber hood tight over their heads with only two slits for nostrils. Their legs were tied to the chair legs, their hands were tied together and attached between their knees with a rope that passed under the chair and back up the chair back to a noose around their necks. If they raised their hands, they would choke themselves.

A slight click and all the lights suddenly went out.

There was a noise behind and Pero turned just in time to see Sergio collapsing to the floor on top of the now equally unconscious Swiss guard. Pero raised his hands to defend against what he was sure was going to be a blow. But no blow came, just a wire noose, a deadly garrote. Off balance as he was, the man spun him around and put his knee in the small of Pero's back. The noose tightened and started choking. Through blurred vision, he saw Mbuno was also struggling.

As black clouds were gathering in Mbuno's mind, images came floating to the surface. A zebra once filmed with a snare still around its throat, cutting into the flesh. It would probably die . . . but not a Meerkat in Botswana. Ferret-looking, the little Meerkat learned to turn in the noose until the larynx was facing the slip knot. No matter how tight the noose, there was still a little bulge at the slipknot. The Meerkat had spun. Once facing the knot, he regained his breath. The noose became useless.

Ever the observant hunter, Mbuno saw, in his mind's eye, how he could strike back.

He twisted, turned, fought, and finally spun to face his attacker. By placing his hands on the man's and pulling, Mbuno prevented him from further tightening the noose wire. Mbuno seemed to be doing what the assailant would expect him to do. Now that the slipknot was over Mbuno's Adam's apple, it still hurt but he could breathe, just a little. The man was trying to apply more pressure. Twenty seconds of this and Mbuno knew he would pass out, and fifteen seconds later, he'd be dead. Mbuno let the man think he was going unconscious. As if he was fainting, Mbuno allowed his left arm to slump and his left hand to drift to the man's torso. The man's eyes, inches from Mbuno's, suddenly showed recognition that Mbuno might be reaching for his weapon, and that accelerated his pressure. The assailant could not let go of either hand.

Mbuno's fingers reached the man's gun in a holster above the waistband of the man's trousers and, desperately, the assailant squeezed Mbuno's arms to prevent Mbuno pulling out the weapon from his shoulder holster.

The man had expected Mbuno to struggle to remove it. He was certain his force on the noose would prevail before Mbuno could extract it. He was wrong. Mbuno had recognized primal animal power in his assailant and that prevented Mbuno from experiencing incapacitating fear. He knew animals and knew this man would want to reach and pull out a weapon. Mbuno did the unexpected. Mbuno simply keyed the safety off and pulled the trigger.

Mbuno had recognized that his assailant didn't want anything—no talk, no threat, nothing except him dead. That focus prevented the man from evaluating Mbuno's possibilities. Mbuno didn't need a weapon. He needed to change the balance of power.

Mbuno didn't care where the shot hit, as long as it hit the man. The bullet exited the barrel of the gun, passed inside the man's trouser belt, chipped the hipbone, continued down along the length of the man's thigh, and stopped at his knee, where it shattered knee bone fragments, destroying the knee and spraying blood. As the assailant released his hold on the noose, Mbuno fell on top of him, kneeing him in the groin. In the dark, Mbuno removed the noose wire and quickly wrapped it around the man's neck and applied pressure with one hand like a lasso. The fingers of Mbuno's other hand found the gun, and he extracted it. He pointed it vaguely at Pero's assailant. In his best imitation of a British accent, Mbuno yelled, "Stop, I shoot." He squeezed off one shot. It passed to the right of the man's left ear, close enough to cause Pero's assailant to release Pero and raise his hands.

At that moment, the lights came on as the police came barreling down the corridor, so Mbuno put the gun on the ground and raised his hands. Sergio and Pero were both on their knees, groaning.

The Swiss are efficient. After they had handcuffed everyone and told them to be quiet, Mbuno's assailant on the floor moaned, handcuffed with the wire noose still loosely looped around his throat. The local police radioed for assistance, and when Major André Schmitz had called in—Pero overheard his name—they shut down all personnel activity and sat, waiting for the bigger boss or bosses to arrive. First four uniformed officers arrived in under twenty minutes by Alouette helicopter, all dressed in crisp uniforms. Sergio was just coming round. A medic was dealing with a two-inch gash on his scalp. Pero could see the bump from six feet away. Sergio was told he was going to hurt and maybe have a concussion. Pero knew that when you are pistol whipped, it really hurts. Or it might have been a lead bag, no one was yet sure.

The man who had tried to garrote Mbuno was writhing under the care of a medic, while another officer went through the man's pockets. They administered morphine, and he succumbed. They carted him out of the small room and into the corridor, but not until they had handcuffed him to a stretcher. They had found a knife, a night vision scope, and another garroting wire in his pockets. Pero's assailant refused to talk, but the contents of his pockets also produced a bottle of chloroform and a rag. There was an empty gun holster that fit the gun he had dropped after bashing Sergio. As for Mbuno's assailant's gun, after smelling the barrel, they seemed satisfied it was the same gun Mbuno had fired. They looked inquiringly at the little man. Mbuno nodded. They nodded back. But he still wasn't allowed to move.

Meanwhile, Danny and Heep were assisted, carefully removing their hoods. Then they were given water to drink, as their ropes were also unwound and unknotted. Heep, much to his credit, simply said "hello," and stayed otherwise silent waiting for a cue from Pero. Danny, frightened as he was, looked around the room and asked a million questions. He got no answers. So, in the end, he sat down and was silent. His trousers were soiled, as were Heep's. As prisoners, they had not even been given bathroom facilities.

A short but fit looking man, mid-forties, in civilian clothing, no tie, walked authoritatively into the room and flipped open his warrant card. The local police and the late arrival officers all saluted. After a few brief questions, they indicated Mbuno was the man who had been holding the gun. He stood in front of them all and was handed a small plastic tray with the contents of all their pockets. Picking up Pero's passport and satellite cell phone, he asked, "And you are?"

"Pero Baltazar, American. I came here to rescue my friends." Heep and Danny started telling their version. They were told to be quiet. "The man there on the floor is Sergio Negroni, that's his plane out there, his *private* plane.

There's a Major André Schmitz who can vouch for him, he's on his way."

He gave Pero a curt nod, "Does it hurt?" He pointed to his neck. The noose was still hanging there.

It was hurting, Pero had to admit, but he felt no blood seeping. Meanwhile, a medic came over and first examined Mbuno's trousers and legs because of the assailant's blood splatter. On orders from the man in charge, one of them took Mbuno's handcuffs off. Another put his hands under Pero's ski parka and green coat and padded him down, between the legs as well. Finding nothing on his person, he asked Pero to remove his trousers and jackets. He did. The Russian bag, having been in the inside green jacket pocket had been missed. Pero dumped them all, carelessly, on the floor, in a heap of nylon and Gore-Tex. Next was Mbuno's turn. He was thoroughly searched. The officer motioned to them both to raise their hands. They did, and the wound on Pero's stomach became visible. The medic gave it a quick inspection, puffing some powder over the slit. The head police officer stood there, thinking, saying nothing. Pero followed his lead. For Mbuno, silence was always preferable for a Waliangulu when dealing with authority.

As it started to ring, the head officer handed Pero the satellite phone.

"May I answer?"

The officer nodded.

"Hello?" Pero heard the static. He shrugged his shoulders. The officer took the phone and listened. He turned it off. He took a digital recorder from his pocket and switched it on to record.

"Now, you three, and you three only, tell me what happened one at a time, you first." He pointed at Pero. They all did, one by one, exactly, from the time Sergio, Mbuno, and Pero landed. The officer's eyes got wider when Mbuno described shooting the man.

When they were all finished, the officer asked, "Now, who was he or the other man?" he pointed to the other assailant, now sitting on the floor, refusing to speak.

"We have no idea."

"Who are they?" Indicating Danny and Heep still getting medical attention. Pero introduced them. The officer's jaw dropped. He hadn't recognized the disheveled Danny at first. "Really?" Pero told him yes, really, abducted this morning from Berlin. Pero told him he had followed a lead and asked Negroni and Mbuno to help rescue them.

"Why didn't you ask the police?"

"A German policeman, an ex-Stasi, helped abduct them. I didn't know who to trust. And when I asked Sergio Negroni, he said he knew who to trust, so he called Major Schmitz, who is his personal houseguest. He telephoned him."

That got the chief police officer's attention, "Personal houseguest?" Pero nodded. An officer came in and whispered in his ear. To Pero and Mbuno, he said, "You may sit." They sat. To Danny and Heep he said, "Sit tight. Wait." The regular uniformed police officer stood at attention. The chief police officer left the room giving orders to keep the guns trained on the assailants. Mostly, the local cops had eyes on Danny. They knew the real article when they saw it.

No more than fifteen minutes after the chief officer had arrived, perhaps thirty-five or forty minutes after they had rescued Danny and Heep, Major André Schmitz arrived. Sergio was sitting up by now, still a little woozy, holding an icepack to his head. André first kneeled by him and they talked intimately back and forth for a moment or two. Pero caught words, like radioactive and kidnapped. Sergio ended with, "We rescued these men, and then Mbuno there saved all our lives."

With that, Mbuno's hand was shaken and Danny and Heep were allowed to get up and move around. The medic helped move them. Mbuno protested his role in the action, starting to lay on the credit where he wanted it: anywhere but on him. Mbuno had learned decades before that white men, mzungus, preferred not to have a Liangulu hero. "No, no, it was Mr. Sergio who led us here and Mr. Pero who knew where they were. Without them we would have never found them."

Le Lion looked at Pero and smiled. He was smart, knew what Mbuno was doing. By diffusing hero credit, there might be no tale for the police to report to the media. After all, they had knocked a man unconscious, pointed guns at another, set off a fire alarm, and, not least, shot a man severely.

Major Schmitz seemed to understand. "Sergio, there will, however, be one more newspaper clipping to add to your collection. The apprehension of these criminals will make front pages around the world. May I credit you as being part of the rescue?"

Sergio nodded weakly. "As long as it is no big deal."

The other officer, taking his cues from Major Schmitz, understood, "We shall, of course, say it was a police rescue."

After the euphoria of rescue had worn off, the reaction to Heep and Danny's ordeal began to surface as the medics still attended to them. Heep had welts around his neck from where the rubber hood had cut into the soft flesh. His nose was red, sore, and swollen from where the slits in the rubber mask had squeezed his nostrils, the breathing holes being stuffed with hard plastic tubing. As Heep pulled the tubes out, his nostrils bled, at first profusely.

Danny wasn't much better. The medics cracked some cold gel-packs and told both men to hold them in place. Heep couldn't stand to put anything on or near his face. Pero was worried at Heep's reaction. Pero couldn't blame him for being frightened, those masks spelled death any way you looked at them. Heep was very pale, eyes downcast.

"Heep," Pero was holding his shoulders, his arms straight, trying to get him to look up at him. "Heep, come on Heep. Don't go there my friend, it'll be alright." He said it softly.

Danny looked over. He saw Heep was beginning to zone out. Going introvert was the way he saw it. Danny waved off his medic and limped over. "Hey Heep, what the hell am I going to do tomorrow on the set, this nose looks like Rudolf the Red Nose Reindeer for fuck's sake." Heep glanced up. Danny yelled at him, acting the prima donna star, "Well, it's your damn movie. I give you your big chance, and this is how you behave? Heep, do your damn job!"

Heep stood, paused, and looked as if he would explode at Danny . . . then smiled, looked around, pointed at Pero and simply said, "Oh God, you've learned that trick from him!" But he had stopped looking so scared. He was gathering himself together. "Okay, okay. Well, if we're going to film tomorrow, we had better get back to Berlin then."

The men, the medics, and the police officers, realizing a corner had been turned, all smiled. Then, first Pero and then Sergio laughed hard. Mbuno was nodding contentedly.

Heep said, "Thanks, Danny."

"Hey, you're the one who kept me sane all those hours, least I could do."

The Swiss police medics looked at them as if they were a little bit crazy.

Perhaps they were. They had been tortured and were destined to be executed. Yet, Danny had just performed, as actors do. Heep had regained control, as directors do. Neither should be going anywhere except to the hospital for medical attention and then therapy, in that order. But the moment that was a dark corner, once turned, should be safely behind them.

Danny, his nostrils still dripping blood, wanted to know, "Pero, how the hell did you find us?" But Pero told Danny they would discuss that later. Instead, he introduced Sergio and Heep also hugged Mbuno and said, "Jambo mzee, jambo. Asante!" (*Hello chief, hello. Thank you!*).

The fog in Pero's brain began to clear. It helped to have the wire noose off from around his neck. The medic was rubbing salve on the welts with Danny looking on, curiously peering at the welts, professional curiosity of an actor, ever the observer.

But for Pero, something Major Schmitz had said to Sergio was like an alarm bell getting louder in Pero's head. *Sergio on the front pages? Telling people? Wait, there's something we haven't dealt with, that we haven't answered.*

Pero loudly told everyone to stand still.

"Major Schmitz, please secure the building, I beg you, or else a major catastrophe will occur. No one must be allowed to leave here. Something is missing—a crime so great, millions could die." In that instant, Pero had everyone's attention. Danny's mouth was, once again, wide open.

"Everything Negroni told you is true, but what we need to find out is: where is the thing that is secreted here? There's a ton of gold at Zurich airport that had a huge radiation signature."

If Pero had his attention before, as Schmitz stepped up to face Pero, he had his burning curiosity now.

"That gold is Nazi concentration camp gold. When it was hidden, it concealed something. It was not accidentally radiated." Pero watched Schmitz nod as if he knew about the gold, "but hides a shipment of maybe a third of a ton of unstable Uranium 234, made by the Nazis prior to 1943. Here, where we are, this company, Brinker, especially *all the employees here*, are guided by a man called Tische, head of TruVereinsbank.

They were going to receive that shipment, extract the uranium, and, somehow, make it into nuclear fuel rods. Those rods could be used as replacement fuel rods in an IAEA verification accounting. Like a doppelganger switch, the fake rods for real ones. Swapping for real, secret, and deadly arms-grade fuel rods to make nuclear bombs. These new rods made of the old uranium, pretending to be expleted plutonium rods would sell to the highest bidder, possibly a rogue nation. We don't know who, yet."

The major held up his hand, commanding silence, "Who's we?" The major asked sternly.

Oh hell. Pero thought. Before he got to that, he needed to get assistance.

"Look, I promise to tell you, but will you please get the two men who abducted these two men? They went to the local hotel for the night. It's imperative they do not report to Tische. And for God's sake round up all the employees here and their families. Tische's real name is, by the way, Stasi Oberführer Heinrich Aue. I think there's a massive conspiracy here." Pero had realized there was no way the bosses or employees of Brinker couldn't have known what they were dealing with. "Look, the radioactive precautions they would have to take here, that they must have been preparing for, would mean they had to know—and had to be keeping it secret."

Schmitz turned and barked orders. Officers sprinted.

Give the major his due, Pero thought, *he is quick*. Schmitz had ordered the arrest of the men at the hotel and every person associated with the Brinker facility, no matter where they were—at home, in a car, anywhere. He gave his men and the local police twenty minutes to round them all up. "And in case you are wondering, Herr Baltazar, even the cell phones here have stopped working now, temporarily." He had a little smile. Pero was sure the landline phones were out as well. Schmitz was clamping down, fast. Pero was pleased and showed it.

"Okay, who am I? I was a simple film and television producer, traveling the globe, sometimes I was supposed to help out the CIA in passing along a document. Instead . . ." and he explained it all. While he tried to present the evidence as he knew it and events he had experienced, his mind was searching for something, something just out of reach.

Pero knew he needed help. The time for secrecy was past. But he also knew there was an important piece missing from events . . . where would the fuel rods be made and who were they to be shipped to? And had others been shipped out already? Now that Heep and Danny were safe, he thought that his part of the job was done—someone else could do the tracking from now on. *Let someone else track down the loose ends.* He was to be proved wrong.

Pero sat on a guard's chair as the medic massaged salve on his neck and continued to tell his tale. Danny and Heep stood over him, their trousers still smelling of urine. They didn't care, they were alive. Pero didn't care, they were safe. He felt exhausted, on an adrenalin downer, but he finished the telling.

Danny patted Pero's back and said, "Hell of a partner, you are. Far as I am concerned, I am certainly lucky to work with you, not the other way around. Damn, but we'll use all this." He meant in the filming, in the script.

Heep walked in front of Pero and kissed the top of his head. "That's for Mary, too."

Since he was done explaining, he asked the major if he there was any way he could call Berlin to tell them Danny and Heep were safe. It was 6:30 a.m., and they would be worried stiff.

"No, Mr. Baltazar, I think we need to prepare our plan of attack before we do that. You see, before your friend Negroni called me, I had a call from a friend of mine in the States, your Mr. Lewis. He asked me to, how do you say it? Ah, yes, to lend you a hand, not much more. I would say he was less forthcoming than you were, but he did say you are new to this level of operational activity, although he has trusted you for minor work for thirty years. The Kenya story was interesting—especially Mr. Mbuno there." He nodded and smiled at Mbuno. "I find your honesty refreshing. Maybe we can catch these *ungeziefer.*" (vermin). He said it with conviction. For Pero, the cavalry had arrived.

But Pero felt he needed to check in with Lewis. He needed information that Lewis should have by now. With stray thoughts still bouncing around his head, he realized there was still a mystery to solve.

Chapter 14

Schönefeld

Pero figured the satellite phone would work despite the local cell towers being blocked by the police. Standing outside the Brinker factory with the direct satellite antenna up and working, he dialed, put the phone on a Police BMW hood, and keyed speaker to "on." He put his finger to his lips to signal silence. Danny Redmond and Heep, now dressed in Police overalls to change from their urine soaked clothing, stood next to Sergio, the major, Mbuno, and Pero. They all listened intently for the connection to Langley while a Brinker factory wing behind them burned. It was a minor fire that Major Schmitz had started to create a plausible diversion for the fire and police activity to placate nosy and concerned local citizens. The plant was locally known to house toxic chemicals. The fire made a good cover. It destroyed an electric tower of no consequence, and could be reported in tomorrow's papers to be the reason for the telephone blackout for the region.

Unfortunately, the sound of the firefighting wasn't loud enough to disguise Lewis's anger. As usual, he wasn't pleased with Pero soliciting non-professional help, namely Sergio and Redmond, and telling them everything. "Baltazar, how many more people have you involved now?"

"I've lost count. But we did rescue them and as Negroni could probably buy the CIA and Redmond could help get a President elected, perhaps you should be more grateful. And, anyway, you called Major Schmitz . . ."

"Yes, but I didn't feel I had to tell him . . . oh, no. I am on speaker again aren't I? Damn, Baltazar, you might warn me."

Pero answered sarcastically, "Oh, dear, so sorry."

"Yeah, well I have news for you. You all it seems. Mr. Redmond, you are under oath not to ever repeat any of this to anyone, get it?" Danny said that he did. "We suspect that there's more than irradiated gold involved here . . ."

Pero had to interrupt him. It was too embarrassing having Lewis tell Major Schmitz something, again, that he had explained not ten minutes ago. "Ah, Lewis, they know all that, a third of a ton of Uranium 234, to be used as sheep dressed as wolf in heavy water pits to skew the IAEA verification accounting somewhere."

"How the hell did you know that?" Silence from Pero. "Hmm . . . Professor Turner figured that out, and you didn't tell me? Why?" Again, he didn't answer. Then, "You think I would have forgotten about Heeper and Redmond, given them up as collateral losses, lost the priority of saving them?" The silence on Pero's end must have been annoying Lewis. "Okay, okay, well maybe greater priority would have kicked in and they might have been not the number one priority. But you took a chance with world events that you had no right to take."

"Charles?" The major addressed him by his first name, "André here. You are right, you should have been told, just as you should have told me the truth about all of this. But let's deal with what we have now. We have rescued the men, and we have proof against Tische. We have arrested, or my men are currently arresting, all the employees of Brinker. I suggest you arrest their agents in the States as well."

"Agreed, André. Will do."

The major continued, "We captured the two ex-Stasi in the local Banhof Hotel, the ones who took them prisoner, kidnapped them in Berlin. They are being held on criminal charges, international criminal charges, but we still do not have the police sample, the bag of liquid, back to re-open the case in Zurich. And we still have no way to proceed to determine where these materials were going to be made into fuel rods Baltazar is talking about. I take it you agree with that scenario? The fuel rods I mean?"

"Yes, our experts and," Lewis emphasized this for Pero, "*upstairs* agrees this has the highest probability and is a number one priority for every government office worldwide. We must find where these were going to be made into rods and where they had been already sold and were going to be sold. And the history of all those dealings. Tische's prosecution is unimportant until we find that out."

Pero chimed in, "As you probe around wasting time, Tische will disappear into the woodwork like his father before him. He's Tische today, he could be Aue tomorrow . . ."

The major interrupted, "You seem obsessed with Tisch . . ."

Lewis cut in, "He's right. If Tische gets away, he'll revert to his father's real name the next day. The red line file I told you about? It told me the truth about Tische. The man he called *Vater* was a very high-ranking SS officer: Oberführer Josef Spacil, former head of Amt II of the Reichssicherheitshauptamt, known as the RSHA, the head Nazi Department of Security, in Berlin. He pretended to be an army sergeant, Joseph Aue, to get captured by the US, not the Russians. He knew what the Russians would do to him—slice and dice him, no doubt, for his activities in the Ukraine in 1943. But in Allied prison, he was identified by a fellow SS officer and re-arrested by CIC, by one Adam Fellars, commanding Detachment 307, on June 16, 1945. He tried to bargain his freedom with a one million dollar—real 1946 dollars—gold cache. Remember, gold was thirty dollars an ounce back then. CIC turned him over to the newly forming OSS secret activities group, later to become the CIA in 1947, Fellars again controlling the money. Fellars also controlled the Japanese money MacArthur recovered and hid from our Federal Government. This money became the backbone of CIA clandestine ops. In 1964 when Tische's father died, in Stuttgart by the way, still under the false name and papers the CIA provided, Aue, as he was then called, defected to the East. He rose to prominence quickly, adopting his real name, Tische. We suspect he used secret gold still hidden in East Germany or Czechoslovakia to leverage authority. But he was also a secret double agent for us—secret even from most people here at Langley."

Lewis took a breath and continued, "So, he rose to become the third overall in charge at the Treuhand. He was a useful double agent. He did hate Communism. When Treuhand became westernized, he moved over to the West. He apparently was still helping to manage hidden assets and provide corporate assistance to our operations." Lewis could hear the men in Switzerland making disapproving comments, "Yeah, I hear that. Look, no one here is proud of this, and I wouldn't be telling you any of this unless there was now an urgent mandate to break him. And, frankly, if the DG wasn't likely to resign tomorrow, anyway. The Senate has called for hearings, beginning on Monday." Two days away.

Pero had to ask, "You said, real name Tische . . ."

"Yes, his adopted father, Oberführer Joseph Spacil had a daughter only, his wife died of typhus caused by living near one of the disease-riddled death camps in the Ukraine that he was in charge of. He adopted a Jewish boy there, Jewish father, non-Jewish mother, a Pole. Names were Jerome Tische and Hannah Tische. We don't know how, but Spacil took their son, made him his."

"But Lewis, that's incredible! A Jewish boy, orphaned, is raised by an SS officer who later supposedly turned CIA informant? Then this boy becomes an agent himself, working for the very people his adoptive father opposed in the war? Does this make sense to you?"

Mbuno chimed in, "Animals do not behave that way."

"Mbuno, is that you? You there too? Oh, good Lord . . . Well, he's not an animal, although he may act like one. He's an opportunist, grabbing what he can. He saw a way to fame and riches and took it. Although analysts here now suspect the driving force is something else, power mixed with idealism. He may still be a Nazi."

"How high did his father get . . . what's the Amt II division you spoke of?"

"You don't get any higher. The head of Amt II was in charge of the Nazi program to expatriate so-called 'Enemies of the State' and Jews and expropriate the possessions of the deprived persons—gold from teeth fillings, for example, paintings, anything. Spacil was in Berlin when Hitler killed himself. He kept a blood-soaked flag as a souvenir, said it was taken from around the Fuhrer's body. It was stolen when Spacil died. He was in Gestapo headquarters, Berlin, ordering mass exterminations from June 1944 on."

Pero suddenly realized that the man, the father, Aue, was a killer, a serial, mass killer. How much of that had rubbed off on his son? "Where was the boy, Tische, during 1944 and 1945?"

"In Berlin, a dedicated Hitler Youth, defending Berlin. He was caught by the French stabbing a soldier in the dark."

Pero knew, then, where Tische's love of the stiletto had come from. "He was arrested as a minor, never tried, held, and then released, on good conduct in May of 1946. He joined his father in Stuttgart, under our umbrella, our care."

Major Schmitz had a question for Lewis: "Charles, we know the uranium material was to be ground up, smelted maybe, here and shipped, but we can find no shipping containers suitable for such radioactive material. Just the usual airfreight containers and truck containers. There are rail wagons as well, but they don't seem used, much."

Pero had an idea. "Where are these wagons, Major?" Pero had been looking across the runway. The major pointed to the side of the Brinker complex at the closed garage doors. Pero continued, "Are your communications blackout orders effective for the whole region, including that factory over there?" He pointed across the runway at the dark hulk a half mile away.

"Yes, all of Schaffhausen is incommunicado."

"Lewis, you still have that list of TruVereinsbank companies? Can you read the companies, starting with the letter P to me, please?"

"One moment. Here it is. Okay, it starts with Pi . . ." Pero stopped him. It was too obvious. Excitedly, he said, "Mbuno had it right, the hyena keeps all the same meat in the same place." Adrenaline flowing again, he pointed. "Major, that's your extruding plant. I'll bet the train tracks connect to there. Place a third of a ton of uranium beads, now mixed with cadmium and cesium, into an old wooden rail truck, push it across to the robotic watch components' factory, have them extrude the metal, truck it back here, and fly it out. Very low tech in a sense, almost no human hands involved, very safe, and no public roads. Who's the head of that factory? Who owns the Pi watch company?"

The major called a lieutenant over and asked him to find out. He got on his army radio. The men stood around looking across at the factory lights now coming on in the early dawn in preparation for the first workers to arrive. They all stood there listening to the slight hiss from Pero's speakerphone still connected to Lewis. They all watched the distant little harmless sodium lights starting to illuminate the Swiss watch factory. The lieutenant came back, "Frau Renate Spacil is the Geschäftsführer."

Lewis chimed in, "Oh my God. Remember that Spacil was the Oberführer of Amt II. His daughter, Joseph Spacil's daughter Renate, is now the head of Pi watches, is that possible?"

Sometimes the obvious is overlooked, but sometimes it is too good to ignore.

The major barked an order to a lieutenant, "Get the army, use my authority, seal that factory, no one goes in or out. Anyone there or arriving there, hold them, no one talks, no one calls, use force. Now!" The lieutenant took off running toward the radio setup.

* * *

Pero knew that belief is a fundamental trait of humankind. It is what separates mankind from animals. They used to say it was opposable thumbs, but other creatures have alternate ways to manipulate with dexterity. Then they said it was the ability to communicate, but any dog owner will tell you dogs do the same, as do dolphins and whales, even if it is not with the same refinement as humans. Then they claimed it was the ability to dream or imagine, and then science showed that dreaming and imagination are essential to any cognitive thought process, so even ants had that one licked.

But the ability to believe in an abstract principle and to dedicate your whole life and your children's lives to that process, that seems to be a human characteristic. At times, it is a dangerous one.

* * *

Thirty minutes later, in the sleepy village, only three miles from the Pi factory, the major set another fire, this time to a car on the street outside a very luxurious house with old world charm. That early in the morning, the sounds of the crackling gas and windows shattering, combined with the stench of burning rubber awakened the whole street. While the fire department doused the flames, uniformed officers went from door to door, politely knocking, asking whose car it was. The major and a uniformed officer knocked on the door of the closest house and, as it opened, rushed and grabbed the man who kept asking what they wanted. They silenced him and handed him to more uniformed officers. From behind them, four of the major's best men rushed the house. It took only minutes to secure the rooms and floors. The occupants included: one maid, one servant, the butler they had captured, and Tische's adopted sister.

Renate Spacil was seventy-five if she was a day. Tall, thin, elegant, and blue-eyed (gone to blue-gray with age). She commanded the room. Admittedly, it was her rococo living room, but even disturbed from her bed, standing there on the silk carpeting, she had a presence they all could feel. Her German was *hohes Deutsch*, the aristocratic German of the Weimar period before Hitler. The Nazi elite spoke *hohes Deutsch*, thinking it gave them class to hide their bestiality. Her English was also starchy and precise.

"What is it you wish, gentlemen?"

Major Schmitz stepped forward. "Madam, you are under arrest."

She reached for the phone, "And what is the charge?"

"Do not touch that phone." She removed her fingers, folded her hands in front of her nightgown. "Treason and other such crimes to be determined. You will be placed in custody presently." He was waiting for a female officer to take her in charge.

"No, I will not. You will regret this intrusion, Major. When you have finished your bluster and bravado, you will allow me to call Judge Remke who will order you to leave me alone."

He decided to shake her confidence. "I am glad you mentioned him. He will now be arrested as we speak." He snapped his fingers and a junior officer left the room hurriedly.

Her eyelids fluttered once, twice, and she resumed her calm composure.

Schmitz continued, calmly, with authority, "Now, you will sit, and when the policewoman arrives, you will be completely bodily searched, your staff will be searched, and your house will be torn apart. We will find everything. We have your brother . . ." again the eyelids fluttered, "so your *übles geschäft*," (evil business), "is at an end." With that, she exhaled and sat, waiting, beginning to look somewhat vulnerable, an animal who realized she was trapped. The years had, perhaps, weakened her father's indoctrinated resolve.

Mbuno's words came back into his head at that moment, so Pero said it aloud "The hyena always has a special place he keeps food." Heep and Major Schmitz nodded.

Pero kneeled before her and said, calmly, "Renate, where is your father's flag?" Very fleetingly her eyes darted to the left and then came back to rest on her hands folded in her lap. It was so brief. If he hadn't been watching only her eyes, he wouldn't have seen them dance. He walked over to the ornate Viennese chest of drawers, with a pink marble top, and pulled on the ormolu handles of the top drawer. There, in a glass box, folded Swastika uppermost, was Hitler's flag, the icon of their true belief intact, now a family tradition, an icon still to be worshiped.

As he lifted it out, Renate sprang up and threw herself at Pero—all one hundred pounds and seventy-five years, like a screeching banshee, "Nein!" Schmitz grabbed her and muscled her back into her chair. Schmitz didn't like Nazis, not even old woman Nazis. He almost struck her. The uniformed officer stopped him.

The woman officer arrived, and she handcuffed Renate Spacil and led her away. Schmitz ordered, "A thorough body search, everything." Then he commanded his twelve men present to sweep the house, "Everything, nothing is to be left to chance. This man here," he pointed to Pero, "has a theory that has proven correct again." He pointed to the glass case with the flag. "Examine that most carefully and everything else that is in this house. And I mean everything."

Having given orders, the major strode out into the morning and waited for Danny, Mbuno, Heep, and Pero to pile into a police car. They proceeded to the landing strip and Sergio's plane. When they got there, Sergio looked better. "It just a little bump really." He laughed, but no one else thought it funny.

A call came from Lewis as they gathered at the steps of Sergio's plane, "Baltazar, urgent matters. The man who tried to impede you, the one Mbuno shot? He was a contractee of the agency, British actually, ex-SAS, one of six given authority to take orders from Tische—everything authorized by upstairs. Five of these agents are still at large. We cannot recall them, we don't know how. Sorry about that." He made it sound so casual. It wasn't. Pero's neck still hurt. "Another thing, we have lost sight of Tische and can offer no additional assistance in Germany. The only four service people we can count on are protecting your people there at the hotel. The rest may be riddled with ex-Stasi spies reporting to Tische. We can't take the chance of using the police for the same reasons."

Pero was now angry. They had let Tische escape. "Lewis, unless Tische is in custody, this thing is not over. You have no idea what you are playing with. These people are not desperate, they are fanatic—worse than the al-Shabaab in Kenya. First, unless we get something out of his sister, he's the only one who knows—or is our lead to—the whereabouts of other caches of gold and/or uranium. Or what—or if—he has already sold and to whom. Second, he has CIA agents at his disposal as well as ex-Stasi. Our friends are at risk. Third, he used the term 'we' several times when threatening me. I don't think he was talking only about his sister, although that may be partly true. You had to see her reaction to me touching their Nazi flag. She was absolutely crazed. I suspect we're talking about a legacy here, a legacy from his SS father for the Fatherland. Whether it's the money or the disruptions and chaos such third party bombs would cause, leading to an opening for a new world order, again, I have no idea, nor do I care. What I am absolutely sure of—and I am sure Danny and Heep now also will agree," they were nodding before he said it, "is that he is a fanatic, part of a fanatic organization of Nazis left over from the war. Cut off the head of this snake and there's another there to take its place. Catch him, interrogate him, break him, and you stand a chance to catch the network. You guys at the CIA permitted this, it's time you put a stop to it."

"Nice speech Baltazar. I happen to agree, and I have no doubt the Senate will agree in hearings next week. But what are you going to do now? Your mission is over. Hand the sample to the major and let him take over."

The major, standing next to Pero, looked at him questioningly. Pero hadn't remembered, until then, that he still had the evidence Schmitz needed. "Nope, I am not going to give the major the sample and retire from the field." The major tilted his head, puzzled. "I am going to take it to Tische as planned. Something tells me he'll turn up. Then we'll get him. Look, Lewis, if we don't stop him now, what are you going to do when another uranium swap is made or perhaps has already been made? Without catching him, without breaking this ring, the whole world is in danger. There is only a day left to catch him. If he thinks I can give him the sample, so he can stop the impounding of his gold and uranium in Swiss customs, then he'll turn up, I know he will. The bag is the only link to him and the uranium. If he gets it, he's legally clear."

Mbuno spoke up, "Hyenas never give up their prey."

Pero nodded, "Right. He still thinks he's got Danny and Heep, so he'll be sure I'll turn up. He knows he'll get what he wants. His ego would not permit failure. He sees me as weak. He knows I value them more than any package I am carrying, even if I know what it is. We have only this one chance to catch him."

"Who will you get to help you?"

Pero looked around. "I have friends here." Everyone nodded. "And I am including the major. Stay out of the way, Lewis, we're going to finish this mission. Tische must not get away." He closed the phone, severing the connection and looked at the men around him. To show his good faith, he took the Russian bag out of his pocket and handed it to the major. As the major started to open it, Pero placed his hands over his as Sam had done for him, and shook his head. "It's too hot, too dangerous."

Schmitz looked around at Danny, Heep, Mbuno, Pero, and Negroni and calmly said, "Ja. Berlin in March, it's cold and damp. We had better be going."

Sergio Negroni had a headache, but he said he was fine to fly. Danny Redmond was typed—trained and certified—on his own Citation private jet, a lot smaller than the Boeing 737, but, banged up or not, he was more than useful in the right seat. Sergio and Danny seemed to hit it off. Heep, André Schmitz, two of his men, Mbuno, and Pero sat in the leather seats and strategized all the way to Berlin's third airport, Schönefeld

* * *

Berlin's Schönefeld Airport was built as the Henschel Aircraft Works in 1934. When the Russians took over the region, seven miles south of the center of Berlin in 1945, they blew the whole place up in a spectacular fashion. Henschel's were bombers used to help kill 500,000 Russians during the war. At first, it became a Soviet Air Base and then, as the years went by, Aeroflot and East German Lufthansa began to fly in and out of there as well. The runway was long and ATC was better than the alternate airports. After the fall of the wall in 1989, the airport fell into relative disuse since Tegel was more modern.

But for private aircraft, Schönefeld was perfect. Sergio and Danny filed a flight plan and with authority being given by Major Schmitz, no Swiss authority asked questions.

Cell phones have a bad reputation in the air. They do cause interference to instruments, especially GPS and other navigational aids. The interference is problematical, especially in older aircraft without proper radio shielding in the cockpit. Sergio's BBJ was brand new. Cell phones worked fine.

Heep was, thank God, back to his old self. Schmitz allowed him to call Mary in Florida. It was a tearful conversation, but it made him less anxious.

Meanwhile, Mbuno talked to Amogh and all was going well there. Mbuno made sure the two morani guards he had asked to protect Niamba in the hospital had shown up. Amogh said they had, and everyone was frightened at first because the morani were carrying five-foot spears, in the hospital. The administration had tried to get them to leave, but Amogh had everything sorted out just fine. Niamba had found it all amusing. Mbuno seemed relieved.

As the sun's first light rose over Lake Constance, they took off. Pero knew they were flying, a short flight of less than an hour, into Tische's stronghold. Schmitz explained that for anyone not familiar with the power of secret police and illegal organizations, it may be hard to understand the dread one feels. Like confronting a great white shark. You know it will bite first and ask questions later—or simply finish the meal. Facing an all-or-nothing opponent, you either win or lose, there is no compromise. "If we go up against Tische, we go up against his whole organization; there will be no mercy from them." The SS and their successors, the Stasi, were known and feared for their ability to enter any battle with this mentality. Pero had no illusions about Tische, the blood lust he had shown in the museum concentration camp railcar, the pleasure in the lust to kill, well, Pero knew Tische's desires to be real.

Lewis and André were on the speakerphone, again using Pero's cell phone. Lewis was explaining, "But we may not be able to contact these men, the very nature of their job was to act on one set of command-and-control instructions until completion." They were talking about the CIA contractees, under Tische's control.

Schmitz was adamant, "You must keep trying. Can you send a text message to their phones? How about one from the DG?"

"Okay, André, I'll try that, but would you expect them to listen to a countermanding text message?"

"No, maybe not . . ."

Pero chimed in, "No wait, Guys, you don't want to call them off. If you do, Lewis, Tische will bolt and we'll lose him. Let him think he's still in command. I wish there was a way to make them accessible when we want, not when he wants . . . the last minute, tell them to back off, that sort of thing."

"Baltazar, that's the best idea yet. André, we'll tell them the report times have changed, direct to the DG's office. I'll put Bergen on it. We'll have them report in every thirty minutes . . . that's the best we can do and still maintain Tische's illusion. Agreed?"

Pero stopped him, "No, make it twenty-six minutes. I want an odd number they will know is odd."

"Why Pero?"

"Because if I have to confront one of them, I'll know something specific, it may give me the split second I can use to stop them." Pero was fingering his neck. Would the assailant have stopped if he had said twenty-six minutes?

Danny shouted back from the cockpit and said the plane was passing over Ulm. Pero asked Lewis, "Any news on the field agent missing around Ulm?"

"Yes, not good I am afraid. He was found dead at an autobahn service/gas station, in his car. He had no visible wounds except one—the flesh on his chest by his heart had sloughed off, literally peeled and disintegrated."

André looked puzzled. Pero asked, "How long did he have the package?"

"Best we can tell, three or four days. He posted it, internal mail from Ulm to Phillips in Berlin."

"Did he have a gun holster?"

"Let me see . . . yes he did, no gun though, didn't like working with one."

"The package killed him. He must have had it in there unshielded." André, who had the Russian bag next to him on the table, moved to the next seat. "Relax, Major, that's a Russian lead ball bearing bag. Sam says it'll hold for a while."

Lewis voiced concern, Pero knew because he used his first name: "How long did you hold the bag Pero?"

"Not long enough, I hope. Sam gave me and I am taking, iodine pills, ex-Chernobyl issue, again from Sam."

"Christ, sorry."

André wasn't sure if he should be sitting next to Pero either. "Herr Baltazar, you take risks I am incapable of taking. I am, how do you say it? In awe."

"No, Major, stupid, just plain stupid and," he paused for effect with Lewis, "The CIA dumped this on me."

"Okay, Pero, enough with the lectures. I said I was sorry, okay?"

"Actually Charles," he called him by his first name, "I just like making your life miserable. You did all right under the circumstances."

"Thanks, Baltazar." Using his last name no doubt meant he wanted to get back to their professional relationship. "Hang on, something is coming in, or should I say someone."

They heard a door being buzzed open and voices. "I have Baltazar on the line here with Major André Schmitz of Switzerland, head of their Internal State Security division. If you want to address them . . ."

"Hello? Can you hear me?"

Schmitz responded, "Yes, we're at 34,000 feet over Southern Germany making our way to Berlin. Who's speaking?"

"The director general of the CIA. Okay, I'll get right to it . . . even though you've done a great job there, what you have done to American prestige and standing internationally is inexcusable. I order you to stand down and return to Washington immediately."

He made all on board instantly angry. Pero responded, "The Swiss major as well?"

"Obviously not. That you Baltazar? No, just you. And bring along that actor and your Dutch friend, we'll want words with them as well."

"Is that an order?"

"Yes."

"Bullshit. You can kiss my ass. Sorry Lewis, but who in the hell does this clown think he is . . ."

"You, you . . ."

"Shut up DG. I hope this is being recorded for the Senate. You empowered a Nazi and the Nazi's son to handle secret funds, outside of Senate or Congressional control, and then you gave him our agents to kill other CIA agents to protect his identity. You were too stupid to know about his uranium side-line, thereby undermining SALT I and SALT II treaties and the IAEA. Reagan is spinning in his grave. The media will have a field day. So, just who harmed America? And you have the gall to think you are going to call me on the carpet? Guess again."

"CIA DG? Major Schmitz here. We're making a full report to the IAEA and the World Court, I'll be sure to mention your name, personally."

The phone was silent. Some noise like a slamming door was heard from Lewis' office and then nothing.

"Lewis? Is he still listening?"

There was a chuckle, "Oh, no, Baltazar, he left. He went purple and left. He may be resigning tomorrow, but today you've made one powerful enemy there."

"Bergen here, I got it all. And if you don't spill these beans, Lewis, I'll have to admit to the Senate Foreign Relations Review Committee that I have the tape. I have been making loads of copies, just in case. This has gone far enough."

"Oh, yes I agree. So much so that I partied in a third party—a White House special counsel. You there George?"

A distant, cold, deep voice answered, "Yes." Nothing else.

"Tomorrow should be interesting Baltazar. You've kicked this sleeping dog and shot at it as well."

"What was the DG going on about when he said *what you have done to American prestige and standing internationally is inexcusable*? How can what we have done be considered damaging to American prestige and standing?"

"Oh, you don't know . . . Ambassador Pontnoire, the fellow whose plane you saved? Well, he issued a State Department three red line," meaning ultra-secret, "report to the Senate Intelligence Committee. His report explained that he had learned that the CIA was using Nazi extermination camp gold-teeth ingots from US Treasury assets. He also pried into his CIA resident's reports on the package and added, in his report, that the Treasury was involved in illegal shipments of Uranium to circumvent IAEA verification to rogue nations. He even gave you credit Pero, saying that the plot had been uncovered by one Pero Baltazar. Overall, that's why the Senate told the DG he had to resign effective tomorrow. The President agreed. Oh, and the President's only angry comment, that we got here internally, was that you, perhaps, might consider reporting to his office in the future so he didn't have to get the news after the fact. That right George?"

Again, that cold, distant voice, "Yes."

Pero, although shocked that his name was being used, he nevertheless knew he had to get them all back on track, "Well, we still have Tische to go."

"Oh, come on, still going through with that? I am not sure it's wise. We'll get him."

Pero looked at the major and Heep.

The major answered for them all. They had been strategizing, planning. "The fish is on the line, we want to reel him in now and also see what other fish we can catch. To do that we need a favor. Allow us, the Swiss, to prepare to release the shipment at Zurich airport—start issuing shipping paperwork. Let them think they can make off with it, we'll track it—we know where it is going and if it doesn't go there, the Brinker factory, we'll uncover another secret. But, most importantly, it will give Tische a sense that he is winning—with only the sample that could incriminate him. He needs that sample. I need him to focus on his weakest link, the package. We plan to give it to him."

Lewis wasn't so sure, "When that happens, he'll call his men to kill and remove Heeper and Redmond's bodies. He'll get no reply, he'll know . . ."

"No, he won't. Communications in and around the Bodensee region—Lake Constance to you Charles—is broken. The papers tomorrow, sorry, this morning, will show a pylon, a tower, fell down in Schaffhausen cutting off phones, all phones. If he sends a message, he wouldn't expect a reply. His sister is a bigger problem, but we let it be known to the newspapers that, in the dark caused by the blackout after the tower fell down, the head of the great Pi factory in Schaffhausen, Frau Spacil, was injured and is in the hospital. She really is in the hospital. It was the only secure place we had for someone of her age and condition. She has a bad heart. We want her alive, to question her. Before this call to you, my men had received a message from Zurich that they had found a series of microdots in the glass flag case. We're working on those now."

Pero thought and Mbuno nodded, reading his thoughts, *the hyena keeps all the same meat in the same place.* Pero looked admiringly at Mbuno.

Moments later, Sergio, popping two Panadol tablets for his headache, prepared the plane for landing, with Danny assisting. Pero took the opportunity to call Susanna to give her the good news but warned her to keep it secret. She assured him they weren't going out of their room for any reason, so it would remain safe. Sam had arrived and was working with Bertha on chemical analysis to help identify the radiation signature in rogue nations' atomic reactors—spotting the fake rods, the sheep in the wolf's bath of heavy water, was how they put it. She would tell Bertha and Sam the good news.

What Pero did not explain right away was that they were still going after Tische. Somehow, he was sure Susanna would not be happy to hear that.

Chapter 15

Potsdamer Platz

As the plane dipped a wing, settled, corrected, and then resumed gliding down to Berlin on final, Pero called Susanna back again. He explained that they were landing and would soon be on the way to help with a plan and with reinforcements. She was greatly relieved. There had been two attempts on them in the past hour using room service and maid service, neither of which they had ordered. The two men guarding them, Bernd and Wolfgang, were armed and determined. When the real maid knocked and let herself into the suite, Susanna saw the guards draw their guns, so she and Bertha ran into the bathroom and laid in the tub for protection while Sam guarded the bathroom door. After getting rid of the maid, the next people to arrive were the real police. Some of them were the nice cops from the shoot, so Bernd and Wolfgang decided to also ask them to help.

When the two women and Sam emerged from the bathroom, all they could see were six armed men in the living room, so they went back to the bathroom and decided to stay there. So far, everything was okay. After all, it was just over twenty-four hours since Pero had left and Heep and Danny had been kidnapped. Susanna explained that other than the three of them in the bathroom of Danny's suite, there were the six police in the main part of the suite and all the film crew in the sixth floor lounge with two other guards, both police force friends of the friendly police from the shoot.

Pero thought, correctly, that Tische would expect Pero or perhaps an assistant to put protection on for the crew. It wouldn't scare him off. Tische would, hopefully, see it as depleting Pero's resources. As far as Tische knew, there was only one free agent not under guard—Pero. Tische would feel sure he still had Danny and Heep, and certainly, he would have no knowledge of Sergio, Mbuno, or Major Schmitz as long as nothing leaked from Schaffhausen or Washington.

Sam's arrival might have worried Tische. But perhaps he hadn't gotten a good ID on him yet. If he did, he might assume the man from CERN had come to collect the package. All the better for Pero's plan because it would confirm, in Tische's mind, that Pero hadn't gotten to CERN and still carried the package.

Sam had been frisked and scanned with a hand scanner when he arrived at the airport, so he was clean. Tische might know that if he was looking for someone from CERN. But Pero hoped it was just a carpet sweep, not a target for Sam. In the event he was right.

Susanna told Pero that Bertha and Sam were still getting on like comrades of old. They finished each other's sentences when talking physics and chemistry. Susanna had to admit when pressed by Pero, who asked her how she fit into the conversations and calculations, that Sam thought her command of mathematics was "almost as good as your sister's." She was shy about it. Pero was impressed.

Pero explained to the men aboard the plane that he would need her special microphone for the meeting that night. His problem was that he dreaded telling her he was going after Tische. Added to which, he needed cover to get in and out of the hotel—if he could at all. In his head, the same worry played out again and again, *If I were Tische, I would hijack me either coming back to Berlin, trying to get to the Steigenberger, or at the restaurant rendezvous Tische has prepared at Borchardt's, whichever comes first.*

In discussions during the flight, all six of them had decided it was safer to assume that Tische would have eyes and ears everywhere. Schmitz agreed, "If he controls the ex-Stasi police, then he's got resources of over a thousand ex-East Berlin police officers and ex-Stasi. He can watch everywhere."

Arriving at Schönefeld airport, Danny took over and taxied Sergio's plane over to the Globe-Ground VIP apron. He shut it down, lowered the stairway, and lead the team into the suite of waiting rooms. Government officials and corporate giants use those services daily. However, seven-thirty in the morning was not their usual time for an arrival, especially one that was unexpected.

Sergio's presence fixed all that. The plane's tail was brightly lit, and Pero thought *well, it's not everyone who has a Boeing BBJ more plush and more capable of flying long-distance than even the German Chancellor has.* So, Sergio put his credit card down, Amex Black, and said to charge anything. Airport security was present in the form of a sleepy inspector, no police to be seen. The uniformed private security agent stared at the passengers who were all avoiding direct facial scrutiny, pretending to be rich jetsetters uninterested in minor functionaries. Sergio and his guests were all clinking champagne glasses in private conversation when the official was told by Schmitz, pretending to be a butler, that Herr Negroni was only there for dinner in Berlin that night and would be leaving. Presto, the customs agent left.

No passport control was necessary since the major had arranged for the Swiss ATC to tell Berlin ATC that the plane was inbound from Friedrichshafen Airport, on the German side of Lake Constance. Their clandestine flight cover was intact. Berlin customs and immigration had no cause to investigate. Tische would not have anticipated the take-off airport switch even if he knew Pero had access to a private plane. So, they felt confident their presence was secret.

Once the minor official left, they discussed the need for transportation. Pero said, "We need a plan for Tische's meeting later on. But before we can decide on that, any way I look at this, we have a problem of Danny being recognized. And then there's the problem of us getting into the hotel and then out to dinner without Tische knowing where or who we are. And with the bag."

Sergio was watching Pero, who had a makeshift napkin ice bag on his scalp wound. "Figured it out yet, la loutre?" Sergio smiled then frowned, "But you know Pero, something is bothering me. How did the DG get named by Pontnoire in his three line, red whatever Lewis called it, message? Pontnoire's the anti-Nazi ambassador, right? So, I get that he was rooting out Nazi sympathizers, he's been open about that in the press. But how did Pontnoire know about the gold and the Nazi connection with the CIA?"

Pero nodded. "Lewis mentioned that the local CIA Station man reporting to the ambassador would have told him about the gold and uranium, so he'd be informed about local issues. Local One is the name for the ambassador in any city."

"But how did Local One know to name the DG?"

It was an obvious question, Pero realized and felt stupid, shaking his head. *Typical of the businessperson to focus on details.* The answer eluded Pero. But it gave him an idea. He called Lewis.

"Baltazar here, can you patch me through to Local One, Berlin?"

"You're kidding. No way, your mission is over, we've got orders. White House says so."

"Ah, so I guess I'll have to call Local One on a land line?"

"Well, you have a cell phone and the embassy is in the directory, but I am advising you not to call them, repeat not. I've told you four hundred and two times not to call."

"Uh-huh, I got that. I understand. Out."

"What did Lewis say?" André wanted to know.

"He gave me the ambassador's extension number."

In Germany, offices and large organizations, even hotels, secure a short phone number ending in a zero and build a phone switching system for themselves, like a mini-phone company in the basement. Then, say you are in room 601, all you do is tell your family that your number is the same as the hotel number, but to leave off the end zero and replace it with 601. They can dial you direct, without the hotel operator answering.

The American Embassy number in Berlin is 8305-0, so Ambassador Pontnoire's direct number was 8305-402. Simple as that. Pero dialed, speaker on.

"Pontnoire."

"Mr. Ambassador, Pero Baltazar here . . ."

"Ah, the man himself, the deadheading Delta pilot. Quite a ruckus you've kicked up ever since. Your discovery has had, ah, repercussions."

"If you call getting the DG of the CIA fired, you're right, but that may be your doing. How did you know he was involved?"

"Security personnel here are under my authority—but they were also taking direct orders from him, not the usual chain of command. The people here tell me everything or else I have them transferred to Greenland."

Pero and those listening smiled, "Okay, but now I need your help in getting the ringleader, TruVereinsbank Geschäftsführer

Tische. He's the one who's ex-Stasi. Can we talk without Washington knowing the gist?"

"No, I cannot promise that. I know Tische, don't care for him or his history much. However, on the secrecy front, I feel compelled to tell you that for at least three days I won't be sending any briefs back to State. Seems my report at the Senate has made me something of a pariah."

"Yeah, welcome to the club. The CIA—no, sorry, the White House—has ordered us to stand down. And those are orders we are expected to obey. However, we want this bastard."

"What about your two comrades, Mr. Heeper and Mr. Redmond?"

"Okay, can I trust you? I guess I have to . . ."

"You can, you should, and I do you, so please proceed . . ."

"They are here next to me. Thanks to Sergio Negroni and a daring raid, we rescued them." Pero was adding fuel to the Sergio fire of fame. "We also have a Swiss Major Schmitz and two of his colleagues—definitely not Stasi or Nazi—here to help. Problem is, I've been advised that there are five agents from the CIA, contracted operatives, attached to the man we're after, and they may or may not be able to be called off."

"Yes, I got some feedback the CIA had been supporting him. What do you propose?"

"The man we're after wants a sample of radiated banknotes . . ."

"What? Explain."

"Mr. Ambassador, it's a long story, here's the précis . . ." Pero ran through events. When he got to landing in Berlin, he turned back to their needs, "But if Tische gets the ex-police evidence that I am carrying, what the CIA called a package, you know the one?"

"I do."

"Well, he'll think he's in the clear if he gets that package. He doesn't know we've rescued Danny Redmond and Heeper, that we've got the shipment under close watch in Switzerland, thanks to major Schmitz, and that we've rounded up his people in Switzerland and his sister—who was, by the way, helping to run the operation."

"You're kidding. You've been busier than I was lead to believe."

"Mr. Ambassador, may I ask you who tipped you off to ask your people for the DG and CIA connection?"

"I was told you would ask, and the answer is no. Let's just say an advisor to the President owed me a favor."

"Okay, but are you willing to help us a bit more? We need cover. You have security, especially because of your anti-Nazi position, security that are not going to be ex-Stasi either."

"They're not, of that I am sure. You want to borrow them?"

"If possible, maybe two? The meeting place with Tische is at a restaurant, Borchardt's, tonight at eight. If we could seal the place and capture him, we would have an asset we could leverage for all the names, or at the very least, we could sever the head of this snake."

"I can arrange that. Two men. Anything else?"

"Can I send two people to your office or the residence and have you keep them there, safe? I need them out of the line of fire—and to keep Tische from finding out they're there safe. And away from danger."

"Names for the security people here?"

"Bill Heeper and Danny Redmond—but please no leaks."

"Ah, the rescued. Okay, no leaks. Guaranteed. I can arrange for them to be safe here in the embassy official residence, but I cannot control them if they want to leave, it's policy . . ."

"Understood, that's up to me—to convince them. I'll do that. And thank you." The two men then arranged the time for Heep and Danny to arrive at the ambassador's residence, confirmed the address, and the ambassador agreed that his men would be at Borchardt by 7:45 having dinner. He'd get them a reservation, no problem, clear the restaurant if need be. He ate there often, with journalists, so he knew the staff. Borchardt's is the haunt of journalists and actors.

Pero was formulating plans as he spoke. He turned to his friends, left the phone on speaker and said, "Okay, the ambassador is on board. Sergio, I know you want to be part of the action, but you're my wild card here. I need you to act, be free to move, clear of me—certainly not associate yourself in any way with us, to provide cover and lodging. Then, at the last moment, turn up with the major's two men, unexpected, at Borchardt's at eight tonight. Can do?"

"Yes, but . . ."

"Sergio, listen. When we leave here, Danny, Heep, and I with the major, I need you to wait and then make a splash entrance in Berlin. Something separate from our activity. Your usual fanfare arrival, limousines, hotel—the best, the Adlon would be good. Book an extra room for your guest. They'll assume it's a mistress. Be there around noon. And then, when we're all ready, you'll turn up to dinner. You will become, by your very normal presence, invisible to Tische. It's the only way I can see you getting in and clear—transparency. You won't be on the agents' or Tische's radar—getting into the restaurant on time and with reinforcements."

"Okay, Pero. I get it, come ready to assist but be unknown to Tische. I'll get a full readout on him. I have good computers on board," he indicated the plane out the window, "and I'll be ready." Pero was sure there would be photographs of the head of the TruVereinsbank on the Internet. *Why wouldn't there be, he is a public figure of good standing.* But Sergio needed to ask, "Who's the extra room for?"

"Me, if I can make it. No check-in. Your cloak of invisibility should work."

"*Fantastico*, it'll work just fine."

"Danny and you Heep, I need you to stay out of sight. If Tische sees you, the game is up."

"We could stay here in the plane . . ."

Sergio answered, "No, there's no way to protect you. Too many people will be here during the day servicing my baby."

Pero agreed, "And there are five agents on the loose with orders from Tische. The blackout in Schaffhausen will make him nervous . . ."

Mbuno chimed in, "The hyena always starts to look about, nervous, he can smell something's wrong, but he's usually too determined to change his course."

"Hyena Mbuno?" Heep looked at him intently. "You still think he is really a hyena?"

"Interesting," said the ambassador on the speakerphone, "And who exactly is Mr. Mbuno?"

"A Kenyan safari guide. My brother." Pero watched Heep's eyebrows rise. "The hyena link, Mbuno gave me the idea, Mr. Ambassador. His advice was to search my thoughts for the animal Tische reminded me of and track him that way. Hyena came to mind for me and Heep." He faced Heep, "Heep, you know how they keep all their food in meat lockers, caches? It's how we narrowed it down to Brinker's."

Heep was impressed, "Damn. Hyena's meat locker, huh? Yeah, it fits."

Danny was looking confused. "Somebody want to try to explain this again?"

Heep responded, "I'll explain it all to you Danny on the way to the ambassador's residence. That right, Pero?

And then I'll explain it to you, Mr. Ambassador," Pero nodded. Heep continued, "It's a thing Mbuno does, relates all human-animal behavior to nature. Damn thing usually works too. Hey, Pero, how're we going to get this famous face," he pointed to Redmond, "through Berlin unnoticed?"

Sergio had the answer. He went out, up the plane's stairway and into the back of the plane and came back with sunglasses, winter parkas with hoods and fur edges, and Ugg Après ski boots. "A little overdressed for Berlin in March, but it'll cover almost anything."

"Yeah, only my red nose sticking out." Danny laughed. He toed off his shoes, slipped the left boot on, reached over and took a flat bottle opener off the bar, put it in the right boot, and slipped that on. "Let's hope I don't have to walk far. Damn thing hurts." He finished dressing and Heep did the same. "See you soon, Mr. Ambassador."

"It'll be my pleasure, Mr. Redmond. Over." And he clicked off.

"One last thing," Pero addressed them all, "if I get caught, don't hesitate to get Tische anyway you can. Something about the prepared elaborate planning here tells me this is a huge operation Tische has going, has had for decades. I am pretty damn sure this is not a one-off." No one responded. The thought had occurred to them as well.

The major was to take them to the residence and then proceed alone on to the hotel, to Susanna, Bertha, and Sam. Mbuno and the Swiss guards would travel with Sergio.

As Pero changed into a pair of Sergio's pants and a sweater, he was glad no one pressed him on his plans. They were at risk and solo. He knew his face was the one Tische would want his men to look for. Nab Pero and there was no need for a restaurant rendezvous. However, even with the beginning of a plan, his planning wasn't completely clear in his head yet, and he feared it would need changing on the fly anyway. He would have to deal with one issue at a time. No doubt the five Tische controlled agents were calculating Pero's odds of evading recognition and capture at the same precise moment. He needed to outwit them. The problem was, they were experienced field operatives, the real journeymen or, perhaps, assassins. Pero had no illusions. His plan called for a diversion.

He decided his first stop was to be Kaufhaus des Westens, locally known as KaDeWe.

KaDeWe has been, like Harrods in London, the centerpiece for elegant shopping in Berlin since before WWI. Situated on the fashionable Kurfurstendamm, the store occupies a whole street block, is nine stories high, and sells everything. The place is always packed, although elegant, refined. The crowd was easy to get lost in. Since the 1920s, locals have always shortened its name to the acronym, KDW, or pronounced in German, *kah day vay*. Finally, the store gave in and changed its trading name to KaDeWe, pronounced the same but written as a logo.

March was liquidation of excess stock time. Pero knew there would be loads of unwanted winter designs and colors on sale.

Pero had to make some assumptions. With only five men, even with additional ex-Stasi, Tische couldn't cover every entrance to Berlin. Pero assumed he would watch the regular airport—Tegel—and the train stations as well as the Steigenberger Hotel and any other place Pero had been, including the museum and the aquarium. So, wearing Sergio's spare camel coat—he had a whole wardrobe back there—with the Russian bag in his pocket, Pero turned up the coat collar and simply walked out of the airport.

Next to the airport was the head stop for the S-Bahn. Pero bought a ticket, inserted it into the time stamping machine—*ding*—checked it was dated, and went up the stairs to the platform for the S9. It was sitting there, doors open. No one else was on the train. Before the doors closed, as he waited for the departure time, two men got on in gray-blue worker's clothes, a black coat over the top. They were discussing the most recent football scandal where someone had taken a bribe to throw a match. They got in the same carriage two doors down from Pero.

The S-Bahn departed and trundled along. He looked at the *fahrplan*, the timetable, adhered to the ceiling like a giant label. He counted the stops. Everyone who rides subways does that. Ten stops before he would need to alight. People got on and off. He paid no attention. Even if someone got on looking for him, it would be one heck of a fluke if they spotted him in the eight carriages out of the thousands in Berlin, at this particular time, on this particular stretch. If fate was being that unkind, he realized there was little he could do.

Ten stops later, the speaker announced his stop "Ostkreuz" and he got off and looked for the transfer to the other S-Bahn, S3 train. Down the steps, hurry along with early morning workers, up the steps, the S3 pulled in, everyone waiting got on. The train was getting crowded, working people mostly. Pero stuck out in the camelhair coat, so he sat, looking hung over. Two women made disparaging remarks about him being unshaven. *Have to do something about that*, he thought.

"Die nexte halt ist Warschauer Strasse." At the next stop, he had to change.

The train slowed, the doors opened, and he waited and then made a dash for the door. No one else made the last second jump. He found the steps down for the U-Bahn connection. This station was the head stop for the U1, direction Uhlandstrasse. The train was waiting. He got on and studied the map, again. Ten more stops. The train was filling up. At the last second, two men got on. They looked about, pointed past Pero, and walked over. The people they knew made room on the red and black vinyl bench. *Still clear,* Pero thought. The train trundled on the elevated section through the morning mist before diving into the tunnel.

"Die nexte halt ist Wittenbergplatz." This was his stop, coming up. He didn't stand, he waited. People started to assemble by the door, their eyes focused on the little white circle with the red lights on each door. When they went to green, you could touch it and the doors would open. If no one wanted to alight, the doors stayed shut, keeping the heat in.

The driver applied the brakes, and the train slid to an almost stop. U-Bahns always seem to be still moving when the doors are opened by passengers pushing the green door lock release button. People began to alight. Pero made a last second dash for the exit and suddenly saw, in front of him, a man watching the train. He had a small photo in his hand. Pero stepped back inside as the doors closed. Pero was sure the man had not seen him, so he turned his back to the doors. The U-Bahn sped away. Pero's fear came on with equal speed.

"Die nexte halt is Kurfurstendamm." It was the end stop. He should have known someone would have been posted at the Wittenbergplatz stop—it was closest to the hotel and Los Angeles Platz. Damn, so is Kurfurstendamm. Somehow, he needed to get off this train undetected.

The U-Bahn he was on was made up of several shorter trains linked together, one driver up front. There was an extra driver's compartment in the fourth car. He quickly made his way there, through the adjoining doors, getting looks as he went along. He didn't have any intention of trying to open that driver's door, but it was the only solid wall in these trains of glass that he could hide behind. *Damn, I'm hiding like a rat trapped in the corner of a barn.*

The train slid into the station just as he stepped behind the driver's compartment, his back against the wall, breathing pounding in his ears. People got out, everyone he thought. No one got on, but he wasn't sure. He had stopped breathing. The speakers were giving instructions. He didn't listen. He was listening for the sound of recognition.

The doors closed, and the train went forward into the tunnel and a switching yard, lights out. He was alone. In a few seconds it stopped, and he heard the driver making his way back through the length of the train to take his seat at the other end. The U-Bahn N1 was about to go back the way it had come. So Pero pretended to be asleep on the seat, arms folded, slightly snoring.

In his street German, the driver woke him up with, "Hey, wake up, you can't sleep here." He asked where Pero was going and for his ticket. Pero showed him the properly stamped ticket, and he seemed satisfied. Pero explained he had been up all night and was going home, late. If it was okay, he would ride back and get off at his stop. The driver said it was irregular but agreed it was okay. He walked away.

Pero was alone in the darkened car. His thoughts were whirring. *How the hell did Tische have so many people covering the stations? Did he own Berlin?* And then it came to him. He remembered that the men, his watchers, were all police, probably ex-East Germany police, following orders, and maybe they could give orders to non-Stasi police. It caused him to rethink his plans. Sitting in the car, waiting for the train to start up, he realized he would have to be especially careful approaching the Hotel Adlon later that morning. If there were that many pairs of eyes searching for him, if he was followed, Tische would gain the advantage.

In a few moments, the lights came back on and shortly after that, the train moved off—screeching across the points to change tracks and head back into the Kurfurstendamm station. Pero peeked out the window. He knew there should be no one watching on this side, it was a head stop, the train coming into the station empty, so it would be easier to watch the steps leading to the platform in case anyone wanted to get on. On the opposite incoming platform, a man was standing tapping a photograph on the knuckles of his left hand. Pero spun around and resumed his fake sleeping position.

He realized he couldn't get off at Wittenbergplatz, the stop nearest the hotel where the crew was staying. He figured Tische's force would be watching both sides of the station there. So he went past the station he wanted and headed toward Nollendorfplatz. He peered carefully through the scratched glass. There was no one around. Getting off swiftly, he went up the stairs, onto the street, and walked back, passing the Wittenbergplatz and the station by skirting the edge, watching windows when someone seemed interested and, generally, acting the tourist. At one point in his new fright, he had thought of going to the hotel but going over his plans made in the airplane, had realized that was impossible, it would draw too much attention to his whereabouts, making Tische's job easier.

Now, seeing how many eyes Tische had, he realized more than ever he needed to create a diversion. His plan had been simply, to change appearance, disguise himself. Now he knew a real diversion was the only way.

He went into the side entrance of KaDeWe. He thought he could be certain there would be no one in there to spot him among the crowds. Sales were on and the store was already packed.

On the third floor, there was the rack with the same day-glow green jackets the grip had bought for him . . . When was it? *Oh God, only two days ago.* Pero took twelve of them, on hangers, and went and paid. He used the cash he still had on him, trying to avoid a credit card trace. The coats were on sale, a bargain price he felt. They were Tommy Hilfiger licensed winter goods on sale for March. *Not bad at the price.* Trivia seemed comforting in his stressful situation.

Pero had quickly formulated a plan, and the coats would keep several people warm, if a little harassed. KaDeWe packaged them up in their thick dark blue and black signature bags and he went to the sixth floor and bought a suitcase, a cheap one. Pero kept all the receipts in his pocket. He repacked the coats into the suitcase and left the building. At the door, he was stopped. He produced the receipts and got an apology. He didn't mind. He did look disreputable, unshaven for two days.

Wait a minute, I can take care of that here too. He went to the perfume counter and asked if he could get men's aftershave. "Certainly sir . . ." and he was led away to the Hermes counter. He changed his mind, rubbing his beard. *No point in aftershave without a shave . . .* The counter assistant suggested the fourth floor, electrical goods. He went back up the escalator, found the shaver counter, and bought a cheap portable one with batteries. By the time he had descended the escalator to get his free sample dose of aftershave, he was clean shaven— even though the escalator passengers were scowling at a man shaving in public. Leaving the aftershave counter moments later, he finally smelled better too.

He was stopped at the door again by store security, which raised his fears once more. So much for blaming his shifty looks on the two-day beard. KaDeWe security for shoplifters was ironclad. He showed the receipts again, and he was allowed to exit.

In the street, his heightened fear made him cautious. He retraced his careful path to the Nollendorfplatz station and rode the U2, direction Pankow, four stops to Potsdamer Platz, the old center of Berlin and now a student and tourist heaven.

As the center of the New Berlin, Potsdamer Platz was normally crawling with police. If they had his description, they could only have the one with the day-glow green winter jacket. It was the only one Tische and the agents on the TGV train had seen. He was hoping they didn't have anything more recent. The Day-Glo coat description was his secret weapon.

Outside the Mies van der Rohe-inspired Potsdamer Platz train canopies, structures that looked like giant black metal tables with glass tops under which the mice—humankind—went about daily lives, he set up shop on a granite stone wall. It was almost 11:30, early lunchtime, with plenty of foot traffic. He saw several uniformed officers, usually in pairs, but they were more interested in traffic movement, bicycle paths, and people not allowed jaywalking. Berlin is strict on jaywalking.

Opening the suitcase, in his best German, French, and English, he said, "Show your student card and get a free Tommy Hilfiger jacket!" In ten minutes, he had a crowd, in three more he had a traffic police officer telling him to knock it off. Pero didn't care, all twelve jackets were being sported, admired, green day-glow outside, as he had helped each student put them on. He watched as many of his green gang made their way into the various station openings, two of them taking the escalator down to the U2 line. He gave the last one the suitcase as well.

It was a pathetic diversion, but it might confuse long enough to use up Tische's resources and allow him to meet with Sergio later at the Adlon. He followed two students and walked the two blocks to loiter in the Arcade, a shopping mall, pretending to look at the shops. He planned to speak on the cell phone, just like every other modern normal businessperson.

He keyed Susanna's number and asked if the major had arrived. He had. Susanna was trying to teach him the intricacies of the microphone. But that wasn't the first thing on her mind. First Pero got a tongue-lashing.

"What do you mean by not telling me what you are doing? We are sitting here worried, we hear Danny and Heep are safe at the ambassador's residenz, the major was *most* informative, but you . . . you . . . you promised, and you broke your promise."

"What promise was that Susanna? Didn't we free Danny and Heep?"

"Yes, but you also say you would keep safe and to come back. He is here, der major, why are you not here?" Pero wasn't sure how to feel about his own reaction to this tirade. He was, on the one hand, flattered that she cared. It was a long time since any woman cared that much. It was in her voice. On the other hand, didn't he have enough to worry about? *Give me a break*, was on his mind. *Oh, hell.* So, instead he merely said, "Yes dear," a bit sarcastic.

"*Ach*, stupid man, it is not a game." And she left, handing the phone on to Andre Schmitz.

"She's really, really angry." And he laughed. Pero heard Susanna telling him off in swift German. "Yes, she's really, really angry." At that point, he heard Susanna laugh and what he guessed was Sam and Bertha as well.

"Can I speak to Sam?" Schmitz passed the phone. "Sam? I heard some disquieting news. An agent who had the package for about four days died. Horribly."

"Radiation poisoning?"

"If you can call it that. He was found dead, and the skin and tissue around his heart, his chest, was all decayed. The best guess is that he was keeping it in a shoulder holster under his armpit."

"That doesn't make sense, Pero, that film bag was a toy, but it should have reduced the radiation by, I think, a factor of twenty or so. Still . . ."

"He didn't have the film bag, just the sample."

"Oh God." He paused, thinking, he could almost hear the scientific wheels turning. "He would have had brain swelling as well. All his systems would have begun to go critical within two days. His skin was . . . what . . . shed like a snake's?"

"Something like that."

"Then he died in agony, started twenty-one to thirty hours after he held that bag unprotected."

"Okay, but here's my question to you: why would Mil Intel or the people in Mannheim—what did you say they were, atomic trigger experts? Anyway, why would they give him the package without any protection?"

"If they did, Pero, they meant him to die. That's murder, plain and simple. One more thing, my man," he meant Bergen head of communications at the CIA, "found out that Brinker has had metals exchanges with North Korea, made several last year . . ."

Aghast, Pero almost shouted, "What? How is that possible?"

"Brinker is Swiss, they are neutral. Nothing being transported was on the embargo list, just some lead and, get this, aluminum rods." Sam paused, someone was talking to him, and Pero could hear him explaining again. He came back on, "The major says he'll lead an immediate investigation. Lord, Pero, do you think that's where that regime got the fuel for their bombs?"

Pero was still shocked, "I guess so . . . We really need to catch this bastard. Stopping him is not enough. Listen, ask the major to find out all he can about the microdots—he'll explain. We need to know if we have enough leads . . ."

"Want to drop the plan to capture Tische?"

"No, I am sure not, but what happens if we lose him? No Sam, we have a plan, we want him physically and legally." Pero asked Sam to give the phone back to Susanna. They talked about the microphone and she suggested that she come and fit it to his lapel and that she would teach him how to handle the recording functions. He told her that the microphone would be on him, but Schmitz needed to have the controls. He wanted her to teach André how to use it. He explained he was sure it was important that a police officer made the recording, to use in court. She gave in, reluctantly. "It means you will not come here now."

"Susanna, I cannot, there are Tische's cops, ex-Stasi no doubt, everywhere. I tried to get off at Wittenbergplatz and just spotted two in time. I can't come there. It would be too easy for Tische to capture me or maybe lead killers to you. There are five we know of in the city, taking orders from Tische, but I suspect he has the regular police helping as well, at least for identification. We're setting a trap, at Borchardt's, and then it will be all over. You're safe there, Bertha is with you, Sam is strong, and you have two capable guards."

"Nein, we now have six. The local police have joined us. Bertha is famous. They want to serve her. They know each other, no one new. Two were the ones who didn't like that Stasi officer at the Technisches Museum. The others are their friends."

Pero was pleased there were so many reinforcements protecting them. "That same Stasi officer is probably the one orchestrating this gauntlet for me. Okay, you are safe, right?" She was forced to agree. What he didn't want to deal with—not now, not yet—was that she wasn't only worried about being safe herself. "Just, please, be patient a little while longer. Please put the major back on."

"Mr. Baltazar?"

"Ready to leave André?"

"I will be in about twenty minutes. Susanna has to go over the controls one more time, then I'll be ready. Where will we meet?"

"At the Hotel Adlon, on Unter den Linden. Take a taxi. I was just going to call Sergio. He should have a room, an extra room, ready by now. I'll get the room number and call your cell phone with the number."

The major was skeptical. "Is that wise? The Hotel Adlon?"

"For Negroni, it's the perfect place. Top flight, luxury, it would be expected. Also, it's a three block walk to Borchardt."

"No, I mean, you getting into the Adlon, undetected."

"Look, the Adlon was a Communist Intourist Hotel, very grand, loads of stairways, lots of crystal—and tons of servants' entrances. The place is like a sieve. When they hold galas and functions there, they need four times the number of guards, just to cover the fire escapes at ground level. And the luxury shops have their own entrances to the street and into the hotel. It's like Swiss cheese when it comes to security. Now, the floors, they are secure, cameras, staff, everywhere. But I'll be with Negroni, which should be okay."

"So you calculate getting in, for you is no problem?"

"I think it'll be okay, there are too many entrances for them to watch."

"How do I get in?"

"When I call, I'll give you the room number to Negroni's mistress' room, just come up and bring something you are delivering, maybe flowers. Got to go." They hung up.

Pero shivered involuntarily.

Eyes squinting, without being seen, he was watching a man follow a green day-glow jacket. The student he had given it to took off his cap as he entered the heated Arcade entrance and the man following spotted red hair and turned away. How many people did Tische have on call? This was miles away from anywhere he had been before. It made Pero more nervous. More than nervous, afraid.

He had to get to the Hotel Adlon safely. The route, from there, was straight: over to the Brandenburg Gate, down Unter den Linden, number seventeen, and enter. Sounded easy. He realized it might not be. With his eyes only, not turning his head, he followed the man who had checked out the student and saw him stop to talk to another two men. One had a photograph in his hand, the other wore a raincoat with a belt tied in a knot. Even from this distance, Pero could see the man was muscular and capable. The chiseled facial features were a giveaway. Pero needed to go out the back of the Arcade.

Halfway down the length of the mall, he turned right, went through the doors, and followed the narrow alleyway toward Potsdamer Strasse and the Sony Center. He looked left and right, crossed against the light, an offense in Berlin, onto the grass median and then jaywalked again into the FilmMuseum Berlin, embedded in the Sony Center. Fortunately, no traffic cop questioned him.

On the ground floor, he bought a ticket, like any tourist, and went up to the museum exhibit entrance on the second floor. He got off the open glass elevator, walked to the left and around to the steps, walked down a half flight and waited and looked through the clear glass side of the eight-floor building. He could see the entire internal plaza of the Sony Center, with its giant glass umbrella suspended magically over the top, the fountain playing in the center, tourists everywhere. The sun had come out, and people were eating lunch sitting on the stone bench diagonally across the center. Two of his green jackets were present. One had a tail. The tail grabbed the jacket, the girl wearing it turned and the tail let go. He could see Tische's agent's arm gestures apologizing from where Pero was, a floor and a half up.

What Pero hadn't calculated was that once the call went out that a green jacket had been spotted. Tische's men would converge on the spot. As more and more sightings were made, they converged in greater numbers. As he was, stupidly, still in the region, he had brought them to himself. *Idiot*, he thought. His diversion had backfired. He was sure they knew that if they had asked even one student, it was a man of his description who had handed them out. The camelhair coat was now a liability. He needed to change it.

The FilmMuseum Berlin houses one of the great collections of pre-eminent art form of the twentieth and twenty-first centuries: film. People going to museums like to eat. Downstairs was a trendy café named after the Berlin and Hollywood director, Billy Wilder, with posters from his films—*The Fortune Cookie, Some Like It Hot*, and others—decorating the walls. Pero went down the galvanized open steel stairs for lunch.

There he hung up his coat on the communal rack, sat, and watched who came in last, about his size. When Pero paid his bill, he left and lifted the other man's coat—a gray-black wool business coat, three-quarter length—instead of the Sergio's camelhair one. On the street, he found a cap in the pocket and put it on and, with nerves jangling, blithely walked past the man in the raincoat who was still scanning the Sony Center. Pero hurried toward the Brandenburg Gate two blocks away.

Passing the Holocaust memorial, with its granite blocks looking like dense, but hollow, tombs, representing the millions who died, he called Sergio. Sergio answered first ring.

"I lost your camelhair coat. Sorry."

"That's okay, you still in one piece?"

"Yes, too many close calls. There is a ton of security everywhere."

"I know, even my passport was scanned by the front desk—police orders—when I checked in. Mbuno's passport made them double check. That may not be so good for you if Tische knows Mbuno's name. I put him down as my safari guide. And they want me to give them my mistress' passport when she arrives. They claim it's a terrorist threat warning issued by the police. What the *Americani* call Red Level."

"He's got contacts and power, that's for sure. Is the room available?"

"Yes, I've got the key—Room 822, next to mine, up here under the eaves. But, Pero, it would be better if I get a woman to check in there first. The electronic key will tell them someone's in the room, lights and so forth trigger computer responses, your every comfort taken care of." Pero knew what he meant. If you turned off the room air conditioner these days and opened the window, the front desk would call up to ask you if everything was all right with the room. You change something, they know. Use the key, they know.

"I don't know what to do about that Sergio."

"I do, but you're not going to be happy. I've been talking to Sam."

"And?"

"A woman will be here in about twenty minutes. Unless you say no. You come on over and up to my suite, 824. You are Signore Lontra. I told them I am expecting you. Oh, and I brought fresh clothes. And a razor."

"I did the shaving part already, spent the morning shopping. Okay, we'll do it your way, I am on my way."

Passing down the east side of the Adlon, the line of luxury shops was impressive. Pero chose a jewelry shop, browsed and bought a fancy key ring and walked out of the store using the back door, into the Adlon foyer. He held the brightly wrapped box he had just purchased like a talisman. It said, to anyone watching, he's conducting normal business here.

Pero walked over to the elevators and asked the bellhop standing there if he could get him the room number for Signore Negroni's suite. He went away, and a manager came back, black tails, looking officious. Pero explained what he wanted.

"And we are?"

"Signore Lontra, I was expected." The manager bowed his head. He already knew her name. They are efficient at the Adlon. The manager himself pressed the call lift button.

Lontra means otter, in Italian. It was all Pero could do not to smile standing next to the manager, awaiting the elevator to open. *Sergio is still such a kid.* The doors finally opened, and the manager waved for Pero to enter. Reaching around the door-jamb, the manager stuck his elevator card in the slot, pressed number eight, and wished Pero a good day.

"Grazie monsignor gentile," Pero said in Italian, completing the farce.

On the eighth floor, he walked left to Sergio's suite and knocked on the door. Sergio opened the door and saw that the major's two police officers were there with him, guns drawn. Pero went in.

"Pero, you have got to come listen to this . . ." Sergio walked over to a small Grundig radio on the table in front of the couch and chairs in his living room. The radio was on a police band. The babble was constant and perhaps a bit comical. "They've got sightings of a man in a green day-glow jacket coming from all around the city. So far, they are all students. Something about a man in a camel coat handing them out. Genius, pure genius." Even the two cops were enjoying Pero's ruse. The discomfort of their fellow officers was amusing to them.

"Well, I needed a diversion. Problem was, I attracted attention, too much attention, and before I could get away, I saw the usual local cops being directed by a man in a raincoat, very tough looking. I suspect he's a professional." Pero meant an agent or one of Tische's ex-Stasi men. "They're looking for a camelhair coat now. Poor fellow, I swapped this one with, he might have a tough time until they know it's not me."

"So, what's next?"

"I need to talk with the ambassador, make sure he's got a reservation at Borchardt's. Have you?"

"I don't ever make one, I don't want to start acting differently now. They'll seat me. But Pero, what do you want us three to do when we're there?" He indicated the two officers.

"Right now, I am not sure. It's a matter of an opposing army. If they have loads of people, we need loads of people. I don't want a war, but I don't want to be a pushover either. I want to get out of this alive. All I need to do is get him, on tape, to admit to kidnapping. Then the police can have him, right there in the restaurant—and squeeze the bastard for the rest of the information. With you and these two officers—thank you, by the way, in case I haven't said it before," they did that little Swiss-German head bow of recognition. "Anyway, with the ambassador's two men with the major, we'll have six. And don't forget, the ambassador's two men are in the system here. If they yell police, then the police must respond in his favor—ex-Stasi opposition or not, Tische's power base or not. Agreed?"

"Sounds right, especially if the ambassador is there."

"I was worried about that. He's a risk taker, and it sounded to me as if he left that possibility open. Frankly, I'd prefer if he's not there, it's too great a risk."

"On the other hand, Pero, my guess is that the man is running for President in two years . . . Don't look so shocked. Why do you think he hasn't fought his forced retirement and why he's always pushing the media? Anyway, my guess is that he'll be there." Power politics was Sergio's world. Pero trusted him to know.

"Okay, then we'll be seven with a high-profile ally. That might help if any of those five agents come into play or lord knows how many other ex-Stasi foot soldiers Tische has. They would have to be really stupid to take an order to act against the ambassador. The first five we know about from Lewis are ex-CIA or CIA contractees. Let's hope they can think for themselves."

"Pero, not everyone is like you. The real professionals don't think as much as act." The phone rang. Sergio answered like he was in Italy: "Pronto? Ah, please escort her up to my suite and have the maid turn down her bed, immediately. Danke." And he hung up.

"Sergio, who's this?"

"My mistress, the Countess von Trappe, and her bodyguard. I just bought her a fifty thousand Euro coat to prove it—the manager went personally to pay for it for me."

There was a knock at the door and the manager, clicking his heels in servitude, showed a big puffy, arctic fox clad, vision of beauty into the room followed by her bodyguard, André. "Carissima." Sergio oozed. The manager left, backward.

She stood looking at Pero. He stood there, dumbfounded.

"Hello, Pero."

Chapter 16

Borchardt

Pero wasn't angry. Susanna had expected him to be. But he needed to know how their change in plans would affect his planning for the rendezvous with Tische. If Tische now connected Susanna to the Adlon and Negroni, that element of surprise was lost. It was the major who had solved the problem and explained.

"I arrested her. I put the cuffs on her and with the two friendly police officers, summoned up a police car and hauled her away. We went to the airport and checked her in on the next flight out, like a deportation. I saw several confirming people making sure, you know ones I was sure would report to the police and then on to Tische. Susanna went through control and security, and she was waiting for the Swiss plane that would take us to Switzerland. I had extradition papers—faxed openly to the Hotel Steigenberger. The police and Tische, no doubt, will have a copy of the papers by now. Susanna Reidermaier wanted in connection with the theft of industrial secrets related to recording systems."

"How'd you get away?"

"Down the steps. Passengers went into the plane. The first class curtain was drawn as we boarded down the Jetway. Instead of boarding, we walked down the Jetway side steps to the cargo area on the tarmac, then around back, into the police car. We were lying down while they drove at breakneck speed to a suburban taxi stand. Then a taxi to the furrier Sergio had called and a quick change for me too and then a limo, blackened windows, again thanks to Sergio, to here." He was really into this cloak-and-dagger stuff. "And how do you like my new coat?" He spun around, the fine tailoring evident, Sergio's money proving useful again.

"Don't get cocky, Major, these guys are killers. You think it's all okay? No tails?"

"I am very sure." He got serious. "I know my job. The arrest warrant was real. The plane ticket and check-in were real. Susanna looked terrified in handcuffs, and the Swiss flight has us as 'on board', arriving," he looked at his watch, "in about twenty minutes." If they check that end, then perhaps they'll find out. But I doubt it. First, I have officers in Zurich sealing the plane and keeping people waiting while they "remove the prisoner" supposedly in the cockpit, behind the curtain, which will remain drawn. Second, one of the flight staff will be wearing Susanna's coat or one like it. It's a silly ruse, but should work."

"Okay, sorry I doubted you." Pero took a breath, "You're here, now tell me the real reason you brought Susanna along."

Sergio and André looked at each other and then at Susanna. She spoke up: "Because, you idiot, I wanted them to. And I am the expert. Without me, your plan has no meaning. The microphone has to be on you, the major agrees so don't scowl. Now, let's get the SilkeWire planted on your jacket." Sergio showed her the clothing he had selected for Pero, and she set about sewing the thread into place.

Pero realized there was no point in fighting. She was here. "Susanna, do you have a second wire with you?"

"What do you need it for?"

"I was thinking, if he steals the bag," Pero held up the Russian bag, "then maybe we'll still get some sound from that."

"I have only one recorder receiver, so the channels would overlap, and we would have to be within radio range, about three hundred meters. But I have two senders, yes. But that bag, it is radioactive, nein?" Pero said it was, inside. "Then we will have to put a wire in the bag which feeds to the sender before the inside, how do you say it? Between the layers on the outside."

"How about a sock? Put the wire and sender in the sock, and I'll slip the Russian bag inside that."

"That will work, but any radioactivity and the microphone and sender will be kaput, you understand?" He said he did.

Sergio asked, "How much time have we got?"

Pero looked at his watch, "It's one-fifteen, so about five to six hours. From seven thirty on, all attention will be focused on Borchardt, so any agent in the field will be there or watching access points. I don't trust Tische's men not to hijack taxis as they pull up, nor do I think he would hesitate to have his agents lift me off the street right in front. They do have the corrupt police on their side, and I don't want to start a war, a gun battle."

"So, how are you going to get in?"

Major Schmitz had been looking at Sergio's computer printouts. "Do what he doesn't expect, hijack him from his office or from his home. See here?" He pointed at the printed map, "He needs to pass along the Französische Strasse coming from Friedrichstrasse or at least cross Friedrichstrasse. The plan could be to get into his car somewhere there. If two of you will help me." Pero nodded. Then Schmitz spent the next ten minutes going over his plan. Everyone thought it would work. And if it didn't, there was still the open restaurant option, find a way in and start recording.

Pero was tired. He needed rest, they all did. They needed to be fresh, even the major agreed. Pero asked, "Sergio, anywhere I can lie down for a while?" Sergio said Pero could take the mistress' room through the connecting door.

Pero lay down on top of the duvet on his side, not able to sleep on his stomach yet because of the stab wound. It seemed to be healing, but it was very sore after the previous night's physical activity. Just before he drifted off to sleep, he felt a body get in behind him. "Move over a bit." He did and Susanna put her arm along his side and her hand on his shoulder and they fell asleep, soundly, together.

Almost immediately, it seemed, Sergio was waking him. "Six thirty Pero, time you got up." Pero was alone in the bed. While he had slept, the major had catnapped in a stuffed armchair and looked disheveled. He was talking with Susanna, going over the radio controls. She was showing, helping him, thread the earpiece up his sweater and shirt. He practiced turning his head away so as to not show the wire too obviously. The earpiece wire was flesh-colored, a stage wire. The color would help hide it.

Mbuno was sitting, on the wide windowsill watching the street eight floors below, his tracker skills sharpening his eye for detail. Before he could be asked, he told Pero there was no unusual police activity below.

Sergio and the two police officers were sitting intently watching news TV and listening to the Grundig radio, set to the police frequency. There seemed less activity across the airwaves than before. Pero asked if there was any change. Sergio explained that the activity on the radio had been reduced. The police seemed to be calling off the general search, but perhaps only reducing the extra manpower. Schmitz explained that hopefully that would reduce Tische's forces—his closest police stooges and, not to forget, the five agents.

Pero wanted an update on that. He went to the window, opened it, and dialed up the satellite phone. "Lewis here. Go ahead Baltazar."

"Any progress on those agents? I would love them called off in about an hour."

"I repeat your orders are to stand down and cease and desist, I've told you twenty-six times. Any command being given for field agents to stand down in one hour have nothing whatsoever to do with you. Do you understand?" He was yelling but without, it seemed to Pero, any conviction.

"Yes, thank you. Out." And he hung up. Pero told the crew, "He'll order them to stand down in an hour from now. There's no guarantee that such an order will be effective. We just have to hope." As he pulled on his shoes, he added, "Look, if you come across one of them and have a chance to speak to them, you have a secret password, twenty-six. Lewis has confirmed the number has been given to them, I hope. Since twenty-six is a strange number, they will have to check it out. It'll at least cause them to hesitate. The moment they call Langley, they'll stop whatever they are doing, Lewis sounded pretty adamant."

Schmitz didn't tell anyone that he felt that there was no hope those agents would join their side. He suspected that the White House or CIA orders wouldn't permit that much support.

Berlin at night is magical. There are lights, shadows, mystery, and playfulness that is unlike other European cities. Strangers talk to strangers, looks are exchanged, no one is excluded from the atmosphere or, more accurately, from the anticipation that a party is about to happen, somewhere.

The Unter den Linden, leading to the Friedrichstrasse that, in turn, crosses the Französische Strasse—all these streets proclaim, "Be Berlin, come join the party." Couples walk hand in hand or arm in arm. People of every ethnicity, sexual persuasion, or religion are more than tolerated. They are the norm, not to be noticed as being different. After ten p.m. things change, only the serious revelers remain—those who do not have work in the morning. But until then, the streets are full if it is not raining, with people just happy to be out and about, on the town, like an Easter parade without the bonnets.

One of the places late night revelers gather in is Borchardt's. The restaurant has a high eighteen-foot ceiling with art-deco lights. There is a full-length bar on the left as you enter, ending with a small round standing bar for people waiting to be seated. There are decorative pillars rising from the floor to the ceiling, around which are seating alcoves and banquette sections all around the room. In summer, there is a little outdoor garden for dining, opening back onto the main dining room via tall and wide French windows. Any time of year, Borchardt's is noisy, boisterous, and intellectually stimulating.

People always gather outside Borchardt's door, some wanting tables, some hoping to see celebrities, always a few paparazzi, and some functionaries waiting for their lords and masters to be finished eating. The outside crowd creates the atmosphere celebrities crave—exclusivity and privilege given to those who enter.

At Borchardt's, at midnight, the next day's papers are handed out. Half the journalists who contributed read them to see how their words had been chopped. Actors read them for reviews and the earliest nibble at gossip. Writers check reviews, and bankers check economic forecasts. Before that bewitching hour, trendy people, intellectuals, and politicians gather to eat the plain but perfectly prepared food, drink, and smoke. Conversation drifts from table to table. It's loud but intimate, casual yet elegant, bustling but exclusive. It is chic.

Using his computer, Sergio pulled up dozens of press photos showing the make and model of Tische's car—Mercedes, black, stretch. Pero thought, *what else could it be? It's the modern day panzerkampfwagen!* There was the chance that Tische would get a police escort, but Pero and the major hoped not. Mbuno assured them, "The hyena male travels alone, he is always confident." Still, Pero knew Tische had agents aplenty all around.

A little before the deadline, on a walk-by to reconnoiter, Mbuno, in nondescript clothing, again bought by Sergio, spotted a few loitering professional looking men near the top of the block where Borchardt's was. Mbuno went back to Pero's dark doorway and identified them because there was nothing else on the block in either direction.

What Major André Schmitz wanted to do was illegal. He wanted to decoy the car to a stop and then shoot the car dead. Tires, engine, Schmitz didn't care. He knew that discharging a firearm was against the law and the police would arrive. Under Schmitz's instructions, Pero hoped to have Tische out of the car and onto the pavement by then.

Arresting Tische was not enough. They needed a confession. They needed to get him to a public place where he would feel safe and talkative. The cattle car had given Pero the idea. When Tische had the upper hand, he became talkative. Or at least that's what Pero hoped for.

What happened was even simpler. Pero was standing in the shadows of the YSL shop watching for the car. André, by then re-costumed in the standard Stasi leather jacket was on the corner. He stepped into the street tapping a Polaroid on the knuckles of his left hand. As Tische's Mercedes advanced toward him, André could see the man on the back seat lean forward to peer through the windshield. André started waving at the car simulating that he had something to say and the car slowed and pulled over. A car behind the limo honked and sped past, its driver gesticulating madly, visibly annoyed.

André walked up to the driver's and backseat passenger's windows as they both powered down. Mbuno ran out from his hiding in the shadows of the YSL shop to the driver's door, using André's body to hide his face and skin color from Tische. Mbuno stuck Sergio's nine millimeter Beretta in the driver's face.

André drew his revolver and pointed it at Tische, put his hand into the car, and opened the driver's latch as Mbuno moved quickly. Mbuno was an expert in close combat. The driver had lost consciousness before his head hit the empty seat on the right of the gear stick. André reached further in, took out the keys, and threw them away. Mbuno sat sideways in the driver's seat and aimed the gun at Tische as André withdrew, keeping watch up and down the block. Pero emerged from the shop shadows and quickly approached the car.

From down the block, two men were walking, quickly toward them. A gun battle was about to begin. André warned Pero.

Pero spoke quickly, "Herr Tische, I have what you want, you have what I want. Let's make the exchange, as planned, and you can leave without getting shot." Mbuno clicked off the gun safety.

Tische knew Pero would know that if he was shot, Danny and Heep were going to die, he was sure his orders would be carried out. And Tische was sure Pero and these other two would know that. But Tische wanted the bag as promised. Feeling he had the upper hand still, "You will not shoot. But I agree." So he got out of the car and barked a command at the advancing men, "*Verlassen sie uns allein*" (leave us alone).

Pero casually asked him if he still wanted dinner.

Tische declared through clenched teeth, lips pulled back, "Why not." It wasn't a question, more like an order. He did not seem to Pero to be a man who was asked many questions nor asked questions unless he had a purpose. He was used to being in command. Pero calculated that was the best way to put him at ease, remembering Mbuno's words about male hyena being "always confident."

Mbuno handed the gun to the major and walked off into the night seemingly away from Borchardt's. Tische's eyes flicked recognition, acceptance—Pero was sure he knew then who Mbuno was. The three of them, the major, Pero, and Tische walked the two blocks to Borchardt, past the two stalled men, who stepped back into the waiting small crowd by the entrance. When they walked into Borschardt's, brushing past three men in the crowded entryway, Pero and the major worried those three were also Tische's. One had a British raincoat on, no belt. Pero felt a bead of sweat drip down his spine.

Once inside, the major left their side and stood alone at the bar. Pero saw him keep a hand on the gun pocket and the other in his waist pocket where Susanna had put the recorder. Pero had an urge to lower his chin and say "Testing, one, two, three . . ."

The waiters fussed over Tische. They knew him well. He had a regular table on the far side of the room away from the hustle and bustle of the center of the room. Tische ordered a whiskey and soda and Pero ordered a glass of red house wine. The waiters placed the menus on the table and both men pretended to look at them.

"You did not check your coat, Herr Baltazar."

"Nor did you Herr Tische."

"Ach, but I do not have anything valuable in mine, and I hope you do."

Pero thought the time for games was over, but he still needed to pretend a little longer, "Look, Tische, this isn't a movie. I know what you want, and you know what I want. Why the hell did you take Redmond and Heeper?"

"It was necessary." Evidence. They had him. But Pero wanted more if he could get Tische to talk, Pero felt they needed to keep recording. "Leverage is always necessary to ensure the outcome. Oh, yes, I read that report on Kenya. You are adaptive, most adaptive, but the enemy there was stupid. We are not stupid. We have your friends and will have them tortured, most horribly unless I get what I want tonight. No promises, no delays. I get what I want or they get tortured. Day by day until they die. The sooner you deliver what I want, the better for them." It struck Pero then that this was a truly evil man.

Behind Pero's head, Tische was watching the door to the restaurant. Pero was watching the door too, reflected in the French window behind Tische. The ambassador was arriving with two men. Outside, the dynamic of the people waiting for a table or hanging around changed. Pero saw some of the men he had assumed were Tische's exchange glances. With the ambassador there, the possibility of any struggle on Tische's behalf changed, not in their favor.

Just as suddenly, two men, in American suits, who had been standing at the bar, one of whom was looking at his cell phone, looked at each other, shrugged their shoulders and left. Pero watched Tische's eyes follow their departure. Tische's eyes said he was not pleased.

The men who left were plainly not Germans. "Sorry to see them go? Your players?"

"Nein, yours it seems. Well done Mr. Baltazar. But the game is not over yet. Now my leverage also needs insurance. So I need more leverage." A man pushed his way in and advanced to their table. He was in full uniform. It was the *Polizeibeamter*, the ex-Stasi cop, from the Technisches Museum encounter. Tische greeted him, "*Abend, Hans.*"

"Mein Chef." He replied and sat next to Pero. He pulled out his gun, making sure Pero saw its nasty muzzle, and placed it under the table pointing at Pero's stomach.

"Hans will shoot you here. He's an officer. He can unless you give me the package now." It was blunt, no finesse. It was exactly what Pero should do before his position deteriorated any further—give him the package. Pero and Tische had seen the contracted agents leaving. Pero could only guess what was happening outside. What was happening outside was not Tische's concern. Inside, right there, at that table was his to command, and he was not about to be distracted from his goal.

"When you tell me where they are."

"Tomorrow, I will call, they will be safe until then. You have my word."

Pero paused as if he was making up his mind. "Okay. I give. Where will you call?" Pero reached for the bag inside the coat, in his jacket pocket. He pulled it out, the Russian bag holding the liquid inside the sock and passed it to Tische.

Tische studied the outside. Turning it over, studying it. Wondering.

Pero wanted that reaction, "It's what you wanted, now get out."

Tische's face darkened. He leaned on the table. Pero felt that intimate sensation of Tische's bloodlust again.

Tische grinned. "Ah, so, you know something I need to know. That was too easy. You will tell me what you know now or I will have Hans shoot you anyway."

Pero was incredulous, raising his voice, "You have a gun pointed at my belly in the hand of this crooked cop and you say it's too easy? I just can't make you happy. Can I Tische?

Okay, here's what I know, Herr Aue . . ." and he let it hang. Pero turned his head to talk to the waiter, who was hovering again, but he had seen Tische's shoulder move his hand that was under the table and it was going to contact Hans. There could only be one reason for that. Pero kicked his legs out and fell backward.

The bullet from Hans' gun pierced the wooden seat bottom of Pero's falling chair and went on to shatter the French window behind. Quickly, Hans stood, ordering everyone to sit, declaring that this was a police matter, he was apprehending a terrorist. Hans was watching Pero as he said that, gun leveled at Pero's chest. With his other hand, he was motioning Pero to stand.

From the bar, André took six quick steps over to Hans and chopped his hand upwards. The gun went off again—aimed at the ceiling—and then André jabbed him in the throat cutting off his air. The police gun clattered to the floor.

Still lying on the floor, Pero noticed feet passing by his head, people panicking and heading in every direction. André, as he subdued Hans with handcuffs, handed Pero the small metal box containing Susanna's digital recorder and nodded toward the kitchen. Pero, still on the floor, still shocked at being shot at, was slow on the uptake.

The ambassador's men had immediately stood and bodily protected the ambassador. The ambassador shouted, "Any CIA here, drop your weapons and disengage, this is an order from Local One." It made the papers the next day. Sergio, Mbuno, the two Swiss police aides, and Susanna arrived about then. The two Swiss officers plunged into the fray, taking on three of Hans' fellow ex-Stasi, peeling them off the bar or getting them up from tables near Tische's. Because Local One was there, German State Security had men on hand, but they didn't know who to arrest or shoot. They guarded the ambassador and barked orders for everyone to stop.

From his vantage point, slowly getting up from the floor, Pero watched Mbuno trip one of the men. Then Sergio disarmed a leather-coated goon coming into the restaurant, one of the ones from the street. Pero watched Sergio hand the confiscated pistol to a uniformed police officer as the officer came in from the street. The police officer looked surprised. When the thug Mbuno had tripped tried to get up again, Sergio hit him, paparazzi cameras flashing, and Mbuno sat on the man's back, pinning him to the restaurant entrance floor.

Sergio smiled at the photographers and his front-page moment of fame was certain—once again.

But Tische had slipped out through the kitchen. Pero's fog of very nearly being shot began to lift. He turned to run after Tische, finally figuring out what the major had wanted him to do when he handed him the metal box: keep recording.

Chapter 17

U-Bahn Halt: Alt-Tegel

Like most kitchens in busy, gourmet establishments, the Borchardt's kitchen was small and crowded. Cooking so many meals required a ballet of timing and movement—an elderly, but determined man running through, crashing into everything, and you have chaos. Tische had gained distance from the dazed Pero, but there was little Pero could do to catch up until they reached the street. As Tische spun out the back door, slipping on the cream, he had made a sous-chef spill, Pero spotted him turning to run up the block, northward. Tische had a hundred-foot lead. Pero ran after him.

Although Pero was gaining, it was not fast enough. Pero was not a fast runner. Tische reached the U-Bahn station, Oranienburger Tor and went down the steps to the U6 train that was waiting, about to depart, doors open.

Sirens could be heard back at the restaurant and Pero wondered if anyone knew where they were running. In desperation, Pero took the steps three at a time and, thankfully, got to the bottom just as the normal loud tone was sounding for closing doors. He jumped into the first car he came to, and the train moved off. With every stop the train made, he leapt out and walked up a car, but he could spot Tische doing the same. Pero wasn't in a rush to apprehend him, he just didn't want too much distance between them. Pero was not sure if Tische was armed. But Pero was sure that if Tische felt Pero was coming on to attack, he would turn and fight—never run away. Hyenas confront attackers, chattering all the time.

As the U-Bahn sped north past the eighth stop, it emerged from the tunnel into the open night air. Emerging from the tunnel inside West Berlin and onto the elevated section in the old Eastern sector, Pero could see through the windows that Tische was in the fourth carriage from the front, while he, Pero, was in the car behind. At the next stop, Pero planned to move into Tische's carriage and talk with him. Pero hoped the recorder would still be working.

"Die nexte halt ist Kurtchumacher Platz" the speakers blared. Pero looked through the connecting windows and saw Tische smiling, all teeth, back at him.

As the train came into the station, the last of the passengers in Pero's car got off except for two. There were three in Tische's still, hopefully giving Pero some cover or at least witnesses. Carefully, hiding, checking that the recording buttons were still on, Pero left his carriage and walked forward to Tische's car. Keeping at arm's length, he addressed Tische, "Herr Aue?"

Tische seemed resigned if unbeaten, "It is clever of you to figure this out. No doubt your bosses have calculated that my usefulness is over. Pity, it was an easy association and good cover while it lasted. Now we will have to carry on without their bungling."

Pero thought *There is that "we" again.* Pero nodded, "Herr Aue, what do you hope to gain? The uranium is useless."

"Ach, so that is what you know. But it not so, you are wrong. In the right hands, in the right way, it is most useful. It is part of a planned existence, a new order. We are patient."

"Like your father was patient?" Pero asked as he took a standing position, leaning on the train doors that would open each stop. Tische was opposite him, swaying with the train, uninterested in holding the handrail.

"Mein foter," he used the Yiddish word, "was weak. He couldn't see. Mein Vater," he used the German word, "was pure, *perfekt.*"

"Before or after he killed your foter?"

"I warned you once before not to be sentimental Herr Baltazar, it is a game you are ill-equipped to play. You know nothing, will learn nothing."

The train stopped again. Doors opened, closed. Two fewer people left in their car. Their discourse was painfully slow for Pero. He was impatient to get Tische to reveal all. But Tische would speak, chattering really, and it was clear he would only answer or ask questions after minutes of silence.

"On the contrary Hitler Jugend Spacil, I have learned much." It shocked Tische, but only for an instant.

"And so? So what is your next trick? You think to shock me into penitence dummer kleiner mann?"

Pero knew Tische was partially right. A little man he might be, in a big game, but not dummer, stupid.

Tische sneered, showing teeth, and sarcastically added, "Ach so, you think I was the poor orphan indoctrinated boy of Spacil or Aue. So what? I did my time in that filthy French prison. My real Vater rescued me. My foter never could have."

"You are right, he couldn't. Did Spacil execute him in the Ukraine, did you know about it?"

The train stopped again, the carriage emptied completely. Pero moved a pace sideways and away. Tische was making him increasingly afraid.

Tische laughed, "Frightened? Again, you show signs of the TV generation you grew up in—soft, weak, and melodramatic. You cannot understand power, Herr Baltazar, its intoxication, its value, its cleanliness for the soul. Did I know—did I know?" He laughed again and was enjoying the exchange, "I watched him execute first meine mame, she begged him to save me . . . He said he would. He was most gentle, one bullet. The blood spattered mein foter. And my Vater's shiny black boots. After he shot mein foter, he made me clean his boots, standing there next to my dead parents, fallen together, weak even in death. Then he took me back to his quarters, and he had slaves bring me food and clothes, fine leather shoes. He had power, you see, he knew how to provide, to show the way. My birth parents were weak, inferior. She for sleeping with a Jew, he for being what he was, unclean and unworthy. Mein Vater made me a German, not weak. So did I know? Oh yes, I watched and I learned. It was eine wertvolle lektion, a good lesson. Vater Spacil made sure I learned it again and again. I became better at exterminating them than he did. Later, in Berlin, I enjoyed eliminating the homosexual French soldiers." He laughed and sneered, "So, Herr Baltazar, keep your petty American values to yourself."

The train slowed to a stop, and the doors opened, "Otisstrasse," was proclaimed and the doors closed. Then there was no one aboard in any part of the train, just the two men hurtling into the night. Pero was wondering if André or perhaps Mbuno were tracking the U-Bahn's passage. Feeling more afraid now that they were alone, Pero wanted to shake Tische's confidence, "Your sister is not so sure."

His head snapped around and Tische lunged at Pero. Again, Pero hadn't seen the dagger come out. Tische brought it up under Pero's chin and pricked the skin. "What about meine schwester?"

"Well, you have a sister, Spacil had a daughter, and records don't show she died, so she's around somewhere." Pero could see his bluff worked as Tische took the point away from Pero's throat but kept it handy.

"By now your friends are dead, that demonstration at Borchardt was their death warrant, just the same as if you pulled the trigger. My men will have seen to it."

"And the shipment?"

The next stop, brightly lit, diverted him. "Holzhauser Strasse." The doors opened, Tische blocked Pero's exit and said nothing until the doors closed.

"The gold with the uranium? It will be loaded by now. Our lawyers had it released this afternoon. You have lost, Herr Baltazar, and your friends are dead. All for this little package as the CIA called it." He pulled it out and held it up. "The field agent was given instructions to carry it on his person, he was supposed to bring it somewhere and then die, thereby closing the trail, but he never made it. He mailed it to that *verdammt* embassy man. You were supposed to help me move it or find it, without knowing." His eyes lost focus as he reminisced, "After we had arranged the purchase of the *geld*—a simple hint to a minor official in the Treasury. We told him how he could get a pay grade improvement, a salary increase of sixty dollars a month for doing a good government job, but only if he released twenty million in gold for a Treasury profit. Hah! After that, all I had to do was arrange your presence here on that *scheisse kleine filme!*" (shitty little film) "Even the stupid masters in Langley, desperate to cover up the secret funding and close the trail of their complicity, didn't guess they provided your name and file as an expendable agent. You were so easy to follow and control, you were to lead me to the package, where it was being taken. If the radiation killed you, so what? Same as happened to the other man. But you are, I will admit, most adaptive. Where did you hide this?" He dangled the sock with the Russian lead ball bag inside.

"In the aquarium."

"Ach so, my man thought so, but he couldn't find it."

"Well, it was well hidden in a plant. Don't blame him."

"Most generous." He held the sock covered bag up to the light, as if he could tell what it was.

Pero prayed that they were still recording.

Tische continued, "Do you know what is really in here?"

"Some radioactive salts, lethal material, and some liquid, I was told."

"Nein, it is a sample of the future, Herr Baltazar. The future. It gives us money and power. Leverage. With a lever you can move the world, Archimedes said that. He was right. With this lever, we will move the world again and again."

The train speaker cut in, "Die nexte halt ist Borsigwerke." Tische wasn't paying attention to the stops anymore. Pero quickly looked up at the roof label and saw there was only one stop left, the head stop, Alt-Tegel, just before the airport. Out the windows, it was a grim part of the city, industrial, unlit.

"But Herr Tische, Aue or Spacil—which do you want me to call you?"

"Spacil, a name of pride."

"Gut, Herr Spacil, what is in the package that is so damn important? It's just water and some flakes of paper."

Tische's curiosity got the better of him. He reached into the sock, opened the Russian bag, and took out the package. The heavy water bag was still vacuum-sealed, not leaking.

He held it up to the light. "Do you see those tiny particles in there, Herr Baltazar?"

Pero pretended to peer closer, then backed away. With the swaying of the train, Pero was suddenly up against the doors, with no room to run. "Yes, looks like the paper bits as I was told it was."

"Ach, yes, paper now, but when they were placed in that cave in the Jura . . ."

Pero thought, *So Sam was right, the calcium carbonate was from the Jura. He would be so pleased to be right again.* And then he realized, doing a mental reset, that it was a foolish time to be thinking off target from the murderous intent of Tische still holding the stiletto. *Concentrate Pero, concentrate.*

Spacil continued, almost softly, speaking to himself, "But in 1945 they were Reich marks, already valueless. *Mein Vater* knew this, but he knew soldiers would be attracted to a mass of them. They would report the find or show them off, word would spread and lead them to a cache of gold we wanted them to take and keep secret, safe for our future. This gold, hiding our secret, which was in the same cache as all that worthless money, this gold would be taken and stolen, to be slipped into the other gold the Allies were stealing from Germany. And this gold would have to be kept safe, safe until we needed it again. The Americans in CIC never knew what it really was. The Treasury didn't want to know. Mein Vater was the only one, a true genius. He was the one who used Jüdisch *geld* to make it easy to identify later. Now it is only meine schwester and I, we know, we are releasing the dragon, red golden dragon. This sample would have given people the key to our plans, we couldn't have that."

"Die nächster halt is Alt-Tegel, letzter halt, alle absteigen" The train speaker declared, *everybody off at the next station.*

"What dragon is that Spacil?"

"The one you Americans were too stupid not to use on the Russians, the one that will unbalance the world, the one which will allow us to rise up again. *Die zukunft!* Tomorrow! Herr Baltazar, it is our motto. It was mein Vater's motto. Simple but true." He paused, the train was slowing down. "Did you know the German officers only ever told the truth at the Nuremberg Trials? Not one of them ever told a lie. All mein Vater's associates used to marvel at their honesty. We knew not one allied soldier could have ever told the truth the way they did. And the irony, not lost on mein Vater, was that the Americans never learned from listening to the truth, they remained—still remain—blind."

The train stopped, the doors opened. He had his stiletto out front, between them, pointing at Pero's gut. "Walk Herr Baltazar, over there, it is a good place for you to die." Pero did as he was told and backed up to a poster advertising an action film, cars crashing, Bourne something or other. "Your little game has failed." Tische checked right and left down the damp and still platform. "Oh, yes, the history lesson." He was enjoying the captive audience. "Goering said it perfectly: if you want to control the masses, first you frighten them, then you tell them they are in greater danger, and then you swear to protect them. They are yours. He said all this in his papers while in American prison awaiting execution. He denied them the privilege of killing him, mein Vater helped. And now good-bye Herr Baltazar."

The empty train started up, passing down the platform. The passing interior lights glinted on the stiletto blade, pointed at Pero's liver. Pero had no doubt Tische would know exactly where to aim. "That flag sure does look good inside the glass box."

"Was?" Tische exploded in rage. "Was did you say?" He stuck the stiletto into Pero's side. But Tische's outrage had caused a hesitation, so quickly Pero tried to make a hollow, move the entry point away from his liver. The blade slid in all too easily. Tische twisted the blade. "You vil tell me now!"

The steel in the abdomen flesh was hurting terribly. Pero couldn't get a breath.

"Now! You vil tell me now, or I will make the pain much worse."

"The Hitler flag, the Swiss have it, microdots and all." Tische's eyes teared up and went redder. He twisted the knife again. Pero was at the limit he could endure. Pero had one hand on the now bloody dagger, the other pushing on Tische's chest. Tische held the vacuum sample bag in his fist, pushing Pero's chest with his knuckles—pinning Pero against the poster while with his other hand, he was trying to force the dagger deeper.

But Tische was squeezing the bag and so Pero decided to help him. He took his hand off Tische's chest and put his hand on Tische's hand that was holding the bag and squeezed, and then harder.

Tische looked down, just for a second. He tried forcing the blade to go in deeper, but only managed to topple both of them over. Tische's back hit the hard concrete with Pero on top. Pero kept his pressure on the bag, willing it to burst while the blade dug deeper.

Finally, the vacuum bag popped.

At that moment, Tische looked at the liquid spraying out, jerked his whole body to get Pero off him and then backed away, crawling in fear. As he crept off, the blade came out.

Tische, stumbling, crawling, went as far as he could and then sat upright, abruptly, back against the concrete wall under another garish poster advertising beer. Lying on the ground, Pero kept one hand on the wound, the fresh one, a few inches to the left of the first one.

Tische Aue Spacil sat there and started twitching, then thrashing. The heavy water had saturated his eyes, face, and chest. He had received direct, immediate contact. It was burning into his flesh, his eyeballs. A thousand radiation treatments in one second. He started screaming. He kept screaming for what seemed like ages until he stopped and then people arrived.

Pero didn't know who was who, or why. He couldn't focus. The pain of the wound was too much.

Out of the fog, he heard his name and hands moving him to a laying-down position on a mattress of some sort, things being stuck in his arms. He heard *Addiena's* voice saying it was all right, then he heard Susanna's pleading "Oh, don't die, don't die, you stupid man, you promised . . ."

Somehow, he summoned the strength to reply. "What die? And not feed you bananas my little Bonobo?" And he went to sleep for a while. He was very tired.

But not dead, he thought, *not quite yet.*

Chapter 18

Charité Mitte

The Humboldt University Hospital, on Schumann Strasse, dates from 1801 and has always been a center for the most advanced modern medical care. It was just as well, for Pero had enough tubes sticking out of him to resemble a robot having its oil changed. He found he could stand the ache of most of them except for the catheter allowing him to urinate without getting out of bed.

Overall, he was a good patient. Over the years, Pero had found he enjoyed hospitals. They were places where he could get to escape the stress of normal life, watch mindless TV, get three square meals a day, and have people fussing over him. *So,* he thought, *what's not to like? The short beds and my toes hitting the end keeping me from a good night's sleep for one.*

He had been in hospitals in places around the world often enough. He had had malaria, twice, then there was back surgery after he fell off a Land Rover roof in Kenya, a knee operation for torn cartilage, the wrist, the ribs, and, not least, an embarrassing infected behind in Kenya that Mbuno would not let him forget. Lying there, Pero ruefully thought that perhaps he should, at fifty-five, slow things down a bit.

Patience in the hospital is boring. Or, rather, the patient hopes it is boring. Boring means the patient is not unconscious or really hurting. There in Humboldt's Charité Mitte Klinik, Pero had loads of time on his hands. He was happily bored.

Tische's stiletto had nicked the liver, severe shock had set in, but Pero survived. André, on encouragement from Mbuno, had the good sense to run after the two men. He was running like mad when Mbuno informed him that hyena kill for fun. André had, as a precaution, called for an ambulance at each U-bahn stop.

The ambulance medics arrived on the platform just as Tische stopped convulsing. They couldn't revive him. The shock was too much for his heart.

While Pero lay there in the hospital, he didn't know that the ambulance technicians were still undergoing anti-radiation treatment somewhere in the *klinik*. Alt-Tegel station had been declared closed. Pero, in turn, was stuck in a room by himself, in a ward sectioned off from the rest of the hospital, with a Geiger counter slowly clicking above the bed-head. Sam's iodine pills had saved his life. Heep's antibiotics prevented infection too. The liver is the only major organ that can repair itself. Pero's was. He was healing.

Pero felt sorry for the hospital staff. Apparently, for the first ten days while he was unconscious, until they were sure he was safe and not contaminated, the staff had to rotate ten-minute shifts to attend to him. Thankfully, he was not all that radioactive. He had no swelling or anything more dire than what Sam had warned about. He just had what they referred to as "background" emission—that seemed to worry them sufficiently.

When he had regained consciousness, they moved him from ICU to the separate, secure, ward room. Since then, his strength seemed to be returning albeit too slowly for his liking. On the first day that he was allowed any real contact, he had been on two tiring phone calls for what seemed like hours. That was his limit for a few days, two calls only, then more rest. It all seemed exhausting.

Of the calls he had received, those with the most pull put through first. In his first permitted phone call, Lewis forbade him from explaining the bag and its contents.

"Baltazar, get this straight: you are not, repeat not, to involve anyone else in this mess? Get it? We will not tolerate you telling all our secrets to everyone. Get it? Is that clear?"

Pero took his time, drank a little water from the glass straw and asked, "You do know I've only been out of the coma for six hours and you are already yelling at me?"

"Yes. It's important."

"I am tired. Okay, fine. Glad to see you're putting the CIA first. What do I explain to the doctors here?"

"You don't, leave that to us." He softened, "Look, Pero, I am sorry, but really you could cause a panic, many people could get hurt, please just shut up for once."

Pero dropped his head back on the pillow, feeling very weary—more than he wanted to admit. He knew Lewis was right. He wasn't a very good field agent, he talked too much, he involved way too many people. *But, dammit, we got the job done!* Tische was dead, and yes he knew Tische would have been more useful alive. Pero was sorry about that. If he had been a real field agent, he would have had to allow Tische to kill him and escape. Tische wasn't going to get away, Pero had known that then and was now feeling a little guilty for the pleasure of killing the bastard. To anyone who asked, he just said it was his stupid doggedness to get the full story on tape that kept him goading Tische on.

Pero slapped his forehead, clearing his thoughts, *No, that is a lie Pero. Don't lie to yourself. You wanted to make sure it was only him and his sister running this thing. That's what you found out, that's what will give access to all the other investigations.* Pero had known, instinctively perhaps, that if you have the head of an organization, you can trace back down the pyramid to the players. The other way was never so easy. Tische was the head, the rest would be investigated and exposed.

So he told Lewis he was resigning as a field agent once again and for the foreseeable future, as a hunter-runner as well. Lewis didn't argue. Pero calculated that, despite his success, he must have aggravated Lewis' ulcer too much.

The afternoon call was from the ambassador. He wanted all the details. Pero referred him to Lewis. Then the ambassador revealed that it was Lewis who had leaked the material for his three red line paper to State and the Senate Intelligence Committee. And then he shocked Pero, "Your father called and gave me the name and number of the key players in the Senate. I worked with your father over the years, a great man, much like you." Then he gave a little chuckle, "Well, not at all like you, obviously, you do get into the fray, don't you?"

"I had not meant to, Mr. Ambassador. It just turned out that way."

"Again?"

"Again." And then, as requested, Pero told him the tale of the last train ride.

"As I said, the fray. Glad you have survived. Now, news. Doctor Turner and Doctor Reidermaier are traveling with me to Geneva for a conference," the ambassador meant he had a conference to attend, "they make a strange couple. He's way over six feet and she's barely over five—but as minds go, they make an astounding pair."

"You sure they are a pair? Not just colleagues?"

"No, they are a pair, holding hands, finishing each other's sentences and beaming. It's written all over them. Mary-Kate and I had them staying with us at the residence these past weeks," he meant his wife, "and they used only one room, seemed very happy. I didn't really understand their nicknames, though." He waited for Pero to ask what they were. Pero obliged. "Giraffe and Tickbird. Can you make heads or tails of that?"

Pero laughed, a bit too much, it hurt. "Giraffe has been his nickname since school. Slow, deliberate, tall, and able to see and feed where others never go. Tickbirds live in complete symbiosis with giraffes. They need the giraffe to be host for their food and in return they warn the giraffe of impending danger. If you ever see them together, the tickbird seems to be whispering in the giraffe's ear."

The ambassador laughed, "Yes, yes, that fits them perfectly. I'll have to explain that to Mary-Kate."

"What about Heep and Danny Redmond?"

"When the fracas was over, they bolted from the residence and became your unofficial bodyguards along with André Schmitz. They stayed two days until Lewis and I convinced them it was safe and that we'd protect you." Pero already knew there were two heavily armed and competent Marines outside his door. "So they went back to work. I am sure they'll want to be your first visitors. Mr. Redmond seems to think you can walk on water, says you saved his life twice."

"No, Sergio did that, saved yours too, it seems." A nurse had shown Pero the Zeitung headline saying that Sergio Negroni had single-handedly saved the US ambassador from attack by neo-Nazis.

"Ahem, yes, Sergio told me your modus operandi, he's taking the media credit, but he used his influence—it is quite considerable you know—to force an official, but secret, three red line, statement concerning your exploits, pointing the finger of pride, rightly at you. He said something about payback for the outgoing DG. And let's not forget that remarkable man, Mbuno."

Feeling the conversation was getting too revealing, Pero wanted, badly, to change the subject. Any official recognition—no matter how secret—could lead to danger for Mbuno in Kenya's uncertain political climate. "And the investigation into Tische's activities?"

"In the works. Some will be hushed up. Several governments are involved who should have—could have—known better. The microdots were vintage World War Two and showed the exact hiding place of all the stashes, coordinated by Spacil in Berlin in 1945. The list tied up with Fellar's lists, which the Senate has now acquired. There are four shipments still in US Treasury deposits that have changed to a nice color pink. As you can imagine, they are being dealt with. The Spacil factory computers, with experts called in to break complex codes, have already revealed past and planned shipments of replacement fuel rods flown out to all the suspect rogue nations. The Pi factory private jet has been impounded. It has a lead-lined cargo section. The IAEA and the foreign desks of every civilized nation will be busy for months to come. As I have a copy, I'll follow this personally."

Pero did not respond. He remembered Sergio's comment about a presidential run. The ambassador must have known that being at the front of such an investigation would help his presidential chances. Pero, instead, thanked him and pleaded fatigue and said good-bye.

That night he had terrible dreams. He cried out in his sleep and nurses rushed in to see what was wrong. When woken, all he could remember was an image of a plane whose passengers had flesh that was slowly melting, faces masked in horror.

The doctors checked him out the next morning. They confirmed he was making excellent progress and that both wounds were healing perfectly. The first wound was more of a problem. The superglue had closed the wound, which then became septic. While he was unconscious, they had cut it open, allowed it to drain and now it was time to remove the final stitches and pull the drainage tube. *One less dripping pipe sticking out of me*, Pero mused. They told him he could have the other drainage tubes removed in the next day or two. Everyone seemed overly happy with the output of urine compared with the input of saline and what he was drinking. When consulting the chart, all the staff nodded sagely at his good progress.

"So, any permanent damage?" He had to know.

"Ja, but it is not serious unless you drink too much." They meant alcohol. Pero didn't drink regularly or to excess, so he nodded and told them that was not a problem. They continued with their report, "You will be able to resume normal activities within the month, maybe five weeks."

Pero thanked them, and just before they left, the older doctor reached up and turned off the Geiger counter. He looked down. Danger over, his smile said.

The phone rang, it was Heep, Mary, Danny, Sam, and Bertha, and Sergio on a conference call, Sergio's doing. After the usual questions, they all seemed happy with his progress and Danny made dogmatic noises about Pero getting back to work.

"Honestly, how long do you think we can cover for you?" When Pero didn't answer, Danny rather sheepishly said, "Sorry, Pero, just trying a little humor."

Pero tried to keep the humor out of his voice, "Much appreciated, Danny, but if I had reacted, you wouldn't have had to grovel just now and apologize to a sick man who's waiting for worker's comp to kick in."

Danny exploded in laughter. "Bastard. Oh, hey, I learned your nickname, Otter. Suits you to a T, water-walker that you are. What happened to that bag of water anyway?"

Sam chimed in, "Danny, you're not supposed to ask about that. Sorry, Pero."

"No, it's okay," Pero answered, "if it's psychological problems you're worried about, skip it. I have none. If it's state secrets you're worried about, share them among yourselves openly. You know too much not to dot the I's and cross the T's." Danny, ever curious as actors usually are, asked again. Pero put his head back on the pillows and listened as things were explained to him by Sam and Sergio.

Finally, "Jesus Christ. What a way to go. Serves the bastard right. And his sister?"

Bertha explained, "That's where Susanna is now, breaking all their little codes."

Sam kicked in, "Yeah, hey, Pero, you can't believe what she's done for cryptography with that little microphone . . ."

"SilkeWire . . ." Bertha corrected him.

"Sorry, SilkeWire programming. She's running a subroutine across his encoding, you know like on the sat phones? Well, her subroutine does almost mechanically what the enigma machine did, only using binary differential calculus as a base set parameter. In short, she's able to construct or deconstruct code in three dimensions with time as the constant."

Pero sighed, "Ah, Sam, you've lost me . . ."

"Well, Pero, it's like this . . ."

Pero could just hear Bertha whispering in Giraffe's ear, "Not now *Liebling*, he's tired."

"Oh, sorry, Pero. Hey, I'll explain all this to you another day. Did you know Bertha and I . . .?" He left it hanging.

"Yes, the ambassador told me. I couldn't be happier. Finally a mind equal to your own."

"It's not only the mind, Pero, she also has great . . ."

"Ach, you will not explain that on this phone!"

"Sorry dear. Well, Pero, we'll get off the line, leave you with Danny, Heep, Mary, and Sergio. We'll talk soon. Will you come to the wedding?"

Bertha shouted, "Was? You haven't even asked me yet proper and you tell everybody on *die telephon*?" But her tone said she was happy, really happy.

"Hey Pero, get back in, the water's great! Bye." And he was gone, Bertha too.

"I was going to get off the phone too, Pero," it was Sergio, and it sounded like he was calling from his plane.

"Me too, Pero," came Danny's voice, "I am up here with Sergio, we're over Switzerland, the beautiful Alps, you can't imagine . . . well, yes you can, sorry. Feel better Pero. Bye."

Sergio continued: "It's Saturday, in case you didn't know, and I've got a party to go to tonight at the chalet. Wish you could join us. Anytime you need a lift again, you let me know. It was an honor and, la loutre, comme auparavant." Pero thought, *yes, it was like before, good memories, good friends, new and old.*

"Bye, Sergio, Lion, thank you, old friend, for . . . well . . . being you. Couldn't get any better." He meant it, Sergio would understand.

"Well, tell my ex-wives. Bye, Pero." And he clicked off.

"You too tired to talk some more Pero?" It was Mary. She sounded near.

"You with Heep?"

"Yes, I flew in a few days after. Initially, I called a few times for you in the hospital, got Danny and Heep and that nice André, who wouldn't leave the hospital for a few days, so I came to join them. I've been enjoying Berlin, now I know why you always love it so." He could hear her intake of breath, "Heep and I are expecting." She said it so suddenly, it caught Pero unawares.

"Congratulations! Damn Heep, at your age?"

"To make a child with Mary is all I could think about, it's all we want."

"That's wonderful." Suddenly Pero felt sad. Time was passing. It wasn't just that the clock was ticking, it was the increasing remoteness of possibility, the diminishing chances of renewal as the years clicked by.

His friends knew him well, "Don't be sad Pero." It was Mary, her voice barely above a whisper. He wasn't sure she had intended that he could hear.

"He's not sad, Mary, he saved the world, yet again. He has this great movie to produce. Mbuno's wife is doing well. Mbuno and Niamba are happy eating fish south of Rome. All's well that ends well. How can he be sad?"

Pero answered for her, "Mary's right Heep. It's what Mbuno said, that I was lone. Acting as one, not sharing. I envy you the kid, Mary and Heep, especially for the togetherness it brings." There it was, in a nutshell. His thoughts turned inward, *all this adventure, all this suffering, all this anguish and my pathetic ego kicks in, and I come down to basic animal needs.*

Pero had realized he didn't want to be *lone* anymore.

"Mary, we'll leave Pero, it's been a long call. We'll see him tomorrow. One last thing Pero," Heep had been saving something, he could sense it in his voice. "Your first visitor is coming this afternoon, get some rest, but keep your appetite. She lovingly said she will forgive you, you dummer mann, as you promised bananas." And they clicked off, laughing, "Bye!"

Much to his surprise, as Pero was lying here, dead phone receiver in hand, he was suddenly full of expectation and, finally, beginning to feel happy. In fact, he was feeling happier than he had felt for years. As he replaced the phone receiver into its cradle, it occurred to him that he might have to get used to being in love all over again.

Bonobos indeed . . .

End